THE
GREATEST MASTERPIECES
OF
RUSSIAN LITERATURE

FYODOR M. DOSTOEVSKY

THE
POSSESSED
II

Translated from the Russian
by Constance Garnett

Original Frontispiece and Illustrations
by Philippe Jullian

Distributed by
HERON BOOKS

Published by arrangement with
William Heinemann Ltd.

© *1968, Illustrations, Edito-Service S.A., Geneva*

Fyodor M. Dostoevsky

PART II

(continued)

CHAPTER VI

PYOTR STEPANOVITCH IS BUSY

I

THE date of the fête was definitely fixed, and Von Lembke became more and more depressed. He was full of strange and sinister forebodings, and this made Yulia Mihailovna seriously uneasy. Indeed, things were not altogether satisfactory. Our mild governor had left the affairs of the province a little out of gear; at the moment we were threatened with cholera; serious outbreaks of cattle plague had appeared in several places; fires were prevalent that summer in towns and villages; whilst among the peasantry foolish rumours of incendiarism grew stronger and stronger. Cases of robbery were twice as numerous as usual. But all this, of course, would have been perfectly ordinary had there been no other and more weighty reasons to disturb the equanimity of Andrey Antonovitch, who had till then been in good spirits.

What struck Yulia Mihailovna most of all was that he became more silent and, strange to say, more secretive every day. Yet it was hard to imagine what he had to hide. It is true that he rarely opposed her and as a rule followed her lead without question. At her instigation, for instance, two or three regulations of a risky and hardly legal character were introduced with the object of strengthening the authority of the governor. There were several ominous instances of transgressions being condoned with the same end in view; persons who deserved to be sent to prison and Siberia were, solely because she insisted, recommended for promotion. Certain complaints and inquiries were deliberately and systematically ignored. All this came out later on. Not only did Lembke sign everything, but he did not even go into the question of the share taken by his wife in the execution of his duties. On the other hand, he began at times to be

1

restive about "the most trifling matters", to the surprise of Yulia Mihailovna. No doubt he felt the need to make up for the days of suppression by brief moments of mutiny. Unluckily, Yulia Mihailovna was unable, for all her insight, to understand this honourable punctiliousness in an honourable character. Alas, she had no thought to spare for that, and that was the source of many misunderstandings.

There are some things of which it is not suitable for me to write, and indeed I am not in a position to do so. It is not my business to discuss the blunders of administration either, and I prefer to leave out this administrative aspect of the subject altogether. In the chronicle I have begun I've set before myself a different task. Moreover, a great deal will be brought to light by the Commission of Inquiry which has just been appointed for our province; it's only a matter of waiting a little. Certain explanations, however, cannot be omitted.

But to return to Yulia Mihailovna. The poor lady (I feel very sorry for her) might have attained all that attracted and allured her (renown and so on) without any such violent and eccentric actions as she resolved upon at the very first step. But either from an exaggerated passion for the romantic or from the frequently blighted hopes of her youth, she felt suddenly, at the change of her fortunes, that she had become one of the specially elect, almost God's anointed, "over whom there gleamed a burning tongue of fire", and this tongue of flame was the root of the mischief, for, after all, it is not like a chignon, which will fit any woman's head. But there is nothing of which it is more difficult to convince a woman than of this; on the contrary, anyone who cares to encourage the delusion in her will always be sure to meet with success. And people vied with one another in encouraging the delusion in Yulia Mihailovna. The poor woman became at once the sport of conflicting influences, while fully persuaded of her own originality. Many clever people feathered their nests and took advantage of her simplicity during the brief period of her rule in the province. And what a jumble there was under this assumption of independence! She was fascinated at the same time by the aristocratic element and the system of big landed properties and the increase of the governor's power, and the democratic element, and the new reforms and discipline, and free-thinking and stray Socialistic notions, and the correct tone of the aristocratic *salon* and the free-and-easy, almost pot-house, manners of the young people that surrounded her. She

2

dreamed of "giving happiness" and reconciling the irreconcil-
able, or, rather, of uniting all and everything in the adoration of
her own person. She had favourites too; she was particularly
fond of Pyotr Stepanovitch, who had recourse at times to the
grossest flattery in dealing with her. But she was attracted by
him for another reason, an amazing one, and most characteristic
of the poor lady: she was always hoping that he would reveal
to her a regular conspiracy against the government. Difficult
as it is to imagine such a thing, it really was the case. She
fancied for some reason that there must be a nihilist plot concealed in the province. By his silence at one time and his hints
at another Pyotr Stepanovitch did much to strengthen this
strange idea in her. She imagined that he was in communica-
tion with every revolutionary element in Russia, but at the
same time passionately devoted to her. To discover the plot,
to receive the gratitude of the government, to enter on a brilliant
career, to influence the young "by kindness", and to restrain
them from extremes—all these dreams existed side by side in
her fantastic brain. She had saved Pyotr Stepanovitch, she had
conquered him (of this she was for some reason firmly convinced); she would save others. None, none of them should
perish, she would save them all; she would pick them out; she
would send in the right report of them; she would act in the
interests of the loftiest justice, and perhaps posterity and
Russian liberalism would bless her name; yet the conspiracy
would be discovered. Every advantage at once.

Still it was essential that Andrey Antonovitch should be in
rather better spirits before the festival. He must be cheered up
and reassured. For this purpose she sent Pyotr Stepanovitch
to him in the hope that he would relieve his depression by some
means of consolation best known to himself, perhaps by giving
him some information, so to speak, first hand. She put implicit
faith in his dexterity.

It was some time since Pyotr Stepanovitch had been in Mr.
von Lembke's study. He popped in on him just when the
sufferer was in a most stubborn mood.

II

A combination of circumstances had arisen which Mr. von
Lembke was quite unable to deal with. In the very district
where Pyotr Stepanovitch had been having a festive time a sub-

3

lieutenant had been called up to be censured by his immediate superior, and the reproof was given in the presence of the whole company. The sub-lieutenant was a young man fresh from Petersburg, always silent and morose, of dignified appearance though small, stout, and rosy-cheeked. He resented the reprimand and suddenly, with a startling shriek that astonished the whole company, he charged at his superior officer with his head bent down like a wild beast's, struck him, and bit him on the shoulder with all his might; they had difficulty in getting him off. There was no doubt that he had gone out of his mind; anyway, it became known that of late he had been observed performing incredibly strange actions. He had, for instance, flung two ikons belonging to his landlady out of his lodgings and smashed up one of them with an axe; in his own room he had, on three stands resembling lecterns, laid out the works of Vogt, Moleschott, and Büchner, and before each lectern he used to burn a church wax-candle. From the number of books found in his rooms it could be gathered that he was a well-read man. If he had had fifty thousand francs he would perhaps have sailed to the island of Marquesas like the "cadet" to whom Herzen alludes with such sprightly humour in one of his writings. When he was seized, whole bundles of the most desperate manifestos were found in his pockets and his lodgings.

Manifestos are a trivial matter too, and to my thinking not worth troubling about. We have seen plenty of them. Besides, they were not new manifestos; they were, it was said later, just the same as had been circulated in the X province, and Liputin, who had travelled in that district and the neighbouring province six weeks previously, declared that he had seen exactly the same leaflets there then. But what struck Andrey Antonovitch most was that the overseer of Shpigulin's factory had brought the police just at the same time two or three packets of exactly the same leaflets as had been found on the lieutenant. The bundles, which had been dropped in the factory in the night, had not been opened, and none of the factory-hands had had time to read one of them. The incident was a trivial one, but it set Andrey Antonovitch pondering deeply. The position presented itself to him in an unpleasantly complicated light.

In this factory the famous "Shpigulin scandal" was just then brewing, which made so much talk among us and got into the Petersburg and Moscow papers with all sorts of variations. Three weeks previously one of the hands had fallen ill and died of Asiatic cholera; then several others were stricken down. The whole town was in a panic, for the cholera was coming nearer and nearer and had reached the neighbouring province. I may observe that satisfactory sanitary measures had been, so far as possible, taken to meet the unexpected guest. But the factory belonging to the Shpigulins, who were millionaires and well-connected people, had somehow been overlooked. And there was a sudden outcry from everyone that this factory was the hot-bed of infection, that the factory itself, and especially the quarters inhabited by the workpeople, were so inveterately filthy that even if cholera had not been in the neighbourhood there might well have been an outbreak there. Steps were immediately taken, of course, and Andrey Antonovitch vigorously insisted on their being carried out without delay within three weeks. The factory was cleansed, but the Shpigulins, for some unknown reason, closed it. One of the Shpigulin brothers always lived in Petersburg and the other went away to Moscow when the order was given for cleansing the factory. The overseer proceeded to pay off the workpeople and, as it appeared, cheated them shamelessly. The hands began to complain among themselves, asking to be paid fairly, and foolishly went to the police, though without much disturbance, for they were not so very much excited. It was just at this moment that the manifestos were brought to Andrey Antonovitch by the overseer.

Pyotr Stepanovitch popped into the study unannounced, like an intimate friend and one of the family; besides, he had a message from Yulia Mihailovna. Seeing him, Lembke frowned grimly and stood still at the table without welcoming him. Till that moment he had been pacing up and down the study and had been discussing something *tête-à-tête* with his clerk Blum, a very clumsy and surly German whom he had brought with him from Petersburg, in spite of the violent opposition of Yulia Mihailovna. On Pyotr Stepanovitch's entrance the clerk had moved to the door, but had not gone out. Pyotr Stepanovitch even fancied that he exchanged significant glances with his chief.

"Aha, I've caught you at last, you secretive monarch of the town!" Pyotr Stepanovitch cried out, laughing, and laid his hand over the manifesto on the table. "This increases your collection, eh?"

Andrey Antonovitch flushed crimson; his face seemed to twitch.

"Leave off, leave off at once!" he cried, trembling with rage. "And don't you dare . . . sir . . ."

"What's the matter with you? You seem to be angry!"

5

"Allow me to inform you, sir, that I've no intention of putting up with your *sans façon* henceforward, and I beg you to remember . . ."

"Why, damn it all, he is in earnest!"

"Hold your tongue, hold your tongue"—Von Lembke stamped on the carpet—"and don't dare . . ."

God knows what it might have come to. Alas, there was one circumstance involved in the matter of which neither Pyotr Stepanovitch nor even Yulia Mihailovna herself had any idea. The luckless Andrey Antonovitch had been so greatly upset during the last few days that he had begun to be secretly jealous of his wife and Pyotr Stepanovitch. In solitude, especially at night, he spent some very disagreeable moments.

"Well, I imagined that if a man reads you his novel two days running till after midnight and wants to hear your opinion of it, he has of his own act discarded official relations, anyway. . . . Yulia Mihailovna treats me as a friend; there's no making you out," Pyotr Stepanovitch brought out, with a certain dignity indeed. "Here is your novel, by the way." He laid on the table a large heavy manuscript rolled up in blue paper.

Lembke turned red and looked embarrassed.

"Where did you find it?" he asked discreetly, with a rush of joy which he was unable to suppress, though he did his utmost to conceal it.

"Only fancy, done up like this, it rolled under the chest of drawers. I must have thrown it down carelessly on the chest when I went out. It was only found the day before yesterday, when the floor was scrubbed. You did set me a task, though!"

Lembke dropped his eyes sternly.

"I haven't slept for the last two nights, thanks to you. It was found the day before yesterday, but I kept it, and have been reading it ever since. I've no time in the day, so I've read it at night. Well, I don't like it; it's not my way of looking at things. But that's no matter; I've never set up for being a critic, but I couldn't tear myself away from it, my dear man, though I didn't like it! The fourth and fifth chapters are . . . they really are . . . damn it all, they are beyond words! And what a lot of humour you've packed into it; it made me laugh! How you can make fun of things *sans que cela paraisse!* As for the ninth and tenth chapters, it's all about love; that's not my line, but it's effective though. I was nearly blubbering over Egrenev's letter, though you've shown him up so cleverly. . . . You know, it's touching, though at the same time you want to show the false side of him, as it were, don't you? Have I guessed rightly? But I could simply beat you for the ending. For what are you setting up? Why, the same old idol of domestic happiness, begetting children and making money; 'they were married and lived happy ever afterwards'—come, it's too much! You will enchant your readers, for even I couldn't put the book down; but that makes it all the worse! The reading public is as stupid as ever, but it's the duty of sensible people to wake them up, while you . . . But that's enough. Good-bye. Don't be cross another time; I came in to you because I had a couple of words to say to you, but you are so unaccountable . . ."

Andrey Antonovitch meantime took his novel and locked it up in an oak bookcase, seizing the opportunity to wink to Blum to disappear. The latter withdrew with a long, mournful face.

"I am not unaccountable, I am simply . . . nothing but annoyances," he muttered, frowning but without anger, and sitting down to the table. "Sit down and say what you have to say. It's a long time since I've seen you, Pyotr Stepanovitch, only don't burst upon me in the future with such manners . . . sometimes, when one has business, it's . . ."

"My manners are always the same. . . ."

"I know, and I believe that you mean nothing by it, but sometimes one is worried. . . . Sit down."

Pyotr Stepanovitch immediately lolled back on the sofa and drew his legs under him.

III

"What sort of worries? Surely not these trifles?" He nodded towards the manifesto. "I can bring you as many of them as you like; I made their acquaintance in X province."

"You mean at the time you were staying there?"

"Of course, it was not in my absence. I remember there was a hatchet printed at the top of it. Allow me." (He took up the manifesto.) "Yes, there's the hatchet here too; that's it, the very same."

"Yes, here's a hatchet. You see, a hatchet."

"Well, is it the hatchet that scares you?"

"No, it's not . . . and I am not scared; but this business . . . it is a business; there are circumstances."

"What sort? That it's come from the factory? He he! But do you know, at that factory the workpeople will soon be writing manifestos for themselves."

"What do you mean?" Von Lembke stared at him severely.

"What I say. You've only to look at them. You are too soft, Andrey Antonovitch; you write novels. But this has to be handled in the good old way."

"What do you mean by the good old way? What do you mean by advising me? The factory has been cleaned; I gave the order and they've cleaned it."

"And the workmen are in rebellion. They ought to be flogged. every one of them; that would be the end of it."

"In rebellion? That's nonsense; I gave the order and they've cleaned it."

"Ech, you are soft, Andrey Antonovitch!"

"In the first place, I am not so soft as you think, and in the second place . . ." Von Lembke was piqued again. He had exerted himself to keep up the conversation with the young man from curiosity, wondering if he would tell him anything new.

"Ha ha, an old acquaintance again," Pyotr Stepanovitch interrupted, pouncing on another document that lay under a paper-weight, something like a manifesto, obviously printed abroad and in verse. "Oh, come, I know this one by heart, 'A Noble Personality". Let me have a look at it—yes, 'A Noble Personality' it is. I made acquaintance with that personality abroad. Where did you unearth it?"

"You say you've seen it abroad?" Von Lembke said eagerly.

"I should think so, four months ago, or maybe five."

"You seem to have seen a great deal abroad." Von Lembke looked at him subtly.

Pyotr Stepanovitch, not heeding him, unfolded the document and read the poem aloud:

"A NOBLE PERSONALITY

"He was not of rank exalted,
He was not of noble birth.
He was bred among the people
In the breast of Mother Earth.
But the malice of the nobles
And the Tsar's revengeful wrath
Drove him forth to grief and torture
On the martyr's chosen path.
He set out to teach the people
Freedom, love, equality,
To exhort them to resistance;

8

But to flee the penalty
Of the prison, whip and gallows,
To a foreign land he went.
While the people waited hoping
From Smolensk to far Tashkent,
Waited eager for his coming
To rebel against their fate,
To arise and crush the Tsardom
And the nobles' vicious hate,
To share all the wealth in common,
And the antiquated thrall
Of the church, the home and marriage
To abolish once for all."

"You got it from that officer, I suppose, eh?" asked Pyotr Stepanovitch.

"Why, do you know that officer, then, too?"

"I should think so. I had a gay time with him there for two days; he was bound to go out of his mind."

"Perhaps he did not go out of his mind."

"You think he didn't because he began to bite?"

"But, excuse me, if you saw those verses abroad and then, it appears, at that officer's . . ."

"What, puzzling, is it? You are putting me through an examination, Andrey Antonovitch, I see. You see," he began suddenly with extraordinary dignity, "as to what I saw abroad I have already given explanations, and my explanations were found satisfactory, otherwise I should not have been gratifying this town with my presence. I consider that the question as regards me has been settled, and I am not obliged to give any further account of myself, not because I am an informer, but because I could not help acting as I did. The people who wrote to Yulia Mihailovna about me knew what they were talking about, and they said I was an honest man. . . . But that's neither here nor there; I've come to see you about a serious matter, and it's as well you've sent your chimney-sweep away. It's a matter of importance to me, Andrey Antonovitch. I shall have a very great favour to ask of you."

"A favour? H'm . . . by all means; I am waiting and, I confess, with curiosity. And I must add, Pyotr Stepanovitch, that you surprise me not a little."

Von Lembke was in some agitation. Pyotr Stepanovitch crossed his legs.

9

"In Petersburg," he began, "I talked freely of most things, but there were things—this, for instance" (he tapped the "Noble Personality" with his finger), "about which I held my tongue—in the first place, because it wasn't worth talking about, and secondly, because I only answered questions. I don't care to put myself forward in such matters; in that I see the distinction between a rogue and an honest man forced by circumstances. Well, in short, we'll dismiss that. But now . . . now that these fools . . . now that this has come to the surface and is in your hands, and I see that you'll find out all about it—for you are a man with eyes and one can't tell beforehand what you'll do—and these fools are still going on, I . . . I . . . well, the fact is, I've come to ask you to save one man, a fool too, most likely mad, for the sake of his youth, his misfortunes, in the name of your humanity. . . . You can't be so humane only in the novels you manufacture!" he said, breaking off with coarse sarcasm and impatience.

In fact, he was seen to be a straightforward man, awkward and impolitic from excess of humane feeling and perhaps from excessive sensitiveness—above all, a man of limited intelligence, as Von Lembke saw at once with extraordinary subtlety. He had indeed long suspected it, especially when during the previous week he had, sitting alone in his study at night, secretly cursed him with all his heart for the inexplicable way in which he had gained Yulia Mihailovna's good graces.

"For whom are you interceding, and what does all this mean?" he inquired majestically, trying to conceal his curiosity.

"It . . . it's . . . damn it! It's not my fault that I trust you! Is it my fault that I look upon you as a most honourable and, above all, a sensible man . . . capable, that is, of understanding . . . damn . . ."

The poor fellow evidently could not master his emotion.

"You must understand at last," he went on, "you must understand that in pronouncing his name I am betraying him to you—I am betraying him, am I not? I am, am I not?"

"But how am I to guess if you don't make up your mind to speak out?"

"That's just it; you always cut the ground from under one's feet with your logic, damn it. . . . Well, here goes . . . this 'noble personality', this 'student' . . . is Shatov . . . that's all."

"Shatov? How do you mean it's Shatov?"

"Shatov is the 'student' who is mentioned in this. He lives

10

here, he was once a serf, the man who gave that slap. . . ."

"I know, I know." Lembke screwed up his eyes. "But excuse me, what is he accused of? Precisely and, above all, what is your petition?"

"I beg you to save him, do you understand? I used to know him eight years ago, I might almost say I was his friend," cried Pyotr Stepanovitch, completely carried away. "But I am not bound to give you an account of my past life," he added, with a gesture of dismissal. "All this is of no consequence; it's the case of three men and a half, and with those that are abroad you can't make up a dozen. But what I am building upon is your humanity and your intelligence. You will understand and you will put the matter in its true light, as the foolish dream of a man driven crazy . . . by misfortunes, by continued misfortunes, and not as some impossible political plot or God knows what!"

He was almost gasping for breath.

"H'm. I see that he is responsible for the manifestos with the axe," Lembke concluded almost majestically. "Excuse me, though, if he were the only person concerned, how could he have distributed it both here and in other districts and in the X province . . . and, above all, where did he get them?"

"But I tell you that at the utmost there are not more than five people in it—a dozen perhaps. How can I tell?"

"You don't know?"

"How should I know?—damn it all."

"Why, you knew that Shatov was one of the conspirators."

"Ech!" Pyotr Stepanovitch waved his hand as though to keep off the overwhelming penetration of the inquirer. "Well, listen. I'll tell you the whole truth: of the manifestos I know nothing—that is, absolutely nothing. Damn it all, don't you know what nothing means? . . . That sub-lieutenant, to be sure, and somebody else and someone else here . . . and Shatov perhaps and someone else too—well, that's the lot of them . . . a wretched lot. . . . But I've come to intercede for Shatov. He must be saved, for this poem is his, his own composition, and it was through him it was published abroad; that I know for a fact, but of the manifestos I really know nothing."

"If the poem is his work, no doubt the manifestos are too. But what data have you for suspecting Mr. Shatov?"

Pyotr Stepanovitch, with the air of a man driven out of all patience, pulled a pocket-book out of his pocket and took a note out of it.

"Here are the facts," he cried, flinging it on the table.

11

Lembke unfolded it; it turned out to be a note written six months before from here to some address abroad. It was a brief note, only two lines:

"I can't print 'A Noble Personality' here, and in fact I can do nothing; print it abroad.

"Iv. Shatov."

Lembke looked intently at Pyotr Stepanovitch. Varvara Petrovna had been right in saying that he had at times the expression of a sheep.

"You see, it's like this," Pyotr Stepanovitch burst out. "He wrote this poem here six months ago, but he couldn't get it printed here, in a secret printing press, and so he asks to have it printed abroad. . . . That seems clear."

"Yes, that's clear, but to whom did he write? That's not clear yet," Lembke observed with the most subtle irony.

"Why, Kirillov, of course; the letter was written to Kirillov abroad. . . . Surely you knew that? What's so annoying is that perhaps you are only putting it on before me, and most likely you knew all about this poem and everything long ago! How did it come to be on your table? It found its way there somehow! Why are you torturing me, if so?"

He feverishly mopped his forehead with his handkerchief.

"I know something, perhaps." Lembke parried dexterously. "But who is this Kirillov?"

"An engineer who has lately come to the town. He was Stavrogin's second, a maniac, a madman; your sub-lieutenant may really only be suffering from temporary delirium, but Kirillov is a thoroughgoing madman—thoroughgoing, that I guarantee. Ah, Andrey Antonovitch, if the government only knew what sort of people these conspirators all are, they wouldn't have the heart to lay a finger on them. Every single one of them ought to be in an asylum; I had a good look at them in Switzerland and at the congresses."

"From which they direct the movement here?"

"Why, who directs it? Three men and a half. It makes one sick to think of them. And what sort of movement is there here? Manifestos! And what recruits have they made? Sub-lieutenants in brain fever and two or three students! You are a sensible man: answer this question. Why don't people of consequence join their ranks? Why are they all students and half-baked boys of twenty-two? And not many of those. I dare say there are thousands of bloodhounds on their track, but have they tracked out many of them? Seven! I tell you it makes one sick."

Lembke listened with attention but with an expression that seemed to say: "You don't feed nightingales on fairy-tales."

"Excuse me, though. You asserted that the letter was sent abroad, but there's no address on it; how do you come to know that it was addressed to Mr. Kirillov and abroad too and . . . and . . . that it really was written by Mr. Shatov?"

"Why, fetch some specimen of Shatov's writing and compare it. You must have some signature of his in your office. As for its being addressed to Kirillov, it was Kirillov himself showed it me at the time."

"Then you were yourself . . ."

"Of course I was, myself. They showed me lots of things out there. And as for this poem, they say it was written by Herzen to Shatov when he was still wandering abroad, in memory of their meeting, so they say, by way of praise and recommenda-tion—damn it all . . . and Shatov circulates it among the young people as much as to say: 'This was Herzen's opinion of me.'"

"Ha ha!" cried Lembke, feeling he had got to the bottom of it at last. "That's just what I was wondering: one can under-stand the manifesto, but what's the object of the poem?"

"Of course you'd see it. Goodness knows why I've been babbling to you. Listen. Spare Shatov for me and the rest may go to the devil—even Kirillov, who is in hiding now, shut up in Filipov's house, where Shatov lodges too. They don't like me because I've turned round . . . but promise me Shatov and I'll dish them all up for you. I shall be of use, Andrey Antonovitch! I reckon nine or ten men make up the whole wretched lot. I am keeping an eye on them myself, on my own account. We know of three already: Shatov, Kirillov, and that sub-lieutenant. The others I am only watching carefully . . . though I am pretty sharp-sighted too. It's the same over again as it was in the X province: two students, a schoolboy, two noblemen of twenty, a teacher, and a half-pay major of sixty, crazy with drink, have been caught with manifestos; that was all—you can take my word for it, that was all; it was quite a surprise that that was all. But I must have six days. I have reckoned it out—six days, not less. If you want to arrive at any result, don't disturb them for six days and I can kill all the birds with one stone for you; but if you flutter them before, the birds

will fly away. But spare me Shatov. I speak for Shatov. . . .
The best plan would be to fetch him here secretly, in a friendly
way, to your study and question him without disguising the
facts. . . . I have no doubt he'll throw himself at your feet
and burst into tears! He is a highly strung and unfortunate
fellow; his wife is carrying on with Stavrogin. Be kind to him
and he will tell you everything, but I must have six days. . . .
And, above all, above all, not a word to Yulia Mihailovna. It's
a secret. May it be a secret?''

"What?'' cried Lembke, opening wide his eyes. "Do you
mean to say you said nothing of this to Yulia Mihailovna?''

"To her? Heaven forbid! Ech, Andrey Antonovitch! You
see, I value her friendship and I have the highest respect for
her . . . and all the rest of it . . . but I couldn't make such
a blunder. I don't contradict her, for, as you know yourself, it's
dangerous to contradict her. I may have dropped a word to her,
for I know she likes that, but to suppose that I mentioned names
to her as I have to you or anything of that sort! My good sir!
Why am I appealing to you? Because you are a man, anyway.
a serious person with old-fashioned firmness and experience in
the service. You've seen life. You must know by heart every
detail of such affairs, I expect, from what you've seen in Petersburg. But if I were to mention those two names, for instance,
to her, she'd stir up such a hubbub. . . . You know, she would
like to astonish Petersburg. No, she's too hot-headed, she
really is.''

"Yes, she has something of that *fougue*,'' Andrey Antonovitch muttered with some satisfaction, though at the same time
he resented this unmannerly fellow's daring to express himself
rather freely about Yulia Mihailovna. But Pyotr Stepanovitch
probably imagined that he had not gone far enough and that
he must exert himself further to flatter Lembke and make a
complete conquest of him.

"*Fougue* is just it,'' he assented. "She may be a woman of
genius, a literary woman, but she would scare our sparrows.
She wouldn't be able to keep quiet for six hours, let alone six
days. Ech, Andrey Antonovitch, don't attempt to tie a woman
down for six days! You do admit that I have some experience—
in this sort of thing, I mean; I know something about it, and
you know that I may very well know something about it. I am
not asking for six days for fun but with an object.''

"I have heard . . .'' (Lembke hesitated to utter his thought)
"I have heard that on your return from abroad you made some

14

expression . . . as it were of repentance, in the proper quarter?"

"Well, that's as it may be."

"And, of course, I don't want to go into it. . . . But it has seemed to me all along that you've talked in quite a different style—about the Christian faith, for instance, about social institutions, about the government even. . . ."

"I've said lots of things, no doubt, I am saying them still; but such ideas mustn't be applied as those fools do it, that's the point. What's the good of biting his superior's shoulder? You agreed with me yourself, only you said it was premature."

"I didn't mean that when I agreed and said it was premature."

"You weigh every word you utter, though. He he! You are a careful man!" Pyotr Stepanovitch observed gaily all of a sudden. "Listen, old friend. I had to get to know you; that's why I talked in my own style. You are not the only one I get to know like that. Maybe I needed to find out your character."

"What's my character to you?"

"How can I tell what it may be to me?" He laughed again. "You see, my dear and highly respected Andrey Antonovitch, you are cunning, but it's not come to *that* yet and it certainly never will come to it, you understand? Perhaps you do understand. Though I did make an explanation in the proper quarter when I came back from abroad, and I really don't know why a man of certain convictions should not be able to work for the advancement of his sincere convictions . . . but nobody *there* has yet instructed me to investigate your character and I've not undertaken any such job from *them*. Consider: I need not have given those two names to you. I might have gone straight *there;* that is where I made my first explanations. And if I'd been acting with a view to financial profit or my own interest in any way, it would have been a bad speculation on my part, for now they'll be grateful to you and not to me at headquarters. I've done it solely for Shatov's sake." Pyotr Stepanovitch added generously, "for Shatov's sake, because of our old friendship. . . . But when you take up your pen to write to head-quarters, you may put in a word for me, if you like. . . . I'll make no objection, he he! *Adieu,* though; I've stayed too long and there was no need to gossip so much!" he added with some amiability, and he got up from the sofa.

"On the contrary, I am very glad that the position has been defined, so to speak." Von Lembke too got up and he too

15

looked pleasant, obviously affected by the last words. "I accept your services and acknowledge my obligation, and you may be sure that anything I can do by way of reporting your zeal . . ."

"Six days—the great thing is to put it off for six days, and that you shouldn't stir for those six days, that's what I want."

"So be it."

"Of course, I don't tie your hands and shouldn't venture to. You are bound to keep watch, only don't flutter the nest too soon; I rely on your sense and experience for that. But I should think you've plenty of bloodhounds and trackers of your own in reserve, ha ha!" Pyotr Stepanovitch blurted out with the gaiety and irresponsibility of youth.

"Not quite so." Lembke parried amiably. "Young people are apt to suppose that there is a great deal in the background. . . . But, by the way, allow me one little word: if this Kirillov was Stavrogin's second, then Mr. Stavrogin too . . ."

"What about Stavrogin?"

"I mean, if they are such friends?"

"Oh no, no, no! There you are quite out of it, though you are cunning. You really surprise me. I thought that you had some information about it. . . . H'm . . . Stavrogin—it's quite the opposite, quite. . . . *Avis au lecteur.*"

"Do you mean it? And can it be so?" Lembke articulated mistrustfully. "Yulia Mihailovna told me that from what she heard from Petersburg he is a man acting on some sort of instructions, so to speak. . . ."

"I know nothing about it; I know nothing, absolutely nothing. *Adieu. Avis au lecteur!*" Abruptly and obviously Pyotr Stepanovitch declined to discuss it.

He hurried to the door.

"Stay, Pyotr Stepanovitch, stay," cried Lembke. "One other tiny matter and I won't detain you."

He drew an envelope out of a table drawer.

"Here is a little specimen of the same kind of thing, and I let you see it to show how completely I trust you. Here, and tell me your opinion."

In the envelope was a letter, a strange anonymous letter addressed to Lembke and only received by him the day before. With intense vexation Pyotr Stepanovitch read as follows:

"YOUR EXCELLENCY,—For such you are by rank. Herewith I make known that there is an attempt to be made on the life

16

of personages of general's rank and on the Fatherland. For it's working up straight for that. I myself have been disseminating unceasingly for a number of years. There's infidelity too. There's a rebellion being got up and there are some thousands of manifestos, and for every one of them there will be a hundred running with their tongues out, unless they've been taken away beforehand by the police. For they've been promised a mighty lot of benefits, and the simple people are foolish, and there's vodka too. The people will attack one after another, taking them to be guilty, and, fearing both sides, I repent of what I had no share in, my circumstances being what they are. If you want information to save the Fatherland, and also the Church and the ikons, I am the only one that can do it. But only on condition that I get a pardon from the Secret Police by telegram at once, me alone, but the rest may answer for it. Put a candle every evening at seven o'clock in the porter's window for a signal. Seeing it, I shall believe and come to kiss the merciful hand from Petersburg. But on condition there's a pension for me, for else how am I to live? You won't regret it for it will mean a star for you. You must go secretly or they'll wring your neck. Your excellency's desperate servant falls at your feet.

"REPENTANT FREE-THINKER INCOGNITO."

Von Lembke explained that the letter had made its appearance in the porter's room when it was left empty the day before.

"So what do you think?" Pyotr Stepanovitch asked almost rudely.

"I think it's an anonymous skit by way of a hoax."

"Most likely it is. There's no taking you in."

"What makes me think that is that it's so stupid."

"Have you received such documents here before?"

"Once or twice, anonymous letters."

"Oh, of course they wouldn't be signed. In a different style. In different handwritings?"

"Yes."

"And were they buffoonery like this one?"

"Yes, and you know . . . very disgusting."

"Well, if you had them before, it must be the same thing now."

"Especially because it's so stupid. Because these people are educated and wouldn't write so stupidly."

"Of course, of course."

"But what if this is someone who really wants to turn informer?"

"It's not very likely," Pyotr Stepanovitch rapped out dryly. "What does he mean by a telegram from the Secret Police and a pension? It's obviously a hoax."

"Yes, yes," Lembke admitted, abashed.

"I tell you what: you leave this with me. I can certainly find out for you before I track out the others."

"Take it," Lembke assented, though with some hesitation. "Have you shown it to anyone?"

"Is it likely! No."

"Not to Yulia Mihailovna?"

"Oh, Heaven forbid! And for God's sake don't you show it her!" Lembke cried in alarm. "She'll be so upset . . . and will be dreadfully angry with me."

"Yes, you'll be the first to catch it; she'd say you brought it on yourself if people write like that to you. I know what women's logic is. Well, good-bye. I dare say I shall bring you the writer in a couple of days or so. Above all, our compact!"

IV

Though Pyotr Stepanovitch was perhaps far from being a stupid man, Fedka the convict had said of him truly "that he would make up a man himself and go on living with him too". He came away from Lembke fully persuaded that for the next six days, anyway, he had put his mind at rest, and this interval was absolutely necessary for his own purposes. But it was a false idea and founded entirely on the fact that he had made up for himself once for all an Andrey Antonovitch who was a perfect simpleton.

Like every morbidly suspicious man, Andrey Antonovitch was always exceedingly and joyfully trustful the moment he got on to sure ground. The new turn of affairs struck him at first in a rather favourable light in spite of some fresh and troublesome complications. Anyway, his former doubts fell to the ground. Besides, he had been so tired for the last few days, so exhausted and helpless, that his soul involuntarily yearned for rest. But alas! he was again uneasy. The long time he had spent in Petersburg had left ineradicable traces in his heart. The official and even the secret history of the "younger generation" was fairly familiar to him—he was a curious man and used to collect manifestos—but he could never understand a word of it. Now he felt like a man lost in a forest. Every instinct told him that there was something in Pyotr Stepanovitch's words utterly incongruous, anomalous, and grotesque, "though there's no telling what may not happen with this 'younger generation', and the devil only knows what's going on among them", he mused, lost in perplexity.

And at this moment, to make matters worse, Blum poked his head in. He had been waiting not far off through the whole of Pyotr Stepanovitch's visit. This Blum was actually a distant relation of Andrey Antonovitch, though the relationship had always been carefully and timorously concealed. I must apologise to the reader for devoting a few words here to this insignificant person. Blum was one of that strange class of "unfortunate" Germans who are unfortunate not through lack of ability but through some inexplicable ill luck. "Unfortunate" Germans are not a myth, but really do exist even in Russia, and are of a special type. Andrey Antonovitch had always had a quite touching sympathy for him, and wherever he could, as he rose himself in the service, had promoted him to subordinate positions under him; but Blum had never been successful Either the post was abolished after he had been appointed to it, or a new chief took charge of the department; once he was almost arrested by mistake with other people. He was precise, but he was gloomy to excess and to his own detriment. He was tall and had red hair; he stooped and was depressed and even sentimental; and in spite of his being humbled by his life, he was obstinate and persistent as an ox, though always at the wrong moment. For Andrey Antonovitch he, as well as his wife and numerous family, had cherished for many years a reverent devotion. Except Andrey Antonovitch no one had ever liked him. Yulia Mihailovna would have discarded him from the first, but could not overcome her husband's obstinacy. It was the cause of their first conjugal quarrel. It had happened soon after their marriage, in the early days of their honeymoon, when she was confronted with Blum, who, together with the humiliating secret of his relationship, had been until then carefully concealed from her. Andrey Antonovitch besought her with clasped hands, told her pathetically all the story of Blum and their friendship from childhood, but Yulia Mihailovna considered herself disgraced for ever, and even had recourse to fainting. Von Lembke would not budge an inch, and declared that he would not give up Blum or part from him for anything in the world, so that she was surprised at last and was obliged to put up with Blum. It was settled, however, that the relationship should be concealed even more carefully than before, if possible, and that even Blum's Christian name and patronymic should be changed, because he too was for some reason called Andrey Antonovitch. Blum knew no one in the town except the German chemist, had not called on anyone, and led, as he always did, a lonely and niggardly existence. He had long been aware of Andrey Antonovitch's literary peccadilloes. He was generally summoned to listen to secret *tête-à-tête* readings of his novel; he would sit like a post for six hours at a stretch, perspiring and straining his utmost to keep awake and smile. On reaching home he would groan with his long-legged and lanky wife over their benefactor's unhappy weakness for Russian literature.

Andrey Antonovitch looked with anguish at Blum.

"I beg you to leave me alone, Blum," he began with agitated haste, obviously anxious to avoid any renewal of the previous conversation which had been interrupted by Pyotr Stepanovitch.

"And yet this may be arranged in the most delicate way and with no publicity; you have full power." Blum respectfully but obstinately insisted on some point, stooping forward and coming nearer and nearer by small steps to Andrey Antonovitch.

"Blum, you are so devoted to me and so anxious to serve me that I am always in a panic when I look at you."

"You always say witty things, and sleep in peace, satisfied with what you've said, but that's how you damage yourself."

"Blum, I have just convinced myself that it's quite a mistake, quite a mistake."

"Not from the words of that false, vicious young man whom you suspect yourself? He has won you by his flattering praise of your talent for literature."

"Blum, you understand nothing about it; your project is absurd, I tell you. We shall find nothing and there will be a fearful upset and laughter too, and then Yulia Mihailovna . . ."

"We shall certainly find everything we are looking for." Blum advanced firmly towards him, laying his right hand on his heart. "We will make a search suddenly early in the morning, carefully showing every consideration for the person himself and strictly observing all the prescribed forms of the law. The young men, Lyamshin and Telyatnikov, assert positively that we shall find all we want. They were constant visitors there. Nobody is favourably disposed to Mr. Verhovensky. Madame Stavrogin has openly refused him her graces, and every honest man, if

20

only there is such a one in this coarse town, is persuaded that a hotbed of infidelity and social doctrines has always been concealed there. He keeps all the forbidden books, Ryliev's 'Reflections', all Herzen's works. . . . I have an approximate catalogue, in case of need."

"Oh heavens! Everyone has these books; how simple you are, my poor Blum."

"And many manifestos," Blum went on without heeding the observation. "We shall end by certainly coming upon traces of the real manifestos here. That young Verhovensky I feel very suspicious of."

"But you are mixing up the father and the son. They are not on good terms. The son openly laughs at his father."

"That's only a mask."

"Blum, you've sworn to torment me! Think! he is a conspicuous figure here, after all. He's been a professor, he is a well-known man. He'll make such an uproar and there will be such gibes all over the town, and we shall make a mess of it all. . . . And only think how Yulia Mihailovna will take it."

Blum pressed forward and did not listen.

"He was only a lecturer, only a lecturer, and of a low rank when he retired." He smote himself on the chest. "He has no marks of distinction. He was discharged from the service of suspicion of plots against the government. He has been under secret supervision, and undoubtedly still is so. And in view of the disorders that have come to light now, you are undoubtedly bound in duty. You are losing your chance of distinction by letting slip the real criminal."

"Yulia Mihailovna! Get away, Blum," Von Lembke cried suddenly, hearing the voice of his spouse in the next room.

Blum started, but did not give in.

"Allow me, allow me," he persisted, pressing both hands still more tightly on his chest.

"Get away!" hissed Andrey Antonovitch. "Do what you like . . . afterwards. Oh, my God!"

The curtain was raised and Yulia Mihailovna made her appearance. She stood still majestically at the sight of Blum, casting a haughty and offended glance at him, as though the very presence of this man was an affront to her. Blum respectfully made her a deep bow without speaking and, doubled up with veneration, moved towards the door on tiptoe with his arms held a little away from him.

Either because he really took Andrey Antonovitch's last

hysterical outbreak as a direct permission to act as he was asking, or whether he strained a point in this case for the direct advantage of his benefactor, because he was too confident that success would crown his efforts; anyway, as we shall see later on, this conversation of the governor with his subordinate led to a very surprising event which amused many people, became public property, moved Yulia Mihailovna to fierce anger, utterly disconcerting Andrey Antonovitch and reducing him at the crucial moment to a state of deplorable indecision.

V

It was a busy day for Pyotr Stepanovitch. From Von Lembke he hastened to Bogoyavlensky Street, but as he went along Bykovy Street, past the house where Karmazinov was staying, he suddenly stopped, grinned, and went into the house. The servant told him that he was expected, which interested him, as he had said nothing beforehand of his coming.

But the great writer really had been expecting him, not only that day, but the day before and the day before that. Three days before he had handed him his manuscript *Merci* (which he had meant to read at the literary matinée at Yulia Mihailovna's fête). He had done this out of amiability, fully convinced that he was agreeably flattering the young man's vanity by letting him read the great work beforehand. Pyotr Stepanovitch had noticed long before that this vainglorious, spoiled gentleman, who was so offensively unapproachable for all but the elect, this writer "with the intellect of a statesman", was simply trying to curry favour with him, even with avidity. I believe the young man guessed at last that Karmazinov considered him, if not the leader of the whole secret revolutionary movement in Russia, at least one of those most deeply initiated into the secrets of the Russian revolution who had an incontestable influence on the younger generation. The state of mind of "the cleverest man in Russia" interested Pyotr Stepanovitch, but hitherto he had, for certain reasons, avoided explaining himself.

The great writer was staying in the house belonging to his sister, who was the wife of a *kammerherr* and had an estate in the neighbourhood. Both she and her husband had the deepest reverence for their illustrious relation, but to their profound regret both of them happened to be in Moscow at the time of his visit, so that the honour of receiving him fell to the lot of an old lady, a poor relation of the kammerherr's, who had for years lived in the family and looked after the housekeeping. All the household had moved about on tiptoe since Karmazinov's arrival. The old lady sent news to Moscow almost every day, how he had slept, what he had deigned to eat, and had once sent a telegram to announce that after a dinner-party at the mayor's he was obliged to take a spoonful of a well-known medicine. She rarely plucked up courage to enter his room, though he behaved courteously to her, but dryly, and only talked to her of what was necessary.

When Pyotr Stepanovitch came in he was eating his morning cutlet with half a glass of red wine. Pyotr Stepanovitch had been to see him before and always found him eating this cutlet, which he finished in his presence without ever offering him anything. After the cutlet a little cup of coffee was served. The footman who brought in the dishes wore a swallow-tail coat, noiseless boots and gloves.

"Ha ha!" Karmazinov got up from the sofa, wiping his mouth with a table-napkin, and came forward to kiss him with an air of unmixed delight—after the characteristic fashion of Russians if they are very illustrious. But Pyotr Stepanovitch knew by experience that, though Karmazinov made a show of kissing him, he really only proffered his cheek, and so this time he did the same: the cheeks met. Karmazinov did not show that he noticed it, sat down on the sofa, and affably offered Pyotr Stepanovitch an easy chair facing him, in which the latter stretched himself at once.

"You don't . . . wouldn't like some lunch?" inquired Karmazinov, abandoning his usual habit, but with an air, of course, which would prompt a polite refusal. Pyotr Stepanovitch at once expressed a desire for lunch. A shade of offended surprise darkened the face of his host, but only for an instant; he nervously rang for the servant and, in spite of all his breeding, raised his voice scornfully as he gave orders for the second lunch to be served.

"What will you have, cutlet or coffee?" he asked once more.

"A cutlet and coffee, and tell him to bring some more wine. I am hungry," answered Pyotr Stepanovitch, calmly scrutinising his host's attire. Mr. Karmazinov was wearing a sort of indoor wadded jacket with pearl buttons, but it was too short, which was far from becoming to his rather comfortable stomach and the solid curves of his hips. But tastes differ. Over his knees he had a checkered woollen plaid reaching to the floor, though it was warm in the room.

"Are you unwell?" commented Pyotr Stepanovitch.

"No, not unwell, but I am afraid of being so in this climate," answered the writer in his squeaky voice, though he uttered each word with a soft cadence and agreeable gentlemanly lisp. "I've been expecting you since yesterday."

"Why? I didn't say I'd come."

"No, but you have my manuscript. Have you . . . read it?"

"Manuscript? Which one?"

Karmazinov was terribly surprised.

"But you've brought it with you, haven't you?" He was so disturbed that he even left off eating and looked at Pyotr Stepanovitch with a face of dismay.

"Ah, that *Bonjour* you mean. . . ."

"*Merci.*"

"Oh, all right. I'd quite forgotten it and hadn't read it; I haven't had time. I really don't know, it's not in my pockets . . . it must be on my table. Don't be uneasy, it will be found."

"No, I'd better send to your rooms at once. It might be lost; besides, it might be stolen."

"Oh, who'd want it! But why are you so alarmed? Why, Yulia Mihailovna told me you always have several copies made —one kept at a notary's abroad, another in Petersburg, a third in Moscow, and then you send some to a bank, I believe."

"But Moscow might be burnt again and my manuscript with it. No, I'd better send at once."

"Stay, here it is!" Pyotr Stepanovitch pulled a roll of note-paper out of a pocket at the back of his coat. "It's a little crumpled. Only fancy, it's been lying there with my pocket-handkerchief ever since I took it from you; I forgot it."

Karmazinov greedily snatched the manuscript, carefully examined it, counted the pages, and laid it respectfully beside him on a special table, for the time, in such a way that he would not lose sight of it for an instant.

"You don't read very much, it seems?" he hissed, unable to restrain himself.

"No, not very much."

"And nothing in the way of Russian literature?"

"In the way of Russian literature? Let me see, I have read something. . . . 'On the Way' or 'Away!' or 'At the Parting

of the Ways'—something of the sort; I don't remember. It's a long time since I read it, five years ago. I've no time."

A silence followed.

"When I came I assured everyone that you were a very intelligent man, and now I believe everyone here is wild over you."

"Thank you," Pyotr Stepanovitch answered calmly.

Lunch was brought in. Pyotr Stepanovitch pounced on the cutlet with extraordinary appetite, had eaten it in a trice, tossed off the wine and swallowed his coffee.

"This boor," thought Karmazinov, looking at him askance as he munched the last morsel and drained the last drops—"this boor probably understood the biting taunt in my words . . . and no doubt he has read the manuscript with eagerness; he is simply lying with some object. But possibly he is not lying and is only genuinely stupid. I like a genius to be rather stupid. Mayn't he be a sort of genius among them? Devil take the fellow!"

He got up from the sofa and began pacing from one end of the room to the other for the sake of exercise, as he always did after lunch.

"Leaving here soon?" asked Pyotr Stepanovitch from his easy chair, lighting a cigarette.

"I really came to sell an estate and I am in the hands of my bailiff."

"You left, I believe, because they expected an epidemic out there after the war?"

"N-no, not entirely for that reason," Mr. Karmazinov went on, uttering his phrases with an affable intonation, and each time he turned round in pacing the corner there was a faint but jaunty quiver of his right leg. "I certainly intend to live as long as I can." He laughed, not without venom. "There is something in our Russian nobility that makes them wear out very quickly, from every point of view. But I wish to wear out as late as possible, and now I am going abroad for good; there the climate is better, the houses are of stone, and everything stronger. Europe will last my time, I think. What do you think?"

"How can I tell?"

"H'm. If the Babylon out there really does fall, and great will be the fall thereof (about which I quite agree with you, yet I think it will last my time), there's nothing to fall here in Russia, comparatively speaking. There won't be stones to fall,

everything will crumble into dirt. Holy Russia has less power
of resistance than anything in the world. The Russian peasantry
is still held together somehow by the Russian God; but according to the latest accounts the Russian God is not to be relied
upon, and scarcely survived the emancipation; it certainly gave
Him a severe shock. And now, what with railways, what with
you . . . I've no faith in the Russian God."

"And how about the European one?"

"I don't believe in any. I've been slandered to the youth
of Russia. I've always sympathised with every movement
among them. I was shown the manifestos here. Everyone
looks at them with perplexity because they are frightened at
the way things are put in them, but everyone is convinced of
their power even if they don't admit it to themselves. Everybody has been rolling down-hill, and everyone has known for
ages that they have nothing to clutch at. I am persuaded of
the success of this mysterious propaganda, if only because
Russia is now pre-eminently the place in all the world where
anything you like may happen without any opposition. I
understand only too well why wealthy Russians all flock abroad,
and more and more so every year. It's simply instinct. If the
ship is sinking, the rats are the first to leave it. Holy Russia
is a country of wood, of poverty . . . and of danger, the
country of ambitious beggars in its upper classes, while the
immense majority live in poky little huts. She will be glad of
any way of escape; you have only to present it to her. It's only
the government that still means to resist, but it brandishes its
cudgel in the dark and hits its own men. Everything here is
doomed and awaiting the end. Russia as she is has no future.
I have become a German and I am proud of it."

"But you began about the manifestos. Tell me everything:
how do you look at them?"

"Everyone is afraid of them, so they must be influential.
They openly unmask what is false and prove that there is
nothing to lay hold of among us and nothing to lean upon. They
speak aloud while all is silent. What is most effective about
them (in spite of their style) is the incredible boldness with which
they look the truth straight in the face. To look facts straight
in the face is only possible to Russians of this generation. No, in
Europe they are not yet so bold; it is a realm of stone, there
there is still something to lean upon. So far as I see and am
able to judge, the whole essence of the Russian revolutionary
idea lies in the negation of honour. I like its being so boldly and

fearlessly expressed. No, in Europe they wouldn't understand it yet, but that's just what we shall clutch at. For a Russian a sense of honour is only a superfluous burden, and it always has been a burden through all his history. The open 'right to dishonour' will attract him more than anything. I belong to the older generation and, I must confess, still cling to honour, but only from habit. It is only that I prefer the old forms, granted it's from timidity; you see one must live somehow what's left of one's life.''

He suddenly stopped.

"I am talking," he thought, "while he holds his tongue and watches me. He has come to make me ask him a direct question. And I shall ask him.''

"Yulia Mihailovna asked me by some stratagem to find out from you what the surprise is that you are preparing for the ball to-morrow,'' Pyotr Stepanovitch asked suddenly.

"Yes, there really will be a surprise and I certainly shall astonish . . .'' said Karmazinov with increased dignity. "But I won't tell you what the secret is.''

Pyotr Stepanovitch did not insist.

"There is a young man here called Shatov,'' observed the great writer. "Would you believe it, I haven't seen him.''

"A very nice person. What about him?''

"Oh, nothing. He talks about something. Isn't he the person who gave Stavrogin that slap in the face?''

"Yes.''

"And what's your opinion of Stavrogin?''

"I don't know; he is such a flirt.''

Karmazinov detested Stavrogin because it was the latter's habit not to take any notice of him.

"That flirt,'' he said, chuckling "if what is advocated in your manifestos ever comes to pass, will be the first to be hanged.''

"Perhaps before,'' Pyotr Stepanovitch said suddenly.

"Quite right too,'' Karmazinov assented, not laughing, and with pronounced gravity.

"You have said so once before, and, do you know, I repeated it to him.''

"What, you surely didn't repeat it?'' Karmazinov laughed again.

"He said that if he were to be hanged it would be enough for you to be flogged, not simply as a compliment but to hurt, as they flog the peasants.''

Pyotr Stepanovitch took his hat and got up from his seat.

27

Karmazinov held out both hands to him at parting.

"And what if all that you are . . . plotting for is destined to come to pass . . ." he piped suddenly, in a honeyed voice with a peculiar intonation, still holding his hands in his. "How soon could it come about?"

"How could I tell?" Pyotr Stepanovitch answered rather roughly. They looked intently into each other's eyes.

"At a guess? Approximately?" Karmazinov piped still more sweetly.

"You'll have time to sell your estate and time to clear out too," Pyotr Stepanovitch muttered still more roughly. They looked at one another even more intently.

There was a minute of silence.

"It will begin early next May and will be over by October," Pyotr Stepanovitch said suddenly.

"I thank you sincerely," Karmazinov pronounced in a voice saturated with feeling, pressing his hands.

"You will have time to get out of the ship, you rat," Pyotr Stepanovitch was thinking as he went out into the street. "Well, if that 'imperial intellect' inquires so confidently of the day and the hour and thanks me so respectfully for the information I have given, we mustn't doubt of ourselves. [He grinned.] H'm! But he really isn't stupid . . . and he is simply a rat escaping; men like that don't tell tales!"

He ran to Filipov's house in Bogoyavlensky Street.

VI

Pyotr Stepanovitch went first to Kirillov's. He found him, as usual, alone, and at the moment practising gymnastics, that is, standing with his legs apart, brandishing his arms above his head in a peculiar way. On the floor lay a ball. The tea stood cold on the table, not cleared since breakfast. Pyotr Stepanovitch stood for a minute on the threshold.

"You are very anxious about your health, it seems," he said in a loud and cheerful tone, going into the room. "What a jolly ball, though; foo, how it bounces! Is that for gymnastics too?"

Kirillov put on his coat.

"Yes, that's for the good of my health too," he muttered dryly. "Sit down."

"I'm only here for a minute. Still, I'll sit down. Health is all very well, but I've come to remind you of our agreement. The appointed time is approaching . . . in a certain sense," he concluded awkwardly.

"What agreement?"

"How can you ask?" Pyotr Stepanovitch was startled and even dismayed.

"It's not an agreement and not an obligation. I have not bound myself in any way; it's a mistake on your part."

"I say, what's this you're doing?" Pyotr Stepanovitch jumped up.

"What I choose."

"What do you choose?"

"The same as before."

"How am I to understand that? Does that mean that you are in the same mind?"

"Yes. Only there's no agreement and never has been, and I have not bound myself in any way. I could do as I like and I can still do as I like."

Kirillov explained himself curtly and contemptuously.

"I agree, I agree; be as free as you like if you don't change your mind." Pyotr Stepanovitch sat down again with a satisfied air. "You are angry over a word. You've become very irritable of late; that's why I've avoided coming to see you. I was quite sure, though, you would be loyal."

"I dislike you very much, but you can be perfectly sure—though I don't regard it as loyalty and disloyalty."

"But do you know" (Pyotr Stepanovitch was startled again) "we must talk things over thoroughly again so as not to get in a muddle. The business needs accuracy, and you keep giving me such shocks. Will you let me speak?"

"Speak," snapped Kirillov, looking away.

"You made up your mind long ago to take your life . . . I mean, you had the idea in your mind. Is that the right expression? Is there any mistake about that?"

"I have the same idea still."

"Excellent. Take note that no one has forced it on you."

"Rather not; what nonsense you talk."

"I dare say I express it very stupidly. Of course, it would be very stupid to force anybody to it. I'll go on. You were a member of the society before its organisation was changed, and confessed it to one of the members."

"I didn't confess it, I simply said so."

"Quite so. And it would be absurd to confess such a thing.

What a confession! You simply said so. Excellent."

"No, it's not excellent, for you are being tedious. I am not obliged to give you any account of myself and you can't understand my ideas. I want to put an end to my life, because that's my idea, because I don't want to be afraid of death, because . . . because there's no need for you to know. What do you want? Would you like tea? It's cold. Let me get you another glass."

Pyotr Stepanovitch actually had taken up the teapot and was looking for an empty glass. Kirillov went to the cupboard and brought a clean glass.

"I've just had lunch at Karmazinov's," observed his visitor, "then I listened to him talking, and perspired and got into a sweat again running here. I am fearfully thirsty."

"Drink. Cold tea is good."

Kirillov sat down on his chair again and again fixed his eyes on the farthest corner.

"The idea has arisen in the society," he went on in the same voice, "that I might be of use if I killed myself, and that when you get up some bit of mischief here, and they are looking for the guilty, I might suddenly shoot myself and leave a letter saying I did it all, so that you might escape suspicion for another year."

"For a few days, anyway; one day is precious."

"Good. So for that reason they asked me, if I would, to wait. I said I'd wait till the society fixed the day, because it makes no difference to me."

"Yes, but remember that you bound yourself not to make up your last letter without me and that in Russia you would be at my . . . well, at my disposition, that is for that purpose only. I need hardly say, in everything else, of course, you are free," Pyotr Stepanovitch added almost amiably.

"I didn't bind myself, I agreed, because it makes no difference to me."

"Good, good. I have no intention of wounding your vanity, but . . ."

"It's not a question of vanity."

"But remember that a hundred and twenty thalers were collected for your journey, so you've taken money."

"Not at all." Kirillov fired up. "The money was not on that condition. One doesn't take money for that."

"People sometimes do."

"That's a lie. I sent a letter from Petersburg, and in Petersburg I paid you a hundred and twenty thalers; I put it in your hand . . . and it has been sent off there, unless you've kept it for yourself.''

"All right, all right, I don't dispute anything; it has been sent off. All that matters is that you are still in the same mind."

"Exactly the same. When you come and tell me it's time, I'll carry it all out. Will it be very soon?''

"Not very many days. . . . But remember, we'll make up the letter together, the same night."

"The same day if you like. You say I must take the responsibility for the manifestos on myself?''

"And something else too.''

"I am not going to make myself out responsible for everything.''

"What won't you be responsible for?'' said Pyotr Stepanovitch again.

"What I don't choose; that's enough. I don't want to talk about it any more.''

Pyotr Stepanovitch controlled himself and changed the subject.

"To speak of something else,'' he began, "will you be with us this evening? It's Virginsky's name-day; that's the pretext for our meeting.''

"I don't want to.''

"Do me a favour. Do come. You must. We must impress them by our number and our looks. You have a face . . . well, in one word, you have a fateful face.''

"You think so?'' laughed Kirillov. "Very well, I'll come, but not for the sake of my face. What time is it?''

"Oh, quite early, half-past six. And, you know, you can go in, sit down, and not speak to anyone, however many there may be there. Only, I say, don't forget to bring pencil and paper with you.''

"What's that for?''

"Why, it makes no difference to you, and it's my special request. You'll only have to sit still, speaking to no one, listen, and sometimes seem to make a note. You can draw something, if you like.''

"What nonsense! What for?''

"Why, since it makes no difference to you! You keep saying that it's just the same to you.''

"No, what for?''

"Why, because that member of the society, the inspector, has stopped at Moscow and I told some of them here that possibly the inspector may turn up to-night; and they'll think that you are the inspector. And as you've been here three weeks already, they'll be still more surprised."

"Stage tricks. You haven't got an inspector in Moscow."

"Well, suppose I haven't—damn him!—what business is that of yours and what bother will it be for you? You are a member of the society yourself."

"Tell them I am the inspector; I'll sit still and hold my tongue, but I won't have the pencil and paper."

"But why?"

"I don't want to."

Pyotr Stepanovitch was really angry; he turned positively green, but again he controlled himself. He got up and took his hat.

"Is that fellow with you?" he brought out suddenly, in a low voice.

"Yes."

"That's good. I'll soon get him away. Don't be uneasy."

"I am not uneasy. He is only here at night. The old woman is in the hospital, her daughter-in-law is dead. I've been alone for the last two days. I've shown him the place in the paling where you can take a board out; he gets through, no one sees."

"I'll take him away soon."

"He says he has got plenty of places to stay the night in."

"That's rot; they are looking for him, but here he wouldn't be noticed. Do you ever get into talk with him?"

"Yes, at night. He abuses you tremendously. I've been reading the 'Apocalypse' to him at night, and we have tea. He listened eagerly, very eagerly, the whole night."

"Hang it all, you'll convert him to Christianity!"

"He is a Christian as it is. Don't be uneasy, he'll do the murder. Whom do you want to murder?"

"No, I don't want him for that, I want him for something different. . . . And does Shatov know about Fedka?"

"I don't talk to Shatov, and I don't see him."

"Is he angry?"

"No, we are not angry, only we shun one another. We lay too long side by side in America."

"I am going to him directly."

"As you like."

32

"Stavrogin and I may come and see you from there, about ten o'clock."

"Do."

"I want to talk to him about something important. . . . I say, make me a present of your ball; what do you want with it now? I want it for gymnastics too. I'll pay you for it if you like."

"You can take it without."

Pyotr Stepanovitch put the ball in the back pocket of his coat.

"But I'll give you nothing against Stavrogin," Kirillov muttered after his guest, as he saw him out. The latter looked at him in amazement, but did not answer.

Kirillov's last words perplexed Pyotr Stepanovitch extremely; he had not time yet to discover their meaning, but even while he was on the stairs of Shatov's lodging he tried to remove all trace of annoyance and to assume an amiable expression. Shatov was at home and rather unwell. He was lying on his bed, though dressed.

"What bad luck!" Pyotr Stepanovitch cried out in the doorway. "Are you really ill?"

The amiable expression of his face suddenly vanished; there was a gleam of spite in his eyes.

"Not at all." Shatov jumped up nervously. "I am not ill at all . . . a little headache . . ."

He was disconcerted; the sudden appearance of such a visitor positively alarmed him.

"You mustn't be ill for the job I've come about," Pyotr Stepanovitch began quickly and, as it were, peremptorily. "Allow me to sit down." (He sat down.) "And you sit down again on your bedstead; that's right. There will be a party of our fellows at Virginsky's to-night on the pretext of his birthday; it will have no political character, however—we've seen to that. I am coming with Nikolay Stavrogin. I would not, of course, have dragged you there, knowing your way of thinking at present . . . simply to save your being worried, not because we think you would betray us. But as things have turned out, you will have to go. You'll meet there the very people with whom we shall finally settle how you are to leave the society and to whom you are to hand over what is in your keeping. We'll do it without being noticed; I'll take you aside into a corner; there'll be a lot of people and there's no need for everyone to know. I must confess I've had to keep my tongue wagging on your behalf; but now I believe they've agreed, on condition you hand over the printing-press and all the papers, of course. Then you can go where you please."

Shatov listened, frowning and resentful. The nervous alarm of a moment before had entirely left him.

"I don't acknowledge any sort of obligation to give an account to the devil knows whom," he declared definitely. "No one has the authority to set me free."

"Not quite so. A great deal has been entrusted to you. You hadn't the right to break off simply. Besides, you made no clear statement about it, so that you put them in an ambiguous position."

"I stated my position clearly by letter as soon as I arrived here."

"No, it wasn't clear," Pyotr Stepanovitch retorted calmly. "I sent you 'A Noble Personality' to be printed here, and meaning the copies to be kept here till they were wanted; and the two manifestos as well. You returned them with an ambiguous letter which explained nothing."

"I refused definitely to print them."

"Well, not definitely. You wrote that you couldn't, but you didn't explain for what reason. 'I can't' doesn't mean 'I don't want to'. It might be supposed that you were simply unable through circumstances. That was how they took it, and considered that you still meant to keep up your connection with the society, so that they might have entrusted something to you again and so have compromised themselves. They say here that you simply meant to deceive them, so that you might betray them when you got hold of something important. I have defended you to the best of my powers, and have shown your brief note as evidence in your favour. But I had to admit on rereading those two lines that they were misleading and not conclusive."

"You kept that note so carefully then?"

"My keeping it means nothing; I've got it still."

"Well, I don't care, damn it!" Shatov cried furiously. "Your fools may consider that I've betrayed them if they like—what is it to me? I should like to see what you can do to me?"

"Your name would be noted, and at the first success of the revolution you would be hanged."

"That's when you get the upper hand and dominate Russia?"

"You needn't laugh. I tell you again, I stood up for you. Anyway, I advise you to turn up to-day. Why waste words through false pride? Isn't it better to part friends? In any case you'll have to give up the printing-press and the old type and papers—that's what we must talk about."

"I'll come," Shatov muttered, looking down thoughtfully.

Pyotr Stepanovitch glanced askance at him from his place.

"Will Stavrogin be there?" Shatov asked suddenly, raising his head.

"He is certain to be."

"Ha ha!"

Again they were silent for a minute. Shatov grinned disdainfully and irritably.

"And that contemptible 'Noble Personality' of yours, that I wouldn't print here. Has it been printed?" he asked.

"Yes."

"To make the schoolboys believe that Herzen himself had written it in your album?"

"Yes, Herzen himself."

Again they were silent for three minutes. At last Shatov got up from the bed.

"Go out of my room; I don't care to sit with you."

"I'm going," Pyotr Stepanovitch brought out with positive alacrity, getting up at once. "Only one word: Kirillov is quite alone in the lodge now, isn't he, without a servant?"

"Quite alone. Get along; I can't stand being in the same room with you."

"'Well, you are a pleasant customer now!" Pyotr Stepanovitch reflected gaily as he went out into the street, "and you will be pleasant this evening too, and that just suits me; nothing better could be wished, nothing better could be wished! The Russian God Himself seems helping me."

VII

He had probably been very busy that day on all sorts of errands and probably with success, which was reflected in the self-satisfied expression of his face when at six o'clock that evening he turned up at Stavrogin's. But he was not at once admitted: Stavrogin had just locked himself in the study with Mavriky Nikolaevitch. This news instantly made Pyotr Stepanovitch anxious. He seated himself close to the study door to wait for the visitor to go away. He could hear conversation, but could not catch the words. The visit did not last long;

soon he heard a noise, the sound of an extremely loud and abrupt voice, then the door opened and Mavriky Nikolaevitch came out with a very pale face. He did not notice Pyotr Stepanovitch, and quickly passed by. Pyotr Stepanovitch instantly ran into the study.

I cannot omit a detailed account of the very brief interview that had taken place between the two "rivals"—an interview which might well have seemed impossible under the circumstances, but which had yet taken place.

This is how it had come about. Nikolay Vsyevolodovitch had been enjoying an after-dinner nap on the couch in his study when Alexey Yegorytch had announced the unexpected visitor. Hearing the name, he had positively leapt up, unwilling to believe it. But soon a smile gleamed on his lips—a smile of haughty triumph and at the same time of a blank, incredulous wonder. The visitor, Mavriky Nikolaevitch, seemed struck by the expression of that smile as he came in; anyway, he stood still in the middle of the room, as though uncertain whether to come farther in or to turn back. Stavrogin succeeded at once in transforming the expression of his face, and with an air of grave surprise took a step towards him. The visitor did not take his outstretched hand, but awkwardly moved a chair and, not uttering a word, sat down without waiting for his host to do so. Nikolay Vsyevolodovitch sat down on the sofa facing him obliquely and, looking at Mavriky Nikolaevitch, waited in silence.

"If you can, marry Lizaveta Nikolaevna," Mavriky Nikolaevitch brought out suddenly at last, and what was most curious, it was impossible to tell from his tone whether it was an entreaty, a recommendation, a surrender, or a command.

Stavrogin still remained silent, but the visitor had evidently said all he had come to say and gazed at him persistently, waiting for an answer.

"If I am not mistaken (but it's quite certain), Lizaveta Nikolaevna is already betrothed to you," Stavrogin said at last.

"Promised and betrothed," Mavriky Nikolaevitch assented firmly and clearly.

"You have . . . quarrelled? Excuse me, Mavriky Nikolaevitch."

"No, she 'loves and respects me'; those are her words. Her words are more precious than anything."

"Of that there can be no doubt."

"But let me tell you, if she were standing in the church at her wedding and you were to call her, she'd give up me and everyone and go to you."

"From the wedding?"

"Yes, and after the wedding."

"Aren't you making a mistake?"

"No. Under her persistent, sincere, and intense hatred for you love is flashing out at every moment . . . and madness . . . the sincerest infinite love and . . . madness! On the contrary, behind the love she feels for me, which is sincere too, every moment there are flashes of hatred . . . the most intense hatred! I could never have fancied all these transitions . . . before."

"But I wonder, though, how could you come here and dispose of the hand of Lizaveta Nikolaevna? Have you the right to do so? Has she authorised you?"

Mavriky Nikolaevitch frowned and for a miuute he looked down.

"That's all words on your part," he brought out suddenly, "words of revenge and triumph; I am sure you can read between the lines, and is this the time for petty vanity? Haven't you satisfaction enough? Must I really dot my *i*'s and go into it all? Very well, I will dot my *i*'s, if you are so anxious for my humiliation. I have no right, it's impossible for me to be authorised; Lizaveta Nikolaevna knows nothing about it and her betrothed has finally lost his senses and is only fit for a madhouse, and, to crown everything, has come to tell you so himself. You are the only man in the world who can make her happy, and I am the one to make her unhappy. You are trying to get her, you are pursuing her, but—I don't know why —you won't marry her. If it's because of a lovers' quarrel abroad and I must be sacrificed to end it, sacrifice me. She is too unhappy and I can't endure it. My words are not a sanction, not a prescription, and so it's no slur on your pride. If you care to take my place at the altar, you can do it without any sanction from me, and there is no ground for me to come to you with a mad proposal, especially as our marriage is utterly impossible after the step I am taking now. I cannot lead her to the altar feeling myself an abject wretch. What I am doing here and my handing her over to you, perhaps her bitterest foe, is to my mind something so abject that I shall never get over it."

"Will you shoot yourself on our wedding day?"

"No, much later. Why stain her bridal dress with my blood? Perhaps I shall not shoot myself at all, either now or later."

"I suppose you want to comfort me by saying that?"

"You? What would the blood of one more mean to you?" He turned pale and his eyes gleamed. A minute of silence followed.

"Excuse me for the questions I've asked you," Stavrogin began again; "some of them I had no business to ask you, but one of them I think I have every right to put to you. Tell me, what facts have led you to form a conclusion as to my feelings for Lizaveta Nikolaevna? I mean to a conviction of a degree of feeling on my part as would justify your coming here . . . and risking such a proposal."

"What?" Mavriky Nikolaevitch positively started. "Haven't you been trying to win her? Aren't you trying to win her, and don't you want to win her?"

"Generally speaking, I can't speak of my feeling for this woman or that to a third person or to anyone except the woman herself. You must excuse it, it's a constitutional peculiarity. But to make up for it, I'll tell you the truth about everything else; I am married, and it's impossible for me either to marry or to try 'to win' anyone."

Mavriky Nikolaevitch was so astounded that he started back in his chair and for some time stared fixedly into Stavrogin's face.

"Only fancy, I never thought of that," he muttered. "You said then, that morning, that you were not married . . . and so I believed you were not married."

He turned terribly pale; suddenly he brought his fist down on the table with all his might.

"If after that confession you don't leave Lizaveta Nikolaevna alone, if you make her unhppy, I'll kill you with my stick like a dog in a ditch!"

He jumped up and walked quickly out of the room. Pyotr Stepanovitch, running in, found his host in a most unexpected frame of mind.

"Ah, that's you!" Stavrogin laughed loudly; his laughter seemed to be provoked simply by the appearance of Pyotr Stepanovitch as he ran in with such impulsive curiosity.

"Were you listening at the door? Wait a bit. What have you come about? I promised you something, didn't I? Ah, bah! I remember, to meet 'our fellows'. Let us go. I am delighted. You couldn't have thought of anything more appropriate."

He snatched up his hat and they both went at once out of the house.

"Are you laughing beforehand at the prospect of seeing 'our fellows'?" chirped gaily Pyotr Stepanovitch, dodging round him with obsequious alacrity, at one moment trying to walk beside his companion on the narrow brick pavement and at the next running right into the mud of the road; for Stavrogin walked in the middle of the pavement without observing that he left no room for anyone else.

"I am not laughing at all," he answered loudly and gaily; "on the contrary, I am sure that you have the most serious set of people there."

" 'Surly dullards,' as you once deigned to express it."

"Nothing is more amusing sometimes than a surly dullard."

"Ah, you mean Mavriky Nikolaevitch? I am convinced he came to give up his betrothed to you, eh? I egged him on to do it, indirectly, would you believe it? And if he doesn't give her up, we'll take her, anyway, won't we—eh?"

Pyotr Stepanovitch knew no doubt that he was running some risk in venturing on such sallies, but when he was excited he preferred to risk anything rather than to remain in uncertainty. Stavrogin only laughed.

"'You still reckon you'll help me?" he asked.

"If you call me. But you know there's one way, and the best one."

"'Do I know your way?"

"Oh no, that's a secret for the time. Only remember, a secret has its price."

"I know what it costs," Stavrogin muttered to himself, but he restrained himself and was silent.

"What it costs? What did you say?" Pyotr Stepanovitch was startled.

"I said: 'Damn you and your secret!' You'd better be telling me who will be there. I know that we are going to a name-day party, but who will be there?"

"Oh, all sorts! Even Kirillov."

"All members of circles?"

"Hang it all, you are in a hurry! There's not one circle formed yet."

"How did you manage to distribute so many manifestos then?"

"Where we are going only four are members of the circle. The others on probation are spying on one another with jealous eagerness, and bring reports to me. They are a trustworthy set. It's all material which we must organise, and then we must clear out. But you wrote the rules yourself, there's no need to explain."

"Are things going badly then? Is there a hitch?"

"Going? Couldn't be better. It will amuse you: the first thing which has a tremendous effect is giving them titles. Nothing has more influence than a title. I invent ranks and duties on purpose; I have secretaries, secret spies, treasurers, presidents, registrars, their assistants—they like it awfully, it's taken capitally. Then, the next force is sentimentalism, of course. You know, amongst us socialism spreads principally through sentimentalism. But the trouble is these lieutenants who bite; sometimes you put your foot in it. Then come the out-and-out rogues; well, they are a good sort, if you like, and sometimes very useful; but they waste a lot of one's time, they want incessant looking after. And the most important force of all—the cement that holds everything together—is their being ashamed of having an opinion of their own. That is a force! And whose work is it, whose precious achievement is it, that not one idea of their own is left in their heads! They think originality a disgrace."

"If so, why do you take so much trouble?"

"Why, if people lie simply gaping at everyone, how can you resist annexing them? Can you seriously refuse to believe in the possibility of success? Yes, you have the faith, but one wants will. It's just with people like this that success is possible. I tell you I could make them go through fire; one has only to din it into them that they are not advanced enough. The fools reproach me that I have taken in everyone here over the central committee and 'the innumerable branches'. You once blamed me for it yourself, but where's the deception? You and I are the central committee and there will be as many branches as we like."

"And always the same sort of rabble!"

"Raw material. Even they will be of use."

"You are the chief, you are the head; I shall only be a subordinate, your secretary. We shall take to our barque, you know; the oars are of maple, the sails are of silk, at the helm sits a fair maiden, Lizaveta Nikolaevna . . . hang it, how does it go in the ballad?"

"He is stuck," laughed Stavrogin. "No, I'd better give you my version. Then you reckon on your fingers the forces that make up the circles. All that business of titles and sentimentalism is a very good cement, but there is something better; persuade four members of the circle to do for a fifth on the pretence that he is a traitor, and you'll tie them all together with the blood they've shed as though it were a knot. They'll be your slaves, they won't dare to rebel or call you to account. Ha ha ha!"

"But you . . . you shall pay for those words," Pyotr Stepanovitch thought to himself, "and this very evening, in fact. You go too far."

This or something like this must have been Pyotr Stepanovitch's reflection. They were approaching Virginsky's house.

"You've represented me, no doubt, as a member from abroad, an inspector in connection with the *Internationale?*" Stavrogin asked suddenly.

"No, not an inspector: you won't be an inspector; but you are one of the original members from abroad, who knows the most important secrets—that's your role. You are going to speak, of course?"

"What's put that idea into your head?"

"Now you are bound to speak."

Stavrogin positively stood still in the middle of the street in surprise, not far from a street lamp. Pyotr Stepanovitch faced his scrutiny calmly and defiantly. Stavrogin cursed and went on.

"And are you going to speak?" he suddenly asked Pyotr Stepanovitch.

"No, I am going to listen to you."

"Damn you, you really are giving me an idea?"

"What idea?" Pyotr Stepanovitch asked quickly.

"Perhaps I will speak there, but afterwards I will give you a hiding—and a sound one too, you know."

"By the way, I told Karmazinov this morning that you said he ought to be thrashed, and not simply as a form, but to hurt, as they flog peasants."

"But I never said such a thing; ha ha!"

"No matter. *Se non è vero . . .*"

"Well, thanks. I am truly obliged."

"And another thing. Do you know, Karmazinov says that the essence of our creed is the negation of honour, and that by the open advocacy of a right to be dishonourable a Russian can be won over more easily than by anything."

"An excellent saying! Golden words!" cried Stavrogin. "He's hit the mark there! The right to dishonour—why, they'd all flock to us for that, not one would stay behind! And listen, Verhovensky, you are not one of the higher police, are you?"

"Anyone who has a question like that in his mind doesn't utter it."

"I understand, but we are by ourselves."

"No, so far I am not one of the higher police. Enough, here we are. Compose your features, Stavrogin; I always do mine when I go in. A gloomy expression, that's all, nothing more is wanted! it's a very simple business."

CHAPTER VII

A MEETING

I

VIRGINSKY lived in his own house, or rather his wife's, in Muravyin Street. It was a wooden house of one storey, and there were no lodgers in it. On the pretext of Virginsky's name-day party, about fifteen guests were assembled; but the entertainment was not in the least like an ordinary provincial name-day party. From the very beginning of their married life the husband and wife had agreed once for all that it was utterly stupid to invite friends to celebrate name-days, and that "there is nothing to rejoice about in fact". In a few years they had succeeded in completely cutting themselves off from all society. Though he was a man of some ability, and by no means very poor, he somehow seemed to everyone an eccentric fellow who was fond of solitude, and, what's more, "stuck up in conversation". Madame Virginsky was a midwife by profession, and by that very fact was on the lowest rung of the social ladder, lower even than the priest's wife, in spite of her husband's rank as an officer. But she was conspicuously lacking in the humility befitting her position. And after her very stupid and unpardonable open liaison on principle with Captain Lebyadkin, a notorious rogue, even the most indulgent of our ladies turned away from her with marked contempt. But Madame Virginsky accepted all this as though it were what she wanted. It is remarkable that those very ladies applied to Arina Prohorovna (that is, Madame Virginsky) when they were in an interesting condition, rather than to anyone of the other three accoucheuses of the town. She was sent for even by country families living in the neighbourhood, so great was the belief in her knowledge, luck, and skill in critical cases. It ended in her practising only among the wealthiest ladies; she was greedy of money. Feeling her power to the full, she ended by not putting herself out for anyone. Possibly on purpose, indeed, in her practice in the best houses she used to scare nervous patients by the most incredible and nihilistic disregard of good manners, or by jeering at "everything holy", at the very time when "everything holy" might have come in most useful. Our town doctor, Rozanov— he too was an accoucheur—asserted most positively that on one occasion when a patient in labour was crying out and calling on the name of the Almighty, a free-thinking sally from Arina Prohorovna, fired off like a pistol-shot, had so terrifying an effect on the patient that it greatly accelerated her delivery.

But though she was a nihilist, Madame Virginsky did not, when occasion arose, disdain social or even old-fashioned super-stitions and customs if they could be of any advantage to her-self. She would never, for instance, have stayed away from a baby's christening, and always put on a green silk dress with a train and adorned her chignon with curls and ringlets for such events, though at other times she positively revelled in sloven-liness. And though during the ceremony she always main-tained "the most insolent air", so that she put the clergy to confusion, yet when it was over she invariably handed cham-pagne to the guests (it was for that she came and dressed up), and it was no use trying to take the glass without a contribu-tion to her "porridge bowl".

The guests who assembled that evening at Virginsky's (mostly men) had a casual and exceptional air. There was no supper nor cards. In the middle of the large drawing-room, which was papered with extremely old blue paper, two tables had been put together and covered with a large though not quite clean table-cloth, and on them two samovars were boiling. The end of the table was taken up by a huge tray with twenty-five glasses on it and a basket with ordinary French bread cut into a number of slices, as one sees it in genteel boarding-schools for boys or girls. The tea was poured out by a maiden lady of thirty, Arina Prohorovna's sister, a silent and malevolent creature, with flaxen hair and no eyebrows, who shared her sister's progressive ideas and was an object of terror to Virginsky himself in domestic life. There were only three ladies in the room: the lady of the house, her eyebrowless sister, and Virginsky's sister, a girl who had just arrived from Petersburg. Arina Prohorovna, a good-looking and buxom woman of seven-and-twenty, rather dishevelled, in an everyday greenish woollen dress, was sitting scanning the guests with her bold eyes, and her look seemed in haste to say: "You see I am not in the least afraid of anything." Miss Virginsky, a rosy-cheeked student and a nihilist, who was also good-looking, short, plump, and round as a little ball, had settled herself beside Arina Prohorovna, almost in her travelling clothes. She held a roll of paper in her hand, and scrutinised the guests with impatient and roving eyes. Virginsky himself was rather unwell that evening, but he came in and sat in an easy chair by the tea-table. All the guests were sitting down too, and the orderly way in which they were ranged on chairs suggested a meeting. Evidently all were expecting something and were filling up the interval with loud but irrelevant conversation. When Stavrogin and Verhovensky appeared there was a sudden hush.

But I must be allowed to give a few explanations to make things clear.

I believe that all these people had come together in the agreeable expectation of hearing something particularly interesting, and had notice of it beforehand. They were the flower of the reddest Radicalism of our ancient town, and had been carefully picked out by Virginsky for this "meeting". I may remark, too, that some of them (though not very many) had never visited him before. Of course, most of the guests had no clear idea why they had been summoned. It was true that at that time all took Pyotr Stepanovitch for a fully authorised emissary from aboard; this idea had somehow taken root among them at once and naturally flattered them. And yet among the citizens assembled ostensibly to keep a name-day, there were some who had been approached with definite proposals. Pyotr Verhovensky had succeeded in getting together a "quintet" amongst us like the one he had already formed in Moscow and, as appeared later, in our province among the officers. It was said that he had another in X province. This quintet of the elect were sitting now at the general table, and very skilfully succeeded in giving themselves the air of being quite ordinary people, so that no one could have known them. They were—since it is no longer a secret—first Liputin, then Virginsky himself, then

Shigalov (a gentleman with long ears, the brother of Madame Virginsky), Lyamshin, and lastly a strange person called Tolkatchenko, a man of forty, who was famed for his vast knowledge of the people, especially of thieves and robbers. He used to frequent the taverns on purpose (though not only with the object of studying the people), and plumed himself on his shabby clothes, tarred boots, and crafty wink and a flourish of peasant phrases. Lyamshin had once or twice brought him to Stepan Trofimovitch's gatherings, where, however, he did not make a great sensation. He used to make his appearance in the town from time to time, chiefly when he was out of a job; he was employed on the railway.

Everyone of these fine champions had formed this first group in the fervent conviction that their quintet was only one of hundreds and thousands of similar groups scattered all over Russia, and that they all depended on some immense central but secret power, which in its turn was intimately connected with the revolutionary movement all over Europe. But I regret to say that even at that time there was beginning to be dissension among them. Though they had ever since the spring been expecting Pyotr Verhovensky, whose coming had been heralded first by Tolkatchenko and then by the arrival of Shigalov, though they had expected extraordinary miracles from him, and though they had responded to his first summons without the slightest criticism, yet they had no sooner formed the quintet than they all somehow seemed to feel insulted; and I really believe it was owing to the promptitude with which they consented to join. They had joined, of course, from a not ignoble feeling of shame, for fear people might say afterwards that they had not dared to join; still they felt Pyotr Verhovensky ought to have appreciated their heroism and have rewarded it by telling them some really important bits of news at least. But Verhovensky was not at all inclined to satisfy their legitimate curiosity, and told them nothing but what was necessary; he treated them in general with great sternness and even rather casually. This was positively irritating, and Comrade Shigalov was already egging the others on to insist on his "explaining himself", though, of course, not at Virginsky's, where so many outsiders were present.

I have an idea that the above-mentioned members of the first quintet were disposed to suspect that among the guests of Virginsky's that evening some were members of other groups, unknown to them, belonging to the same secret organisation and founded in the town by the same Verhovensky; so that in fact all present were suspecting one another, and posed in various ways to one another, which gave the whole party a very perplexing and even romantic air. Yet there were persons present who were beyond all suspicion. For instance, a major in the service, a near relation of Virginsky, a perfectly innocent person who had not been invited but had come of himself for the name-day celebration, so that it was impossible not to receive him. But Virginsky was quite unperturbed, as the major was "incapable of betraying them"; for in spite of his stupidity he had all his life been fond of dropping in wherever extreme Radicals met; he did not sympathise with their ideas himself, but was very fond of listening to them. What's more, he had even been compromised indeed. It had happened in his youth that whole bundles of manifestos and of numbers of *The Bell* had passed through his hands, and although he had been afraid even to open them, yet he would have considered it absolutely contemptible to refuse to distribute them—and there are such people in Russia even to this day.

The rest of the guests were either types of honourable *amour-propre* crushed and embittered, or types of the generous impulsiveness of ardent youth. There were two or three teachers, of whom one, a lame man of forty-five, a master in the high school, was a very malicious and strikingly vain person; and two or three officers. Of the latter, one very young artillery officer who had only just come from a military training school, a silent lad who had not yet made friends with anyone, turned up now at Virginsky's with a pencil in his hand, and, scarcely taking any part in the conversation, continually made notes in his note-book. Everybody saw this, but everyone pretended not to. There was, too, an idle divinity student who had helped Lyamshin to put indecent photographs into the gospel-woman's pack. He was a solid youth with a free-and-easy though mistrustful manner, with an unchangeably satirical smile, together with a calm air of triumphant faith in his own perfection. There was also present, I don't know why, the mayor's son, that unpleasant and prematurely exhausted youth to whom I have referred already in telling the story of the lieutenant's little wife. He was silent the whole evening. Finally there was a very enthusiastic and tousle-headed schoolboy of eighteen, who sat with the gloomy air of a young man whose dignity has been wounded, evidently distressed by his eighteen years. This infant was already the head of an independent group of conspirators which had been formed in the highest class of the gymnasium, as it came out afterwards to the surprise of everyone.

I haven't mentioned Shatov. He was there at the farthest corner of the table, his chair pushed back a little out of the row. He gazed at the ground, was gloomily silent, refused tea and bread, and did not for one instant let his cap go out of his hand, as though to show that he was not a visitor, but had come on business, and when he liked would get up and go away. Kirillov was not far from him. He, too, was very silent, but he did not look at the ground; on the contrary, he scrutinised intently every speaker with his fixed, lustreless eyes, and listened to everything without the slightest emotion or surprise. Some of the visitors who had never seen him before stole thoughtful glances at him. I can't say whether Madame Virginsky knew anything about the existence of the quintet. I imagine she knew everything and from her husband. The girl-student, of course, took no part in anything; but she had an anxiety of her own: she intended to stay only a day or two and then to go on farther and farther from one university town to another "to show active sympathy with the sufferings of poor students and to rouse them to protest". She was taking with her some hundreds of copies of lithographed appeal, I believe of her own composition. It is remarkable that the schoolboy conceived an almost murderous hatred for her from the first moment, though he saw her for the first time in his life; and she felt the same for him. The major was her uncle, and met her to-day for the first time after ten years. When Stavrogin and Verhovensky came in, her cheeks were as red as cranberries: she had just quarrelled with her uncle over his views on the woman question.

II

With conspicuous nonchalance Verhovensky lounged in the chair at the upper end of the table, almost without greeting anyone. His expression was disdainful and even haughty. Stavrogin bowed politely, but in spite of the fact that they were all only waiting for them, everybody, as though acting on instruction, appeared scarcely to notice them. The lady of the house turned severely to Stavrogin as soon as he was seated.

"Stavrogin, will you have tea?"

"Please," he answered.

"Tea for Stavrogin," she commanded her sister at the

samovar. "And you, will you?" (This was to Verhovensky.)

"Of course. What a question to ask a visitor! And give me cream too; you always give one such filthy stuff by way of tea, and with a name-day party in the house!"

"What, you believe in keeping name-days too!" the girl-student laughed suddenly. "We were just talking of that."

"That's stale," muttered the schoolboy at the other end of the table.

"What's stale? To disregard conventions, even the most innocent is not stale; on the contrary, to the disgrace of everyone, so far it's a novelty," the girl-student answered instantly, darting forward on her chair. "Besides, there are no innocent conventions," she added with intensity.

"I only meant," cried the schoolboy with tremendous excitement, "to say that though conventions of course are stale and must be eradicated, yet about name-days everybody knows that they are stupid and very stale to waste precious time upon, which has been wasted already all over the world, so that it would be as well to sharpen one's wits on something more useful. . . ."

"You drag it out so, one can't understand what you mean," shouted the girl.

"I think that everyone has a right to express an opinion as well as everyone else, and if I want to express my opinion like anybody else . . ."

"No one is attacking your right to give an opinion," the lady of the house herself cut in sharply. "You were only asked not to ramble because no one can make out what you mean."

"But allow me to remark that you are not treating me with respect. If I couldn't fully express my thought, it's not from want of thought but from too much thought," the schoolboy muttered, almost in despair, losing his thread completely.

"If you don't know how to talk, you'd better keep quiet," blurted out the girl.

The schoolboy positively jumped from his chair.

"I only wanted to state,' he shouted, crimson with shame and afraid to look about him, "that you only wanted to show off your cleverness because Mr. Stavrogin came in—so there!"

"That's a nasty and immoral idea and shows the worthlessness of your development. I beg you not to address me again," the girl rattled off.

"Stavrogin," began the lady of the house, "they've been discussing the rights of the family before you came—this officer

here"—she nodded towards her relation, the major—"and, of course, I am not going to worry you with such stale nonsense, which has been dealt with long ago. But how have the rights and duties of the family come about in the superstitious form in which they exist at present? That's the question. What's your opinion?"

"What do you mean by 'come about'?" Stavrogin asked in his turn.

"We know, for instance, that the superstition about God came from thunder and lightning." The girl-student rushed into the fray again, staring at Stavrogin with her eyes almost jumping out of her head. "It's well known that primitive man, scared by thunder and lightning, made a god of the unseen enemy, feeling their weakness before it. But how did the superstition of the family arise? How did the family itself arise?"

"That's not quite the same thing. . . ." Madame Virginsky tried to check her.

"I think the answer to this question wouldn't be quite discreet," answered Stavrogin.

"How so?" said the girl-student, craning forward suddenly.

But there was an audible titter in the group of teachers, which was at once caught up at the other end by Lyamshin and the schoolboy and followed by a hoarse chuckle from the major.

"You ought to write vaudevilles," Madame Virginsky observed to Stavrogin.

"It does you no credit, I don't know what your name is," the girl rapped out with positive indignation.

"And don't you be too forward," boomed the major. "You are a young lady and you ought to behave modestly, and you keep jumping about as though you were sitting on a needle."

"Kindly hold your tongue and don't address me familiarly with your nasty comparisons. I've never seen you before and I don't recognise the relationship."

"But I am your uncle; I used to carry you about when you were a baby!"

"I don't care what babies you used to carry about. I didn't ask you to carry me. It must have been a pleasure to you to do so, you rude officer. And allow me to observe, don't dare to address me so familiarly, unless it's as a fellow-citizen. I forbid you to do it, once for all."

"There, they are all like that!" cried the major, banging the table with his fist and addressing Stavrogin, who was sitting opposite. "But, allow me, I am fond of Liberalism and modern ideas, and I am fond of listening to clever conversation; masculine conversation, though, I warn you. But to listen to these women, these flighty windmills—no, that makes me ache all over! Don't wriggle about!" he shouted to the girl, who was leaping up from her chair. "No, it's my turn to speak, I've been insulted."

"You can't say anything yourself, and only hinder other people talking," the lady of the house grumbled indignantly.

"No, I will have my say," said the major hotly, addressing Stavrogin. "I reckon on you, Mr. Stavrogin, as a fresh person who has only just come on the scene, though I haven't the honour of knowing you. Without men they'll perish like flies—that's what I think. All their woman question is only lack of originality. I assure you that all this woman question has been invented for them by men in foolishness and to their own hurt. I only thank God I am not married. There's not the slightest variety in them, they can't even invent a simple pattern; they have to get men to invent them for them! Here I used to carry her in my arms, used to dance the mazurka with her when she was ten years old; to-day she's come, naturally I fly to embrace her, and at the second word she tells me there's no God. She might have waited a little, she was in too great a hurry! Clever people don't believe, I dare say; but that's from their cleverness. But you, chicken, what do you know about God? I said to her. 'Some student taught you, and if he'd taught you to light the lamp before the ikons you would have lighted it.' "

"You keep telling lies, you are a very spiteful person. I proved to you just now the untenability of your position," the girl answered contemptuously, as though disdaining further explanations with such a man. "I told you just now that we've all been taught in the Catechism if you honour your father and your parents you will live long and have wealth. That's in the Ten Commandments. If God thought it necessary to offer rewards for love, your God must be immoral. That's how I proved it to you. It wasn't the second word, and it was because you asserted your rights. It's not my fault if you are stupid and don't understand even now. You are offended and you are spiteful—and that's what explains all your generation."

"You're a goose!" said the major.

"And you are a fool!"

"You can call me names!"

"Excuse me, Kapiton Maximitch, you told me yourself you

don't believe in God," Liputin piped from the other end of the table.

"What if I did say so—that's a different matter. I believe, perhaps, only not altogether. Even if I don't believe altogether, still I don't say God ought to be shot. I used to think about God before I left the hussars. From all the poems you would think that hussars do nothing but carouse and drink. Yes, I did drink, maybe, but would you believe it, I used to jump out of bed at night and stood crossing myself before the images with nothing but my socks on, praying to God to give me faith; for even then I couldn't be at peace as to whether there was a God or not. It used to fret me so! In the morning, of course, one would amuse oneself and one's faith would seem to be lost again; and in fact I've noticed that faith always seems to be less in the daytime."

"Haven't you any cards?" asked Verhovensky, with a mighty yawn, addressing Madame Virginsky.

"I sympathise with your question, I sympathise entirely," the girl-student broke in hotly, flushed with indignation at the major's words.

"We are wasting precious time listening to silly talk," snapped out the lady of the house, and she looked reprovingly at her husband.

The girl pulled herself together.

"I wanted to make a statement to the meeting concerning the sufferings of the students and their protest, but as time is being wasted in immoral conversation . . ."

"There's no such thing as moral or immoral," the school-boy brought out, unable to restrain himself as soon as the girl began.

"I knew that, Mr. Schoolboy, long before you were taught it."

"And I maintain," he answered savagely, "that you are a child come from Petersburg to enlighten us all, though we know for ourselves the commandment 'honour thy father and thy mother', which you could not repeat correctly; and the fact that it's immoral everyone in Russia knows from Byelinsky."

"Are we ever to have an end of this?" Madame Virginsky said resolutely to her husband. As the hostess, she blushed for the ineptitude of the conversation, especially as she noticed smiles and even astonishment among the guests who had been invited for the first time.

"Gentlemen," said Virginsky, suddenly lifting up his voice

"if anyone wishes to say anything more nearly connected with our business, or has any statement to make, I call upon him to do so without wasting time."

"I'll venture to ask one question," said the lame teacher suavely. He had been sitting particularly decorously and had not spoken till then. "I should like to know, are we some sort of meeting, or are we simply a gathering of ordinary mortals paying a visit? I ask simply for the sake of order and so as not to remain in ignorance."

This "sly" question made an impression. People looked at each other, everyone expecting someone else to answer, and suddenly all, as though at a word of command, turned their eyes to Verhovensky and Stavrogin.

"I suggest our voting on the answer to the question whether we are a meeting or not," said Madame Virginsky.

"I entirely agree with the suggestion," Liputin chimed in, "though the question is rather vague."

"I agree too." "And so do I," cried voices.

"I too think it would make our proceedings more in order," confirmed Virginsky.

"To the vote then," said his wife. "Lyamshin, please sit down to the piano; you can give your vote from there when the voting begins."

"Again!" cried Lyamshin. "I've strummed enough for you."

"I beg you most particularly, sit down and play. Don't you care to do anything for the cause?"

"But I assure you, Arina Prohorovna, nobody is eavesdropping. It's only your fancy. Besides, the windows are high, and people would not understand if they did hear."

"We don't understand ourselves," someone muttered.

"But I tell you one must always be on one's guard. I mean in case there should be spies," she explained to Verhovensky. "Let them hear from the street that we have music and a name-day party."

"Hang it all!" Lyamshin swore, and sitting down to the piano, began strumming a valse, banging on the keys almost with his fists, at random.

"I propose that those who want it to be a meeting should put up their right hands," Madame Virginsky proposed.

Some put them up, others did not. Some held them up and then put them down again and then held them up again.

"Foo! I don't understand it at all," one officer shouted.

"I don't either," cried the other.

"Oh, I understand," cried a third. "If it's *yes*, you hold your hand up."

"But what does 'yes' mean?"

"Means a meeting."

"No, it means not a meeting."

"I voted for a meeting," cried the schoolboy to Madame Virginsky.

"Then why didn't you hold up your hand?"

"I was looking at you. You didn't hold up yours, so I didn't hold up mine."

"How stupid! I didn't hold up my hand because I proposed it. Gentlemen, now I propose the contrary. Those who want a meeting, sit still and do nothing; those who don't, hold up their right hands."

"Those who don't want it?" inquired the schoolboy.

"Are you doing it on purpose?" cried Madame Virginsky wrathfully.

"No. Excuse me, those who want it, or those who don't want it? For one must know that definitely," cried two or three voices.

"Those who don't want it—those who *don't* want it."

"Yes, but what is one to do, hold up one's hand or not hold it up if one doesn't want it?" cried an officer.

"Ech, we are not accustomed to constitutional methods yet!" remarked the major.

"Mr. Lyamshin, excuse me, but you are thumping so that no one can hear anything," observed the lame teacher.

"But, upon my word, Arina Prohorovna, nobody is listening, really!" cried Lyamshin, jumping up. "I won't play! I've come to you as a visitor, not as a drummer!"

"Gentlemen," Virginsky went on, "answer verbally, are we a meeting or not?"

"We are! We are!" was heard on all sides.

"If so, there's no need to vote, that's enough. Are you satisfied, gentlemen? Is there any need to put it to the vote?"

"No need—no need, we understand."

"Perhaps someone doesn't want it to be a meeting?"

"No, no; we all want it."

"But what does 'meeting' mean?" cried a voice.

No one answered.

"We must choose a chairman," people cried from different parts of the room.

"Our host, of course, our host!"

"Gentlemen, if so," Virginsky, the chosen chairman, began, "I propose my original motion. If anyone wants to say anything more relevant to the subject, or has some statement to make, let him bring it forward without loss of time."

There was a general silence. The eyes of all were turned again on Verhovensky and Stavrogin.

"Verhovensky, have you no statement to make?" Madame Virginsky asked him directly.

"Nothing whatever," he answered, yawning and stretching on his chair. "But I should like a glass of brandy."

"Stavrogin, don't you want to?"

"Thank you, I don't drink."

"I mean don't you want to speak, not don't you want brandy."

"To speak, what about? No, I don't want to."

"They'll bring you some brandy," she answered Verhovensky.

The girl-student got up. She had darted up several times already.

"I have come to make a statement about the sufferings of poor students and the means of rousing them to protest."

But she broke off. At the other end of the table a rival had risen, and all eyes turned to him. Shigalov, the man with the long ears, slowly rose from his seat with a gloomy and sullen air and mournfully laid on the table a thick notebook filled with extremely small handwriting. He remained standing in silence. Many people looked at the notebook in consternation, but Liputin, Virginsky, and the lame teacher seemed pleased.

"I ask leave to address the meeting," Shigalov pronounced sullenly but resolutely.

"You have leave." Virginsky gave his sanction.

The orator sat down, was silent for half a minute, and pronounced in a solemn voice:

"Gentlemen!"

"Here's the brandy," the sister who had been pouring out tea and had gone to fetch brandy rapped out, contemptuously and disdainfully putting the bottle before Verhovensky, together with the wineglass which she brought in her fingers without a tray or a plate.

The interrupted orator made a dignified pause.

"Never mind, go on, I am not listening," cried Verhovensky, pouring himself out a glass.

"Gentlemen, asking your attention and, as you will see

54

later, soliciting your aid in a matter of the first importance,"
Shigalov began again, "I must make some prefatory remarks."

"Arina Prohorovna, haven't you some scissors?" Pyotr
Stepanovitch asked suddenly.

"What do you want scissors for?" she asked, with wide-
open eyes.

"I've forgotten to cut my nails; I've been meaning to for the
last three days," he observed, scrutinising his long and dirty
nails with unruffled composure.

Arina Prohorovna crimsoned, but Miss Virginsky seemed
pleased.

"I believe I saw them just now on the window." She got
up from the table, went and found the scissors, and at once
brought them. Pyotr Stepanovitch did not even look at her,
took the scissors and set to work with them. Arina Prohorovna
grasped that these were realistic manners, and was ashamed of
her sensitiveness. People looked at one another in silence. The
lame teacher looked vindictively and enviously at Verhovensky.
Shigalov went on:

"Dedicating my energies to the study of the social organisation which is in the future to replace the present condition of
things, I've come to the conviction that all makers of social
systems from ancient times up to the present year, 187 — , have
been dreamers, tellers of fairy-tales, fools who contradicted
themselves, who understood nothing of natural science and the
strange animal called man. Plato, Rousseau, Fourier, columns
of aluminium, are only fit for sparrows and not for human
society. But, now that we are all at last preparing to act, a
new form of social organisation is essential. In order to avoid
further uncertainty, I propose my own system of world organisation. Here it is." He tapped the notebook. "I wanted to expound my views to the meeting in the most concise form
possible, but I see that I should need to add a great many
verbal explanations, and so the whole exposition would occupy
at least ten evenings, one for each of my chapters." (There was
the sound of laughter.) "I must add, besides, that my system
is not yet complete." (Laughter again.) "I am perplexed by
my own data and my conclusion is a direct contradiction of the
original idea with which I start. Starting from unlimited
freedom, I arrive at unlimited despotism. I will add, however,
that there can be no solution of the social problem but mine."

The laughter grew louder and louder, but it came chiefly from
the younger and less initiated visitors. There was an expression

of some annoyance on the faces of Madame Virginsky, Liputin, and the lame teacher.

"If you've been unsuccessful in making your system consistent, and have been reduced to despair yourself, what could we do with it?" one officer observed warily.

"You are right, Mr. Officer"—Shigalov turned sharply to him—"especially in using the word despair. Yes, I am reduced to despair. Nevertheless, nothing can take the place of the system set forth in my book, and there is no other way out of it; no one can invent anything else. And so I hasten without loss of time to invite the whole society to listen for ten evenings to my book and then give their opinions of it. If the members are unwilling to listen to me, let us break up from the start—the men to take up service under government, the women to their cooking; for if you reject my solution you'll find no other, none whatever! If they let the opportunity slip, it will simply be their loss, for they will be bound to come back to it again."

There was a stir in the company. "Is he mad, or what?" voices asked.

"So the whole point lies in Shigalov's despair," Lyamshin commented, "and the essential question is whether he must despair or not?"

"Shigalov's being on the brink of despair is a personal question," declared the schoolboy.

"I propose we put it to the vote how far Shigalov's despair affects the common cause, and at the same time whether it's worth while listening to him or not," an officer suggested gaily.

"That's not right." The lame teacher put in his spoke at last. As a rule he spoke with a rather mocking smile, so that it was difficult to make out whether he was in earnest or joking. "That's not right, gentlemen. Mr. Shigalov is too much devoted to his task and is also too modest. I know his book. He suggests as a final solution of the question the division of mankind into two unequal parts. One-tenth enjoys absolute liberty and unbounded power over the other nine-tenths. The others have to give up all individuality and become, so to speak, a herd, and, through boundless submission, will by a series of regenerations attain primæval innocence, something like the Garden of Eden. They'll have to work, however. The measures proposed by the author for depriving nine-tenths of mankind of their freedom and transforming them into a herd through the education of whole generations are very remarkable, founded on the facts of nature and highly logical. One may not agree

56

with some of the deductions, but it would be difficult to doubt the intelligence and knowledge of the author. It's a pity that the time required—ten evenings—is impossible to arrange for, or we might hear a great deal that's interesting."

"Can you be in earnest?" Madame Virginsky addressed the lame gentleman with a shade of positive uneasiness in her voice, "when that man doesn't know what to do with people and so turns nine-tenths of them into slaves? I've suspected him for a long time."

"You say that of your own brother?" asked the lame man.

"Relationship? Are you laughing at me?"

"And besides, to work for aristocrats and to obey them as though they were gods is contemptible!" observed the girl-student fiercely.

"What I propose is not contemptible; it's paradise, an earthly paradise, and there can be no other on earth," Shigalov pronounced authoritatively.

"For my part," said Lyamshin, "if I didn't know what to do with nine-tenths of mankind, I'd take them and blow them up into the air instead of putting them in paradise. I'd only leave a handful of educated people, who would live happily ever afterwards on scientific principles."

"No one but a buffoon can talk like that!" cried the girl, flaring up.

"He is a buffoon, but he is of use," Madame Virginsky whispered to her.

"And possibly that would be the best solution of the problem," said Shigalov, turning hotly to Lyamshin. "You certainly don't know what a profound thing you've succeeded in saying, my merry friend. But as it's hardly possible to carry out your idea, we must confine ourselves to an earthly paradise, since that's what they call it."

"This is pretty thorough rot," broke, as though involuntarily, from Verhovensky. Without even raising his eyes, however, he went on cutting his nails with perfect nonchalance.

"Why is it rot?" The lame man took it up instantly, as though he had been lying in wait for his first words to catch at them. "Why is it rot? Mr. Shigalov is somewhat fanatical in his love for humanity, but remember that Fourier, still more Cabet and even Proudhon himself, advocated a number of the most despotic and even fantastic measures. Mr. Shigalov is perhaps far more sober in his suggestions than they are. I assure you that when one reads his book it's almost impossible

57

not to agree with some things. He is perhaps less far from realism than anyone and his earthly paradise is almost the real one—if it ever existed—for the loss of which man is always sighing."

"I knew I was in for something," Verhovensky muttered again.

"Allow me," said the lame man, getting more and more excited. "Conversations and arguments about the future organisation of society are almost an actual necessity for all thinking people nowadays. Herzen was occupied with nothing else all his life. Byelinsky, as I know on very good authority, used to spend whole evenings with his friends debating and settling beforehand even the minutest, so to speak, domestic, details of the social organisation of the future."

"Some people go crazy over it," the major observed suddenly.

"We are more likely to arrive at something by talking, anyway, than by sitting silent and posing as dictators," Liputin hissed, as though at last venturing to begin the attack.

"I didn't mean Shigalov when I said it was rot," Verhovensky mumbled. "You see, gentlemen"—he raised his eyes a trifle—"to my mind all these books, Fourier, Cabet, all this talk about the right to work, and Shigalov's theories—are all like novels of which one can write a hundred thousand—an æsthetic entertainment. I can understand that in this little town you are bored, so you rush to ink and paper."

"Excuse me," said the lame man, wriggling on his chair, "though we are provincials and of course objects of commiseration on that ground, yet we know that so far nothing has happened in the world new enough to be worth our weeping at having missed it. It is suggested to us in various pamphlets made abroad and secretly distributed that we should unite and form groups with the sole object of bringing about universal destruction. It's urged that, however much you tinker with the world, you can't make a good job of it, but that by cutting off a hundred million heads and so lightening one's burden, one can jump over the ditch more safely. A fine idea, no doubt, but quite as impracticable as Shigalov's theories, which you referred to just now so contemptuously."

"Well, but I haven't come here for discussion." Verhovensky let drop this significant phrase, and, as though quite unaware of his blunder, drew the candle nearer to him that he might see better.

"It's a pity, a great pity, that you haven't come for discussion, and it's a great pity that you are so taken up just now with your toilet."

"What's my toilet to you?"

"To remove a hundred million heads is as difficult as to transform the world by propaganda. Possibly more difficult, especially in Russia," Liputin ventured again.

"It's Russia they rest their hopes on now," said an officer.

"We've heard they are resting their hopes on it," interposed the lame man. "We know that a mysterious finger is pointing to our delightful country as the land most fitted to accomplish the great task. But there's this: by the gradual solution of the problem by propaganda, I shall gain something, anyway—I shall have some pleasant talk, at least, and shall even get some recognition from government for my services to the cause of society. But in the second way, by the rapid method of cutting off a hundred million heads, what benefit shall I get personally? If you began advocating that, your tongue might be cut out."

"Yours certainly would be," observed Verhovensky.

"You see. And as under the most favourable circumstances you would not get through such a massacre in less than fifty or at the best thirty years—for they are not sheep, you know, and perhaps they would not let themselves be slaughtered—wouldn't it be better to pack one's bundle and migrate to some quiet island beyond calm seas and there close one's eyes tranquilly? Believe me"—he tapped the table significantly with his finger—"you will only promote emigration by such propaganda and nothing else!"

He finished evidently triumphant. He was one of the intellects of the province. Liputin smiled shyly, Virginsky listened rather dejectedly, the others followed the discussion with great attention, especially the ladies and officers. They all realised that the advocate of the hundred million heads theory had been driven into a corner, and waited to see what would come of it.

"That was a good saying of yours, though," Verhovensky mumbled more carelessly than ever, in fact with an air of positive boredom. "Emigration is a good idea. But all the same, if in spite of all the obvious disadvantages you foresee, more and more come forward every day ready to fight for the common cause, it will be able to do without you. It's a new religion, my good friend, coming to take the place of the old one. That's why so many fighters come forward, and it's a big movement. You'd better emigrate! And, you know, I should advise Dresden, not 'the calm islands'. To begin with, it's a town that has never been visited by an epidemic, and as you are a man of culture, no doubt you are afraid of death. Another thing, it's near the Russian frontier, so you can more easily receive your income from your beloved Fatherland. Thirdly, it contains what are called treasures of art, and you are a man of æsthetic tastes, formerly a teacher of literature, I believe. And, finally, it has a miniature Switzerland of its own—to provide you with poetic inspiration, for no doubt you write verse. In fact it's a treasure in a nutshell!"

There was a general movement, especially among the officers. In another instant they would have all begun talking at once. But the lame man rose irritably to the bait.

"No, perhaps I am not going to give up the common cause. You must understand that . . ."

"What, would you join the quintet if I proposed it to you?" Verhovensky boomed suddenly, and he laid down the scissors.

Everyone seemed startled. The mysterious man had revealed himself too freely. He had even spoken openly of the "quintet".

"Everyone feels himself to be an honest man and will not shirk his part in the common cause"—the lame man tried to wriggle out of it—"but . . ."

"No, this not a question which allows of a *but*," Verhovensky interrupted harshly and peremptorily. "I tell you, gentlemen, I must have a direct answer. I quite understand that, having come here and having called you together myself, I am bound to give you explanations" (again an unexpected revelation), "but I can give you none till I know what is your attitude to the subject. To cut the matter short—for we can't go on talking for another thirty years as people have done for the last thirty—I ask you which you prefer: the slow way, which consists in the composition of socialistic romances and the academic ordering of the destinies of humanity a thousand years hence, while despotism will swallow the savoury morsels which would almost fly into your mouths of themselves if you'd take a little trouble; or do you, whatever it may imply, prefer a quicker way which will at last untie your hands, and will let humanity make its own social organisation in freedom and in action, not on paper? They shout 'a hundred million heads'; that may be only a metaphor; but why be afraid of it if, with the slow day-dreams on paper, despotism in the course of some hundred years will devour not a hundred but five hundred million heads? Take note too that an incurable invalid will not be cured whatever prescriptions are written for him on paper. On the contrary,

60

if there is delay, he will grow so corrupt that he will infect us too and contaminate all the fresh forces which one might still reckon upon now, so that we shall all at last come to grief together. I thoroughly agree that it's extremely agreeable to chatter liberally and eloquently, but action is a little trying. . . . However, I am no hand at talking; I came here with communications, and so I beg all the honourable company not to vote, but simply and directly to state which you prefer: walking at a snail's pace in the marsh, or putting on full steam to get across it?"

"I am certainly for crossing at full steam!" cried the schoolboy in an ecstasy.

"So am I," Lyamshin chimed in.

"There can be no doubt about the choice," muttered an officer, followed by another, then by someone else. What struck them all most was that Verhovensky had come "with communications" and had himself just promised to speak.

"Gentlemen, I see that almost all decide for the policy of the manifestos," he said, looking round at the company.

"All, all!" cried the majority of voices.

"I confess I am rather in favour of a more humane policy," said the major, "but as all are on the other side, I go with all the rest."

"It appears, then, that even you are not opposed to it," said Verhovensky, addressing the lame man.

"I am not exactly . . ." said the latter, turning rather red, "but if I do agree with the rest now, it's simply not to break up. . . ."

"You are all like that! Ready to argue for six months to practise your Liberal eloquence and in the end you vote the same as the rest! Gentlemen, consider though, is it true that you are all ready?"

(Ready for what? The question was vague, but very alluring.)

"All are, of course!" voices were heard. But all were looking at one another.

"But afterwards perhaps you will resent having agreed so quickly? That's almost always the way with you."

The company was excited in various ways, greatly excited. The lame man flew at him.

"Allow me to observe, however, that answers to such questions are conditional. Even if we have given our decision, you must note that questions put in such a strange way . . ."

"In what strange way?"

"In a way such questions are not asked."

"Teach me how, please. But do you know, I felt sure you'd be the first to take offence."

"You've extracted from us an answer as to our readiness for immediate action; but what right had you to do so? By what authority do you ask such questions?"

"You should have thought of asking that question sooner! Why did you answer? You agree and then you go back on it!"

"But to my mind the irresponsibility of your principal question suggests to me that you have no authority, no right, and only asked from personal curiosity."

"What do you mean? What do you mean?" cried Verhovensky, apparently beginning to be much alarmed.

"Why, that the initiation of new members into anything you like is done, anyway, *tête-à-tête* and not in the company of twenty people one doesn't know!" blurted out the lame man. He had said all that was in his mind because he was too irritated to restrain himself. Verhovensky turned to the general company with a capitally simulated look of alarm.

"Gentlemen, I deem it my duty to declare that all this is folly, and that our conversation has gone too far. I have so far initiaated no one, and no one has the right to say of me that I initiate members. We were simply discussing our opinions. That's so, isn't it? But whether that's so or not, you alarm me very much." He turned to the lame man again. "I had no idea that it was unsafe here to speak of such practically innocent matters except *tête-à-tête*. Are you afraid of informers? Can there possibly be an informer among us here?"

The excitement became tremendous; all began talking.

"Gentlemen, if that is so," Verhovensky went on, "I have compromised myself more than anyone, and so I will ask you to answer one question, if you care to, of course. You are all perfectly free."

"What question? What question?" everyone clamoured.

"A question that will make it clear whether we are to remain together, or take up our hats and go our several ways without speaking."

"The question! The question!"

"If anyone of us knew of a proposed political murder, would he, in view of all the consequences, go to give information, or would he stay at home and await events? Opinions may differ on this point. The answer to the question will tell us clearly whether we are to separate, or to remain together and for far longer than this one evening. Let me appeal to you first.'' He turned to the lame man.

"Why to me first?"

"Because you began it all. Be so good as not to prevaricate; it won't help you to be cunning. But please yourself, it's for you to decide.''

"Excuse me, but such a question is positively insulting.''

"No, can't you be more exact than that?''

"I've never been an agent of the Secret Police,'' replied the latter, wriggling more than ever.

"Be so good as to be more definite, don't keep us waiting.''

The lame man was so furious that he left off answering. Without a word he glared wrathfully from under his spectacles at his tormentor.

"Yes or no? Would you inform or not?'' cried Verhovensky.

"Of course I wouldn't,'' the lame man shouted twice as loudly.

"And no one would, of course not!'' cried many voices.

"Allow me to appeal to you, Mr. Major. Would you inform or not?'' Verhovensky went on. "And note that I appeal to you on purpose.''

"I won't inform.''

"But if you knew that someone meant to rob and murder someone else, an ordinary mortal, then you would inform and give warning?''

"Yes, of course; but that's a private affair, while the other would be a political treachery. I've never been an agent of the Secret Police.''

"And no one here has,'' voices cried again. "It's an unnecessary question. Everyone will make the same answer. There are no informers here.''

"What is that gentleman getting up for?'' cried the girl-student.

"That's Shatov. What are you getting up for?'' cried the lady of the house.

Shatov did, in fact, stand up. He was holding his cap in his hand and looking at Verhovensky. Apparently he wanted to say something to him, but was hesitating. His face was pale and wrathful, but he controlled himself. He did not say one word, but in silence walked towards the door.

"Shatov, this won't make things better for you!'' Verhovensky called after him enigmatically.

"But it will for you, since you are a spy and a scoundrel!" Shatov shouted to him from the door, and he went out.

Shouts and exclamations again.

"That's what comes of a test," cried a voice.

"It's been of use," cried another.

"Hasn't it been of use too late?" observed a third.

"Who invited him? Who let him in? Who is he? Who is Shatov? Will he inform, or won't he?" There was a shower of questions.

"If he were an informer he would have kept up appearances instead of cursing it all and going away," observed someone.

"See, Stavrogin is getting up too. Stavrogin has not answered the question either," cried the girl-student.

Stavrogin did actually stand up, and at the other end of the table Kirillov rose at the same time.

"Excuse me, Mr. Stavrogin," Madame Virginsky addressed him sharply, "we all answered the question, while you are going away without a word."

"I see no necessity to answer the question which interests you," muttered Stavrogin.

"But we've compromised ourselves and you won't," shouted several voices.

"What business is it of mine if you have compromised yourselves?" laughed Stavrogin, but his eyes flashed.

"What business? What business?" voices exclaimed.

Many people got up from their chairs.

"Allow me, gentlemen, allow me," cried the lame man. "Mr. Verhovensky hasn't answered the question either; he has only asked it."

The remark produced a striking effect. All looked at one another. Stavrogin laughed aloud in the lame man's face and went out; Kirillov followed him: Verhovensky ran after them into the passage.

"What are you doing?" he faltered, seizing Stavrogin's hand and gripping it with all his might in his. Stavrogin pulled away his hand without a word.

"Be at Kirillov's directly, I'll come. . . . It's absolutely necessary for me to see you! . . ."

"It isn't necessary for me," Stavrogin cut him short.

"Stavrogin will be there," Kirillov said finally. "Stavrogin, it is necessary for you. I will show you that there."

They went out.

CHAPTER VIII

IVAN THE TSAREVITCH

THEY had gone. Pyotr Stepanovitch was about to rush back to the meeting to bring order into chaos, but probably reflecting that it wasn't worth bothering about, left everything, and two minutes later was flying after the other two. On the way he remembered a short cut to Filipov's house. He rushed along it, up to his knees in mud, and did in fact arrive at the very moment when Stavrogin and Kirillov were coming in at the gate.

"You here already?" observed Kirillov. "That's good. Come in."

"How is it you told us you lived alone," asked Stavrogin, passing a boiling samovar in the passage.

"You will see directly whom it is I live with," muttered Kirillov. "Go in."

They had hardly entered when Verhovensky at once took out of his pocket the anonymous letter he had taken from Lembke, and laid it before Stavrogin. They all then sat down. Stavrogin read the letter in silence.

"Well?" he asked.

"That scoundrel will do as he writes," Verhovensky explained. "So, as he is under your control, tell me how to act. I assure you he may go to Lembke to-morrow."

"Well, let him go."

"Let him go! And when we can prevent him, too!"

"You are mistaken. He is not dependent on me. Besides, I don't care; he doesn't threaten me in any way; he only threatens you."

"You too."

"I don't think so."

"But there are other people who may not spare you. Surely you understand that? Listen, Stavrogin. This is only playing with words. Surely you don't grudge the money?"

"Why, would it cost money?"

"It certainly would; two thousand or at least fifteen hundred. Give it to me to-morrow or even to-day, and to-morrow evening I'll send him to Petersburg for you. That's just what he wants. If you like, he can take Marya Timofyevna. Note that."

There was something distracted about him. He spoke, as it were, without caution, and he did not reflect on his words. Stavrogin watched him, wondering.

"I've no reason to send Marya Timofyevna away."

"Perhaps you don't even want to," Pyotr Stepanovitch smiled ironically.

"Perhaps I don't."

"In short, will there be the money or not?" he cried with angry impatience, and as it were peremptorily, to Stavrogin. The latter scrutinised him gravely.

"There won't be the money."

"Look here, Stavrogin! You know something, or have done something already! You are going it!"

His face worked, the corners of his mouth twitched, and he suddenly laughed an unprovoked and irrelevant laugh.

"But you've had money from your father for the estate," Stavrogin observed calmly. "Maman sent you six or eight thousand for Stepan Trofimovitch. So you can pay the fifteen hundred out of your own money. I don't care to pay for other people. I've given a lot as it is. It annoys me. . . ." He smiled himself at his own words.

"Ah, you are beginning to joke!"

Stavrogin got up from his chair. Verhovensky instantly jumped up too, and mechanically stood with his back to the door, as though barring the way to him. Stavrogin had already made a motion to push him aside and go out, when he stopped short.

"I won't give up Shatov to you," he said. Pyotr Stepanovitch started. They looked at one another.

"I told you this evening why you needed Shatov's blood," said Stavrogin, with flashing eyes. "It's the cement you want to bind your groups together with. You drove Shatov away cleverly just now. You knew very well that he wouldn't promise not to inform and he would have thought it mean to lie to you. But what do you want with me? What do you want with me? Ever since we met abroad you won't let me alone. The explanation you've given me so far was simply raving. Meanwhile you are driving at my giving Lebyadkin fifteen hundred roubles, so as to give Fedka an opportunity to murder him. I know that you think I want my wife murdered too. You think to tie my hands by this crime, and have me in your power. That's it, isn't it? What good will that be to you? What the devil do you want with me? Look at me. Once for all, am I the man for you? And let me alone."

"Has Fedka been to you himself?" Verhovensky asked breathlessly.

"Yes, he came. His price is fifteen hundred too. . . . But here; he'll repeat it himself. There he stands." Stavrogin stretched out his hand.

Pyotr Stepanovitch turned round quickly. A new figure, Fedka, wearing a sheepskin coat, but without a cap, as though he were at home, stepped out of the darkness in the doorway. He stood there laughing and showing his even white teeth. His black eyes, with yellow whites, darted cautiously about the room watching the gentlemen. There was something he did not understand. He had evidently been just brought in by Kirillov, and his inquiring eyes turned to the latter. He stood in the doorway, but was unwilling to come into the room.

"I suppose you got him ready here to listen to our bargaining, or that he may actually see the money in our hands. Is that it?" asked Stavrogin; and without waiting for an answer he walked out of the house. Verhovensky, almost frantic, overtook him at the gate.

"Stop! Not another step!" he cried, seizing him by the arm. Stavrogin tried to pull away his arm, but did not succeed. He was overcome with fury. Seizing Verhovensky by the hair with his left hand he flung him with all his might on the ground and went out at the gate. But he had not gone thirty paces before Verhovensky overtook him again.

"Let us make it up; let us make it up!" he murmured in a spasmodic whisper.

Stavrogin shrugged his shoulders, but neither answered nor turned round.

"Listen. I will bring you Lizaveta Nikolaevna to-morrow; shall I? No? Why don't you answer? Tell me what you want. I'll do it. Listen. I'll let you have Shatov. Shall I?"

"Then it's true that you meant to kill him?" cried Stavrogin.

"What do you want with Shatov? What is he to you?" Pyotr Stepanovitch went on, gasping, speaking rapidly. He was in a frenzy, and kept running forward and seizing Stavrogin by the elbow, probably unaware of what he was doing. "Listen. I'll let you have him. Let's make it up. Your price is a very great one, but . . . Let's make it up!"

Stavrogin glanced at him at last, and was amazed. The eyes, the voice, were not the same as always, or as they had been in the room just now. What he saw was almost another face. The intonation of the voice was different. Verhovensky besought, implored. He was a man from whom what was most

67

THE POSSESSED

precious was being taken or had been taken, and who was still stunned by the shock.

"But what's the matter with you?" cried Stavrogin. The other did not answer, but ran after him and gazed at him with the same imploring but yet inflexible expression.

"Let's make it up!" he whispered once more. "Listen. Like Fedka, I have a knife in my boot, but I'll make it up with you!"

"But what do you want with me, damn you?" Stavrogin cried, with intense anger and amazement. "Is there some mystery about it? Am I a sort of talisman for you?"

"Listen. We are going to make a revolution," the other muttered rapidly, and almost in delirium. "You don't believe we shall make a revolution? We are going to make such an upheaval that everything will be uprooted from its foundation. Karmazinov is right that there is nothing to lay hold of. Karmazinov is very intelligent. Another ten such groups in different parts of Russia—and I am safe."

"Groups of fools like that?" broke reluctantly from Stavrogin.

"Oh, don't be so clever, Stavrogin; don't be so clever yourself. And you know you are by no means so intelligent that you need wish others to be. You are afraid, you have no faith. You are frightened at our doing things on such a scale. And why are they fools? They are not such fools. No one has a mind of his own nowadays. There are terribly few original minds nowadays. Virginsky is a pure-hearted man, ten times as pure as you or I; but never mind about him. Liputin is a rogue, but I know one point about him. Every rogue has some point in him. . . . Lyamshin is the only one who hasn't, but he is in my hands. A few more groups and I should have money and passports everywhere; so much at least. Suppose it were only that? And safe places, so that they can search as they like. They might uproot one group but they'd stick at the next. We'll set things in a ferment. . . . Surely you don't think that we two are not enough?"

"Take Shigalov, and let me alone. . . ."

"Shigalov is a man of genius! Do you know he is a genius like Fourier, but bolder than Fourier; stronger. I'll look after him. He's discovered 'equality'!"

"He is in a fever; he is raving; something very queer has happened to him," thought Stavrogin, looking at him once more. Both walked on without stopping.

"He's written a good thing in that manuscript," Verhovensky

went on. "He suggests a system of spying. Every member of the society spies on the others, and it's his duty to inform against them. Everyone belongs to all and all to everyone. All are slaves and equal in their slavery. In extreme cases he advocates slander and murder, but the great thing about it is equality. To begin with, the level of education, science, and talents is lowered. A high level of education and science is only possible for great intellects, and they are not wanted. The great intellects have always seized the power and been despots. Great intellects cannot help being despots and they've always done more harm than good. They will be banished or put to death. Cicero will have his tongue cut out, Copernicus will have his eyes put out, Shakespeare will be stoned—that's Shigalovism. Slaves are bound to be equal. There has never been either freedom or equality without despotism, but in the herd there is bound to be equality, and that's Shigalovism! Ha ha ha! Do you think it strange? I am for Shigalovism."

Stavrogin tried to quicken his pace and to reach home as soon as possible. "If this fellow is drunk, where did he manage to get drunk?" crossed his mind. "Can it be the brandy?"

"Listen, Stavrogin. To level the mountains is a fine idea, not an absurd one. I am for Shigalov. Down with culture. We've had enough science! Without science we have material enough to go on for a thousand years, but one must have discipline. The one thing wanting in the world is discipline. The thirst for culture is an aristocratic thirst. The moment you have family ties or love you get the desire for property. We will destroy that desire; we'll make use of drunkenness, slander, spying; we'll make use of incredible corruption; we'll stifle every genius in its infancy. We'll reduce all to a common denominator! Complete equality! 'We've learned a trade, and we are honest men; we need nothing more,' that was an answer given by English working-men recently. Only the necessary is necessary, that's the motto of the whole world henceforward. But it needs a shock. That's for us, the directors, to look after. Slaves must have directors. Absolute submission, absolute loss of individuality, but once in thirty years Shigalov would let them have a shock and they would all suddenly begin eating one another up, to a certain point, simply as a precaution against boredom. Boredom is an aristocratic sensation. The Shigalovians will have no desires. Desire and suffering are our lot, but Shigalovism is for the slaves."

"You exclude yourself?" Stavrogin broke in again.

"You, too. Do you know, I have thought of giving up the world to the Pope. Let him come forth, on foot, and barefoot, and show himself to the rabble, saying: 'See what they have brought me to!' and they will all rush after him, even the troops. The Pope at the head, with us round him, and below us—Shigalovism. All that's needed is that the *Internationale* should come to an agreement with the Pope; so it will. And the old chap will agree at once. There's nothing else he can do. Remember my words! Ha ha! Is it stupid? Tell me, is it stupid or not?"

"That's enough!" Stavrogin muttered with vexation.

"Enough! Listen. I've given up the Pope! Damn Shigalovism! Damn the Pope! We must have something more everyday. Not Shigalovism, for Shigalovism is a rare specimen of the jeweller's art. It's an ideal; it's in the future. Shigalov is an artist and a fool like every philanthropist. We need coarse work, and Shigalov despises coarse work. Listen. The Pope shall be for the west, and you shall be for us, you shall be for us!"

"Let me alone, you drunken fellow!" muttered Stavrogin, and he quickened his pace.

"Stavrogin, you are beautiful," cried Pyotr Stepanovitch, almost ecstatically. "Do you know that you are beautiful? What's the most precious thing about you is that you sometimes don't know it. Oh, I've studied you! I often watch you on the sly! There's a lot of simple-heartedness and naïveté about you still. Do you know that? There still is, there is! You must be suffering and suffering genuinely from that simple-heartedness. I love beauty. I am a nihilist, but I love beauty. Are nihilists incapable of loving beauty? It's only idols they dislike, but I love an idol. You are my idol! You injure no one, and everyone hates you. You treat everyone as an equal, and yet everyone is afraid of you—that's good. Nobody would slap you on the shoulder. You are an awful aristocrat. An aristocrat is irresistible when he goes in for democracy! To sacrifice life, your own or another's, is nothing to you. You are just the man that's needed. It's just such a man as you that I need. I know no one but you. You are the leader, you are the sun and I am your worm."

He suddenly kissed his hand. A shiver ran down Stavrogin's spine, and he pulled away his hand in dismay. They stood still.

"Madman!" whispered Stavrogin.

"Perhaps I am raving; perhaps I am raving," Pyotr Stepano-vitch assented, speaking rapidly. "But I've thought of the first step! Shigalov would never have thought of it. There are lots of Shigalovs, but only one man, one man in Russia has hit on the first step and knows how to take it. And I am that man! Why do you look at me? I need you, you; without you I am nothing. Without you I am a fly, a bottled idea; Columbus without America."

Stavrogin stood still and looked intently into his wild eyes.

"Listen. First of all we'll make an upheaval," Verhovensky went on in desperate haste, continually clutching at Stavrogin's left sleeve. "I've already told you. We shall penetrate to the peasantry. Do you know that we are tremendously powerful already? Our party does not consist only of those who commit murder and arson, fire off pistols in the traditional fashion, or bite colonels. They are only a hindrance. I don't accept any-thing without discipline. I am a scoundrel, of course, and not a socialist. Ha ha! Listen. I've reckoned them all up: a teacher who laughs with children at their God and at their cradle is on our side. The lawyer who defends an educated murderer because he is more cultured than his victims and could not help murdering them to get money is one of us. The schoolboys who murder a peasant for the sake of sensation are ours. The juries who acquit every criminal are ours. The prosecutor who trembles at a trial for fear he should not seem advanced enough is ours, ours. Among officials and literary men we have lots, lots, and they don't know it themselves. On the other hand, the docility of schoolboys and fools has reached an extreme pitch; the schoolmasters are bitter and bilious. On all sides we see vanity puffed up out of all proportion; brutal, monstrous appetites. . . . Do you know how many we shall catch by little, ready-made ideas? When I left Russia, Littré's dictum that crime is insanity was all the rage; I come back and I find that crime is no longer insanity, but simply common sense, almost a duty; anyway, a gallant protest. 'How can we expect a cul-tured man not to commit a murder, if he is in need of money?' But these are only the firstfruits. The Russian God has already been vanquished by cheap vodka. The peasants are drunk, the mothers are drunk, the children are drunk, the churches are empty, and in the peasant courts one hears: 'Two hundred lashes or stand us a bucket of vodka.' Oh, this generation has only to grow up. It's only a pity we can't afford to wait, or we might have let them get a bit more tipsy! Ah, what a pity there's no proletariat! But there will be, there will be; we are going that way. . . ."

"It's a pity, too, that we've grown greater fools," muttered Stavrogin, moving forward as before.

"Listen. I've seen a child of six years of age leading home his drunken mother, whilst she swore at him with foul words. Do you suppose I am glad of that? When it's in our hands, maybe we'll mend things . . . if need be, we'll drive them for forty years into the wilderness. . . . But one or two generations of vice are essential now; monstrous, abject vice by which a man is transformed into a loathsome, cruel, egoistic reptile. That's what we need! And what's more, a little 'fresh blood' that we may get accustomed to it. Why are you laughing? I am not contradicting myself. I am only contradicting the philanthropists and Shigalovism, not myself! I am a scoundrel, not a socialist. Ha ha ha! I'm only sorry there's no time. I promised Karmazinov to begin in May, and to make an end by October. Is that too soon? Ha ha! Do you know what, Stavrogin? Though the Russian people use foul language, there's nothing cynical about them so far. Do you know the serfs had more self-respect than Karmazinov? Though they were beaten they always preserved their gods, which is more than Karmazinov's done."

"Well, Verhovensky, this is the first time I've heard you talk, and I listen with amazement," observed Stavrogin. "So you are really not a socialist, then, but some sort of . . . ambitious politician?"

"A scoundrel, a scoundrel! You are wondering what I am. I'll tell you what I am directly, that's what I am leading up to. It was not for nothing that I kissed your hand. But the people must believe that we know what we are after, while the other side do nothing but 'brandish their cudgels and beat their own followers'. Ah, if we only had more time! That's the only trouble, we have no time. We will proclaim destruction. . . . Why is it, why is it that idea has such a fascination? But we must have a little exercise; we must. We'll set fires going. . . . We'll set legends going. Every scurvy 'group' will be of use. Out of those very groups I'll pick you out fellows so keen they'll not shrink from shooting, and be grateful for the honour of a job, too. Well, and there will be an upheaval! There's going to be such an upset as the world has never seen before. . . . Russia will be overwhelmed with darkness, the earth will weep for its old gods. . . . Well, then we shall bring forward . . . whom?"

"Whom."

"Ivan the Tsarevitch."

"Who-m?"

"Ivan the Tsarevitch. You! You!"

Stavrogin thought a minute.

"A pretender?" he asked suddenly, looking with intense surprise at his frantic companion. "Ah! so that's your plan at last!"

"We shall say that he is 'in hiding',," Verhovensky said softly, in a sort of tender whisper, as though he really were drunk indeed. "Do you know the magic of that phrase, 'he is in hiding'? But he will appear, he will appear. We'll set a legend going better than the Skoptsis'. He exists, but no one has seen him. Oh, what a legend one can set going! And the great thing is it will be a new force at work! And we need that; that's what they are crying for. What can Socialism do? it's destroyed the old forces but hasn't brought in any new. But in this we have a force, and what a force! Incredible. We only need one lever to lift up the earth. Everything will rise up!"

"Then have you been seriously reckoning on me?" Stavrogin said with a malicious smile.

"Why do you laugh, and so spitefully? Don't frighten me. I am like a little child now. I can be frightened to death by one smile like that. Listen. I'll let no one see you, no one. So it must be. He exists, but no one has seen him; he is in hiding. And do you know, one might show you, to one out of a hundred thousand, for instance. And the rumour will spread over all the land: 'We've seen him, we've seen him.'" Ivan Filipovitch, the God of Sabaoth,* has been seen, too, when he ascended into heaven in his chariot in the sight of men. They saw him with their own eyes. And you are not an Ivan Filipovitch. You are beautiful and proud as a god; you are seeking nothing for yourself, with the halo of a victim round you, 'in hiding'. The great thing is the legend. You'll conquer them, you'll have only to look, and you will conquer them. He is 'in hiding', and will come forth bringing a new truth. And, meanwhile, we'll pass two or three judgments as wise as Solomon's. The groups, you know, the quintets—we've no need of newspapers. If out of ten thousand petitions only one is granted, all would come with petitions. In every parish, every peasant will know that

*The reference is to the legend current in the sect of Flagellants.—Translator's note.

there is somewhere a hollow tree where petitions are to be put. And the whole land will resound with the cry: 'A new just law is to come', and the sea will be troubled and the whole gimcrack show will fall to the ground, and then we shall consider how to build up an edifice of stone. For the first time! *We* are going to build it, we, and only we!"

"Madness," said Stavrogin.

"Why, why don't you want it? Are you afraid? That's why I caught at you, because you are afraid of nothing. Is it unreasonable? But you see, so far I am Columbus without America. Would Columbus without America seem reasonable?"

Stavrogin did not speak. Meanwhile they had reached the house and stopped at the entrance.

"Listen," Verhovensky bent down to his ear. "I'll do it for you without money. I'll settle Marya Timofyevna to-morrow! . . . Without the money, and to-morrow I'll bring you Liza. Will you have Liza to-morrow?"

"Is he really mad?" Stavrogin wondered, smiling. The front door was opened.

"Stavrogin—is America ours?" said Verhovensky, seizing his hand for the last time.

"What for?" said Nikolay Vsyevolodovitch, gravely and sternly.

"You don't care, I knew that!" cried Verhovensky in an access of furious anger. "You are lying, you miserable, profligate, perverted, little aristocrat! I don't believe you, you've the appetite of a wolf! . . . Understand that you've cost me such a price, I can't give you up now! There's no one on earth but you! I invented you abroad; I invented it all, looking at you. If I hadn't watched you from my corner, nothing of all this would have entered my head!"

Stavrogin went up the steps without answering.

"Stavrogin!" Verhovensky called after him, "I give you a day . . . two, then . . . three, then; more than three I can't— and then you're to answer!"

CHAPTER IX

A RAID AT STEPAN TROFIMOVITCH'S

MEANWHILE an incident had occurred which astounded me and shattered Stepan Trofimovitch. At eight o'clock in the morning Nastasya ran round to me from him with the news that her master was "raided". At first I could not make out what she meant; I could only gather that the "raid" was carried out by officials, that they had come and taken his papers, and that a soldier had tied them up in a bundle and "wheeled them away in a barrow". It was a fantastic story. I hurried at once to Stepan Trofimovitch.

I found him in a surprising condition: upset and in great agitation, but at the same time unmistakably triumphant. On the table in the middle of the room the samovar was boiling, and there was a glass of tea poured out but untouched and forgotten. Stepan Trofimovitch was wandering round the table and peeping into every corner of the room, unconscious of what he was doing. He was wearing his usual red knitted jacket, but seeing me, he hurriedly put on his coat and waistcoat—a thing he had never done before when any of his intimate friends found him in his jacket. He took me warmly by the hand at once.

"Enfin un ami!" (He heaved a deep sigh.) *"Cher,* I've sent to you only, and no one knows anything. We must give Nastasya orders to lock the doors and not admit anyone, except, of course, *them. . . . Vous comprenez?"*

He looked at me uneasily, as though expecting a reply. I made haste, of course, to question him, and from his disconnected and broken sentences, full of unnecessary parentheses, I succeeded in learning that at seven o'clock that morning an official of the province had 'all of a sudden' called on him.

"Pardon, j'ai oublié son nom. Il n'est pas du pays, but I think he came to the town with Lembke, *quelque chose de bête et d'Allemand dans la physionomie. Il s'appelle Rosenthal."*

"Wasn't it Blum?"

"Yes, that was his name. *Vous le connaissez? Quelque chose d'hébété et de très content dans la figure, pourtant très sévère, roide et sérieux.* A type of the police, of the submissive subordinates, *je m'y connais.* I was still asleep, and, would you believe it, he asked to have a look at my books and manuscripts! *Oui, je m'en souviens, il a employé ce mot.* He did not arrest me, but only the books. *Il se tenait à distance,* and when he began to explain his visit he looked as though I . . . *enfin il avait l'air de croire que je tomberai sur lui immédiatement et que je commencerai à le battre comme plâtre. Tous ces gens du bas étage sont comme ça* when they have to do with a gentleman. I need hardly say I understood it all at once. *Voilà vingt ans que je m'y prépare.* I opened all the drawers and handed him all the keys; I gave them myself, I gave him all. *J'étais digne et calme.* From the books he took the foreign edition of Herzen, the bound volume of "The Bell", four copies of my poem, *et enfin tout ça.* Then he took my letters and my papers *et quelques-unes de mes ébauches historiques, critiques et politiques.* All that they carried off. Nastasya says that a soldier wheeled them away in a barrow and covered them with an apron; *oui, c'est cela,* with an apron."

It sounded like delirium. Who could make head or tail of it? I pelted him with questions again. Had Blum come alone, or with others? On whose authority? By what right? How had he dared? How did he explain it?

"*Il était seul, bien seul,* but there was someone else *dans l'antichambre, oui, je m'en souviens, et puis* . . . Though I believe there was someone else besides, and there was a guard standing in the entry. You must ask Nastasya; she knows all about it better than I do. *J'étais surexcité, voyez-vous. Il parlait, il parlait* . . . *un tas de choses;* he said very little though, it was I said all that. . . . I told him the story of my life, simply from that point of view, of course. *J'étais surexcité, mais digne, je vous assure.* . . . I am afraid, though, I may have shed tears. They got the barrow from the shop next door."

"Oh, heavens! how could all this have happened? But for mercy's sake, speak more exactly, Stepan Trofimovitch. What you tell me sounds like a dream."

"*Cher,* I feel as though I were in a dream myself. . . . *Savez-vous! Il a prononcé le nom de Telyatnikof,* and I believe that that man was concealed in the entry. Yes, I remember, he suggested calling the prosecutor and Dmitri Dmitritch, I believe . . . *qui me doit encore quinze roubles* I won at cards, *soit dit en passant. Enfin, je n'ai pas trop compris.* But I got the better of them, and what do I care for Dmitri Dmitritch? I believe I begged him very earnestly to keep it quiet; I begged him particularly, most particularly. I am afraid I demeaned myself, in fact, *comment croyez-vous? Enfin il a consenti.* Yes, I remember, he suggested that himself—that it would be better to keep it quiet, for he had only come 'to have a look round' *et rien de plus,* and nothing more, nothing more . . . and that if they find nothing, nothing will happen. So that we ended it all *en amis, je suis tout à fait content.*"

"Why, then he suggested the usual course of proceedings in such cases and regular guarantees, and you rejected them yourself," I cried with friendly indignation.

"Yes, it's better without the guarantees. And why make a

scandal? Let's keep it *en amis* so long as we can. You know, in our town, if they get to know it . . . *mes ennemis, et puis, à quoi bon, le procureur, ce cochon de notre procureur, qui deux fois m'a manqué de politesse et qu'on a rossé à plaisir l'autre année chez cette charmante et belle Natalya Pavlovna quand il se cacha dans son boudoir. Et puis, mon ami,* don't make objections and don't depress me, I beg you, for nothing is more unbearable when a man is in trouble than for a hundred friends to point out to him what a fool he has made of himself. Sit down though and have some tea. I must admit I am awfully tired. . . . Hadn't I better lie down and put vinegar on my head? What do you think?"

"Certainly," I cried, "ice even. You are very much upset. You are pale and your hands are trembling. Lie down, rest, and put off telling me. I'll sit by you and wait."

He hesitated, but I insisted on his lying down. Nastasya brought a cup of vinegar. I wetted a towel and laid it on his head. Then Nastasya stood on a chair and began lighting a lamp before the ikon in the corner. I noticed this with surprise; there had never been a lamp there before and now suddenly it had made its appearance.

"I arranged for that as soon as they had gone away," muttered Stepan Trofimovitch, looking at me slyly. "*Quand on a de ces choses-là dans sa chambre et qu'on vient vous arrêter* it makes an impression and they are sure to report that they have seen it. . . ."

When she had done the lamp, Nastasya stood in the doorway, leaned her cheek in her right hand, and began gazing at him with a lachrymose air.

"*Eloignez-la* on some excuse," he nodded to me from the sofa. "I can't endure this Russian sympathy, *et puis ça m'embête.*"

But she went away of herself. I noticed that he kept looking towards the door and listening for sounds in the passage.

"*Il faut être prêt, voyez-vous,*" he said, looking at me significantly, "*chaque moment* . . . they may come and take one and, phew!—a man disappears."

"Heavens! who'll come? Who will take you?"

"*Voyez-vous, mon cher,* I asked straight out when he was going away, what would they do to me now?"

"You'd better have asked them where you'd be exiled!" I cried out in the same indignation.

"That's just what I meant when I asked, but he went away

without answering. *Voyez-vous:* as for linen, clothes, warm
things especially, that must be as they decide; if they tell me
to take them—all right, or they might send me in a soldier's
overcoat. But I thrust thirty-five roubles" (he suddenly
dropped his voice, looking towards the door by which Nastasya
had gone out) "in a slit in my waistcoat pocket, here, feel. . . .
I believe they won't take the waistcoat off, and left seven roubles
in my purse to keep up appearances, as though that were all I
have. You see, it's in small change and the coppers are on the
table, so they won't guess that I've hidden the money, but will
suppose that that's all. For God knows where I may have to
sleep to-night!"

I bowed my head before such madness. It was obvious that
a man could not be arrested and searched in the way he was
describing, and he must have mixed things up. It's true it all
happened in the days before our present, more recent regulations. It is true, too, that according to his own account they
had offered to follow the more regular procedure, but he "got
the better of them" and refused. . . . Of course not long ago
a governor might, in extreme cases. . . . But how could this
be an extreme case? That's what baffled me.

"No doubt they had a telegram from Petersburg," Stepan
Trofimovitch said suddenly.

"A telegram? About you? Because of the works of Herzen
and your poem? Have you taken leave of your senses? What
is there in that to arrest you for?"

I was positively angry. He made a grimace and was evidently
mortified—not at my exclamation, but at the idea that there was
no ground for arrest.

"Who can tell in our day what he may not be arrested for?"
he muttered enigmatically.

A wild and nonsensical idea crossed my mind.

"Stepan Trofimovitch, tell me as a friend," I cried, "as a real
friend, I will not betray you: do you belong to some secret
society or not?"

And on this, to my amazement, he was not quite certain
whether he was or was not a member of some secret society.

"That depends, *voyez-vous.*"

"How do you mean 'it depends'?"

"When with one's whole heart one is an adherent of progress
and . . . who can answer it? You may suppose you don't belong,
and suddenly it turns out that you do belong to something."

"Now is that possible? It's a case of yes or no."

"Cela date de Pétersbourg when she and I were meaning to found a magazine there. That's what's at the root of it. She gave them the slip then, and they forgot us, but now they've remembered. *Cher, cher,* don't you know me?" he cried hysterically. "And they'll take us, put us in a cart, and march us off to Siberia for ever, or forget us in prison."

And he suddenly broke into bitter weeping. His tears positively streamed. He covered his face with his red silk handkerchief and sobbed, sobbed convulsively for five minutes. It wrung my heart. This was the man who had been a prophet among us for twenty years, a leader, a patriarch, the Kukolnik who had borne himself so loftily and majestically before all of us, before whom we bowed down with genuine reverence, feeling proud of doing so—and all of a sudden here he was sobbing, sobbing like a naughty child waiting for the rod which the teacher is fetching for him. I felt fearfully sorry for him. He believed in the reality of that "cart" as he believed that I was sitting by his side, and he expected it that morning, at once, that very minute, and all this on account of his Herzen and some poem! Such complete, absolute ignorance of everyday reality was touching and somehow repulsive.

At last he left off crying, got up from the sofa and began walking about the room again, continuing to talk to me, though he looked out of the window every minute and listened to every sound in the passage. Our conversation was still disconnected. All my assurances and attempts to console him rebounded from him like peas from a wall. He scarcely listened, but yet what he needed was that I should console him and keep on talking with that object. I saw that he could not do without me now, and would not let me go for anything. I remained, and we spent more than two hours together. In conversation he recalled that Blum had taken with him two manifestos he had found.

"Manifestos!" I said, foolishly frightened. "Do you mean to say you . . ."

"Oh, ten were left here," he answered with vexation (he talked to me at one moment in a vexed and haughty tone and at the next with dreadful plaintiveness and humiliation), "but I had disposed of eight already, and Blum only found two."

And he suddenly flushed with indignation.

"Vous me mettez avec ces gens-là! Do you suppose I could be working with those scoundrels, those anonymous libellers, with my son Pyotr Stepanovitch, *avec ces esprits forts de la lâcheté?* Oh, heavens!"

"Bah! haven't they mixed you up perhaps? . . . But it's nonsense, it can't be so," I observed.

"*Savez-vous*," broke from him suddenly, "I feel at moments *que je ferai là-bas quelque esclandre*. Oh, don't go away, don't leave me alone! *Ma carrière est finie aujourd'hui, je le sens.* Do you know, I might fall on somebody there and bite him, like that lieutenant."

He looked at me with a strange expression—alarmed, and at the same time anxious to alarm me. He certainly was getting more and more exasperated with somebody and about something as time went on and the police-cart did not appear; he was positively wrathful. Suddenly Nastasya, who had come from the kitchen into the passage for some reason, upset a clothes-horse there. Stepan Trofimovitch trembled and turned numb with terror as he sat; but when the noise was explained, he almost shrieked at Nastasya and, stamping, drove her back to the kitchen. A minute later he said, looking at me in despair:

"I am ruined! *Cher*"—he sat down suddenly beside me and looked piteously into my face—"*cher*, it's not Siberia I am afraid of, I swear. *Oh, je vous jure!*" (Tears positively stood in his eyes.) "It's something else I fear."

I saw from his expression that he wanted at last to tell me something of great importance which he had till now refrained from telling.

"I was afraid of disgrace," he whispered mysteriously.

"What disgrace? On the contrary! Believe me, Stepan Trofimovitch, that all this will be explained to-day and will end to your advantage. . . ."

"Are you so sure that they will pardon me?"

"Pardon you? What! What a word! What have you done? I assure you you've done nothing."

"*Qu'en savez-vous?* all my life has been . . . *cher* . . . They'll remember everything . . . and if they find nothing, it will be *worse still*," he added all of a sudden, unexpectedly.

"How do you mean it will be worse?"

"It will be worse."

"I don't understand."

"My friend, let it be Siberia, Archangel, loss of rights—if I must perish, let me perish! But . . . I am afraid of something else." (Again whispering, a scared face, mystery.)

"But of what? Of what?"

"They'll flog me," he pronounced, looking at me with a face of despair.

80

"Who'll flog you? What for? Where?" I cried, feeling alarmed that he was going out of his mind.

"Where? Why there . . . where 'that's' done."

"But where is it done?"

"Eh, *cher*," he whispered almost in my ear. "The floor suddenly gives way under you, you drop half through. . . . Everyone knows that."

"Legends!" I cried, guessing what he meant. "Old tales. Can you have believed them till now?" I laughed.

"Tales! But there must be foundation for them; flogged men tell no tales. I've imagined it ten thousand times."

"But you, why you? You've done nothing, you know."

"That makes it worse. They'll find out I've done nothing and flog me for it."

"And you are sure that you'll be taken to Petersburg for that."

"My friend, I've told you already that I regret nothing, *ma carrière est finie*. From that hour when she said good-bye to me at Skvoreshniki my life has had no value for me . . . but disgrace, disgrace, *que dira-t-elle* if she finds out?"

He looked at me in despair. And the poor fellow flushed all over. I dropped my eyes too.

"She'll find out nothing, for nothing will happen to you. I feel as if I were speaking to you for the first time in my life, Stepan Trofimovitch, you've astonished me so this morning."

"But, my friend, this isn't fear. For even if I am pardoned, even if I am brought here and nothing is done to me—then I am undone. *Elle me soupçonnera toute sa vie*—me, me, the poet, the thinker, the man whom she has worshipped for twenty-two years!"

"It will never enter her head."

"It will," he whispered with profound conviction. "We've talked of it several times in Petersburg, in Lent, before we came away, when we were both afraid. . . . *Elle me soupçonnera toute sa vie* . . . and how can I disabuse her? It won't sound likely. And in this wretched town who'd believe it? *c'est invraisemblable*. . . . *Et puis les femmes*, she will be pleased. She will be genuinely grieved like a true friend, but secretly she will be pleased. . . . I shall give her a weapon against me for the rest of my life. Oh, it's all over with me! Twenty years of such perfect happiness with her . . . and now!"

He hid his face in his hands.

"Stepan Trofimovitch, oughtn't you to let Varvara Petrovna know at once of what has happened?" I suggested

81

"God preserve me!" he cried, shuddering and leaping up from his place. "On no account, never, after what was said at parting at Skvoreshniki—never!"

His eyes flashed.

We went on sitting together another hour or more, I believe, expecting something all the time—the idea had taken such hold of us. He lay down again, even closed his eyes, and lay for twenty minutes without uttering a word, so that I thought he was asleep or unconscious. Suddenly he got up impulsively, pulled the towel off his head, jumped up from the sofa, rushed to the looking-glass, with trembling hands tied his cravat, and in a voice of thunder called to Nastasya, telling her to give him his overcoat, his new hat and his stick.

"I can hear no more," he said in a breaking voice. "I can't, I can't! I am going myself."

"Where?" I cried, jumping up too.

"To Lembke. *Cher,* I ought, I am obliged. It's my duty. I am a citizen and a man, not a worthless chip. I have rights; I want my rights. . . . For twenty years I've not insisted on my rights. All my life I've neglected them criminally . . . but now I'll demand them. He must tell me everything—everything. He received a telegram. He dare not torture me; if so, let him arrest me, let him arrest me!"

He stamped and vociferated almost with shrieks.

"I approve of what you say," I said, speaking as calmly as possible, on purpose, though I was very much afraid for him. "Certainly it is better than sitting here in such misery, but I can't approve of your state of mind. Just see what you look like and in what a state you are going there! *Il faut être digne et calme avec Lembke.* You really might rush at someone there and bite him."

"I am giving myself up. I am walking straight into the jaws of the lion. . . ."

"I'll go with you."

"I expected no less of you, I accept your sacrifice, the sacrifice of a true friend; but only as far as the house, only as far as the house. You ought not, you have no right to compromise yourself further by being my confederate. *Oh, croyez-moi, je serai calme.* I feel that I am at this moment *à la hauteur de tout ce qu'il y a de plus sacré.*" . . .

"I may perhaps go into the house with you," I interrupted him. "I had a message from their stupid committee yesterday through Vysotsky that they reckon on me and invite me to the

fête to-morrow as one of the stewards or wnatever it is . . . one
of the six young men whose duty it is to look after the trays,
wait on the ladies, take the guests to their places, and wear a
rosette of crimson and white ribbon on the left shoulder. I
meant to refuse, but now why shouldn't I go into the house on
the excuse of seeing Yulia Mihailovna herself about it? . . .
So we will go in together.''

He listened, nodding, but I think he understood nothing.
We stood on the threshold.

"Cher"—he stretched out his arm to the lamp before the
ikon—*"cher,* I have never believed in this, but . . . so be it,
so be it!'' He crossed himself. *"Allons!"*

''Well, that's better so,'' I thought as I went out on to the
steps with him. ''The fresh air will do him good on the way,
and we shall calm down, turn back, and go home to bed. . . .''

But I reckoned without my host. On the way an adventure
occurred which agitated Stepan Trofimovitch even more, and
finally determined him to go on . . . so that I should never
have expected of our friend so much spirit as he suddenly displayed that morning. Poor friend, kind-hearted friend!

CHAPTER X

FILIBUSTERS. A FATAL MORNING

I

THE adventure that befell us on the way was also a surprising one. But I must tell the story in due order. An
hour before Stepan Trofimovitch and I came out into the street,
a crowd of people, the hands from Shpigulins' factory, seventy
or more in number, had been marching through the town, and
had been an object of curiosity to many spectators. They
walked intentionally in good order and almost in silence. Afterwards it was asserted that these seventy had been elected out of
the whole number of factory hands, amounting to about nine
hundred, to go to the governor and to try and get from him, in
the absence of their employer, a just settlement of their grievances against the manager, who, in closing the factory and dis-
missing the workmen, had cheated them all in an impudent
way—a fact which has since been proved conclusively. Some
people still deny that there was any election of delegates, main-

taining that seventy was too large a number to elect, and that the crowd simply consisted of those who had been most unfairly treated, and that they only came to ask for help in their own case, so that the general "mutiny" of the factory workers, about which there was such an uproar later on, had never existed at all. Others fiercely maintained that these seventy men were not simple strikers but revolutionists, that is, not merely that they were the most turbulent, but that they must have been worked upon by seditious manifestos. The fact is, it is still uncertain whether there had been any outside influence or incitement at work or not. My private opinion is that the workmen had not read the seditious manifestos at all, and if they had read them, would not have understood one word, for one reason because the authors of such literature write very obscurely in spite of the boldness of their style. But as the workmen really were in a difficult plight and the police to whom they appealed would not enter into their grievances, what could be more natural than their idea of going in a body to "the general himself" if possible, with the petition at their head, forming up in an orderly way before his door, and as soon as he showed himself, all falling on their knees and crying out to him as to providence itself? To my mind there is no need to see in this a mutiny or even a deputation, for it's a traditional, historical mode of action; the Russian people have always loved to parley with "the general himself" for the mere satisfaction of doing so, regardless of how the conversation may end.

And so I am quite convinced that, even though Pyotr Stepanovitch, Liputin, and perhaps some others—perhaps even Fedka too—had been flitting about among the workpeople talking to them (and there is fairly good evidence of this), they had only approached two, three, five at the most, trying to sound them, and nothing had come of their conversation. As for the mutiny they advocated, if the factory-workers did understand anything of their propaganda, they would have left off listening to it at once as to something stupid that had nothing to do with them. Fedka was a different matter: he had more success, I believe, than Pyotr Stepanovitch. Two workmen are now known for a fact to have assisted Fedka in causing the fire in the town which occurred three days afterwards, and a month later three men who had worked in the factory were arrested for robbery and arson in the province. But if in these cases Fedka did lure them to direct and immediate action, he could only have succeeded with these five, for we heard of nothing of the sort being done by others.

Be that as it may, the whole crowd of workpeople had at last reached the open space in front of the governor's house and were drawn up there in silence and good order. Then, gaping openmouthed at the front door, they waited. I am told that as soon as they halted they took off their caps, that is, a good half-hour before the appearance of the governor, who, as ill-luck would have it, was not at home at the moment. The police made their appearance at once, at first individual policemen and then as large a contingent of them as could be gathered together; they began, of course, by being menacing, ordering them to break up. But the workmen remained obstinately, like a flock of sheep at a fence, and replied laconically that they had come to see "the general himself"; it was evident that they were firmly determined. The unnatural shouting of the police ceased, and was quickly succeeded by deliberations, mysterious whispered instructions, and stern, fussy perplexity, which wrinkled the brows of the police officers. The head of the police preferred to await the arrival of the "governor himself". It was not true that he galloped to the spot with three horses at full speed, and began hitting out right and left before he alighted from his carriage. It's true that he used to dash about and was fond of dashing about at full speed in a carriage with a yellow back, and while his trace-horses, who were so trained to carry their heads that they looked "positively perverted", galloped more and more frantically, rousing the enthusiasm of all the shopkeepers in the bazaar, he would rise up in the carriage, stand erect, holding on by a strap which had been fixed on purpose at the side, and with his right arm extended into space like a figure on a monument, survey the town majestically. But in the present case he did not use his fists, and though as he got out of the carriage he could not refrain from a forcible expression, this was simply done to keep up his popularity. There is a still more absurd story that soldiers were brought up with bayonets, and that a telegram was sent for artillery and Cossacks; those are legends which are not believed now even by those who invented them. It's an absurd story, too, that barrels of water were brought from the fire brigade, and that people were drenched with water from them. The simple fact is that Ilya Ilyitch shouted in his heat that he wouldn't let one of them come dry out of the water; probably this was the foundation of the barrel legend which got into the columns of the Petersburg and Moscow newspapers. Probably the most accurate version was that at first all the available police formed a cordon round the crowd, and a messenger was sent for Lembke, a police superintendent, who dashed off in the carriage belonging to the head of the police on the way to Skvoreshniki, knowing that Lembke had gone there in his carriage half an hour before.

But I must confess that I am still unable to answer the question how they could at first sight, from the first moment, have transformed an insignificant, that is to say an ordinary, crowd of petitioners, even though there were several of them, into a rebellion which threatened to shake the foundations of the state. Why did Lembke himself rush at that idea when he arrived twenty minutes after the messenger? I imagine (but again it's only my private opinion) that it was to the interest of Ilya Ilyitch, who was a crony of the factory manager's, to represent the crowd in this light to Lembke, in order to prevent him from going into the case; and Lembke himself had put the idea into his head. In the course of the last two days he had had two unusual and mysterious conversations with him. It is true they were exceedingly obscure, but Ilya Ilyitch was able to gather from them that the governor had thoroughly made up his mind that there were political manifestos, and that Shpigulins' factory hands were being incited to a Socialist rising, and that he was so persuaded of it that he would perhaps have regretted it if the story had turned out to be nonsense. "He wants to get distinction in Petersburg," our wily Ilya Ilyitch thought to himself as he left Von Lembke; "well, that just suits me."

But I am convinced that poor Andrey Antonovitch would not have desired a rebellion even for the sake of distinguishing himself. He was a most conscientious official, who had lived in a state of innocence up to the time of his marriage. And was it his fault that, instead of an innocent allowance of wood from the government and an equally innocent Minnchen, a princess of forty summers had raised him to her level? I know almost for certain that the unmistakable symptoms of the mental condition which brought poor Andrey Antonovitch to a well-known establishment in Switzerland, where, I am told, he is now regaining his energies, were first apparent on that fatal morning. But once we admit that unmistakable signs of something were visible that morning, it may well be allowed that similar symptoms may have been evident the day before, though not so clearly. I happen to know from the most private sources (well, you may assume that Yulia Mihailovna later on, not in triumph but *almost* in remorse—for a woman is incapable of *complete* remorse—revealed part of it to me herself) that Andrey

86

Antonovitch had gone into his wife's room in the middle of the previous night, past two o'clock in the morning, had waked her up, and had insisted on her listening to his "ultimatum". He demanded it so insistently that she was obliged to get up from her bed in indignation and curl-papers, and, sitting down on a couch, she had to listen, though with sarcastic disdain. Only then she grasped for the first time how far gone her Andrey Antonovitch was, and was secretly horrified. She ought to have thought what she was about and have been softened, but she concealed her horror and was more obstinate than ever. Like every wife she had her own method of treating Andrey Antono-vitch, which she had tried more than once already and with it driven him to frenzy. Yulia Mihailovna's method was that of contemptuous silence, for one hour, two, a whole day, and almost for three days and nights—silence whatever happened, whatever he said, whatever he did, even if he had clambered up to throw himself out of a three-storey window—a method unendurable for a sensitive man! Whether Yulia Mihailovna meant to punish her husband for his blunders of the last few days and the jealous envy he, as the chief authority in the town, felt for her administrative abilities; whether she was indignant at his criticism of her behaviour with the young people and local society generally, and lack of comprehension of her subtle and far-sighted political aims; or was angry with his stupid and senseless jealousy of Pyotr Stepanovitch—however that may have been, she made up her mind not to be softened even now, in spite of its being three o'clock at night, and though Andrey Antonovitch was in a state of emotion such as she had never seen him in before.

Pacing up and down in all directions over the rugs of her boudoir, beside himself, he poured out everything, everything, quite disconnectedly, it's true, but everything that had been rankling in his heart, for—"it was outrageous". He began by saying that he was a laughing-stock to everyone and "was being led by the nose". "Curse the expression," he squealed, at once catching her smile, "let it stand, it's true. . . . . No, madam, the time has come; let me tell you it's not a time for laughter and feminine arts now. We are not in the boudoir of a mincing lady, but like two abstract creatures in a balloon who have met to speak the truth." (He was no doubt confused and could not find the right words for his ideas, however just they were.) "It is you, madam, you who have destroyed my happy past. I took up this post simply for your sake, for the sake of

87

your ambition. . . . You smile sarcastically? Don't triumph, don't be in a hurry. Let me tell you, madam, let me tell you that I should have been equal to this position, and not only this position but a dozen positions like it, for I have abilities; but with you, madam, with you—it's impossible, for with you here I have no abilities. There cannot be two centres, and you have created two—one of mine and one in your boudoir—two centres of power, madam, but I won't allow it, I won't allow it! In the service, as in marriage, there must be one centre, two are impossible. . . . How have you repaid me?" he went on. "Our marriage has been nothing but your proving to me all the time, every hour, that I am a nonentity, a fool, and even a rascal, and I have been all the time, every hour, forced in a degrading way to prove to you that I am not a nonentity, not a fool at all, and that I impress everyone with my honourable character. Isn't that degrading for both sides?"

At this point he began rapidly stamping with both feet on the carpet, so that Yulia Mihailovna was obliged to get up with stern dignity. He subsided quickly, but passed to being pathetic and began sobbing (yes, sobbing!), beating himself on the breast almost for five minutes, getting more and more frantic at Yulia Mihailovna's profound silence. At last he made a fatal blunder, and let slip that he was jealous of Pyotr Stepanovitch. Realising that he had made an utter fool of himself, he became savagely furious, and shouted that he "would not allow them to deny God" and that he would "send her *salon* of irresponsible infidels packing", that the governor of a province was bound to believe in God "and so his wife was too", that he wouldn't put up with these young men; that "you, madam, for the sake of your own dignity, ought to have thought of your husband and to have stood up for his intelligence even if he were a man of poor abilities (and I'm by no means a man of poor abilities!), and yet it's your doing that everyone here despises me, it was you put them all up to it!" He shouted that he would annihilate the woman question, that he would eradicate every trace of it, that to-morrow he would forbid and break up their silly fête for the benefit of the governesses (damn them!), that the first governess he came across to-morrow morning he would drive out of the province "with a Cossack! I'll make a point of it!" he shrieked. "Do you know," he screamed, "do you know that your rascals are inciting men at the factory, and that I know it? Let me tell you, I know the names of four of these rascals and that I am going out of my mind, hopelessly, hopelessly! . . ."

But at this point Yulia Mihailovna suddenly broke her silence and sternly announced that she had long been aware of these criminal designs, and that it was all foolishness, and that he had taken it too seriously, and that as for these mischievous fellows, she knew not only those four but all of them (it was a lie); but that she had not the faintest intention of going out of her mind on account of it, but, on the contrary, had all the more confidence in her intelligence and hoped to bring it all to a harmonious conclusion: to encourage the young people, to bring them to reason, to show them suddenly and unexpectedly that their designs were known, and then to point out to them new aims for rational and more noble activity.

Oh, how can I describe the effect of this on Andrey Antonovitch! Hearing that Pyotr Stepanovitch had duped him again and had made a fool of him so coarsely, that he had told her much more than he had told him, and sooner than him, and that perhaps Pyotr Stepanovitch was the chief instigator of all these criminal designs—he flew into a frenzy. "Senseless but malignant woman," he cried, snapping his bonds at one blow, "let me tell you, I shall arrest your worthless lover at once, I shall put him in fetters and send him to the fortress, or—I shall jump out of window before your eyes this minute!"

Yulia Mihailovna, turning green with anger, greeted this tirade at once with a burst of prolonged, ringing laughter, going off into peals such as one hears at the French theatre when a Parisian actress, imported for a fee of a hundred thousand to play a coquette, laughs in her husband's face for daring to be jealous of her.

Von Lembke rushed to the window, but suddenly stopped as though rooted to the spot, folded his arms across his chest, and, white as a corpse, looked with a sinister gaze at the laughing lady. "Do you know, Yulia, do you know," he said in a gasping and suppliant voice, "do you know that even I can do something?" But at the renewed and even louder laughter that followed his last words he clenched his teeth, groaned, and suddenly rushed, not towards the window, but at his spouse, with his fist raised! He did not bring it down—no, I repeat again and again, no; but it was the last straw. He ran to his own room, not knowing what he was doing, flung himself, dressed as he was, face downwards on his bed, wrapped himself convulsively, head and all, in the sheet, and lay so for two hours—incapable of sleep, incapable of thought, with a load on his heart and blank, immovable despair in his soul. Now and then he shivered all over with an agonising, feverish tremor. Disconnected and irrelevant things kept coming into his mind: at one minute he thought of the old clock which used to hang on his wall fifteen years ago in Petersburg and had lost the minute-hand; at another of the cheerful clerk, Millebois, and how they had once caught a sparrow together in Alexandrovsky Park and had laughed so that they could be heard all over the park, remembering that one of them was already a college assessor. I imagine that about seven in the morning he must have fallen asleep without being aware of it himself, and must have slept with enjoyment, with agreeable dreams.

Waking about ten o'clock, he jumped wildly out of bed, remembering everything at once, and slapped himself on the head; he refused his breakfast, and would see neither Blum nor the chief of the police nor the clerk who came to remind him that he was expected to preside over a meeting that morning; he would listen to nothing, and did not want to understand. He ran like one possessed to Yulia Mihailovna's part of the house. There Sofya Antropovna, an old lady of good family who had lived for years with Yulia Mihailovna, explained to him that his wife had set off at ten o'clock that morning with a large company in three carriages to Varvara Petrovna Stavrogin's, to Skvoreshniki, to look over the place with a view to the second fête which was planned for a fortnight later, and that the visit to-day had been arranged with Varvara Petrovna three days before. Overwhelmed with this news, Andrey Antonovitch returned to his study and impulsively ordered the horses. He could hardly wait for them to be got ready. His soul was hungering for Yulia Mihailovna—to look at her, to be near her for five minutes; perhaps she would glance at him, notice him, would smile as before, forgive him . . . O-oh! "Aren't the horses ready?" Mechanically he opened a thick book lying on the table. (He sometimes used to try his fortune in this way with a book, opening it at random and reading the three lines at the top of the right-hand page.) What turned up was: *"Tout est pour le mieux dans le meilleur des mondes possibles."*—Voltaire, *Candide*. He uttered an ejaculation of contempt and ran to get into the carriage: "Skvoreshniki!"

The coachman said afterwards that his master urged him on all the way, but as soon as they were getting near the mansion he suddenly told him to turn and drive back to the town, bidding him "Drive fast; please drive fast!" Before they reached the town wall "master told me to stop again, got out of the carriage, and went across the road into the field; I thought he felt ill, but he stopped and began looking at the flowers, and so he stood for a time. It was strange, really; I began to feel quite uneasy." This was the coachman's testimony. I remember the weather that morning: it was a cold, clear, but windy September day; before Andrey Antonovitch stretched a forbidding landscape of bare fields from which the crop had long been harvested; there were a few dying yellow flowers, pitiful relics blown about by the howling wind. Did he want to compare himself and his fate with those wretched flowers battered by the autumn and the frost? I don't think so; in fact I feel sure it was not so, and that he realised nothing about the flowers in spite of the evidence of the coachman and of the police superintendent, who drove up at that moment and asserted afterwards that he found the governor with a bunch of yellow flowers in his hand. This police superintendent, Flibusterov by name, was an ardent champion of authority who had only recently come to our town, but had already distinguished himself and become famous by his inordinate zeal, by a certain vehemence in the execution of his duties, and his inveterate inebriety. Jumping out of the carriage, and not the least disconcerted at the sight of what the governor was doing, he blurted out all in one breath, with a frantic expression, yet with an air of conviction, that "There's an upset in the town".

"Eh? What?" said Andrey Antonovitch, turning to him with a stern face, but without a trace of surprise or any recollection of his carriage and his coachman, as though he had been in his own study.

"Police-superintendent Flibusterov, your Excellency. There's a riot in the town."

"Filibusters?" Andrey Antonovitch said thoughtfully.

"Just so, your Excellency. The Shpigulin men are making a riot."

"The Shpigulin men! . . ."

The name "Shpigulin" seemed to remind him of something. He started and put his finger to his forehead: "The Shpigulin men!" In silence, and still plunged in thought, he walked without haste to the carriage, took his seat, and told the coachman to drive to the town. The police-superintendent followed in the droshky.

I imagine that he had vague impressions of many interesting things of all sorts on the way, but I doubt whether he had any definite idea or any settled intention as he drove into the open space in front of his house. But no sooner did he see the resolute and orderly ranks of "the rioters", the cordon of police, and helpless (and perhaps purposely helpless) chief of police, and the general expectation of what he was the object, than all the blood rushed to his heart. With a pale face he stepped out of his carriage.

"Caps off!" he said breathlessly and hardly audibly. "On your knees!" he squealed, to the surprise of everyone, to his own surprise too, and perhaps the very unexpectedness of the position was the explanation of what followed. Can a sledge on a switchback at carnival stop short as it flies down the hill? What made it worse, Andrey Antonovitch had been all his life serene in character, and never shouted or stamped at anyone; and such people are always the most dangerous if it once happens that something sets their sledge sliding down-hill. Everything was whirling before his eyes.

"Filibusters!" he yelled still more shrilly and absurdly, and his voice broke. He stood, not knowing what he was going to do, but knowing and feeling in his whole being that he certainly would do something directly.

"Lord!" was heard from the crowd. A lad began crossing himself; three or four men actually did try to kneel down, but the whole mass moved three steps forward, and suddenly all began talking at once: "Your Excellency . . . we were hired for a term . . . the manager . . . you mustn't say," and so on and so on. It was impossible to distinguish anything.

Alas! Andrey Antonovitch could distinguish nothing: the flowers were still in his hands. The riot was as real to him as the prison carts were to Stepan Trofimovitch. And flitting to and fro in the crowd of "rioters" who gazed open-eyed at him, he seemed to see Pyotr Stepanovitch, who had egged them on— Pyotr Stepanovitch, whom he hated and whose image had never left him since yesterday.

"Rods!" he cried even more unexpectedly. A dead silence followed.

From the facts I have learnt and those I have conjectured, this must have been what happened at the beginning; but I have no such exact information for what followed, nor can I conjecture it so easily. There are some facts, however.

In the first place, rods were brought on the scene with strange rapidity; they had evidently been got ready beforehand in expectation by the intelligent chief of the police. Not more than two, or at most three, were actually flogged, however; that fact I wish to lay stress on. It's an absolute fabrication to say that the whole crowd of rioters, or at least half of them, were punished. It is a nonsensical story, too, that a poor but respectable lady was caught as she passed by and promptly thrashed; yet I read myself an account of this incident afterwards among the provincial items of a Petersburg newspaper. Many people in the town talked of an old woman called Avdotya Petrovna Tarapygin, who lived in the almshouse by the cemetery. She was said, on her way home from visiting a friend, to have forced her way into the crowd of spectators through natural curiosity. Seeing what was going on, she cried out: "What a shame!" and spat on the ground. For this it was said she had been seized and flogged too. This story not only appeared in print, but in our excitement we positively got up a subscription for her benefit. I subscribed twenty kopecks myself. And would you believe it? It appears now that there was no old woman called Tarapygin living in the almshouse at all! I went to inquire at the almshouse by the cemetery myself; they had never heard of anyone called Tarapygin there, and, what's more, they were quite offended when I told them the story that was going round. I mention this fabulous Avdotya Petrovna because what happened to her (if she really had existed) very nearly happened to Stepan Trofimovitch. Possibly, indeed, his adventure may have been at the bottom of the ridiculous tale about the old woman, that is, as the gossip went on growing he was transformed into this old dame.

What I find most difficult to understand is how he came to slip away from me as soon as he got into the square. As I had a misgiving of something very unpleasant, I wanted to take him round the square straight to the entrance to the governor's, but my own curiosity was roused, and I stopped only for one minute to question the first person I came across, and suddenly I looked round and found Stepan Trofimovitch no longer at my side. Instinctively I darted off to look for him in the most dangerous place; something made me feel that his sledge, too, was flying down-hill. And I did, as a fact, find him in the very centre of things. I remember I seized him by the arm; but he looked quietly and proudly at me with an air of immense authority.

"*Cher,*" he pronounced in a voice which quivered on a breaking note, "if they are dealing with people so unceremoniously before us, in an open square, what is to be expected from *that*

93

man, for instance . . . if he happens to act on his own authority?''

And shaking with indignation and with an intense desire to defy them, he pointed a menacing, accusing finger at Flibusterov, who was gazing at us open-eyed two paces away.

"*That* man!'' cried the latter, blind with rage. "What man? And who are you?'' He stepped up to him, clenching his fist. "Who are you?'' he roared ferociously, hysterically, and desperately. (I must mention that he knew Stepan Trofimovitch perfectly well by sight.) Another moment and he would have certainly seized him by the collar; but luckily, hearing him shout, Lembke turned his head. He gazed intensely but with perplexity at Stepan Trofimovitch, seeming to consider something, and suddenly he shook his hand impatiently. Flibusterov was checked. I drew Stepan Trofimovitch out of the crowd, though perhaps he may have wished to retreat himself.

"Home, home,'' I insisted; "it was certainly thanks to Lembke that we were not beaten.''

"Go, my friend; I am to blame for exposing you to this. You have a future and a career of a sort before you, while I— *mon heure est sonnée.*''

He resolutely mounted the governor's steps. The hall-porter knew me; I said that we both wanted to see Yulia Mihailovna. We sat down in the waiting-room and waited. I was unwilling to leave my friend, but I thought it unnecessary to say anything more to him. He had the air of a man who had consecrated himself to certain death for the sake of his country. We sat down, not side by side, but in different corners—I nearer to the entrance, he at some distance facing me, with his head bent in thought, leaning lightly on his stick. He held his wide-brimmed hat in his left hand. We sat like that for ten minutes.

II

Lembke suddenly came in with rapid steps, accompanied by the chief of police, looked absent-mindedly at us and, taking no notice of us, was about to pass into his study on the right, but Stepan Trofimovitch stood before him blocking his way. The tall figure of Stepan Trofimovitch, so unlike other people's, made an impression. Lembke stopped.

"Who is this?'' he muttered, puzzled, as if he were questioning the chief of police, though he did not turn his head towards him, and was all the time gazing at Stepan Trofimovitch.

"Retired college assessor, Stepan Trofimovitch Verhovensky, your Excellency," answered Stepan Trofimovitch, bowing majestically. His Excellency went on staring at him with a very blank expression, however.

"What is it?" And with the curtness of a great official he turned his ear to Stepan Trofimovitch with disdainful impatience, taking him for an ordinary person with a written petition of some sort.

"I was visited and my house was searched to-day by an official acting in your Excellency's name; therefore I am desirous . . ."

"Name? Name?" Lembke asked impatiently, seeming suddenly to have an inkling of something. Stepan Trofimovitch repeated his name still more majestically.

"A-a-ah! It's . . . that hotbed . . . You have shown yourself, sir, in such a light. . . . Are you a professor? a professor?"

"I once had the honour of giving some lectures to the young men of the X university."

"The young men!" Lembke seemed to start, though I am ready to bet that he grasped very little of what was going on or even, perhaps, did not know with whom he was talking.

"That, sir, I won't allow," he cried, suddenly getting terribly angry. "I won't allow young men! It's all these manifestos? It's an assault on society, sir, a piratical attack, filibustering. . . . What is your request?"

"On the contrary, your wife requested me to read something to-morrow at her fête. I've not come to make a request, but to ask for my rights. . . ."

"At the fête? There'll be no fête. I won't allow your fête. A lecture? A lecture?" he screamed furiously.

"I should be very glad if you would speak to me rather more politely, your Excellency, without stamping or shouting at me as though I were a boy."

"Perhaps you understand whom you are speaking to?" said Lembke, turning crimson.

"Perfectly, your Excellency."

"I am protecting society while you are destroying it! . . . You . . . I remember about you, though: you used to be a tutor in the house of Madame Stavrogin?"

"Yes, I was in the position . . . of tutor . . . in the house of Madame Stavrogin."

95

"And have been for twenty years the hotbed of all that has now accumulated . . . all the fruits. . . . I believe I saw you just now in the square. You'd better look out, sir, you'd better look out; your way of thinking is well known. You may be sure that I keep my eye on you. I cannot allow your lectures, sir, I cannot. Don't come with such requests to me."

He would have passed on again.

"I repeat that your Excellency is mistaken; it was your wife who asked me to give, not a lecture, but a literary reading at the fête to-morrow. But I decline to do so in any case now. I humbly request that you will explain to me if possible how, why, and for what reason I was subjected to an official search to-day? Some of my books and papers, private letters to me, were taken from me and wheeled through the town in a barrow."

"Who searched you?" said Lembke, starting and returning to full consciousness of the position. He suddenly flushed all over. He turned quickly to the chief of police. At that moment the long, stooping, and awkward figure of Blum appeared in the doorway.

"'Why, this official here," said Stepan Trofimovitch, indicating him. Blum came forward with a face that admitted his responsibility, but showed no contrition.

"*Vous ne faites que des bêtises,*" Lembke threw at him in a tone of vexation and anger, and suddenly he was transformed and completely himself again.

"Excuse me," he muttered, utterly disconcerted and turning absolutely crimson, "all this . . . all this was probably a mere blunder, a misunderstanding . . . nothing but a misunderstanding."

"Your Excellency," observed Stepan Trofimovitch, "once when I was young I saw a characteristic incident. In the corridor of a theatre a man ran up to another and gave him a sounding smack in the face before the whole public. Perceiving at once that his victim was not the person whom he had intended to chastise but someone quite different who only slightly resembled him, he pronounced angrily, with the haste of one whose moments are precious—as your Excellency did just now —'I've made a mistake . . . excuse me, it was a misunderstanding, nothing but a misunderstanding'. And when the offended man remained resentful and cried out, he observed to him, with extreme annoyance: 'Why, I tell you it was a misunderstanding. What are you crying out about?'"

"That's . . . that's very amusing, of course"—Lembke gave

a wry smile—"but . . . but can't you see how unhappy I am myself?"

He almost screamed, and seemed about to hide his face in his hands.

This unexpected and piteous exclamation, almost a sob, was almost more than one could bear. It was probably the first moment since the previous day that he had full, vivid consciousness of all that had happened—and it was followed by complete, humiliating despair that could not be disguised—who knows, in another minute he might have sobbed aloud. For the first moment Stepan Trofimovitch looked wildly at him; then he suddenly bowed his head and in a voice pregnant with feeling pronounced:

"Your Excellency, don't trouble yourself with my petulant complaint, and only give orders for my books and letters to be restored to me . . ."

He was interrupted. At that very instant Yulia Mihailovna returned and entered noisily with all the party which had accompanied her. But at this point I should like to tell my story in as much detail as possible.

III

In the first place, the whole company who had filled three carriages crowded into the waiting-room. There was a special entrance to Yulia Mihailovna's apartments on the left as one entered the house; but on this occasion they all went through the waiting-room—and I imagine just because Stepan Trofimovitch was there, and because all that had happened to him as well as the Shpigulin affair had reached Yulia Mihailovna's ears as she drove into the town. Lyamshin, who for some misdemeanour had not been invited to join the party and so knew all that had been happening in the town before anyone else, brought her the news. With spiteful glee he hired a wretched Cossack nag and hastened on the way to Skvoreshniki to meet the returning cavalcade with the diverting intelligence. I fancy that, in spite of her lofty determination, Yulia Mihailovna was a little disconcerted on hearing such surprising news, but probably only for an instant. The political aspect of the affair, for instance, could not cause her uneasiness; Pyotr Stepanovitch had impressed upon her three of four times that the Shpigulin ruffians ought to be flogged, and Pyotr Stepanovitch certainly had for some time past been a great authority in her eyes. "But

. . . anyway, I shall make him pay for it," she doubtless reflected, the "he", of course, referring to her spouse. I must observe in passing that on this occasion, as though purposely, Pyotr Stepanovitch had taken no part in the expedition, and no one had seen him all day. I must mention too, by the way, that Varvara Petrovna had come back to the town with her guests (in the same carriage with Yulia Mihailovna) in order to be present at the last meeting of the committee which was arranging the fête for the next day. She too must have been interested, and perhaps even agitated, by the news about Stepan Trofimovitch communicated by Lyamshin.

The hour of reckoning for Andrey Antonovitch followed at once. Alas! he felt that from the first glance at his admirable wife. With an open air and an enchanting smile she went quickly up to Stepan Trofimovitch, held out her exquisitely gloved hand, and greeted him with a perfect shower of flattering phrases—as though the only thing she cared about that morning was to make haste to be charming to Stepan Trofimovitch because at last she saw him in her house. There was not one hint of the search that morning; it was as though she knew nothing of it. There was not one word to her husband, not one glance in his direction—as though he had not been in the room. What's more, she promptly confiscated Stepan Trofimovitch and carried him off to the drawing-room—as though he had had no interview with Lembke, or as though it was not worth prolonging if he had. I repeat again, I think that in this, Yulia Mihailovna, in spite of her aristocratic tone, made another great mistake. And Karmazinov particularly did much to aggravate this. (He had taken part in the expedition at Yulia Mihailovna's special request, and in that way had, incidentally, paid his visit to Varvara Petrovna, and she was so poor-spirited as to be perfectly delighted at it.) On seeing Stepan Trofimovitch, he called out from the doorway (he came in behind the rest) and pressed forward to embrace him, even interrupting Yulia Mihailovna.

"What years, what ages! At last . . . *excellent ami.*"

He made as though to kiss him, offering his cheek, of course, and Stepan Trofimovitch was so fluttered that he could not avoid saluting it.

"*Cher,*" he said to me that evening, recalling all the events of that day, "I wondered at that moment which of us was the most contemptible: he, embracing me only to humiliate me, or I, despising him and his face and kissing it on the spot, though I might have turned away. . . . Foo!"

98

"Come, tell me about yourself, tell me everything," Karmazinov drawled and lisped, as though it were possible for him on the spur of the moment to give an account of twenty-five years of his life. But this foolish trifling was the height of *chic*.

"Remember that the last time we met was at the Granovsky dinner in Moscow, and that twenty-four years have passed since then . . ." Stepan Trofimovitch began very reasonably (and consequently not at all in the same *chic* style).

"*Ce cher homme,*" Karmazinov interrupted with shrill familiarity, squeezing his shoulder with exaggerated friendliness. "Make haste and take us to your room, Yulia Mihailovna; there he'll sit down and tell us everything."

"And yet I was never at all intimate with that peevish old woman," Stepan Trofimovitch went on complaining to me that same evening, shaking with anger; "we were almost boys, and I'd begun to detest him even then . . . just as he had me, of course."

Yulia Mihailovna's drawing-room filled up quickly. Varvara Petrovna was particularly excited, though she tried to appear indifferent, but I caught her once or twice glancing with hatred at Karmazinov and with wrath at Stepan Trofimovitch—the wrath of anticipation, the wrath of jealousy and love: if Stepan Trofimovitch had blundered this time and had let Karmazinov make him look small before everyone, I believe she would have leapt up and beaten him. I have forgotten to say that Liza too was there, and I had never seen her more radiant, carelessly light-hearted, and happy. Mavriky Nikolaevitch was there too, of course. In the crowd of young ladies and rather vulgar young men who made up Yulia Mihailovna's usual retinue, and among whom this vulgarity was taken for sprightliness, and cheap cynicism for wit, I noticed two or three new faces: a very obsequious Pole who was on a visit in the town; a German doctor, a sturdy old fellow who kept loudly laughing with great zest at his own wit; and lastly, a very young princeling from Petersburg like an automaton figure, with the deportment of a state dignitary and a fearfully high collar. But it was evident that Yulia Mihailovna had a very high opinion of this visitor, and was even a little anxious of the impression her *salon* was making on him.

"*Cher M. Karmazinov,*" said Stepan Trofimovitch, sitting in a picturesque pose on the sofa and suddenly beginning to lisp as daintily as Karmazinov himself, "*cher M. Karmazinov,* the life of a man of our time and of certain convictions, even after an interval of twenty-five years, is bound to seem monotonous . . ."

The German went off into a loud abrupt guffaw like a neigh, evidently imagining that Stepan Trofimovitch had said something exceedingly funny. The latter gazed on him with studied amazement, but produced no effect on him whatever. The prince, too, looked at the German, turning head, collar and all, towards him and putting up his pince-nez, though without the slightest curiosity.

". . . Is bound to seem monotonous," Stepan Trofimovitch intentionally repeated, drawling each word as deliberately and nonchalantly as possible. "And so my life has been throughout this quarter of a century, *et comme on trouve partout plus de moines que de raison,* and as I am entirely of this opinion, it has come to pass that throughout this quarter of a century I . . ."

"C'est charmant, les moines," whispered Yulia Mihailovna, turning to Varvara Petrovna, who was sitting beside her.

Varvara Petrovna responded with a look of pride. But Karmazinov could not stomach the success of the French phrase, and quickly and shrilly interrupted Stepan Trofimovitch.

"As for me, I am quite at rest on that score, and for the past seven years I've been settled at Karlsruhe. And last year, when it was proposed by the town council to lay down a new water-pipe, I felt in my heart that this question of water-pipes in Karlsruhe was dearer and closer to my heart than all the questions of my precious Fatherland . . . in this period of so-called reform."

"I can't help sympathising, though it goes against the grain," sighed Stepan Trofimovitch, bowing his head significantly.

Yulia Mihailovna was triumphant: the conversation was becoming profound and taking a political turn.

"A drain-pipe?" the doctor inquired in a loud voice.

"A water-pipe, doctor, a water-pipe, and I positively assisted them in drawing up the plan."

The doctor went off into a deafening guffaw. Many people followed his example, laughing in the face of the doctor, who remained unconscious of it and was highly delighted that everyone was laughing.

"You must allow me to differ from you, Karmazinov," Yulia Mihailovna hastened to interpose. "Karlsruhe is all very well, but you are fond of mystifying people, and this time we don't believe you. What Russian writer has presented so many modern types, has brought forward so many contemporary problems,

100

has put his finger on the most vital modern points which make up the type of the modern man of action? You, only you, and no one else. It's no use your assuring us of your coldness towards your own country and your ardent interest in the water-pipes of Karlsruhe. Ha ha!''

"Yes, no doubt," lisped Karmazinov. "I have portrayed in the character of Pogozhev all the failings of the Slavophils and in the character of Nikodimov all the failings of the Westerners. . . ."

"I say, hardly *all!*" Lyamshin whispered slyly.

"But I do this by the way, simply to while away the tedious hours and to satisfy the persistent demands of my fellow-countrymen."

"You are probably aware, Stepan Trofimovitch," Yulia Mihailovna went on enthusiastically, "that to-morrow we shall have the delight of hearing the charming lines . . . one of the last of Semyon Yakovlevitch's exquisite literary inspirations—it's called "Merci". He announces in this piece that he will write no more, that nothing in the world will induce him to, if angels from Heaven or, what's more, all the best society were to implore him to change his mind. In fact he is laying down the pen for good, and this graceful "Merci" is addressed to the public in grateful acknowledgment of the constant enthusiasm with which it has for so many years greeted his unswerving loyalty to true Russian thought."

Yulia Mihailovna was at the acme of bliss.

"Yes, I shall make my farewell; I shall say my *Merci* and depart and there . . . in Karlsruhe . . . I shall close my eyes." Karmazinov was gradually becoming maudlin.

Like many of our great writers (and there are numbers of them amongst us), he could not resist praise, and began to be limp at once, in spite of his penetrating wit. But I consider this is pardonable. They say that one of our Shakespeares positively blurted out in private conversation that "we *great men* can't do otherwise", and so on, and, what's more, was unaware of it.

"There in Karlsruhe I shall close my eyes. When we have done our duty, all that's left for us great men is to make haste to close our eyes without seeking a reward. I shall do so too."

"Give me the address and I shall come to Karlsruhe to visit your tomb," said the German, laughing immoderately.

"They send corpses by rail nowadays," one of the less important young men said unexpectedly.

Lyamshin positively shrieked with delight. Yulia Mihailovna frowned. Nikolay Stavrogin walked in.

"Why, I was told that you were locked up?" he said aloud, addressing Stepan Trofimovitch before everyone else.

"No, it was a case of unlocking," jested Stepan Trofimovitch.

"But I hope that what's happened will have no influence on what I asked you to do," Yulia Mihailovna put in again. "I trust that you will not let this unfortunate annoyance, of which I had no idea, lead you to disappoint our eager expectations and deprive us of the enjoyment of hearing your reading at our literary matinée."

"I don't know, I . . . now . . ."

"Really, I am so unlucky, Varvara Petrovna . . . and only fancy, just when I was so longing to make the personal acquaintance of one of the most remarkable and independent intellects of Russia—and here Stepan Trofimovitch suddenly talks of deserting us."

"Your compliment is uttered so audibly that I ought to pretend not to hear it," Stepan Trofimovitch said neatly, "but I cannot believe that my insignificant presence is so indispensable at your fête to-morrow. However, I . . ."

"Why, you'll spoil him!" cried Pyotr Stepanovitch, bursting into the room. "I've only just got him in hand—and in one morning he has been searched, arrested, taken by the collar by a policeman, and here ladies are cooing to him in the governor's drawing-room. Every bone in his body is aching with rapture; in his wildest dreams he had never hoped for such good fortune. Now he'll begin informing against the Socialists after this!"

"Impossible, Pyotr Stepanovitch! Socialism is too grand an idea to be unrecognised by Stepan Trofimovitch." Yulia Mihailovna took up the gauntlet with energy.

"It's a great idea but its exponents are not always great men, *et brisons-là, mon cher,*" Stepan Trofimovitch ended, addressing his son and rising gracefully from his seat.

But at this point an utterly unexpected circumstance occurred. Von Lembke had been in the room for some time but seemed unnoticed by anyone, though everyone had seen him come in. In accordance with her former plan, Yulia Mihailovna went on ignoring him. He took up his position near the door and with a stern face listened gloomily to the conversation. Hearing an allusion to the events of the morning, he began fidgeting uneasily, stared at the prince, obviously struck by his stiffly starched, prominent collar; then suddenly he seemed to start on

102

hearing the voice of Pyotr Stepanovitch and seeing him burst in; and no sooner had Stepan Trofimovitch uttered his phrase about Socialists than Lembke went up to him, pushing against Lyamshin, who at once skipped out of the way with an affected gesture of surprise, rubbing his shoulder and pretending that he had been terribly bruised.

'Enough!" said Von Lembke to Stepan Trofimovitch, vigorously gripping the hand of the dismayed gentleman and squeezing it with all his might in both of his. "Enough! The filibusters of our day are unmasked. Not another word. Measures have been taken. . . ."

He spoke loudly enough to be heard by all the room, and concluded with energy. The impression he produced was poignant. Everybody felt that something was wrong. I saw Yulia Mihailovna turn pale. The effect was heightened by a trivial accident. After announcing that measures had been taken, Lembke turned sharply and walked quickly towards the door, but he had hardly taken two steps when he stumbled over a rug, swerved forward, and almost fell. For a moment he stood still, looked at the rug at which he had stumbled, and, uttering aloud "Change it!" went out of the room. Yulia Mihailovna ran after him. Her exit was followed by an uproar, in which it was difficult to distinguish anything. Some said he was "deranged", others that he was "liable to attacks"; others put their fingers to their forehead; Lyamshin, in the corner, put his two fingers above his forehead. People hinted at some domestic difficulties—in a whisper, of course. No one took up his hat; all were waiting. I don't know what Yulia Mihailovna managed to do, but five minutes later she came back, doing her utmost to appear composed. She replied evasively that Andrey Antonovitch was rather excited, but that it meant nothing, that he had been like that from a child, that she knew "much better", and that the fête next day would certainly cheer him up. Then followed a few flattering words to Stepan Trofimovitch simply from civility, and a loud invitation to the members of the committee to open the meeting now, at once. Only then, all who were not members of the committee prepared to go home; but the painful incidents of this fatal day were not yet over.

I noticed at the moment when Nikolay Stavrogin came in that Liza looked quickly and intently at him and was for a long time unable to take her eyes off him—so much so that at last it attracted attention. I saw Mavriky Nikolaevitch bend over her from behind; he seemed to mean to whisper something to her, but evidently changed his intention and drew himself up quickly, looking round at everyone with a guilty air. Nikolay Vsyevolodovitch too excited curiosity; his face was paler than usual and there was a strangely absent-minded look in his eyes. After flinging his question at Stepan Trofimovitch he seemed to forget about him altogether, and I really believe he even forgot to speak to his hostess. He did not once look at Liza—not because he did not want to, but I am certain because he did not notice her either. And suddenly, after the brief silence that followed Yulia Mihailovna's invitation to open the meeting without loss of time, Liza's musical voice, intentionally loud, was heard. She called to Stavrogin.

"Nikolay Vsyevolodovitch, a captain who calls himself a relation of yours, the brother of your wife, and whose name is Lebyadkin, keeps writing impertinent letters to me, complaining of you and offering to tell me some secrets about you. If he really is a connection of yours, please tell him not to annoy me, and save me from this unpleasantness."

There was a note of desperate challenge in these words— everyone realised it. The accusation was unmistakable, though perhaps it was a surprise to herself. She was like a man who shuts his eyes and throws himself from the roof.

But Nikolay Stavrogin's answer was even more astounding.

To begin with, it was strange that he was not in the least surprised and listened to Liza with unruffled attention. There was no trace of either confusion or anger in his face. Simply, firmly, even with an air of perfect readiness, he answered the fatal question:

"Yes, I have the misfortune to be connected with that man. I have been the husband of his sister for nearly five years. You may be sure I will give him your message as soon as possible, and I'll answer for it that he shan't annoy you again."

I shall never forget the horror that was reflected on the face of Varvara Petrovna. With a distracted air she got up from her seat, lifting up her right hand as though to ward off a blow. Nikolay Vsyevolodovitch looked at her, looked at Liza, at the spectators, and suddenly smiled with infinite disdain; he walked deliberately out of the room. Everyone saw how Liza leapt up from the sofa as soon as he turned to go and unmistakably made a movement to run after him. But she controlled herself and did not run after him; she went quietly out of the room without saying a word or even looking at anyone, accompanied, of course, by Mavriky Nikolaevitch, who rushed after her.

The uproar and the gossip that night in the town I will not attempt to describe. Varvara Petrovna shut herself up in her town house and Nikolay Vsyevolodovitch, it was said, went straight to Skvoreshniki without seeing his mother. Stepan Trofimovitch sent me that evening to *cette chère amie* to implore her to allow him to come to her, but she would not see me. He was terribly overwhelmed; he shed tears. "Such a marriage! Such a marriage! Such an awful thing in the family!" he kept repeating. He remembered Karmazinov, however, and abused him terribly. He set to work vigorously to prepare for the reading too and—the artistic temperament!—rehearsed before the looking-glass and went over all the jokes and witticisms uttered in the course of his life which he had written down in a separate notebook, to insert into his reading next day.

"My dear, I do this for the sake of a great idea," he said to me, obviously justifying himself. *"Cher ami,* I have been stationary for twenty-five years and suddenly I've begun to move—whither, I know not—but I've begun to move. . . ."

PART III

CHAPTER I

THE FÊTE—FIRST PART

I

THE fête took place in spite of all the perplexities of the pre-ceding "Shpigulin" day. I believe that even if Lembke had died the previous night, the fête would still have taken place next morning—so peculiar was the significance Yulia Mihailovna attached to it. Alas! up to the last moment she was blind and had no inkling of the state of public feeling. No one believed at last that the festive day would pass without some tremendous scandal, some "catastrophe" as some people expressed it, rub-bing their hands in anticipation. Many people, it is true, tried to assume a frowning and diplomatic countenance; but, speak-ing generally, every Russian is inordinately delighted at any public scandal and disorder. It is true that we did feel some-thing much more serious than the mere craving for a scandal: there was a general feeling of irritation, a feeling of implacable resentment; everyone seemed thoroughly disgusted with every-thing. A kind of bewildered cynicism, a forced, as it were, strained cynicism was predominant in everyone. The only people who were free from bewilderment were the ladies, and they were clear on only one point: their remorseless detestation of Yulia Mihailovna. Ladies of all shades of opinion were agreed in this. And she, poor dear, had no suspicion· up to the last hour she was persuaded that she was "surrounded by followers", and that they were still "fanatically devoted to her".

I have already hinted that some low fellows of different sorts had made their appearance amongst us. In turbulent times of upheaval or transition low characters always come to the front everywhere. I am not speaking now of the so-called "advanced" people who are always in a hurry to be in advance of everyone else (their absorbing anxiety) and who always have some more or less definite, though often very stupid, aim. No, I am speaking only of the riff-raff. In every period of transition this riff-raff, which exists in every society, rises to the surface, and is not only without any aim but has not even a symptom of an idea, and merely does its utmost to give expression to

106

THE POSSESSED

uneasiness and impatience. Moreover, this riff-raff almost always falls unconsciously under the control of the little group of "advanced people" who do act with a definite aim, and this little group can direct all this rabble as it pleases, if only it does not itself consist of absolute idiots, which, however, is sometimes the case. It is said among us, now that it is all over, that Pyotr Stepanovitch was directed by the *Internationale,* and Yulia Mihailovna by Pyotr Stepanovitch, while she controlled, under his rule, a rabble of all sorts. The more sober minds amongst us wonder at themselves now, and can't understand how they came to be so foolish at the time.

What constituted the turbulence of our time and what transition it was we were passing through I don't know, nor I think does anyone, unless it were some of those visitors of ours. Yet the most worthless fellows suddenly gained predominant influence, began loudly criticising everything sacred, though till then they had not dared to open their mouths, while the leading people, who had till then so satisfactorily kept the upper hand, began listening to them and holding their peace, some even simpered approval in a most shameless way. People like Lyamshin and Telyatnikov, like Gogol's Tentyotnikov, drivelling home-bred editions of Radishtchev, wretched little Jews with a mournful but haughty smile, guffawing foreigners, poets of advanced tendencies from the capital, poets who made up with peasant coats and tarred boots for the lack of tendencies or talents, majors and colonels who ridiculed the senselessness of the service, and who would have been ready for an extra rouble to unbuckle their swords, and take jobs as railway clerks; generals who had abandoned their duties to become lawyers; advanced mediators, advancing merchants, innumerable divinity students, women who were the embodiment of the woman question—all these suddenly gained complete sway among us and over whom? Over the club, the venerable officials, over generals with wooden legs, over the very strict and inaccessible ladies of our local society. Since even Varvara Petrovna was almost at the beck and call of this rabble, right up to the time of the catastrophe with her son, our other local Minervas may well be pardoned for their temporary aberration. Now all this is attributed, as I have mentioned already, to the *Internationale.* This idea has taken such root that it is given as the explanation to visitors from other parts. Only lately Councillor Kubrikov, a man of sixty-two, with the Stanislav Order on his breast, came forward uninvited and confessed in a voice full of feeling that he had beyond a shadow of doubt been for fully three months under the influence of the *Internationale*. When with every deference for his years and services he was invited to be more definite, he stuck firmly to his original statement, though he could produce no evidence except that "he had felt it in all his feelings", so that they cross-examined him no further.

I repeat again, there was still even among us a small group who held themselves aloof from the beginning, and even locked themselves up. But what lock can stand against a law of nature? Daughters will grow up even in the most careful families, and it is essential for grown-up daughters to dance.

And so all these people, too, ended by subscribing to the governesses' fund.

The ball was assumed to be an entertainment so brilliant, so unprecedented; marvels were told about it; there were rumours of princes from a distance with lorgnettes; of ten stewards, all young dandies, with rosettes on their left shoulder; of some Petersburg people who were setting the thing going; there was a rumour that Karmazinov had consented to increase the subscriptions to the fund by reading his *Merci* in the costume of the governesses of the district; that there would be a literary quadrille all in costume, and every costume would symbolise some special line of thought; and finally that "honest Russian thought" would dance in costume—which would certainly be a complete novelty in itself. Who would resist subscribing? Everyone subscribed.

II

The programme of the fête was divided into two parts: the literary matinée from midday till four o'clock, and afterwards a ball from ten o'clock onwards through the night. But in this very programme there lay concealed germs of disorder. In the first place, from the very beginning a rumour had gained ground among the public concerning a luncheon immediately after the literary matinée, or even while it was going on, during an interval arranged expressly for it—a free luncheon, of course, which would form part of the programme and be accompanied by champagne. The immense price of the tickets (three roubles) tended to confirm this rumour. "As though one would subscribe for nothing? The fête is arranged for twenty-four hours, so food must be provided. People will get hungry." This was how people reasoned in the town. I must admit that Yulia Mihailovna did much to confirm this disastrous rumour by her own heedlessness. A month earlier, under the first spell of the great project, she would babble about it to anyone she met, and even sent a paragraph to one of the Petersburg papers about the toasts and speeches arranged for her fête. What fascinated her most at that time was the idea of these toasts; she wanted to propose them herself and was continually composing them in anticipation. They were to make clear what was their banner (what was it? I don't mind betting that the poor dear composed nothing after all), they were to get into the Petersburg and Moscow papers, to touch and fascinate the higher powers and then to spread the idea over all the provinces of Russia, rousing people to wonder and imitation.

But for toasts, champagne was essential, and as champagne can't be drunk on an empty stomach, it followed that a lunch was essential too. Afterwards, when by her efforts a committee had been formed and had attacked the subject more seriously, it was proved clearly to her at once that if they were going to dream of banquets there would be very little left for the governesses, however well people subscribed. There were two ways out of the difficulty: either Belshazzar's feast with toasts and speeches, and ninety roubles for the governesses, or a considerable sum of money with the fête only as a matter of form to raise it. The committee, however, only wanted to scare her, and had of course worked out a third course of action, which was reasonable and combined the advantages of both, that is, a very decent fête in every respect only without champagne, and so yielding a very respectable sum, much more than ninety roubles. But Yulia Mihailovna would not agree to it: her proud spirit revolted from paltry compromise. She decided at once that if the original idea could not be carried out they should rush to the opposite extreme, that is, raise an enormous subscription that would be the envy of other provinces. "The public must understand," she said at the end of her flaming speech to the committee, "that the attainment of an object of universal human interest is infinitely loftier than the corporeal enjoyments of the passing moment, that the fête in its essence is only the proclamation of a great idea, and so we ought to be content with the most frugal German ball simply as a symbol, that is, if we can't dispense with this detestable ball altogether," so great was the aversion she suddenly conceived for it. But she was pacified at last. It was then that "the literary quadrille" and the other æsthetic items were invented and proposed as substitutes for the corporeal enjoyments. It was then that Karmazinov finally consented to read "Merci" (until then he had only tantalised them by his hesitation) and so eradicate the very idea of victuals from the minds of our incontinent public. So the ball was once more to be a magnificent function, though in a different style. And not to be too ethereal it was decided that tea with lemon and round biscuits should be served at the beginning of the ball, and later on "orchade" and lemonade and at the end even ices —but nothing else. For those who always and everywhere are hungry and, still more, thirsty, they might open a buffet in the farthest of the suite of rooms and put it in charge of Prohorovitch, the head cook of the club, who would, subject to the strict supervision of the committee, serve whatever was wanted, at a fixed charge, and a notice should be put up on the door of the hall that refreshments were extra. But on the morning they decided not to open the buffet at all for fear of disturbing the reading, though the buffet would have been five rooms off the White Hall in which Karmazinov had consented to read "Merci".

It is remarkable that the committee, and even the most practical people in it, attached enormous consequence to this reading. As for people of poetical tendencies, the marshal's wife, for instance, informed Karmazinov that after the reading she would immediately order a marble slab to be put up in the wall of the White Hall with an inscription in gold letters, that on such a day and year, here, in this place, the great writer of Russia and of Europe had read "Merci" on laying aside his pen, and so had for the first time taken leave of the Russian public represented by the leading citizens of our town, and that this inscription would be read by all at the ball, that is, only five hours after "Merci" had been read. I know for a fact that Karmazinov it was who insisted that there should be no buffet in the morning on any account, while he was reading, in spite of some protests from members of the committee that this was rather opposed to our way of doing things.

This was the position of affairs, while in the town people were still reckoning on a Belshazzar feast, that is, on refreshments provided by the committee; they believed in this to the last hour. Even the young ladies were dreaming of masses of sweets and preserves, and something more beyond their imagination. Everyone knew that the subscriptions had reached a huge sum, that all the town was struggling to go, that people were driving

110

in from the surrounding districts, and that there were not tickets enough. It was known, too, that there had been some large subscriptions apart from the price paid for tickets: Varvara Petrovna, for instance, had paid three hundred roubles for her ticket and had given almost all the flowers from her conservatory to decorate the room. The marshal's wife, who was a member of the committee, provided the house and the lighting; the club furnished the music, the attendants, and gave up Prohorovitch for the whole day. There were other contributions as well, though lesser ones, so much so indeed that the idea was mooted of cutting down the price of tickets from three roubles to two. Indeed, the committee were afraid at first that three roubles would be too much for young ladies to pay, and suggested that they might have family tickets, so that every family should pay for one daughter only, while the other young ladies of the family, even if there were a dozen specimens, should be admitted free. But all their apprehensions turned out to be groundless: it was just the young ladies who did come. Even the poorest clerks brought their girls, and it was quite evident that if they had had no girls it would never have occurred to them to subscribe for tickets. One insignificant little secretary brought all his seven daughters, to say nothing of his wife and a niece into the bargain, and every one of these persons held in her hand an entrance ticket that cost three roubles.

It may be imagined what an upheaval it made in the town! One has only to remember that as the fête was divided into two parts every lady needed two costumes for the occasion—a morning one for the matinée and a ball dress for the evening. Many middle-class people, as it appeared afterwards, had pawned everything they had for that day, even the family linen, even the sheets, and possibly the mattresses, to the Jews, who had been settling in our town in great numbers during the previous two years and who became more and more numerous as time went on. Almost all the officials had asked for their salary in advance, and some of the landowners sold beasts they could ill spare, and all simply to bring their ladies got up as marchionesses, and to be as good as anybody. The magnificence of dresses on this occasion was something unheard of in our neighbourhood. For a fortnight beforehand the town was overflowing wtih funny stories which were all brought by our wits to Yulia Mihailovna's court. Caricatures were passed from hand to hand. I have seen some drawings of the sort myself, in Yulia

111

Mihailovna's album. All this reached the ears of the families who were the source of the jokes; I believe this was the cause of the general hatred of Yulia Mihailovna which had grown so strong in the town. People swear and gnash their teeth when they think of it now. But it was evident, even at the time, that if the committee were to displease them in anything, or if anything went wrong at the ball, the outburst of indignation would be something surprising. That's why everyone was secretly expecting a scandal; and if it was so confidently expected, how could it fail to come to pass?

The orchestra struck up punctually at midday. Being one of the stewards, that is, one of the twelve "young men with a rosette", I saw with my own eyes how this day of ignominious memory began. It began with an enormous crush at the doors. How was it that everything, including the police, went wrong that day? I don't blame the genuine public: the fathers of families did not crowd, nor did they push against anyone, in spite of their position. On the contrary, I am told that they were disconcerted even in the street, at the sight of the crowd shoving in a way unheard of in our town, besieging the entry and taking it by assault, instead of simply going in. Meanwhile the carriages kept driving up, and at last blocked the street. Now, at the time I write, I have good grounds for affirming that some of the lowest rabble of our town were brought in without tickets by Lyamshin and Liputin, possibly, too, by other people who were stewards like me. Anyway, some complete strangers, who had come from the surrounding districts and elsewhere, were present. As soon as these savages entered the hall they began asking where the buffet was, as though they had been put up to it beforehand, and learning that there was no buffet they began swearing with brutal directness, and an unprecedented insolence; some of them, it is true, were drunk when they came. Some of them were dazed like savages at the splendour of the hall, as they had never seen anything like it, and subsided for a minute gazing at it open-mouthed. This great White Hall really was magnificent, though the building was falling into decay: it was of immense size, with two rows of windows, with an old-fashioned ceiling covered with gilt carving, with a gallery with mirrors on the walls, red and white draperies, marble statues (nondescript but still statues) with heavy old furniture of the Napoleonic period, white and gold, upholstered in red velvet. At the moment I am describing, a high platform had been put up for the literary gentlemen who were to read, and the whole hall was filled with chairs like the parterre of a theatre with wide aisles for the audience.

But after the first moments of surprise the most senseless questions and protests followed. "Perhaps we don't care for a reading. . . . We've paid our money. . . The audience has been impudently swindled. . . . This is our entertainment, not the Lembkes'!" They seemed, in fact, to have been let in for this purpose. I remember specially an encounter in which the princeling with the stand-up collar and the face of a Dutch doll, whom I had met the morning before at Yulia Mihailovna's, distinguished himself. He had, at her urgent request, consented to pin a rosette of his left shoulder and to become one of our stewards. It turned out that this dumb wax figure could act after a fashion of his own, if he could not talk. When a colossal pock-marked captain, supported by a herd of rabble following at his heels, pestered him by asking "which way to the buffet?" he made a sign to a police sergeant. His hint was promptly acted upon, and in spite of the drunken captain's abuse he was dragged out of the hall. Meantime the genuine public began to make its appearance, and stretched in three long files between the chairs. The disorderly elements began to subside, but the public, even the most "respectable" among them, had a dissatisfied and perplexed air; some of the ladies looked positively scared.

At last all were seated; the music ceased. People began blowing their noses and looking about them. They waited with too solemn an air—which is always a bad sign. But nothing was to be seen yet of the Lembkes. Silks, velvets, diamonds glowed and sparkled on every side; whiffs of fragrance filled the air. The men were wearing all their decorations, and the old men were even in uniform. At last the marshal's wife came in with Liza. Liza had never been so dazzlingly charming or so splendidly dressed as that morning. Her hair was done up in curls, her eyes sparkled, a smile beamed on her face. She made an unmistakable sensation: people scrutinised her and whispered about her. They said that she was looking for Stavrogin, but neither Stavrogin nor Varvara Petrovna was there. At the time I did not understand the expression of her face: why was there so much happiness, such joy, such energy and strength in that face? I remembered what had happened the day before and could not make it out.

But still the Lembkes did not come. This was distinctly a blunder. I learned that Yulia Mihailovna waited till the last minute for Pyotr Stepanovitch, without whom she could not stir a step, though she never admitted it to herself. I must mention, in parenthesis, that on the previous day Pyotr Stepanovitch had at the last meeting of the committee declined to wear the rosette of a steward, which had disappointed her dreadfully, even to the point of tears. To her surprise and, later on, her extreme discomfiture (to anticipate things) he vanished for the whole morning and did not make his appearance at the literary matinée at all, so that no one met him till evening. At last the audience began to manifest unmistakable signs of impatience. No one appeared on the platform either. The back rows began applauding, as in a theatre. The elderly gentlemen and the ladies frowned. "The Lembkes are really giving themselves unbearable airs." Even among the better part of the audience an absurd whisper began to gain ground that perhaps there would not be a fête at all, that Lembke perhaps was really unwell, and so on and so on. But, thank God, the Lembkes at last appeared, she was leaning on his arm; I must confess I was in great apprehension myself about their appearance. But the legends were disproved, and the truth was triumphant. The audience seemed relieved. Lembke himself seemed perfectly well. Everyone, I remember, was of that opinion, for it can be imagined how many eyes were turned on him. I may mention, as characteristic of our society, that there were very few of the better-class people who saw reason to suppose that there was anything wrong with him; his conduct seemed to them perfectly normal, and so much so that the action he had taken in the square the morning before was accepted and approved.

"That's how it should have been from the first," the higher officials declared. "If a man begins as a philanthropist he has to come to the same thing in the end, though he does not see that it was necessary from the point of view of philanthropy itself"—that, at least, was the opinion at the club. They only blamed him for having lost his temper. "It ought to have been done more coolly, but there, he is a new man," said the authorities.

All eyes turned with equal eagerness to Yulia Mihailovna. Of course no one has the right to expect from me an exact account in regard to one point: that is a mysterious, a feminine question. But I only know one thing: on the evening of the previous day she had gone into Andrey Antonovitch's study and was there with him till long after midnight. Andrey Antonovitch was comforted and forgiven. The husband and wife came to

114

a complete understanding, everything was forgotten, and when at the end of the interview Lembke went down on his knees, recalling with horror the final incident of the previous night, the exquisite hand, and after it the lips of his wife, checked the fervent flow of penitent phrases of the chivalrously delicate gentleman who was limp with emotion. Everyone could see the happiness in her face. She walked in with an open-hearted air, wearing a magnificent dress. She seemed to be at the very pinnacle of her heart's desires, the fête—the goal and crown of her diplomacy—was an accomplished fact. As they walked to their seats in front of the platform, the Lembkes bowed in all directions and responded to greetings. They were at once surrounded. The marshal's wife got up to meet them.

But at that point a horrid misunderstanding occurred; the orchestra, apropos of nothing, struck up a flourish, not a triumphal march of any kind, but a simple flourish such as was played at the club when someone's health was drunk at an official dinner. I know now that Lyamshin, in his capacity of steward, had arranged this, as though in honour of the Lembkes' entrance. Of course he could always excuse it as a blunder or excessive zeal. . . . Alas! I did not know at the time that they no longer cared even to find excuses, and that all such considerations were from that day a thing of the past. But the flourish was not the end of it: in the midst of the vexatious astonishment and the smiles of the audience there was a sudden "hurrah" from the end of the hall and from the gallery also, apparently in Lembke's honour. The hurrahs were few, but I must confess they lasted for some time. Yulia Mihailovna flushed, her eyes flashed. Lembke stood still at his chair, and turning towards the voices sternly and majestically scanned the audience. . . . They hastened to make him sit down. I noticed with dismay the same dangerous smile on his face as he had worn the morning before, in his wife's drawing-room, when he stared at Stepan Trofimovitch before going up to him. It seemed to me that now, too, there was an ominous, and, worst of all, a rather comic expression on his countenance, the expression of a man resigned to sacrifice himself to satisfy his wife's lofty aims. . . . Yulia Mihailovna beckoned to me hurriedly, and whispered to me to run to Karmazinov and entreat him to begin. And no sooner had I turned away than another disgraceful incident, much more unpleasant than the first, took place.

On the platform, the empty platform, on which till that

moment all eyes and all expectations were fastened, and where nothing was to be seen but a small table, a chair in front of it, and on the table a glass of water on a silver salver—on the empty platform there suddenly appeared the colossal figure of Captain Lebyadkin wearing a dress-coat and a white tie. I was so astounded I could not believe my eyes. The captain seemed confused and remained standing at the back of the platform. Suddenly there was a shout in the audience: "Lebyadkin! You?" The captain's stupid red face (he was hopelessly drunk) expanded in a broad vacant grin at this greeting. He raised his hand, rubbed his forehead with it, shook his shaggy head and, as though making up his mind to go through with it, took two steps forward and suddenly went off into a series of prolonged, blissful, gurgling, but not loud guffaws, which made him screw up his eyes and set all his bulky person heaving. This spectacle set almost half the audience laughing, twenty people applauded. The serious part of the audience looked at one another gloomily; it all lasted only half a minute, however. Liputin, wearing his steward's rosette, ran on to the platform with two servants; they carefully took the captain by both arms, while Liputin whispered something to him. The captain scowled, muttered "Ah, well, if that's it!" waved his hand, turned his huge back to the public and vanished with his escort. But a minute later Liputin skipped on to the platform again. He was wearing the sweetest of his invariable smiles, which usually suggested vinegar and sugar, and carried in his hands a sheet of note-paper. With tiny but rapid steps he came forward to the edge of the platform.

"Ladies and gentlemen," he said, addressing the public, "through our inadvertency there has arisen a comical mis-understanding which has been removed; but I've hopefully undertaken to do something at the earnest and most respect-ful request of one of our local poets. Deeply touched by the humane and lofty object . . . in spite of his appearance . . . the object which has brought us all together . . . to wipe away the tears of the poor but well-educated girls of our province . . . this gentleman, I mean this local poet . . . although desirous of preserving his incognito, would gladly have heard his poem read at the beginning of the ball . . . that is, I mean, of the matinée. Though this poem is not in the programme . . . for it has only been received half an hour ago . . . yet it has seemed to *us*"—(Us? Whom did he mean by us? I report his con-fused and incoherent speech word for word)—"that through its remarkable naïveté of feeling, together with its equally remark-

able gaiety, the poem might well be read, that is, not as something serious, but as something appropriate to the occasion, that is to the idea . . . especially as some lines . . . And I wanted to ask the kind permission of the audience."

"Read it!" boomed a voice at the back of the hall.

"Then I am to read it?"

"Read it, read it!" cried many voices.

"With the permission of the audience I will read it," Liputin minced again, still with the same sugary smile. He still seemed to hesitate, and I even thought that he was rather excited. These people are sometimes nervous in spite of their impudence. A divinity student would have carried it through without winking, but Liputin did, after all, belong to the last generation.

"I must say, that is, I have the honour to say by way of preface that it is not precisely an ode such as used to be written for fêtes, but is rather, so to say, a jest, but full of undoubted feeling, together with playful humour, and, so to say, the most realistic truthfulness."

"Read it, read it!"

He unfolded the paper. No one of course was in time to stop him. Besides, he was wearing his steward's badge. In a ringing voice he declaimed:

"To the local governesses of the Fatherland from the poet at the fête:

> *"Governesses all, good morrow,*
> *Triumph on this festive day.*
> *Retrograde or vowed George-Sander—*
> *Never mind, just frisk away!"*

"But that's Lebyadkin's! Lebyadkin's!" cried several voices. There was laughter and even applause, though not from very many.

> *"Teaching French to wet-nosed children,*
> *You are glad enough to think*
> *You can catch a worn-out sexton—*
> *Even he is worth a wink!"*

"Hurrah! hurrah!"

> *"But in these great days of progress,*
> *Ladies, to your sorrow know,*

You can't even catch a sexton,
If you have not got a 'dot'.''

"To be sure, to be sure, that's realism. You can't hook a husband without a 'dot'!''

> *"But, henceforth, since through our feasting*
> *Capital has flowed from all,*
> *And we send you forth to conquest*
> *Dancing, dowried from this hall—*
> *Retrograde or vowed George-Sander,*
> *Never mind, rejoice you may,*
> *You're a governess with a dowry,*
> *Spit on all and frisk away!''*

I must confess I could not believe my ears. The insolence of it was so unmistakable that there was no possibility of excusing Liputin on the ground of stupidity. Besides, Liputin was by no means stupid. The intention was obvious, to me, anyway; they seemed in a hurry to create disorder. Some lines in these idiotic verses, for instance the last, were such that no stupidity could have let them pass. Liputin himself seemed to feel that he had undertaken too much; when he had achieved his exploit he was so overcome by his own impudence that he did not even leave the platform but remained standing, as though there were something more he wanted to say. He had probably imagined that it would somehow produce a different effect; but even the group of ruffians who had applauded during the reading suddenly sank into silence, as though they, too, were overcome. What was silliest of all, many of them took the whole episode seriously, that is, did not regard the verses as a lampoon but actually thought it realistic and true as regards the governesses —a poem with a tendency, in fact. But the excessive freedom of the verses struck even them at last; as for the general public they were not only scandalised but obviously offended. I am sure I am not mistaken as to the impression. Yulia Mihailovna said afterwards that in another moment she would have fallen into a swoon. One of the most respectable old gentlemen helped his old wife on to her feet, and they walked out of the hall accompanied by the agitated glances of the audience. Who knows, the example might have infected others if Karmazinov himself, wearing a dress-coat and a white tie and carrying a manuscript in his hand, had not appeared on the platform at that moment. Yulia Mihailovna turned an ecstatic gaze at him as on her deliverer. . . . But I was by that time behind the scenes. I was in quest of Liputin.

"You did that on purpose!" I said, seizing him indignantly by the arm.

"I assure you I never thought . . ." he began, cringing and lying at once, pretending to be unhappy. "The verses had only just been brought and I thought that as an amusing pleasantry. . . ."

"You did not think anything of the sort. You can't really think that stupid rubbish an amusing pleasantry?"

"Yes, I do."

"You are simply lying, and it wasn't brought to you just now. You helped Lebyadkin to compose it yourself, yesterday very likely, to create a scandal. The last verse must have been yours, the part about the sexton too. Why did he come on in a dress-coat? You must have meant him to read it, too, if he had not been drunk?"

Liputin looked at me coldly and ironically.

"What business is it of yours?" he asked suddenly with strange calm.

"What business is it of mine? You are wearing the steward's badge, too. . . . Where is Pyotr Stepanovitch?"

"I don't know, somewhere here; why do you ask?"

"Because now I see through it. It's simply a plot against Yulia Mihailovna so as to ruin the day by a scandal. . . ."

Liputin looked at me askance again.

"But what is it to you?" he said, grinning. He shrugged his shoulders and walked away.

It came over me with a rush. All my suspicions were confirmed. Till then, I had been hoping I was mistaken! What was I to do? I was on the point of asking the advice of Stepan Trofimovitch, but he was standing before the looking-glass, trying on different smiles, and continually consulting a piece of paper on which he had notes. He had to go on immediately after Karmazinov, and was not in a fit state for conversation. Should I run to Yulia Mihailovna? But it was too soon to go to her: she needed a much sterner lesson to cure her of her conviction that she had "a following", and that everyone was "fanatically devoted" to her. She would not have believed me, and would have thought I was dreaming. Besides, what help could she be? "Eh," I thought, "after all, what business is it of mine? I'll take off my badge and go home *when it begins."* That was my mental phrase, "when it begins"; I remember it.

But I had to go and listen to Karmazinov. Taking a last look round behind the scenes, I noticed that a good number of outsiders, even women among them, were flitting about, going in and out. "Behind the scenes" was rather a narrow space completely screened from the audience by a curtain and communicating with other rooms by means of a passage. Here our readers were awaiting their turns. But I was struck at that moment by the reader who was to follow Stepan Trofimovitch. He, too, was some sort of professor (I don't know to this day exactly what he was) who had voluntarily left some educational institution after a disturbance among the students, and had arrived in the town only a few days before. He, too, had been recommended to Yulia Mihailovna, and she had received him with reverence. I know now that he had only spent one evening in her company before the reading; he had not spoken all that evening, had listened with an equivocal smile to the jests and the general tone of the company surrounding Yulia Mihailovna, and had made an unpleasant impression on everyone by his air of haughtiness, and at the same time almost timorous readiness to take offence. It was Yulia Mihailovna herself who had enlisted his services. Now he was walking from corner to corner, and, like Stepan Trofimovitch, was muttering to himself, though he looked on the ground instead of in the looking-glass. He was not trying on smiles, though he often smiled rapaciously. It was obvious that it was useless to speak to him either. He looked about forty, was short and bald, had a greyish beard, and was decently dressed. But what was most interesting about him was that at every turn he took he threw up his right fist, brandished it above his head and suddenly brought it down again as though crushing an antagonist to atoms. He went through this by-play every moment. It made me uncomfortable. I hastened away to listen to Karmazinov.

III

There was a feeling in the hall that something was wrong again. Let me state to begin with that I have the deepest reverence for genius, but why do our geniuses in the decline of their illustrious years behave sometimes exactly like little boys? What though he was Karmazinov, and came forward with as much dignity as five *Kammerherrs* rolled into one? How could he expect to keep an audience like ours listening for a whole hour to a single paper? I have observed, in fact, that however big a genius a man may be, he can't monopolise the attention of an audience at a frivolous literary matinée for more than twenty minutes with impunity. The entrance of the great writer was received, indeed, with the utmost respect: even the severest elderly men showed signs of approval and interest, and the ladies even displayed some enthusiasm. The applause was brief, however, and somehow uncertain and not unanimous. Yet there was no unseemly behaviour in the back rows, till Karmazinov began to speak, not that anything very bad followed then, but only a sort of misunderstanding. I have mentioned already that he had rather a shrill voice, almost feminine in fact, and at the same time a genuinely aristocratic lisp. He had hardly articulated a few words when someone had the effrontery to laugh aloud—probably some ignorant simpleton who knew nothing of the world, and was congenitally disposed to laughter. But there was nothing like a hostile demonstration; on the contrary people said "Sh-h!" and the offender was crushed. But Mr. Karmazinov, with an affected air and intonation, announced that "at first he had declined absolutely to read". (Much need there was to mention it!) "There are some lines which come so deeply from the heart that it is impossible to utter them aloud, so that these holy things cannot be laid before the public"—(Why lay them then?)—"but as he had been begged to do so, he was doing so, and as he was, moreover, laying down his pen for ever, and had sworn to write no more, he had written this last farewell; and as he had sworn never, on any inducement, to read anything in public," and so on, and so on, all in that style.

But all that would not have mattered; everyone knows what authors' prefaces are like, though, I may observe, that considering the lack of culture of our audience and the irritability of the back rows, all this may have had an influence. Surely it would have been better to have read a little story, a short tale such as he had written in the past—over-elaborate, that is, and affected, but sometimes witty. It would have saved the situation. No, this was quite another story! It was a regular oration! Good heavens, what wasn't there in it! I am positive that it would have reduced to rigidity even a Petersburg audience, let alone ours. Imagine an article that would have filled some thirty pages of print of the most affected, aimless prattle; and to make

121

matters worse, the gentleman read it with a sort of melancholy condescension as though it were a favour, so that it was almost insulting to the audience. The subject. . . . Who could make it out? It was a sort of description of certain impressions and reminiscences. But of what? And about what? Though the leading intellects of the province did their utmost during the first half of the reading, they could make nothing of it, and they listened to the second part simply out of politeness. A great deal was said about love, indeed, of the love of the genius for some person, but I must admit it made rather an awkward impression. For the great writer to tell us about his first kiss seemed to my mind a little incongruous with his short and fat little figure . . . Another thing that was offensive; these kisses did not occur as they do with the rest of mankind. There had to be a framework of gorse (it had to be gorse or some such plant that one must look up in a flora) and there had to be a tint of purple in the sky, such as no mortal had ever observed before, or if some people had seen it, they had never noticed it, but he seemed to say: "I have seen it and am describing it to you, fools, as if it were a most ordinary thing." The tree under which the interesting couple sat had of course to be of an orange colour. They were sitting somewhere in Germany. Suddenly they see Pompey or Cassius on the eve of a battle, and both are penetrated by a chill of ecstasy. Some wood-nymph squeaked in the bushes. Gluck played the violin among the reeds. The title of the piece he was playing was given in full, but no one knew it, so that one would have had to look it up in a musical dictionary. Meanwhile a fog came on, such a fog, such a fog, that it was more like a million pillows than a fog. And suddenly everything disappears and the great genius is crossing the frozen Volga in a thaw. Two and a half pages are filled with the crossing, and yet he falls through the ice. The genius is drowning—you imagine he was drowned? Not a bit of it; this was simply in order that when he was drowning and at his last gasp, he might catch sight of a bit of ice, the size of a pea, but pure and crystal "as a frozen tear", and in that tear was reflected Germany, or more accurately the sky of Germany, and its iridescent sparkle recalled to his mind the very tear which "dost thou remember, fell from thine eyes when we were sitting under that emerald tree, and thou didst cry out joyfully: 'There is no crime!' 'No,' I said through my tears, 'but if that is so, there are no righteous either.' We sobbed and parted for ever." She went off somewhere to the sea coast, while he went

122

to visit some caves, and then he descends and descends and descends for three years under Suharev Tower in Moscow, and suddenly in the very bowels of the earth, he finds in a cave a lamp, and before the lamp a hermit. The hermit is praying. The genius leans against a little barred window, and suddenly hears a sigh. Do you suppose it was the hermit sighing? Much he cares about the hermit! Not a bit of it, this sigh simply reminds him of her first sigh, thirty-seven years before, ''in Germany, when, dost thou remember, we sat under an agate-tree and thou didst say to me: 'Why love? See ochra is growing all around and I love thee; but the ochra will cease to grow, and I shall cease to love.' '' Then the fog comes on again, Hoffman appears on the scene, the wood-nymph whistles a tune from Chopin, and suddenly out of the fog appears Ancus Marcius over the roofs of Rome, wearing a laurel wreath. ''A chill of ecstasy ran down our backs and we parted for ever''— and so on and so on.

Perhaps I am not reporting it quite right and don't know how to report it, but the drift of the babble was something of that sort. And after all, how disgraceful this passion of our great intellects for jesting in a superior way really is! The great European philosopher, the great man of science, the inventor, the martyr—all these who labour and are heavy laden, are to the great Russian genius no more than so many cooks in his kitchen. He is the master and they come to him, cap in hand, awaiting orders. It is true he jeers superciliously at Russia too, and there is nothing he likes better than exhibiting the bankruptcy of Russia in every relation before the great minds of Europe, but as regards himself, no, he is at a higher level than all the great minds of Europe; they are only material for his jests. He takes another man's idea, tacks on to it its antithesis, and the epigram is made. There is such a thing as crime, there is no such thing as crime; there is no such thing as justice, there are no just men; atheism, Darwinism, the Moscow bells. . . . But alas, he no longer believes in the Moscow bells; Rome, laurels. . . . But he has no belief in laurels even. . . . We have a conventional attack of Byronic spleen, a grimace from Heine, something of Petchorin—and the machine goes on rolling, whistling, at full speed. ''But you may praise me, you may praise me, that I like extremely; it's only in a manner of speaking that I lay down the pen; I shall bore you three hundred times more, you'll grow weary of reading me. . . .''

Of course it did not end without trouble; but the worst of it was that it was his own doing. People had for some time begun shuffling their feet, blowing their noses, coughing, and doing everything that people do when a lecturer, whoever he may be, keeps an audience for longer than twenty minutes at a literary matinée. But the genius noticed nothing of all this. He went on lisping and mumbling, without giving a thought to the audience, so that everyone began to wonder. Suddenly in a back row a solitary but loud voice was heard:

"Good Lord, what nonsense!"

The exclamation escaped involuntarily, and I am sure was not intended as a demonstration. The man was simply worn out. But Mr. Karmazinov stopped, looked sarcastically at the audience, and suddenly lisped with the deportment of an aggrieved *kammerherr*.

"I'm afraid I've been boring you dreadfully, gentlemen?"

That was his blunder, that he was the first to speak; for provoking an answer in this way he gave an opening for the rabble to speak, too, and even legitimately, so to say, while if he had restrained himself, people would have gone on blowing their noses and it would have passed off somehow. Perhaps he expected applause in response to his question, but there was no sound of applause; on the contrary, everyone seemed to subside and shrink back in dismay.

"You never did see Ancus Marcius, that's all brag," cried a voice that sounded full of irritation and even nervous exhaustion.

"Just so," another voice agreed at once. "There are no such things as ghosts nowadays, nothing but natural science. Look it up in a scientific book."

"Gentlemen, there was nothing I expected less than such objections," said Karmazinov, extremely surprised. The great genius had completely lost touch with his Fatherland in Karlsruhe.

"Nowadays it's outrageous to say that the world stands on three fishes," a young lady snapped out suddenly. "You can't have gone down to the hermit's cave, Karmazinov. And who talks about hermits nowadays?"

"Gentlemen, what surprises me most of all is that you take it all so seriously. However . . . however, you are perfectly right. No one has greater respect for truth and realism than I have. . . ."

Though he smiled ironically he was tremendously overcome. His face seemed to express: "I am not the sort of man you

124

think, I am on your side, only praise me, praise me more, as much as possible, I like it extremely. . . ."

"Gentlemen," he cried, completely mortified at last, "I see that my poor poem is quite out of place here. And, indeed, I am out of place here myself, I think."

"You threw at the crow and you hit the cow," some fool, probably drunk, shouted at the top of his voice, and of course no notice ought to have been taken of him. It is true there was a sound of disrespectful laughter.

"A cow, you say?" Karmazinov caught it up at once, his voice grew shriller and shriller. "As for crows and cows, gentlemen, I will refrain. I've too much respect for any audience to permit myself comparisons, however harmless; but I did think . . ."

"You'd better be careful, sir," someone shouted from a back row.

"But I had supposed that laying aside my pen and saying farewell to my readers, I should be heard . . ."

"No, no, we want to hear you, we want to," a few voices from the front row plucked up spirit to exclaim at last.

"Read, read!" several enthusiastic ladies' voices chimed in, and at last there was an outburst of applause, sparse and feeble, it is true.

"Believe me, Karmazinov, everyone looks on it as an honour . . ." the marshal's wife herself could not resist saying

"Mr. Karmazinov!" cried a fresh young voice in the back of the hall suddenly. It was the voice of a very young teacher from the district school who had only lately come among us, an excellent young man, quiet and gentlemanly. He stood up in his place. "Mr. Karmazinov, if I had the happiness to fall in love as you have described to us, I really shouldn't refer to my love in an article intended for public reading. . . ."

He flushed red all over.

"Ladies and gentlemen," cried Karmazinov, "I have finished. I will omit the end and withdraw. Only allow me to read the six last lines:

"Yes, dear reader, farewell!" he began at once from the manuscript without sitting down again in his chair. "Farewell, reader; I do not greatly insist on our parting friends; what need to trouble you, indeed. You may abuse me, abuse me as you will if it affords you any satisfaction. But best of all if we forget one another for ever. And if you all, readers, were suddenly so kind as to fall on your knees and begin begging me with tears: 'Write, oh, write for us, Karmazinov—for the sake of Russia, for the sake of posterity, to win laurels,' even then I would answer you, thanking you, of course, with every courtesy, 'No, we've had enough of one another, dear fellow-countrymen, *merci!* It's time we took our separate ways!' *Merci, merci, merci!*"

Karmazinov bowed ceremoniously, and, as red as though he had been cooked, retired behind the scenes.

"Nobody would go down on their knees; a wild idea!"

"What conceit!"

"That's only humour," someone more reasonable suggested.

"Spare me your humour."

"I call it impudence, gentlemen!"

"Well, he's finished now, anyway!"

"Ech, what a dull show!"

But all these ignorant exclamations in the back rows (though they were confined to the back rows) were drowned in applause from the other half of the audience. They called for Karmazinov. Several ladies with Yulia Mihailovna and the marshal's wife crowded round the platform. In Yulia Mihailovna's hands was a gorgeous laurel wreath resting on another wreath of living roses on a white velvet cushion.

"Laurels!" Karmazinov pronounced with a subtle and rather sarcastic smile. "I am touched, of course, and accept with real emotion this wreath prepared beforehand, but still fresh and unwithered, but I assure you, mesdames, that I have suddenly become so realistic that I feel laurels would in this age be far more appropriate in the hands of a skilful cook than in mine. . . ."

"Well, a cook is more useful," cried the divinity student, who had been at the "meeting" at Virginsky's.

There was some disorder. In many rows people jumped up to get a better view of the presentation of the laurel wreath.

"I'd give another three roubles for a cook this minute," another voice assented loudly, too loudly; insistently, in fact.

"So would I."

"And I."

"Is it possible there's no buffet? . . ."

"Gentlemen, it's simply a swindle. . . ."

It must be admitted, however, that all these unbridled gentlemen still stood in awe of our higher officials and of the police superintendent, who was present in the hall. Ten minutes later all had somehow got back into their places, but there was not the same good order as before. And it was into this incipient chaos that poor Stepan Trofimovitch was thrust.

IV

I ran out to him behind the scenes once more, and had time to warn him excitedly that in my opinion the game was up, that he had better not appear at all, but had better go home at once on the excuse of his usual ailment, for instance, and I would take off my badge and come with him. At that instant he was on his way to the platform; he stopped suddenly, and haughtily looking me up and down he pronounced solemnly:

"What grounds have you, sir, for thinking me capable of such baseness?"

I drew back. I was as sure as twice two make four that he would not get off without a catastrophe. Meanwhile, as I stood utterly dejected, I saw moving before me again the figure of the professor, whose turn it was to appear after Stepan Trofimovitch, and who kept lifting up his fist and bringing it down again with a swing. He kept walking up and down, absorbed in himself and muttering something to himself with a diabolical but triumphant smile. I somehow almost unintentionally went up to him. I don't know what induced me to meddle again.

"Do you know," I said, "judging from many examples, if a lecturer keeps an audience for more than twenty minutes it won't go on listening. No celebrity is able to hold his own for half an hour."

He stopped short and seemed almost quivering with resentment. Infinite disdain was expressed in his countenance.

"Don't trouble yourself," he muttered contemptuously and walked on. At that moment Stepan Trofimovitch's voice rang out in the hall.

"Oh, hang you all," I thought, and ran to the hall.

Stepan Trofimovitch took his seat in the lecturer's chair in the midst of the still persisting disorder. He was greeted by the first rows with looks which were evidently not over-friendly. (Of late, at the club, people almost seemed not to like him, and treated him with much less respect than formerly.) But it was something to the good that he was not hissed. I had had a strange idea in my head ever since the previous day: I kept fancying that he would be received with hisses as soon as he appeared. They scarcely noticed him, however, in the disorder.

What could that man hope for if Karmazinov was treated like this? He was pale; it was ten years since he had appeared before an audience. From his excitement and from all that I knew so well in him, it was clear to me that he, too, regarded his present appearance on the platform as a turning-point of his fate, or something of the kind. That was just what I was afraid of. The man was dear to me. And what were my feelings when he opened his lips and I heard his first phrase?

"Ladies and gentlemen," he pronounced suddenly, as though resolved to venture everything, though in an almost breaking voice: "Ladies and gentlemen! Only this morning there lay before me one of the illegal leaflets that have been distributed here lately, and I asked myself for the hundredth time: 'Wherein lies its secret?'"

The whole hall became instantly still, all looks were turned to him, some with positive alarm. There was no denying, he knew how to secure their interest from the first word. Heads were thrust out from behind the scenes; Liputin and Lyamshin listened greedily. Yulia Mihailovna waved to me again.

"Stop him, whatever happens, stop him," she whispered in agitation. I could only shrug my shoulders: how could one stop a man resolved to venture everything? Alas, I understood what was in Stepan Trofimovitch's mind.

"Ha ha, the manifestos!" was whispered in the audience; the whole hall was stirred.

"Ladies and gentlemen, I've solved the whole mystery. The whole secret of their effect lies in their stupidity." (His eyes flashed.) "Yes, gentlemen, if this stupidity were intentional, pretended and calculated, oh, that would be a stroke of genius! But we must do them justice: they don't pretend anything. It's the barest, most simple-hearted, most shallow stupidity. *C'est la bêtise dans son essence la·plus pure, quelque chose comme un simple chimique.* If it were expressed ever so little more cleverly, everyone would see at once the poverty of this shallow stupidity. But as it is, everyone is left wondering; no one can believe that it is such elementary stupidity. 'It's impossible that there's nothing more in it,' everyone says to himself and tries to find the secret of it, sees a mystery in it, tries to read between the lines—the effect is attained! Oh, never has stupidity been so solemnly rewarded, though it has so often deserved it. . . . For, *en parenthèse,* stupidity is of as much service to humanity as the loftiest genius. . . ."

"Epigram of 1840" was commented, in a very modest voice,

however, but it was followed by a general outbreak of noise and uproar.

"Ladies and gentlemen, hurrah! I propose a toast to stupidity!" cried Stepan Trofimovitch, defying the audience in a perfect frenzy.

I ran up on the pretext of pouring out some water for him.

"Stepan Trofimovitch, leave off, Yulia Mihailovna entreats you to."

"No, you leave me alone, idle young man," he cried out at me at the top of his voice. I ran away. "Messieurs," he went on, "why this excitement, why the outcries of indignation I hear? I have come forward with an olive branch. I bring you the last word, for in this business I have the last word—and we shall be reconciled."

"Down with him!" shouted some.

"Hush, let him speak, let him have his say!" yelled another section. The young teacher was particularly excited; having once brought himself to speak he seemed now unable to be silent.

"Messieurs, the last word in this business—is forgiveness. I, an old man at the end of my life, I solemnly declare that the spirit of life breathes in us still, and there is still a living strength in the young generation. The enthusiasm of the youth of to-day is as pure and bright as in our age. All that has happened is a change of aim, the replacing of one beauty by another! The whole difficulty lies in the question which is more beautiful, Shakespeare or boots, Raphael or petroleum?"

"It's treachery!" growled some.

"Compromising questions!"

"*Agent provocateur!*"

"But I maintain," Stepan Trofimovitch shrilled at the utmost pitch of excitement, "I maintain that Shakespeare and Raphael are more precious than the emancipation of the serfs, more precious than Nationalism, more precious than Socialism, more precious than the young generation, more precious than chemistry, more precious than almost all humanity because they are the fruit, the real fruit of all humanity and perhaps the highest fruit that can be. A form of beauty is already attained, but for the attaining of which I would not perhaps consent to live. . . . Oh, heavens!" he cried, clasping his hands, "ten years ago I said the same thing from the platform in Petersburg, exactly the same thing, in the same words, and in just the same way they did not understand it, they laughed and hissed as now;

129

shallow people, what is lacking in you that you cannot understand? But let me tell you, let me tell you, without the English, life is still possible for humanity, without Germany, life is possible, without the Russians it is only too possible, without science, without bread, life is possible—only without beauty it is impossible, for there will be nothing left in the world. That's the secret at the bottom of everything, that's what history teaches! Even science would not exist a moment without beauty—do you know that, you who laugh—it will sink into bondage, you won't invent a nail even! . . . I won't yield an inch!" he shouted absurdly in confusion, and with all his might banged his fist on the table.

But all the while that he was shrieking senselessly and incoherently, the disorder in the hall increased. Many people jumped up from their seats, some dashed forward, nearer to the platform. It all happened much more quickly than I describe it, and there was no time to take steps, perhaps no wish to, either.

"It's all right for you, with everything found for you, you pampered creatures!" the same divinity student bellowed at the foot of the platform, grinning with relish at Stepan Trofimovitch, who noticed it and darted to the very edge of the platform.

"Haven't I, haven't I just declared that the enthusiasm of the young generation is as pure and bright as it was, and that it is coming to grief through being deceived only in the forms of beauty! Isn't that enough for you? And if you consider that he who proclaims this is a father crushed and insulted, can one —oh, shallow hearts—can one rise to greater heights of impartiality and fairness? . . . Ungrateful . . . unjust. . . . Why, why can't you be reconciled?"

And he burst into hysterical sobs. He wiped away his dropping tears with his fingers. His shoulders and breast were heaving with sobs. He was lost to everything in the world.

A perfect panic came over the audience, almost all got up from their seats. Yulia Mihailovna, too, jumped up quickly, seizing her husband by the arm and pulling him up too. . . . The scene was beyond all belief.

"Stepan Trofimovitch!" the divinity student roared gleefully. "There's Fedka the convict wandering about the town and the neighbourhood, escaped from prison. He is a robber and has recently committed another murder. Allow me to ask you: if you had not sold him as a recruit fifteen years ago to pay a gambling debt, that is, more simply, lost him at cards, tell me, would he have got into prison? Would he have cut men's throats now, in his struggle for existence? What do you say, Mr. Æsthete?''

I decline to describe the scene that followed. To begin with there was a furious volley of applause. The applause did not come from all—probably from some fifth part of the audience—but they applauded furiously. The rest of the public made for the exit, but as the applauding part of the audience kept pressing forward towards the platform, there was a regular block. The ladies screamed, some of the girls began to cry and asked to go home. Lembke, standing up by his chair, kept gazing wildly about him. Yulia Mihailovna completely lost her head—for the first time during her career amongst us. As for Stepan Trofimovitch, for the first moment he seemed literally crushed by the divinity student's words, but he suddenly raised his arms as though holding them out above the public and yelled:

"I shake the dust from off my feet and I curse you. . . . It's the end, the end. . . .''

And turning, he ran behind the scenes, waving his hands menacingly.

"He has insulted the audience! . . . Verhovensky!'' the angry section roared. They even wanted to rush in pursuit of him. It was impossible to appease them, at the moment, any way, and—a final catastrophe broke like a bomb on the assembly and exploded in its midst: the third reader, the maniac who kept waving his fist behind the scenes, suddenly ran on to the platform.

He looked like a perfect madman. With a broad, triumphant smile, full of boundless self-confidence, he looked round at the agitated hall and he seemed to be delighted at the disorder. He was not in the least disconcerted at having to speak in such an uproar, on the contrary, he was obviously delighted. This was so obvious that it attracted attention at once.

"What's this now?'' people were heard asking. "Who is this? Sh-h! What does he want to say?''

"Ladies and gentlemen,'' the maniac shouted with all his might, standing at the very edge of the platform and speaking with almost as shrill, feminine a voice as Karmazinov's, but without the aristocratic lisp. "Ladies and gentlemen! Twenty years ago, on the eve of war with half Europe, Russia was regarded as an ideal country by officials of all ranks! Literature was in the service of the censorship; military drill was all that was taught at the universities; the troops were trained like a ballet, and the peasants paid the taxes and were mute under the lash of serfdom. Patriotism meant the wringing of bribes from the quick and the dead. Those who did not take bribes were looked upon as rebels because they disturbed the general harmony. The birch copses were extirpated in support of discipline. Europe trembled. . . . But never in the thousand years of its senseless existence had Russia sunk to such ignominy. . . ."

He raised his fist, waved it ecstatically and menacingly over his head and suddenly brought it down furiously, as though pounding an adversary to powder. A frantic yell rose from the whole hall, there was a deafening roar of applause; almost half the audience was applauding: their enthusiasm was excusable. Russia was being put to shame publicly, before everyone. Who could fail to roar with delight?

"This is the real thing! Come, this is something like! Hurrah! Yes, this is none of your æsthetics!"

The maniac went on ecstatically:

"Twenty years have passed since then. Universies have been opened and multiplied. Military drill has passed into a legend; officers are too few by thousands, the railways have eaten up all the capital and have covered Russia as with a spider's web, so that in another fifteen years one will perhaps get somewhere. Bridges are rarely on fire, and fires in towns occur only at regular intervals, in turn, at the proper season. In the law courts judgments are as wise as Solomon's, and the jury only take bribes through the struggle for existence, to escape starvation. The serfs are free, and flog one another instead of being flogged by the land-owners. Seas and oceans of vodka are consumed to support the budget, and in Novgorod, opposite the ancient and useless St. Sophia, there has been solemnly put up a colossal bronze globe to celebrate a thousand years of disorder and confusion; Europe scowls and begins to be uneasy again. . . . Fifteen years of reforms! And yet never even in the most grotesque periods of its madness has Russia sunk . . ."

The last words could not be heard in the roar of the crowd. One could see him again raise his arm and bring it down triumphantly again. Enthusiasm was beyond all bounds: people yelled, clapped their hands, even some of the ladies shouted: "Enough, you can't beat that!" Some might have been drunk. The orator scanned them all and seemed revelling in his own triumph. I caught a glimpse of Lembke in indescribable excitement, pointing something out to somebody. Yulia Mihailovna, with a pale face, said something in haste to the prince, who had run up to her. But at that moment a group of six men, officials more or less, burst on to the platform, seized the orator and dragged him behind the scenes. I can't understand how he managed to tear himself away from them, but he did escape, darted up to the edge of the platform again and succeeded in shouting again, at the top of his voice, waving his fist:

"But never has Russia sunk . . ."

But he was dragged away again. I saw some fifteen men dash behind the scenes to rescue him, not crossing the platform but breaking down the light screen at the side of it. . . . I saw afterwards, though I could hardly believe my eyes, the girl student (Virginsky's sister) leap on to the platform with the same roll under her arm, dressed as before, as plump and rosy as ever, surrounded by two or three women and two or three men, and accompanied by her mortal enemy, the schoolboy. I even caught the phrase:

"Ladies and gentlemen, I've come to call attention to the sufferings of poor students and to rouse them to a general protest . . ."

But I ran away. Hiding my badge in my pocket I made my way from the house into the street by back passages which I knew of. First of all, of course, I went to Stepan Trofimovitch's.

CHAPTER II

THE END OF THE FÊTE

I

HE would not see me. He had shut himself up and was writing. At my repeated knocks and appeals he answered through the door:

"My friend, I have finished everything. Who can ask anything more of me?"

"You haven't finished anything, you've only helped to make a mess of the whole thing. For God's sake, no epigrams, Stepan Trofimovitch! Open the door. We must take steps; they may still come and insult you. . . ."

I thought myself entitled to be particularly severe and even

133

rigorous. I was afraid he might be going to do something still more mad. But to my surprise I met an extraordinary firmness.

"Don't be the first to insult me then. I thank you for the past, but I repeat I've done with all men, good and bad. I am writing to Darya Pavlovna, whom I've forgotten so unpardonably till now. You may take it to her to-morrow, if you like, now *merci.*"

"Stepan Trofimovitch, I assure you that the matter is more serious than you think. Do you think that you've crushed someone there? You've pulverised no one, but have broken yourself to pieces like an empty bottle." (Oh, I was coarse and discourteous; I remember it with regret.) "You've absolutely no reason to write to Darya Pavlovna . . . and what will you do with yourself without me? What do you understand about practical life? I expect you are plotting something else? You'll simply come to grief again if you go plotting something more. . . ."

He rose and came close up to the door.

"You've not been long with them, but you've caught the infection of their tone and language. *Dieu vous pardonne, mon ami, et Dieu vous garde.* But I've always seen in you the germs of delicate feeling, and you will get over it perhaps—*après le temps,* of course, like all of us Russians. As for what you say about my impracticability, I'll remind you of a recent idea of mine: a whole mass of people in Russia do nothing whatever but attack other people's impracticability with the utmost fury and with the tiresome persistence of flies in the summer, accusing everyone of it except themselves. *Cher,* remember that I am excited, and don't distress me. Once more *merci* for everything, and let us part like Karmazinov and the public; that is, let us forget each other with as much generosity as we can. He was posing in begging his former readers so earnestly to forget him; *quant à moi,* I am not so conceited, and I rest my hopes on the youth of your inexperienced heart. How should you remember a useless old man for long? 'Live more,' my friend, as Nastasya wished me on my last name-day (*ces pauvres gens ont quelquefois des mots charmants et pleins de philosophie*). I do not wish you much happiness—it will bore you. I do not wish you trouble either, but, following the philosophy of the peasant, I will repeat simply 'live more' and try not to be much bored; this useless wish I add from myself. Well, good-bye, and good-bye for good. Don't stand at my door, I will not open it."

He went away and I could get nothing more out of him. In spite of his "excitement", he spoke smoothly, deliberately, with weight, obviously trying to be impressive. Of course he was rather vexed with me and was avenging himself indirectly, possibly even for the yesterday's "prison carts" and "floors that give way". His tears in public that morning, in spite of a triumph of a sort, had put him, he knew, in rather a comic position, and there never was a man more solicitous of dignity and punctilio in his relations with his friends than Stepan Trofimovitch. Oh, I don't blame him. But this fastidiousness and irony which he preserved in spite of all shocks reassured me at the time. A man who was so little different from his ordinary self was, of course, not in the mood at that moment for anything tragic or extraordinary. So I reasoned at the time, and, heavens, what a mistake I made! I left too much out of my reckoning.

In anticipation of events I will quote the few first lines of the letter to Darya Pavlovna, which she actually received the following day:

"Mon enfant, my hand trembles, but I've done with everything. You were not present at my last struggle; you did not come to that matinée, and you did well to stay away. But you will be told that in our Russia, which has grown so poor in men of character, one man had the courage to stand up and, in spite of deadly menaces showered on him from all sides, to tell the fools the truth, that is, that they are fools. *Oh, ce sont—des pauvres petits vauriens et rien de plus, des petits*—fools— *voilà le mot!* The die is cast; I am going from this town for ever and I know not whither. Everyone I loved has turned from me. But you, you are a pure and naïve creature; you, a gentle being whose life has been all but linked with mine at the will of a capricious and imperious heart; you who looked at me perhaps with contempt when I shed weak tears on the eve of our frustrated marriage; you who cannot in any case look on me except as a comic figure—for you, for you is the last cry of my heart, for you my last duty, for you alone! I cannot leave you for ever thinking of me as an ungrateful fool, a churlish egoist, as probably a cruel and ungrateful heart—whom, alas, I cannot forget—is every day describing me to you. . . ."*

And so on and so on, four large pages.
Answering his "I won't open" with three bangs with my

fist on the door, and shouting after him that I was sure he would send Nastasya for me three times that day, but I would not come, I gave him up and ran off to Yulia Mihailovna.

II

There I was the witness to a revolting scene: the poor woman was deceived to her face, and I could do nothing. Indeed, what could I say to her? I had had time to reconsider things a little and reflect that I had nothing to go upon but certain feelings and suspicious presentiments. I found her in tears, almost in hysterics, with compresses of eau-de-Cologne and a glass of water. Before her stood Pyotr Stepanovitch, who talked without stopping, and the prince, who held his tongue as though it had been under a lock. With tears and lamentations she reproached Pyotr Stepanovitch for his "desertion". I was struck at once by the fact that she ascribed the whole failure, the whole ignominy of the matinée, everything in fact, to Pyotr Stepanovitch's absence.

In him I observed an important change: he seemed a shade too anxious, almost serious. As a rule he never seemed serious; he was always laughing, even when he was angry, and he was often angry. Oh, he was angry now! He was speaking coarsely, carelessly, with vexation and impatience. He said that he had been taken ill at Gaganov's lodging, where he had happened to go early in the morning. Alas, the poor woman was so anxious to be deceived again! The chief question which I found being discussed was whether the ball, that is, the whole second half of the fête, should or should not take place. Yulia Mihailovna could not be induced to appear at the ball "after the insults she had received that morning"; in other words, her heart was set on being compelled to do so, and by him, by Pyotr Stepanovitch. She looked upon him as an oracle, and I believe if he had gone away she would have taken to her bed at once. But he did not want to go away; he was desperately anxious that the ball should take place and that Yulia Mihailovna should be present at it.

"Come, what is there to cry about? Are you set on having a scene? On venting your anger on somebody? Well, vent it on me; only make haste about it, for the time is passing and you must make up your mind. We made a mess of it with the matinée; we'll pick up on the ball. Here, the prince thinks as

I do. Yes, if it hadn't been for the prince, how would things have ended there?''

The prince had been at first opposed to the ball (that is, opposed to Yulia Mihailovna's appearing at it; the ball was bound to go on in any case), but after two or three such references to his opinion he began little by little to grant his acquiescence.

I was surprised too at the extraordinary rudeness of Pyotr Stepanovitch's tone. Oh, I scout with indignation the contemptible slander which was spread later of some supposed liaison between Yulia Mihailovna and Pyotr Stepanovitch. There was no such thing, nor could there be. He gained his ascendancy over her from the first only by encouraging her in her dreams of influence in society and in the ministry, by entering into her plans, by inventing them for her, and working upon her with the grossest flattery. He had got her completely into his toils and had become as necessary to her as the air she breathed. Seeing me, she cried, with flashing eyes:

"Here, ask him. He kept by my side all the while, just like the prince did. Tell me, isn't it plain that it was all a preconcerted plot, a base, designing plot to damage Andrey Antonovitch and me as much as possible? Oh, they had arranged it beforehand. They had a plan! It's a party, a regular party."

"You are exaggerating as usual. You've always some romantic notion in your head. But I am glad to see Mr. . . ." (He pretended to have forgotten my name.) "He'll give us his opinion."

"My opinion," I hastened to put in, "is the same as Yulia Mihailovna's. The plot is only too evident. I have brought you these ribbons, Yulia Mihailovna. Whether the ball is to take place or not is not my business, for it's not in my power to decide; but my part as steward is over. Forgive my warmth, but I can't act against the dictates of common sense and my own convictions."

"You hear! You hear!" She clasped her hands.

"I hear, and I tell you this." He turned to me. "I think you must have eaten something which has made you all delirious. To my thinking, nothing has happened, absolutely nothing but what has happened before and is always liable to happen in this town. A plot, indeed! It was an ugly failure, disgracefully stupid. But where's the plot? A plot against Yulia Mihailovna, who has spoiled them and protected them and fondly forgiven them all their schoolboy pranks! Yulia

Mihailovna! What have I been hammering into you for the last month continually? What did I warn you? What did you want with all these people—what did you want with them? What induced you to mix yourself up with these fellows? What was the motive, what was the object of it? To unite society? But, mercy on us! will they ever be united?"

"When did you warn me? On the contrary, you approved of it, you even insisted on it. . . . I confess I am so surprised. . . . You brought all sorts of strange people to see me yourself."

"On the contrary, I opposed you; I did not approve of it. As for bringing them to see you, I certainly did, but only after they'd got in by dozens and only of late to make up 'the literary quadrille'—we couldn't get on without these rogues. Only I don't mind betting that a dozen or two more of the same sort were let in without tickets to-day."

"Not a doubt of it," I agreed.

"There, you see, you are agreeing already. Think what the tone has been lately here—I mean in this wretched town. It's nothing but insolence, impudence; it's been a crying scandal all the time. And who's been encouraging it? Who's screened it by her authority? Who's upset them all? Who has made all the small fry huffy? All their family secrets are caricatured in your album. Didn't you pat them on the back, your poets and caricaturists? Didn't you let Lyamshin kiss your hand? Didn't a divinity student abuse an actual state councillor in your presence and spoil his daughter's dress with his tarred boots? Now, can you wonder that the public is set against you?"

"But that's all your doing, yours! Oh, my goodness!"

"No, I warned you. We quarrelled. Do you hear, we quarrelled?"

"Why, you are lying to my face!"

"Of course it's easy for you to say that. You need a victim to vent your wrath on. Well, vent it on me as I've said already. I'd better appeal to you, Mr. . . ." (He was still unable to recall my name.) "We'll reckon on our fingers. I maintain that, apart from Liputin, there was nothing preconcerted, nothing! I will prove it, but first let us analyse Liputin. He came forward with that fool Lebyadkin's verses. Do you maintain that that was a plot? But do you know it might simply have struck Liputin as a clever thing to do. Seriously, seriously. He simply came forward with the idea of making every-

one laugh and entertaining them—his protectress Yulia Mihailovna first of all. That was all. Don't you believe it? Isn't that
in keeping with all that has been going on here for the last
month? Do you want me to tell the whole truth? I declare
that under other circumstances it might have gone off all right.
It was a coarse joke—well, a bit strong, perhaps; but it was
amusing, you know, wasn't it?''

"What! You think what Liputin did was clever?" Yulia
Mihailovna cried in intense indignation. "Such stupidity, such
tactlessness, so contemptible, so mean! It was intentional! Oh,
you are saying it on purpose! I believe after that you are in
the plot with them yourself.''

"Of course I was behind the scenes, I was in hiding, I set
it all going. But if I were in the plot—understand that, anyway—it wouldn't have ended with Liputin. So according to
you I had arranged with my papa too that he should cause such
a scene on purpose? Well, whose fault is it that my papa was
allowed to read? Who tried only yesterday to prevent you
from allowing it, only yesterday?''

"*Oh, hier il avait tant d'esprit,* I was so reckoning on him;
and then he has such manners. I thought with him and
Karmazinov . . . Only think!''

"Yes, only think. But in spite of *tant d'esprit* papa has made
things worse, and if I'd known beforehand that he'd made
such a mess of it, I should certainly not have persuaded you
yesterday to keep the goat out of the kitchen garden, should
I—since I am taking part in this conspiracy against your fête
that you are so positive about? And yet I did try to dissuade
you yesterday; I tried to because I foresaw it. To foresee everything was, of course, impossible; he probably did not know
himself a minute before what he would fire off—these nervous
old men can't be reckoned on like other people. But you can
still save the situation: to satisfy the public, send to him to-
morrow by administrative order, and with all the ceremonies,
two doctors to inquire into his health. Even to-day, in fact,
and take him straight to the hospital and apply cold compresses. Everyone would laugh, anyway, and see that there
was nothing to take offence at. I'll tell people about it in
the evening at the ball, as I am his son. Karmazinov is another
story. He was a perfect ass and dragged out his article for a
whole hour. He certainly must have been in the plot with me!
'I'll make a mess of it too,' he thought, 'to damage Yulia
Mihailovna.' ''

"Oh, Karmazinov! *Quelle honte!* I was burning, burning with shame for his audience!"

"Well, I shouldn't have burnt, but have cooked him instead. The audience was right, you know. Who was to blame for Karmazinov, again? Did I foist him upon you? Was I one of his worshippers? Well, hang him! But the third maniac, the political—that's a different matter. That was everyone's blunder, not only my plot."

"Ah, don't speak of it! That was awful, awful! That was my fault, entirely my fault!"

"Of course it was, but I don't blame you for that. No one can control them, these candid souls! You can't always be safe from them, even in Petersburg. He was recommended to you, and in what terms too! So you will admit that you are bound to appear at the ball to-night. It's an important business. It was you put him on to the platform. You must make it plain now to the public that you are not in league with him, that the fellow is in the hands of the police, and that you were in some inexplicable way deceived. You ought to declare with indignation that you were the victim of a madman. Because he is a madman and nothing more. That's how you must put it about him. I can't endure these people who bite. I say worse things perhaps, but not from the platform, you know. And they are talking about a senator too."

"What senator? Who's talking?'

"I don't understand it myself, you know. Do you know anything about a senator, Yulia Mihailovna?"

"A senator?"

"You see, they are convinced that a senator has been appointed to be governor here, and that you are being superseded from Petersburg. I've heard it from lots of people.'

"I've heard it too," I put in.

"Who said so?" asked Yulia Mihailovna, flushing all over.

"You mean, who said so first? How can I tell? But there it is, people say so. Masses of people are saying so. They were saying so yesterday particularly. They are all very serious about it, though I can't make it out. Of course the more intelligent and competent don't talk, but even some of those listen."

"How mean! And . . . how stupid!"

"Well, that's just why you must make your appearance, to show these fools."

"I confess I feel myself that it's my duty, but . . . what if

140

there's another disgrace in store for us? What if people don't come? No one will come, you know, no one!"

"How hot you are! They not come! What about the new clothes? What about the girls' dresses? I give you up as a woman after that! Is that your knowledge of human nature?'

"The marshal's wife won't come, she won't."

"But, after all, what has happened? Why won't they come?" he cried at last with angry impatience.

"Ignominy, disgrace—that's what's happened. I don't know what to call it, but after it I can't face people."

"Why? How are you to blame for it, after all? Why do you take the blame of it on yourself? Isn't it rather the fault of the audience, of your respectable residents, your patres-familias? They ought to have controlled the roughs and the rowdies—for it was all the work of roughs and rowdies, nothing serious. You can never manage things with the police alone in any society, anywhere. Among us everyone asks for a special policeman to protect him wherever he goes. People don't understand that society must protect itself. And what do our patres-familias, the officials, the wives and daughters, do in such cases? They sit quiet and sulk. In fact there's not enough social initiative to keep the disorderly in check."

"Ah, that's the simple truth! They sit quiet, sulk and . . . gaze about them."

"And if it's the truth, you ought to say so aloud, proudly, sternly, just to show that you are not defeated, to those respectable residents and mothers of families. Oh, you can do it; you have the gift when your head is clear. You will gather them round you and say it aloud. And then a paragraph in the 'Voice' and the 'Financial News'. Wait a bit, I'll undertake it myself, I'll arrange it all for you. Of course there must be more superintendence: you must look after the buffet; you must ask the prince, you must ask Mr. . . . You must not desert us, monsieur, just when we have to begin all over again. And finally, you must appear arm-in-arm with Andrey Antonovitch. . . . How is Andrey Antonovitch?"

"Oh, how unjustly, how untruly, how cruelly you have always judged that angelic man!" Yulia Mihailovna cried in a sudden outburst, almost with tears, putting her handkerchief to her eyes.

Pyotr Stepanovitch was positively taken aback for the moment.

"Good heavens! I . . . What have I said? I've always . . ."

"You never have, never! You have never done him justice."

"There's no understanding a woman," grumbled Pyotr Stepanovitch, with a wry smile.

"He is the most sincere, the most delicate, the most angelic of men! The most kind-hearted of men!"

"Well, really, as for kind-heartedness . . . I've always done him justice. . . ."

"Never! But let us drop it. I am too awkward in my defence of him. This morning that little Jesuit, the marshal's wife, also dropped some sarcastic hints about what happened yesterday."

"Oh, she has no thoughts to spare for yesterday now, she is full of to-day. And why are you so upset at her not coming to the ball to-night? Of course, she won't come after getting mixed up in such a scandal. Perhaps it's not her fault, but still her reputation . . . her hands are soiled."

"What do you mean; I don't understand? Why are her hands soiled?" Yulia Mihailovna looked at him in perplexity.

"I don't vouch for the truth of it, but the town is ringing with the story that it was she brought them together."

"What do you mean? Brought whom together?"

"What, do you mean to say you don't know?" he exclaimed with well-simulated wonder. "Why, Stavrogin and Lizaveta Nikolaevna."

"What? How?" we all cried out at once.

"Is it possible you don't know? Phew! Why, it is quite a tragic romance: Lizaveta Nikolaevna was pleased to get out of that lady's carriage and get straight into Stavrogin's carriage, and slipped off with 'the latter' to Skvoreshniki in full daylight. Only an hour ago, hardly an hour."

We were flabbergasted. Of course we fell to questioning him, but to our wonder, although he "happened" to be a witness of the scene himself, he could give us no detailed account of it. The thing seemed to have happened like this: when the marshal's wife was driving Liza and Mavriky Nikolaevitch from the matinée to the house of Praskovya Ivanovna (whose legs were still bad) they saw a carriage waiting a short distance, about twenty-five paces, to one side of the front door. When Liza jumped out, she ran straight to this carriage; the door was flung open and shut again; Liza called to Mavriky Nikolaevitch: "Spare me," and the carriage drove off at full speed to Skvoreshniki. To our hurried questions whether it was by arrangement? Who was in the carriage? Pyotr Stepanovitch answered that he knew nothing about it; no doubt it had been arranged, but that he did not see Stavrogin himself; possibly the old butler, Alexey Yegorytch, might have been in the carriage. To the question "How did he come to be there, and how did he know for a fact that she had driven to Skvoreshniki?" he answered that he happened to be passing and, at seeing Liza, he had run up to the carriage (and yet he could not make out who was in it, an inquisitive man like him!) and that Mavriky Nikolaevitch, far from setting off in pursuit, had not even tried to stop Liza, and had even laid a restraining hand on the marshal's wife, who was shouting at the top of her voice: "She is going to Stavrogin, to Stavrogin." At this point I lost patience, and cried furiously to Pyotr Stepanovitch:

"It's all your doing, you rascal! This was what you were doing this morning. You helped Stavrogin, you came in the carriage, you helped her into it . . . it was you, you, you! Yulia Mihailovna, he is your enemy; he will be your ruin too! Beware of him!"

And I ran headlong out of the house. I wonder myself and cannot make out to this day how I came to say that to him. But I guessed quite right: it had all happened almost exactly as I said, as appeared later. What struck me most was the obviously artificial way in which he broke the news. He had not told it at once on entering the house as an extraordinary piece of news, but pretended that we knew without his telling us, which was impossible in so short a time. And if we had known it, we could not possibly have refrained from mentioning it till he introduced the subject. Besides, he could not have heard yet that the town was "ringing with gossip" about the marshal's wife in so short a time. Besides, he had once or twice given a vulgar, frivolous smile as he told the story, probably considering that we were fools and completely taken in.

But I had no thought to spare for him; the central fact I believed, and ran from Yulia Mihailovna's, beside myself. The catastrophe cut me to the heart. I was wounded almost to tears; perhaps I did shed some indeed. I was at a complete loss what to do. I rushed to Stepan Trofimovitch's, but the vexatious man still refused to open the door. Nastasya informed me, in a reverent whisper, that he had gone to bed, but I did not believe it. At Liza's house I succeeded in questioning the servants. They confirmed the story of the elopement, but knew nothing themselves. There was great commotion in the house; their mistress had been attacked by fainting fits, and Mavriky Nikolaevitch was with her. I did not feel it possible to ask for Mavriky Nikolaevitch. To my inquiries about Pyotr Stepanovitch they told me that he had been in and out continually of late, sometimes twice in the day. The servants were sad, and showed particular respectfulness in speaking of Liza; they were fond of her. That she was ruined, utterly ruined, I did not doubt; but the psychological aspect of the matter I was utterly unable to understand, especially after her scene with Stavrogin the previous day. To run about the town and inquire at the houses of acquaintances, who would, of course, by now have heard the news and be rejoicing at it, seemed to me revolting, besides being humiliating for Liza. But, strange to say, I ran to see Darya Pavlovna, though I was not admitted (no one had been admitted into the house since the previous morning). I don't know what I could have said to her and what made me run to her. From her I went to her brother's. Shatov listened sullenly and in silence. I may observe that I found him more gloomy than I had ever seen him before; he was awfully preoccupied and seemed only to listen to me with an effort. He said scarcely anything and began walking up and down his cell from corner to corner, treading more noisily than usual. As I was going down the stairs he shouted after me to go to Liputin's: "There you'll hear everything." Yet I did not go to Liputin's, but after I'd gone a good way towards home I turned back to Shatov's again, and, half opening the door without going in, suggested to him laconically and with no kind of explanation: "Won't you go to Marya Timofyevna to-day?" At this Shatov swore at me, and I went away. I note here that I may not forget it that he did purposely go that evening to the other end of the town to see Marya Timofyevna, whom he had not seen for some time. He found her in excellent health and spirits and Lebyadkin dead drunk, asleep on the sofa in the first room. This was at nine o'clock. He told me so himself next day when we met for a moment in the street. Before ten o'clock I made up my mind to go to the ball, but not in the capacity of a steward (besides, my rosette had been left at Yulia Mihailovna's). I was tempted by irresistible curiosity to listen, without asking any questions, to what people were saying in the town about all that had happened. I wanted, too, to have a look at Yulia Mihailovna, if only at a distance. I reproached myself greatly that I had left her so abruptly that afternoon.

All that night, with its almost grotesque incidents, and the terrible *dénouement* that followed in the early morning, still seems to me like a hideous nightmare, and is, for me at least, the most painful chapter in my chronicle. I was late for the ball, and it was destined to end so quickly that I arrived not long before it was over. It was eleven o'clock when I reached the entrance of the marshal's house, where the same White Hall in which the matinée had taken place had, in spite of the short interval between, been cleared and made ready to serve as the chief ballroom for the whole town, as we expected, to dance in. But far as I had been that morning from expecting the ball to be a success, I had had no presentiment of the full truth. Not one family of the higher circles appeared; even the subordinate officials of rather more consequence were absent—and this was a very striking fact. As for ladies and girls, Pyotr Stepanovitch's arguments (the duplicity of which was obvious now) turned out to be utterly incorrect: exceedingly few had come; to four men there was scarcely one lady—and what ladies they were! Regimental ladies of a sort, three doctors' wives with their daughters, two or three poor ladies from the country, the seven daughters and the niece of the secretary whom I have mentioned already, some wives of tradesmen, of post-office clerks and other small fry—was this what Yulia Mihailovna expected? Half the tradespeople even were absent. As for the men, in spite of the complete absence of all persons of consequence, there was still a crowd of them, but they made a doubtful and suspicious impression. There were, of course, some quiet and respectful officers with their wives, some of the most docile fathers of families, like that secretary, for instance, the father of his seven daughters. All these humble, insignificant people had come, as one of these gentlemen expressed it, because it was "inevitable". But, on the other hand, the mass of free-and-easy people and the mass too of those whom Pyotr Stepanovitch and I had suspected of coming in without tickets, seemed even bigger than in the afternoon. So far they were all sitting in the refreshment bar, and had gone straight there on arriving, as though it were the meeting-place they had agreed upon. So at least it seemed to me. The refreshment bar had been placed in a large room, the last of several opening out of one another. Here Prohoritch was installed with all the attractions of the club cuisine and with a tempting display of drinks

THE POSSESSED

and dainties. I noticed several persons whose coats were almost in rags and whose get-up was altogether suspicious and utterly unsuitable for a ball. They had evidently been with great pains brought to a state of partial sobriety which would not last long; and goodness knows where they had been brought from, they were not local people. I knew, of course, that it was part of Yulia Mihailovna's idea that the ball should be of the most democratic character, and that "even working people and shop-men should not be excluded if anyone of that class chanced to pay for a ticket". She could bravely utter such words in her committee with absolute security that none of the working people of our town, who all lived in extreme poverty, would dream of taking a ticket. But in spite of the democratic senti-ments of the committee, I could hardly believe that such sinister-looking and shabby people could have been admitted in the regular way. But who could have admitted them, and with what object? Lyamshin and Liputin had already been deprived of their stewards' rosettes, though they were present at the ball, as they were taking part in the "literary quadrille". But, to my amazement, Liputin's place was taken by the divinity student, who had caused the greatest scandal at the matinée by his skirmish with Stepan Trofimovitch; and Lyamshin's was taken by Pyotr Stepanovitch himself. What was to be looked for under the circumstances?

I tried to listen to the conversation. I was struck by the wild-ness of some ideas I heard expressed. It was maintained in one group, for instance, that Yulia Mihailovna had arranged Liza's elopement with Stavrogin and had been paid by the latter for doing so. Even the sum paid was mentioned. It was asserted that she had arranged the whole fête with a view to it, and that that was the reason why half the town had not turned up at the ball, and that Lembke himself was so upset about it that "his mind had given way", and that, crazy as he was, "she had got him in tow". There was a great deal of laughter too, hoarse, wild and significant. Everyone was criticising the ball, too, with great severity, and abusing Yulia Mihailovna with-out ceremony. In fact it was disorderly, incoherent, drunken and excited babble, so it was difficult to put it together and make anything of it. At the same time there were simple-hearted people enjoying themselves at the refreshment-bar; there were even some ladies of the sort who are surprised and frightened at nothing, very genial and festive, chiefly military ladies with their husbands. They made parties at the little

146

tables, were drinking tea, and were very merry. The refreshment-bar made a snug refuge for almost half of the guests. Yet in a little time all this mass of people must stream into the ballroom. It was horrible to think of it!

Meanwhile the prince had succeeded in arranging three skimpy quadrilles in the White Hall. The young ladies were dancing, while their parents were enjoying watching them. But many of these respectable persons had already begun to think how they could, after giving their girls a treat, get off in good time before "the trouble began". Absolutely everyone was convinced that it certainly would begin. It would be difficult for me to describe Yulia Mihailovna's state of mind. I did not talk to her though I went close up to her. She did not respond to the bow I made her on entering; she did not notice me (really did not notice). There was a painful look in her face and a contemptuous and haughty though restless and agitated expression in her eyes. She controlled herself with evident suffering—for whose sake, with what object? She certainly ought to have gone away, still more to have got her husband away, and she remained! From her face one could see that her eyes were "fully opened", and that it was useless for her to expect anything more. She did not even summon Pyotr Stepanovitch (he seemed to avoid her; I saw him in the refreshment-room, he was extremely lively). But she remained at the ball and did not let Andrey Antonovitch leave her side for a moment. Oh, up to the very last moment, even that morning she would have repudiated any hint about his health with genuine indignation. But now her eyes were to be opened on this subject too. As for me, I thought from the first glance that Andrey Antonovitch looked worse than he had done in the morning. He seemed to be plunged into a sort of oblivion and hardly to know where he was. Sometimes he looked about him with unexpected severity —at me, for instance, twice. Once he tried to say something; he began loudly and audibly but did not finish the sentence, throwing a modest old clerk who happened to be near him almost into a panic. But even this humble section of the assembly held sullenly and timidly aloof from Yulia Mihailovna and at the same time turned upon her husband exceedingly strange glances, open and staring, quite out of keeping with their habitually submissive demeanour.

"Yes, that struck me, and I suddenly began to guess about Andrey Antonovitch," Yulia Mihailovna confessed to me afterwards.

Yes, she was to blame again! Probably when after my departure she had settled with Pyotr Stepanovitch that there should be a ball and that she should be present she must have gone again to the study where Andrey Antonovitch was sitting, utterly "shattered" by the matinée; must again have used all her fascinations to persuade him to come with her. But what misery she must have been in now! And yet she did not go away. Whether it was pride or simply she lost her head, I do not know. In spite of her haughtiness, she attempted with smiles and humiliation to enter into conversation with some ladies, but they were confused, confined themselves to distrustful monosyllables, "Yes" and "No", and evidently avoided her.

The only person of undoubted consequence who was present at the ball was that distinguished general whom I have described already, the one who after Stavrogin's duel with Gaganov "opened the door to public impatience" at the marshal's wife's. He walked with an air of dignity through the rooms, looked about, and listened, and tried to appear as though he had come rather for the sake of observation than for the sake of enjoying himself. . . . He ended by establishing himself beside Yulia Mihailovna and not moving a step away from her, evidently trying to keep up her spirits and reassure her. He certainly was a most kind-hearted man, of very high rank, and so old that even compassion from him was not wounding. But to admit to herself that this old gossip was venturing to pity her and almost to protect her, knowing that he was doing her honour by his presence, was very vexatious. The general stayed by her and never ceased chattering.

"They say a town can't go on without seven righteous men . . . seven, I think it is, I am not sure of the number fixed. . . . I don't know how many of these seven, the certified righteous of the town . . . have the honour of being present at your ball. Yet in spite of their presence I begin to feel unsafe. *Vous me pardonnez, charmante dame, n'est-ce pas?* I speak allegorically, but I went into the refreshment-room and I am glad I escaped alive. . . . Our priceless Prohoritch is not in his place there, and I believe his bar will be destroyed before morning. But I am laughing. I am only waiting to see what the 'literary quadrille' is going to be like, and then home to bed. You must excuse a gouty old fellow. I go early to bed, and I would advise you too to go 'by-by', as they say *aux enfants*. I've come, you know, to have a look at the pretty girls . . .

148

whom, of course, I could meet nowhere in such profusion as here. They all live beyond the river and I don't drive out so far. There's a wife of an officer . . . in the chasseurs I believe he is . . . who is distinctly pretty, distinctly, and . . . she knows it herself. I've talked to the sly puss; she is a sprightly one . . . and the girls too are fresh-looking; but that's all, there's nothing but freshness. Still, it's a pleasure to look at them. There are some rosebuds, but their lips are thick. As a rule there's an irregularity about female beauty in Russia, and . . . they are a little like buns . . . *vous me pardonnez, n'est-ce pas?* . . . with good eyes, however, laughing eyes. . . . These rose-buds are charming for two years when they are young . . . even for three . . . then they broaden out and are spoilt for ever . . . producing in their husbands that deplorable indifference which does so much to promote the woman movement . . . that is, if I understand it correctly. . . . H'm! It's a fine hall; the rooms are not badly decorated. It might be worse. The music might be much worse. . . . I don't say it ought to have been. What makes a bad impression is that there are so few ladies. I say nothing about the dresses. It's bad that that chap in the grey trousers should dare to dance the cancan so openly. I can forgive him if he does it in the gaiety of his heart, and since he is the local chemist. . . . Still, eleven o'clock is a bit early even for chemists. There were two fellows fighting in the refreshment-bar and they weren't turned out. At eleven o'clock people ought to be turned out for fighting, whatever the standard of manners. . . . Three o'clock is a different matter; then one has to make concessions to public opinion—if only this ball survives till three o'clock. Varvara Petrovna has not kept her word, though, and hasn't sent flowers. H'm! She has no thoughts for flowers, *pauvre mère!* And poor Liza! Have you heard? They say it's a mysterious story . . . and Stavrogin is to the front again. . . . H'm! I would have gone home to bed . . . I can hardly keep my eyes open. But when is this 'literary quadrille' coming on?"

At last the "literary quadrille" began. Whenever of late there had been conversation in the town on the ball it had invariably turned on this literary quadrille, and as no one could imagine what it would be like, it aroused extraordinary curiosity. Nothing could be more unfavourable to its chance of success, and great was the disappointment.

The side doors of the White Hall were thrown open and several masked figures appeared. The public surrounded them eagerly. All the occupants of the refreshment-bar trooped to the last man into the hall. The masked figures took their places for the dance. I succeeded in making my way to the front and installed myself just behind Yulia Mihailovna, Von Lembke, and the general. At this point Pyotr Stepanovitch, who had kept away till that time, skipped up to Yulia Mihailovna.

"I've been in the refreshment-room all this time, watching," he whispered, with the air of a guilty schoolboy, which he, how-ever, assumed on purpose to irritate her even more. She turned crimson with anger.

"You might give up trying to deceive me now at least, inso-lent man!" broke from her almost aloud, so that it was heard by other people. Pyotr Stepanovitch skipped away extremely well satisfied with himself.

It would be difficult to imagine a more pitiful, vulgar, dull and insipid allegory than this "literary quadrille". Nothing could be imagined less appropriate to our local society. Yet they say it was Karmazinov's idea. It was Liputin indeed who arranged it, with the help of the lame teacher who had been at the meeting at Virginsky's. But Karmazinov had given the idea and had, it was said, meant to dress up and to take a special and prominent part in it. The quadrille was made up of six couples of masked figures, who were not in fancy dress exactly, for their clothes were like everyone else's. Thus, for instance, one short and elderly gentleman wearing a dress-coat—in fact, dressed like everyone else—wore a venerable grey beard, tied on (and this constituted his disguise). As he danced he pounded up and down, taking tiny and rapid steps on the same spot with a stolid expression of countenance. He gave vent to sounds in a subdued but husky bass, and this huskiness was meant to sug-gest one of the well-known papers. Opposite this figure danced two giants, X and Z, and these letters were pinned on their coats, but what the letters meant remained unexplained. "Honest Russian thought" was represented by a middle-aged gentleman in spectacles, dress-coat and gloves, and wearing fetters (real fetters). Under his arm he had a portfolio contain-ing papers relating to some "case". To convince the sceptical a letter from abroad testifying to the honesty of "honest Russian thought" peeped out of his pocket. All this was explained by the stewards, as the letter which peeped out of his pocket could not be read. "Honest Russian thought" had his right hand raised and in it held a glass as though he wanted to propose a toast. In a line with him on each side tripped a crop-headed

THE POSSESSED

nihilist girl; while *vis-à-vis* danced another elderly gentleman in a dress-coat with a heavy cudgel in his hand. He was meant to represent a formidable periodical (not a Petersburg one), and seemed to be saying: "I'll pound you to a jelly." But in spite of his cudgel he could not bear the spectacles of "honest Russian thought" fixed upon him and tried to look away, and when he did the *pas de deux,* he twisted, turned, and did not know what to do with himself—so terrible, probably, were the stings of his conscience! I don't remember all the absurd tricks they played, however; it was all in the same style, so that I felt at last painfully ashamed. And this same expression, as it were, of shame was reflected in the whole public, even on the most sullen figures that had come out of the refreshment-room. For some time all were silent and gazed with angry perplexity. When a man is ashamed he generally begins to get angry and is disposed to be cynical. By degrees a murmur arose in the audience.

"What's the meaning of it?" a man who had come in from the refreshment-room muttered in one of the groups.

"It's silly."

"It's something literary. It's a criticism of the 'Voice'."

"What's that to me?"

From another group:

"Asses!"

"No, they are not asses; it's we who are the asses."

"Why are you an ass?"

"I am not an ass."

"Well, if you are not, I am certainly not."

From a third group:

"We ought to give them a good smacking and send them flying."

"Pull down the hall!"

From a fourth group:

"I wonder the Lembkes are not ashamed to look on!"

"Why should they be ashamed? You are not."

"Yes, I am ashamed, and he is the governor."

"And you are a pig."

"I've never seen such a commonplace ball in my life," a lady observed viciously, quite close to Yulia Mihailovna, obviously with the intention of being overheard. She was a stout lady of forty with rouge on her cheeks, wearing a bright-coloured silk dress. Almost everyone in the town knew her, but no one received her. She was the widow of a civil councillor, who had left her a wooden house and a small pension; but she lived well and kept horses. Two months previously she had called on Yulia Mihailovna, but the latter had not received her.

"That might have been foreseen," she added, looking insolently into Yulia Mihailovna's face.

"If you could foresee it, why did you come?" Yulia Mihailovna could not resist saying.

"Because I was too simple," the sprightly lady answered instantly, up in arms and eager for the fray; but the general intervened.

"Chère dame"—he bent over to Yulia Mihailovna—"you'd really better be going. We are only in their way and they'll enjoy themselves thoroughly without us. You've done your part, you've opened the ball, now leave them in peace. And Andrey Antonovitch doesn't seem to be feeling quite satisfactorily. . . . To avoid trouble."

But it was too late.

All through the quadrille Andrey Antonovitch gazed at the dancers with a sort of angry perplexity, and when he heard the comments of the audience he began looking about him uneasily. Then for the first time he caught sight of some of the persons who had come from the refreshment-room; there was an expression of extreme wonder in his face. Suddenly there was a loud roar of laughter at a caper that was cut in the quadrille. The editor of the "menacing periodical, not a Petersburg one", who was dancing with the cudgel in his hands, felt utterly unable to endure the spectacled gaze of "honest Russian thought", and not knowing how to escape it, suddenly in the last figure advanced to meet him standing on his head, which was meant, by the way, to typify the continual turning upside down of common sense by the menacing non-Petersburg gazette. As Lyamshin was the only one who could walk standing on his head, he had undertaken to represent the editor with the cudgel. Yulia Mihailovna had had no idea that anyone was going to walk on his head. "They concealed that from me, they concealed it," she repeated to me afterwards in despair and indignation. The laughter from the crowd was, of course, provoked not by the allegory, which interested no one, but simply by a man's walking on his head in a swallow-tail coat. Lembke flew into a rage and shook with fury.

"Rascal!" he cried, pointing to Lyamshin, "take hold of the scoundrel, turn him over . . . turn his legs . . . his head . . . so that his head's up . . . up!"

Lyamshin jumped on to his feet. The laughter grew louder.

"Turn out all the scoundrels who are laughing!" Lembke prescribed suddenly.

There was an angry roar and laughter in the crowd.

"You can't do like that, your Excellency."

"You mustn't abuse the public."

"You are a fool yourself!" a voice cried suddenly from a corner.

"Filibusters!" shouted someone from the other end of the room.

Lembke looked round quickly at the shout and turned pale. A vacant smile came on to his lips, as though he suddenly understood and remembered something.

"Gentlemen," said Yulia Mihailovna, addressing the crowd which was pressing round them, as she drew her husband away —"gentlemen, excuse Andrey Antonovitch. Andrey Antonovitch is unwell . . . excuse . . . forgive him, gentlemen."

I positively heard her say "forgive him". It all happened very quickly. But I remember for a fact that a section of the public rushed out of the hall immediately after those words of Yulia Mihailovna's as though panic-stricken. I remember one hysterical, tearful feminine shriek:

"Ach, the same thing again!"

And in the retreat of the guests, which was almost becoming a crush, another bomb exploded exactly as in the afternoon.

"Fire! All the riverside quarter is on fire!"

I don't remember where this terrible cry rose first, whether it was first raised in the hall, or whether someone ran upstairs from the entry, but it was followed by such alarm that I can't attempt to describe it. More than half the guests at the ball came from the quarter beyond the river, and were owners or occupiers of wooden houses in that district. They rushed to the windows, pulled back the curtains in a flash, and tore down the blinds. The riverside was in flames. The fire, it is true, was only beginning, but it was in flames in three separate places— and that was what was alarming.

"Arson! The Shpigulin men!" roared the crowd.

I remember some very characteristic exclamations:

"I've had a presentiment in my heart that there'd be arson, I've had a presentiment of it these last few days!"

"The Shpigulin men, the Shpigulin men, no one else!"

"We were all lured here on purpose to set fire to it!"

This last most amazing exclamation came from a woman; it was an unintentional involuntary shriek of a housewife whose goods were burning. Everyone rushed for the door. I won't describe the crush in the vestibule over sorting out cloaks, shawls, and pelisses, the shrieks of the frightened women, the weeping of the young ladies. I doubt whether there was any theft, but it was no wonder that in such disorder some went away without their wraps because they were unable to find them, and this grew into a legend with many additions, long preserved in the town. Lembke and Yulia Mihailovna were almost crushed by the crowd at the doors.

"Stop, everyone! Don't let anyone out!" yelled Lembke, stretching out his arms menacingly towards the crowding people. "Everyone without exception to be strictly searched at once!"

A storm of violent oaths rose from the crowd.

"Andrey Antonovitch! Andrey Antonovitch!" cried Yulia Mihailovna in complete despair.

"Arrest her first!" shouted her husband, pointing his finger at her threateningly. "Search her first! The ball was arranged with a view to the fire. . . ."

She screamed and fell into a swoon. (Oh, there was no doubt of its being a real one.) The general, the prince, and I rushed to her assistance; there were others, even among the ladies, who helped us at that difficult moment. We carried the unhappy woman out of this hell to her carriage, but she only regained consciousness as she reached the house, and her first utterance was about Andrey Antonovitch again. With the destruction of all her fancies, the only thing left in her mind was Andrey Antonovitch. They sent for a doctor. I remained with her for a whole hour; the prince did so too. The general, in an access of generous feeling (though he had been terribly scared), meant to remain all night "by the bedside of the unhappy lady", but within ten minutes he fell asleep in an arm-chair in the drawing-room while waiting for the doctor, and there we left him.

The chief of the police, who had hurried from the ball to the fire, had succeeded in getting Andrey Antonovitch out of the hall after us, and attempted to put him into Yulia Mihailovna's carriage, trying all he could to persuade his Excellency "to seek repose". But I don't know why he did not insist. Andrey Antonovitch, of course, would not hear of repose, and was set on going to the fire; but that was not a sufficient reason. It ended in his taking him to the fire in his droshky. He told us afterwards that Lembke was gesticulating all the way and "shouting orders that it was impossible to obey owing to their unusualness." It was officially reported later on that his Excellency had at that time been in a delirious condition "owing to a sudden fright".

There is no need to describe how the ball ended. A few dozen rowdy fellows, and with them some ladies, remained in the hall. There were no police present. They would not let the orchestra go, and beat the musicians who attempted to leave. By morning they had pulled all Prohoritch's stall to pieces, had drunk themselves senseless, danced the Kamarinsky in its unexpurgated form, made the rooms in a shocking mess, and only towards daybreak part of this hopelessly drunken rabble reached the scene of the fire to make fresh disturbances there. The other part spent the night in the rooms dead drunk, with disastrous consequences to the velvet sofas and the floor. Next morning, at the earliest possibility, they were dragged out by their legs into the street. So ended the fête for the benefit of the governesses of our province.

IV

The fire frightened the inhabitants of the riverside just because it was evidently a case of arson. It was curious that at the first cry of "fire" another cry was raised that the Shpigulin men had done it. It is now well known that three Shpigulin men really did have a share in setting fire to the town, but that was all; all the other factory hands were completely acquitted, not only officially but also by public opinion. Besides those three rascals (of whom one has been caught and confessed and the other two have so far escaped), Fedka the convict undoubtedly had a hand in the arson. That is all that is known for certain about the fire till now; but when it comes to conjectures it's a very different matter. What had led these three rascals to do it? Had they been instigated by anyone? It is very difficult to answer all these questions even now.

Owing to the strong wind, the fact that the houses at the riverside were almost all wooden, and that they had been set fire to in three places, the fire spread quickly and enveloped the whole quarter with extraordinary rapidity. (The fire burnt, however, only at two ends; at the third spot it was extinguished almost as soon as it began to burn—of which later.) But the Petersburg and Moscow papers exaggerated our calamity. Not more than a quarter, roughly speaking, of the riverside district was burnt down; possibly less indeed. Our fire brigade, though it was hardly adequate to the size and population of the town, worked with great promptitude and devotion. But it would not have been of much avail, even with the zealous co-operation of the inhabitants, if the wind had not suddenly dropped towards morning. When an hour after our flight from the ball I made my way to the riverside, the fire was at its height. A whole street parallel with the river was in flames. It was as light as day. I won't describe the fire; everyone in Russia knows what it looks like. The bustle and crush was immense in the lanes adjoining the burning street. The inhabitants, fully expecting the fire to reach their houses, were hauling out their belongings, but had not yet left their dwellings, and were waiting meanwhile sitting on their boxes and feather beds under their windows. Part of the male population were hard at work ruthlessly chopping down fences and even whole huts which were near the fire and on the windward side. None were crying except the children, who had been waked out of their sleep, though the women who had dragged out their chattels were lamenting in sing-song voices. Those who had not finished their task were still silent, busily carrying out their goods. Sparks and embers were carried a long way in all directions. People put them out as best they could. Some helped to put the fire out while others stood about, admiring it. A great fire at night always has a thrilling and exhilarating effect. This is what explains the attraction of fireworks. But in that case the artistic regularity with which the fire is presented and the complete lack of danger give an impression of lightness and playfulness like the effect of a glass of champagne. A real conflagration is a very different matter. Then the horror and a certain sense of personal danger, together with the exhilarating effect of a fire at night, produce on the spectator (though of course not in the householder whose goods are being burnt) a certain concussion of the brain and, as it were, a challenge to those destructive instincts which, alas, lie hidden in every heart, even that of the mildest and most domestic little clerk. . . . This sinister sensation is almost always fascinating. "I really don't know whether one can look at a fire without a certain pleasure." This is word for word what Stepan Trofimovitch said to me one night on returning home after he had happened to witness a fire and was still under the influence of the spectacle. Of course, the very man who enjoys the spectacle will rush into the fire himself to save a child or an old woman; but that is altogether a different matter.

Following in the wake of the crowd of sightseers, I succeeded, without asking questions, in reaching the chief centre of danger, where at last I saw Lembke, whom I was seeking at Yulia Mihailovna's request. His position was strange and extraordinary. He was standing on the ruins of a fence. Thirty paces to the left of him rose the black skeleton of a two-storeyed house which had almost burnt out. It had holes instead of windows at each storey, its roof had fallen in, and the flames were still here and there creeping among the charred beams. At the farther end of the courtyard, twenty paces away, the lodge, also a two-storeyed building, was beginning to burn, and the firemen were doing their utmost to save it. On the right, the firemen and the people were trying to save a rather large wooden building which was not actually burning, though it had caught fire several times and was inevitably bound to be burnt in the end. Lembke stood facing the lodge, shouting and gesticulating. He was giving orders which no one attempted to carry out. It seemed to me that everyone had given him up as hopeless and left him. Anyway, though everyone in the vast crowd of all classes, among whom there were gentlemen, and even the cathedral priest, was listening to him with curiosity and wonder, no one spoke to him or tried to get him away. Lembke, with a pale face and glittering eyes, was uttering the most amazing things. To complete the picture, he had lost his hat and was bareheaded.

"It's all incendiarism! It's nihilism! If anything is burning, it's nihilism!" I heard almost with horror; and though there was nothing to be surprised at, yet actual madness, when one sees it, always gives one a shock.

"Your Excellency," said a policeman, coming up to him, "what if you were to try the repose of home? . . . It's dangerous for your Excellency even to stand here."

This policeman, as I heard afterwards, had been told off by the chief of police to watch over Andrey Antonovitch, to do his utmost to get him home, and in case of danger even to use force—a task evidently beyond the man's power.

"They will wipe away the tears of the people whose houses have been burnt, but they will burn down the town. It's all the work of four scoundrels, four and a half! Arrest the scoundrel! He worms himself into the honour of families. They made use of the governesses to burn down the houses. It's vile, vile! Aie, what's he about?" he shouted, suddenly noticing a fireman at the top of the burning lodge, under whom the roof had almost burnt away and round whom the flames were beginning to flare up. "Pull him down! Pull him down! He will fall, he will catch fire, put him out! . . . What is he doing there?"

"He is putting the fire out, your Excellency."

"Not likely. The fire is in the minds of men and not in the roofs of houses. Pull him down and give it up! Better give it up, much better! Let it put itself out. Aie, who is crying now? An old woman! It's an old woman shouting. Why have they forgotten the old woman?"

There actually was an old woman crying on the ground floor of the burning lodge. She was an old creature of eighty, a relation of the shopkeeper who owned the house. But she had not been forgotten; she had gone back to the burning house while it was still possible, with the insane idea of rescuing her feather bed from a corner room which was still untouched. Choking with the smoke and screaming with the heat, for the room was on fire by the time she reached it, she was still trying with her decrepit hands to squeeze her feather bed through a broken window-pane. Lembke rushed to her assistance. Everyone saw him run up to the window, catch hold of one corner of the feather bed and try with all his might to pull it out. As ill luck would have it, a board fell at that moment from the roof and hit the unhappy governor. It did not kill him, it merely grazed him on the neck as it fell, but Andrey Antonovitch's career was over, among us at least; the blow knocked him off his feet and he sank on the ground unconscious.

The day dawned at last, gloomy and sullen. The fire was abating; the wind was followed by a sudden calm, and then a fine drizzling rain fell. I was by that time in another part, some distance from where Lembke had fallen, and here I overheard very strange conversations in the crowd. A strange fact had come to light. On the very outskirts of the quarter, on a piece of waste land beyond the kitchen gardens, not less than fifty paces from any other buildings, there stood a little wooden house which had only lately been built, and this solitary house had been on fire at the very beginning, almost before any other. Even had it burnt down, it was so far from other houses that no other building in the town could have caught fire from it, and, *vice versa*, if the whole riverside had been burnt to the ground, that house might have remained intact, whatever the wind had been. It followed that it had caught fire separately and independently and therefore not accidentally. But the chief point was that it was not burnt to the ground, and at daybreak strange things were discovered within it. The owner of this new house, who lived in the neighbourhood, rushed up as soon as he saw it in flames and with the help of his neighbours pulled apart a pile of faggots which had been heaped up by the side wall and set fire to. In this way he saved the house. But there were lodgers in the house—the captain, who was well known in the town, his sister, and their elderly servant, and these three persons—the captain, his sister, and their servant—had been murdered and apparently robbed in the night. (It was here that the chief of police had gone while Lembke was rescuing the feather bed.)

By morning the news had spread and an immense crowd of all classes, even the riverside people who had been burnt out, had flocked to the waste land where the new house stood. It was difficult to get there, so dense was the crowd. I was told at once that the captain had been found lying dressed on the bench with his throat cut, and that he must have been dead drunk when he was killed, so that he had felt nothing, and he had "bled like a bull"; that his sister Marya Timofyevna had been "stabbed all over" with a knife and she was lying on the floor in the doorway, so that probably she had been awake and had fought and struggled with the murderer. The servant, who had also probably been awake, had her skull broken. The owner of the house said that the captain had come to see him the morning before, and that in his drunken bragging he had shown him a lot of money, as much as two hundred roubles. The captain's shabby old green pocket-book was found empty on the floor, but Marya Timofyevna's box had not been touched, and the silver setting of the ikon had not been removed either; the captain's clothes, too, had not been disturbed. It was evident that the thief had been in a hurry and was a man familiar with the captain's circumstances, who had come only for money and knew where it was kept. If the owner of the house had not run up at that moment the burning faggot stack would certainly have set fire to the house and "it would have been difficult to find out from the charred corpses how they had died."

So the story was told. One other fact was added: that the person who had taken this house for the Lebyadkins was no other than Mr. Stavrogin, Nikolay Vsyevolodovitch, the son of Varvara Petrovna. He had come himself to take it and had had much ado to persuade the owner to let it, as the latter had

intended to use it as a tavern; but Nikolay Vsyevolodovitch was
ready to give any rent he asked and had paid for six months in
advance.

"The fire wasn't an accident," I heard said in the crowd.

But the majority said nothing. People's faces were sullen,
but I did not see signs of much indignation. People persisted,
however, in gossiping about Stavrogin, saying that the murdered
woman was his wife; that on the previous day he had "dis-
honourably" abducted a young lady belonging to the best
family in the place, the daughter of Madame Drozdov, and that
a complaint was to be lodged against him in Petersburg; and
that his wife had been murdered evidently that he might marry
the young lady. Skvoreshniki was not more than a mile and a
half away, and I remember I wondered whether I should not
let them know the position of affairs. I did not notice, however,
that there was anyone egging the crowd on and I don't want
to accuse people falsely, though I did see and recognised at
once in the crowd at the fire two or three of the rowdy lot I
had seen in the refreshment-room. I particularly remember one
thin, tall fellow, a cabinet-maker, as I found out later, with an
emaciated face and a curly head, black as though grimed with
soot. He was not drunk, but in contrast to the gloomy passivity
of the crowd seemed beside himself with excitement. He kept
addressing the people, though I don't remember his words;
nothing coherent that he said was longer than "I say, lads,
what do you say to this? Are things to go on like this?" and
so saying he waved his arms.

CHAPTER III

A ROMANCE ENDED

I

FROM the large ballroom of Skvoreshniki (the room in
which the last interview with Varvara Petrovna and Stepan
Trofimovitch had taken place) the fire could be plainly seen.
At daybreak, soon after five in the morning, Liza was standing
at the farthest window on the right looking intently at the fading
glow. She was alone in the room. She was wearing the dress
she had worn the day before at the matinée—a very smart light

green dress covered with lace, but crushed and put on carelessly and with haste. Suddenly noticing that some of the hooks were undone in front she flushed, hurriedly set it right, snatched up from a chair the red shawl she had flung down when she came in the day before, and put it round her neck. Some locks of her luxuriant hair had come loose and showed below the shawl on her right shoulder. Her face looked weary and care-worn, but her eyes glowed under her frowning brows. She went up to the window again and pressed her burning forehead against the cold pane. The door opened and Nikolay Vsyevolodovitch came in.

"I've sent a messenger on horseback," he said. "In ten minutes we shall hear all about it, meantime the servants say that part of the riverside quarter has been burnt down, on the right side of the bridge near the quay. It's been burning since eleven o'clock; now the fire is going down."

He did not go near the window, but stood three steps behind her; she did not turn towards him.

"It ought to have been light an hour ago by the calendar, and it's still almost night," she said irritably.

" 'Calendars always tell lies,' " he observed with a polite smile, but, a little ashamed, he made haste to add: "It's dull to live by the calendar, Liza."

And he relapsed into silence, vexed at the ineptitude of the second sentence. Liza gave a wry smile.

"You are in such a melancholy mood that you cannot even find words to speak to me. But you need not trouble, there's a point in what you said. I always live by the calendar. Every step I take is regulated by the calendar. Does that surprise you?"

She turned quickly from the window and sat down in a low chair.

"You sit down, too, please. We haven't long to be together and I want to say anything I like. . . . Why shouldn't you, too, say anything you like?"

Nikolay Vsyevolodovitch sat beside her and softly, almost timidly, took her hand.

"What's the meaning of this tone, Liza? Where has it suddenly sprung from? What do you mean by 'we haven't long to be together'? That's the second mysterious phrase since you waked, half an hour ago."

"You are beginning to reckon up my mysterious phrases?" she laughed. "Do you remember I told you I was a dead woman when I came in yesterday? That you thought fit to forget. To forget or not to notice.''

"I don't remember, Liza. Why dead? You must live."

"And is that all? You've quite lost your flow of words. I've lived my hour and that's enough. Do you remember Christopher Ivanovitch?''

"No, I don't," he answered, frowning.

"Christopher Ivanovitch at Lausanne? He bored you dreadfully. He always used to open the door and say: 'I've come for one minute,' and then stay the whole day. I don't want to be like Christopher Ivanovitch and stay the whole day.''

A look of pain came into his face.

"Liza, it grieves me, this unnatural language. This affectation must hurt you, too. What's it for? What's the object of it?''

His eyes glowed.

"Liza," he cried, "I swear I love you now more than yesterday when you came to me!''

"What a strange declaration! Why bring in yesterday and to-day and these comparisons?''

"You won't leave me," he went on, almost with despair; "we will go away together, to-day, won't we? Won't we?''

"Aie, don't squeeze my hand so painfully! Where could we go together to-day? To 'rise again' somewhere? No, we've made experiments enough . . . and it's too slow for me; and I am not fit for it; it's too exalted for me. If we are to go, let it be to Moscow, to pay visits and entertain—that's my ideal, you know; even in Switzerland I didn't disguise from you what I was like. As we can't go to Moscow and pay visits since you are married, it's no use talking of that.''

"Liza! What happened yesterday?''

"What happened is over!''

"That's impossible! That's cruel!''

"What if it is cruel? You must bear it if it is cruel.''

"You are avenging yourself on me for yesterday's caprice, he muttered with an angry smile. Liza flushed.

"What a mean thought!''

"Why then did you bestow on me . . . so great a happiness? Have I the right to know?''

"No, you must manage without rights; don't aggravate the meanness of your supposition by stupidity. You are not lucky to-day. By the way, you surely can't be afraid of public opinion and that you will be blamed for this 'great happiness'?

162

If that's it, for God's sake don't alarm yourself. It's not your doing at all and you are not responsible to anyone. When I opened your door yesterday, you didn't even know who was coming in. It was simply my caprice, as you expressed it just now, and nothing more! You can look everyone in the face boldly and triumphantly!"

"Your words, that laugh, have been making me feel cold with horror for the last hour. That 'happiness' of which you speak frantically is worth . . . everything to me. How can I lose you now? I swear I loved you less yesterday. Why are you taking everything from me to-day? Do you know what it has cost me, this new hope? I've paid for it with life."

"Your own life or another's?"

He got up quickly.

"What does that mean?" he brought out, looking at her steadily.

"Have you paid for it with your life or with mine? is what I mean. Or have you lost all power of understanding?" cried Liza, flushing. "Why did you start up so suddenly? Why do you stare at me with such a look? You frighten me! What is it you are afraid of all the time? I noticed some time ago that you were afraid and you are now, this very minute . . . Good heavens, how pale you are!"

"If you know anything, Liza, I swear I don't . . . and I wasn't talking of *that* just now when I said that I had paid for it with life. . . ."

"I don't understand you," she brought out, faltering apprehensively.

At last a slow brooding smile came on to his lips. He slowly sat down, put his elbows on his knees, and covered his face with his hands.

"A bad dream and delirium. . . . We were talking of two different things."

"I don't know what you were talking about. . . . Do you mean to say you did not know yesterday that I should leave you to-day, did you know or not? Don't tell a lie, did you or not?"

"I did," he said softly.

"Well then, what would you have? You knew and yet you accepted 'that moment' for yourself. Aren't we quits?"

"Tell me the whole truth," he cried in intense distress. "When you opened my door yesterday, did you know your-self that it was only for one hour?"

163

She looked at him with hatred.

"Really, the most sensible person can ask most amazing questions. And why are you so uneasy? Can it be vanity that a woman should leave you first instead of your leaving her? Do you know, Nikolay Vsyevolodovitch, since I've been with you I've discovered that you are very generous to me, and it's just that I can't endure from you."

He got up from his seat and took a few steps about the room.

"Very well, perhaps it was bound to end so. . . . But how can it all have happened?"

"That's a question to worry about! Especially as you know the answer yourself perfectly well, and understand it better than anyone on earth, and were counting on it yourself. I am a young lady, my heart has been trained on the opera, that's how it all began, that's the solution."

"No."

"There is nothing in it to fret your vanity. It is all the absolute truth. It began with a fine moment which was too much for me to bear. The day before yesterday, when I 'insulted' you before everyone and you answered me so chivalrously, I went home and guessed at once that you were running away from me because you were married, and not from contempt for me which, as a fashionable young lady, I dreaded more than anything. I understood that it was for my sake, for me, mad as I was, that you ran away. You see how I appreciate your generosity. Then Pyotr Stepanovitch skipped up to me and explained it all to me at once. He revealed to me that you were dominated by a 'great idea', before which he and I were as nothing, but yet that I was a stumbling-block in your path. He brought himself in, he insisted that we three should work together, and said the most fantastic things about a boat and about maple-wood oars out of some Russian song. I complimented him and told him he was a poet, which he swallowed as the real thing. And as apart from him I had known long before that I had not the strength to do anything for long, I made up my mind on the spot. Well, that's all and quite enough, and please let us have no more explanations. We might quarrel. Don't be afraid of anyone, I take it all on myself. I am horrid and capricious, I was fascinated by that operatic boat, I am a young lady . . . but you know I did think that you were dreadfully in love with me. Don't despise the poor fool, and don't laugh at the tear that dropped just now. I am awfully given to crying with self-pity. Come, that's enough, that's enough. I am no good for anything and you are no good for anything; it's as bad for both of us, so let's comfort ourselves with that. Anyway, it eases our vanity."

"Dream and delirium," cried Stavrogin, wringing his hands, and pacing about the room. "Liza, poor child, what have you done to yourself?"

"I've burnt myself in a candle, nothing more. Surely you are not crying, too? You should show less feeling and better breeding. . . ."

"Why, why did you come to me?"

"Don't you understand what a ludicrous position you put yourself in in the eyes of the world by asking such questions?"

"Why have you ruined yourself, so grotesquely and so stupidly, and what's to be done now?"

"And this is Stavrogin, 'the vampire Stavrogin', as you are called by a lady here who is in love with you! Listen! I have told you already, I've put all my life into one hour and I am at peace. Do the same with yours . . . though you've no need to: you have plenty of 'hours' and 'moments' of all sorts before you."

"As many as you; I give you my solemn word, not one hour more than you!"

He was still walking up and down and did not see the rapid penetrating glance she turned upon him, in which there seemed a dawning hope. But the light died away at the same moment.

"If you knew what it costs me that I can't be sincere at this moment, Liza, if I could only tell you . . ."

"Tell me? You want to tell me something, to me? God save me from your secrets!" she broke in almost in terror.

He stopped and waited uneasily.

"I ought to confess that ever since those days in Switzerland I have had a strong feeling that you have something awful, loathsome, some bloodshed on your conscience . . . and yet something that would make you look very ridiculous. Beware of telling me, if it's true: I shall laugh you to scorn. I shall laugh at you for the rest of your life. . . . Aie, you are turning pale again? I won't, I won't, I'll go at once." She jumped up from her chair with a movement of disgust and contempt.

"Torture me, punish me, vent your spite on me," he cried in despair. "You have the full right. I knew I did not love you and yet I ruined you! Yes, I accepted the moment for my own; I had a hope . . . I've had it a long time . . . my last hope. . . . I could not resist the radiance that flooded my heart when you came in to me yesterday, of yourself, alone, of your own accord. I suddenly believed. . . . Perhaps I have faith in it still."

"I will repay such noble frankness by being as frank. I don't want to be a Sister of Mercy for you. Perhaps I really may become a nurse unless I happen appropriately to die to-day; but if I do I won't be your nurse, though, of course, you need one as much as any crippled creature. I always fancied that you would take me to some place where there was a huge wicked spider, big as a man, and we should spend our lives looking at it and being afraid of it. That's how our love would spend itself. Appeal to Dashenka; she will go with you anywhere you like."

"Can't you help thinking of her even now?"

"Poor little spaniel! Give her my greetings. Does she know that even in Switzerland you had fixed on her for your old age? What prudence! What foresight! Aie, who's that?"

At the farther end of the room a door opened a crack; a head was thrust in and vanished again hurriedly.

"Is that you, Alexey Yegorytch?" asked Stavrogin.

"No, it's only I." Pyotr Stepanovitch thrust himself half in again. "How do you do, Lizaveta Nikolaevna? Good morning, anyway. I guessed I should find you both in this room. I have come for one moment literally, Nikolay Vsyevolodovitch. I was anxious to have a couple of words with you at all costs . . . absolutely necessary . . . only a few words!"

Stavrogin moved towards him but turned back to Liza at the third step.

"If you hear anything directly, Liza, let me tell you I am to blame for it!"

She started and looked at him in dismay; but he hurriedly went out.

II

The room from which Pyotr Stepanovitch had peeped in was a large oval vestibule. Alexey Yegorytch had been sitting there before Pyotr Stepanovitch came in, but the latter sent him away. Stavrogin closed the door after him and stood expectant. Pyotr Stepanovitch looked rapidly and searchingly at him.

"Well?"

"If you know already," said Pyotr Stepanovitch hurriedly,

his eyes looking as though they would dive into Stavrogin's soul, "then, of course, we are none of us to blame, above all not you, for it's such a concatenation . . . such a coincidence of events . . . in brief, you can't be legally implicated and I've rushed here to tell you beforehand."

"Have they been burnt? murdered?"

"Murdered but not burnt, that's the trouble, but I give you my word of honour that it's not been my fault, however much you may suspect me, eh? Do you want the whole truth: you see the idea really did cross my mind—you hinted it yourself, not seriously, but teasing me (for, of course, you would not hint it seriously), but I couldn't bring myself to it, and wouldn't bring myself to it for anything, not for a hundred roubles—and what was there to be gained by it, I mean for me, for me. . . ." (He was in desperate haste and his talk was like the clacking of a rattle.) "But what a coincidence of circumstances: I gave that drunken fool Lebyadkin two hundred and thirty roubles of my own money (do you hear, my own money, there wasn't a rouble of yours and, what's more, you know it your-self, the day before yesterday, in the evening—do you hear, not yesterday after the matinée, but the day before yesterday, make a note of it: it's a very important coincidence, for I did not know for certain at that time whether Lizaveta Nikolaevna would come to you or not; I gave my own money simply because you distinguished yourself by taking it into your head to betray your secret to everyone. Well, I won't go into that . . . that's your affair . . . your chivalry . . . but I must own I was amazed, it was a knock-down blow. And forasmuch as I was exceeding weary of these tragic stories—and let me tell you, I talk seriously though I do use Biblical language—as it was all upsetting my plans in fact, I made up my mind at any cost, and without your knowledge, to pack the Lebyadkins off to Petersburg, especially as he was set on going himself. I made one mistake: I gave the money in your name; was it a mistake or not? Perhaps it wasn't a mistake, eh? Listen now, listen how it has all turned out. . . ."

In the heat of his talk he went close up to Stavrogin and took hold of the revers of his coat (really, it may have been on pur-pose). With a violent movement Stavrogin struck him on the arm.

"Come, what is it . . . give over . . . you'll break my arm . . . what matters is the way things have turned out," he rattled on, not in the least surprised at the blow. "I forked out the money in the evening on condition that his sister and he should set off early next morning; I trusted that rascal Liputin with the job of getting them into the train and seeing them off. But that beast Liputin wanted to play his schoolboy pranks on the public—perhaps you heard? At the matinée? Listen, listen: they both got drunk, made up verses of which half are Liputin's; he rigged Lebyadkin out in a dress-coat, assuring me meanwhile that he had packed him off that morning, but he kept him shut somewhere in a back room, till he thrust him on the platform at the matinée. But Lebyadkin got drunk quickly and unexpectedly. Then came the scandalous scene you know of, and then they got him home more dead than alive, and Liputin filched away the two hundred roubles, leaving him only small change. But it appears unluckily that already that morning Lebyadkin had taken that two hundred roubles out of his pocket, boasted of it and shown it in undesirable quarters. And as that was just what Fedka was expecting, and as he had heard something at Kirillov's (do you remember, your hint?) he made up his mind to take advantage of it. That's the whole truth. I am glad, anyway, that Fedka did not find the money, the rascal was reckoning on a thousand, you know! He was in a hurry and seems to have been frightened by the fire himself. . . . Would you believe it, that fire came as a thunderbolt for me. Devil only knows what to make of it! It is taking things into their own hands. . . . You see, as I expect so much of you I will hide nothing from you: I've long been hatching this idea of a fire because it suits the national and popular taste; but I was keeping it for a critical moment, for that precious time when we should all rise up and . . . And they suddenly took it into their heads to do it, on their own initiative, without orders, now at the very moment when we ought to be lying low and keeping quiet! Such presumption! . . . The fact is, I've not got to the bottom of it yet, they talk about two Shpigulin men . . . but if there are any of *our* fellows in it, if any one of them has had a hand in it—so much the worse for him! You see what comes of letting people get ever so little out of hand! No, this democratic rabble, with its quintets, is a poor foundation; what we want is one magnificent, despotic will, like an idol, resting on something fundamental and external. . . . Then the quintets will cringe into obedience and be obsequiously ready on occasion. But, anyway, though, they are all crying out now that Stavrogin wanted his wife to be burnt and that that's what caused the fire in the town, but . . ."

"Why, are they all saying that?"

"Well, not yet, and I must confess I have heard nothing of the sort, but what one can do with people, especially when they've been burnt out! *Vox populi, vox Dei*. A stupid rumour is soon set going. But you really have nothing to be afraid of. From the legal point of view you are all right, and with your conscience also. For you didn't want it done, did you? There's no clue, nothing but the coincidence. . . . The only thing is Fedka may remember what you said that night at Kirillov's (and what made you say it?), but that proves nothing and we shall stop Fedka's mouth. I shall stop it to-day. . . ."

"And weren't the bodies burnt at all?"

"Not a bit; that ruffian could not manage anything properly. But I am glad, anyway, that you are so calm . . . for though you are not in any way to blame, even in thought, but all the same. . . . And you must admit that all this settles your difficulties capitally: you are suddenly free and a widower and can marry a charming girl this minute with a lot of money, who is already yours, into the bargain. See what can be done by crude, simple coincidence—eh?"

"Are you threatening me, you fool?"

"Come, leave off, leave off! Here you are, calling me a fool, and what a tone to use! You ought to be glad, yet you . . . I rushed here on purpose to let you know in good time. . . . Besides, how could I threaten you? As if I cared for what I could get by threats! I want you to help from goodwill and not from fear. You are the light and the sun. . . . It's I who am terribly afraid of you, not you of me! I am not Mavriky Nikolaevitch. . . . And only fancy, as I flew here in a racing droshky I saw Mavriky Nikolaevitch by the fence at the farthest corner of your garden . . . in his greatcoat, drenched through, he must have been sitting there all night! Queer goings on! How mad people can be!"

"Mavriky Nikolaevitch? Is that true?"

"Yes, yes. He is sitting by the garden fence. About three hundred paces from here, I think. I made haste to pass him, but he saw me. Didn't you know? In that case I am glad I didn't forget to tell you. A man like that is more dangerous than anyone if he happens to have a revolver about him, and then the night, the sleet, or natural irritability—for after all he is in a nice position, ha ha! What do you think? Why is he sitting there?"

"He is waiting for Lizaveta Nikolaevna, of course."

"Well! Why should she go out to him? And . . . in such rain too . . . what a fool!"

"She is just going out to him!"

"Eh! That's a piece of news! So then . . . But listen, her position is completely changed now. What does she want with Mavriky now? You are free, a widower, and can marry her to-morrow! She doesn't know yet—leave it to me and I'll arrange it all for you. Where is she? We must relieve her mind too."

"Relieve her mind?"

"Rather! Let's go."

"And do you suppose she won't guess what those dead bodies mean?" said Stavrogin, screwing up his eyes in a peculiar way.

"Of course she won't," said Pyotr Stepanovitch with all the confidence of a perfect simpleton, "for legally . . . Ech, what a man you are! What if she did guess?. Women are so clever at shutting their eyes to such things, you don't understand women! Apart from its being altogether to her interest to marry you now, because there's no denying she's disgraced herself; apart from that, I talked to her of 'the boat' and I saw that one could affect her by it, so that shows you what the girl is made of. Don't be uneasy, she will step over those dead bodies without turning a hair—especially as you are not to blame for them; not in the least, are you? She will only keep them in reserve to use them against you when you've been married two or three years. Every woman saves up something of the sort out of her husband's past when she gets married, but by that time . . . what may not happen in a year? Ha ha!"

"If you've come in a racing droshky, take her to Mavriky Nikolaevitch now. She said just now that she could not endure me and would leave me, and she certainly will not accept my carriage."

"What! Can she really be leaving? How can this have come about?" said Pyotr Stepanovitch, staring stupidly at him.

"She's guessed somehow during this night that I don't love her . . . which she knew all along, indeed."

"But don't you love her?" said Pyotr Stepanovitch, with an expression of extreme surprise. "If so, why did you keep her when she came to you yesterday, instead of telling her plainly like an honourable man that you didn't care for her? That was horribly shabby on your part; and how mean you make me look in her eyes!"

Stavrogin suddenly laughed.

170

"I am laughing at my monkey," he explained at once.

"Ah! You saw that I was putting it on!" cried Pyotr Stepanovitch, laughing too, with great enjoyment. "I did it to amuse you! Only fancy, as soon as you came out to me I guessed from your face that you'd been 'unlucky'. A complete fiasco, perhaps. Eh? There! I'll bet anything," he cried, almost gasping with delight, "that you've been sitting side by side in the drawing-room all night wasting your precious time discussing something lofty and elevated . . . There, forgive me, forgive me; it's not my business. I felt sure yesterday that it would all end in foolishness. I brought her to you simply to amuse you, and to show you that you wouldn't have a dull time with me. I shall be of use to you a hundred times in that way. I always like pleasing people. If you don't want her now, which was what I was reckoning on when I came, then . . ."

"So you brought her simply for my amusement?"

"Why, what else?"

"Not to make me kill my wife?"

"Come. You've not killed her? What a tragic fellow you are!"

"It's just the same; you killed her."

"I didn't kill her! I tell you I had no hand in it. . . . You are beginning to make me uneasy, though. . . ."

"Go on. You said, 'If you don't want her now, then . . .'"

"Then, leave it to me, of course. I can quite easily marry her off to Mavriky Nikolaevitch, though I didn't make him sit down by the fence. Don't take that notion into your head. I am afraid of him, now. You talk about my droshky, but I simply dashed by. . . . What if he has a revolver? It's a good thing I brought mine. Here it is." He brought a revolver out of his pocket, showed it, and hid it again at once. "I took it as I was coming such a long way. . . . But I'll arrange all that for you in a twinkling: her little heart is aching at this moment for Mavriky; it should be, anyway. . . . And, do you know, I am really rather sorry for her? If I take her to Mavriky she will begin about you directly; she will praise you to him and abuse him to his face. You know the heart of woman! There you are, laughing again! I am awfully glad that you are so cheerful now. Come, let's go. I'll begin with Mavriky right away, and about them . . . those who've been murdered . . . hadn't we better keep quiet now? She'll hear later on, anyway."

"What will she hear? Who's been murdered? What were

THE POSSESSED

you saying about Mavriky Nikolaevitch?'' said Liza, suddenly
opening the door.

"Ah! You've been listening?''

"What were you saying just now about Mavriky Nikolaevitch? Has he been murdered?''

"Ah! Then you didn't hear? Don't distress yourself,
Mavriky Nikolaevitch is alive and well, and you can satisfy
yourself of it in an instant, for he is here by the wayside, by
the garden fence . . . and I believe he's been sitting there all
night. He is drenched through in his greatcoat! He saw me as
I drove past.''

"That's not true. You said 'murdered'. . . . Who's been
murdered?'' she insisted with agonising mistrust.

"The only people who have been murdered are my wife, her
brother Lebyadkin, and their servant,'' Stavrogin brought out
firmly.

Liza trembled and turned terribly pale.

"A strange brutal outrage, Livazeta Nikolaevna. A stupid
case of robbery,'' Pyotr Stepanovitch rattled off at once.
"Simply robbery, under cover of the fire. The crime was committed by Fedka the convict, and it was all that fool Lebyadkin's fault for showing everyone his money. . . . I rushed here
with the news . . . it fell on me like a thunderbolt. Stavrogin
could hardly stand when I told him. We were deliberating here
whether to tell you at once or not?''

"Nikolay Vsyevolodovitch, is he telling the truth?'' Liza
articulated faintly.

"No; it's false.''

"False!'' said Pyotr Stepanovitch, starting. "What do you
mean by that?''

"Heavens! I shall go mad!'' cried Liza.

"Do you understand, anyway, that he is mad now!'' Pyotr
Stepanovitch cried at the top of his voice. "After all, his wife
has just been murdered. You see how white he is. . . . Why,
he has been with you the whole night. He hasn't left your side
a minute. How can you suspect him?''

"Nikolay Vsyevolodovitch, tell me, as before God, are you
guilty or not, and I swear I'll believe your word as though it
were God's, and I'll follow you to the end of the earth. Yes, I
will. I'll follow you like a dog.''

"Why are you tormenting her, you fantastic creature?'' cried
Pyotr Stepanovitch in exasperation. "Lizaveta Nikolaevna,
upon my oath, you can crush me into powder, but he is not

172

guilty. On the contrary, it has crushed him, and he is raving, you see that. He is not to blame in any way, not in any way, not even in thought! . . . It's all the work of robbers who will probably be found within a week and flogged. . . . It's all the work of Fedka the convict, and some Shpigulin men, all the town is agog with it. That's why I say so too."

"Is that right? Is that right?" Liza waited trembling for her final sentence.

"I did not kill them, and I was against it, but I knew they were going to be killed and I did not stop the murderers. Leave me, Liza," Stavrogin brought out, and he walked into the drawing-room.

Liza hid her face in her hands and walked out of the house. Pyotr Stepanovitch was rushing after her, but at once hurried back and went into the drawing-room.

"So that's your line? That's your line? So there's nothing you are afraid of?" He flew at Stavrogin in an absolute fury, muttering incoherently, scarcely able to find words and foaming at the mouth.

Stavrogin stood in the middle of the room and did not answer a word. He clutched a lock of his hair in his left hand and smiled helplessly. Pyotr Stepanovitch pulled him violently by the sleeve.

"Is it all over with you? So that's the line you are taking? You'll inform against all of us, and go to a monastery yourself, or to the devil. . . . But I'll do for you, though you are not afraid of me!"

"Ah! That's you chattering!" said Stavrogin, noticing him at last. "Run," he said, coming to himself suddenly, "run after her, order her carriage, don't leave her. . . . Run, run! Take her home so that no one may know . . and that she mayn't go there . . . to the bodies . . . to the bodies. . . . Force her to get into the carriage . . . Alexey Yegorytch! Alexey Yegorytch!"

"Stay, don't shout! By now she is in Mavriky's arms. . . . Mavriky won't put her into your carriage. . . . Stay! There's something more important than the carriage!"

He seized his revolver again. Stavrogin looked at him gravely.

"Very well, kill me," he said softly, almost conciliatorily.

"Foo. Damn it! What a maze of false sentiment a man can get into!" said Pyotr Stepanovitch, shaking with rage. "Yes, really, you ought to be killed! She ought simply to spit at you! Fine sort of 'magic boat', you are; you are a broken-down, leaky old hulk! . . . You ought to pull yourself together, if only from spite! Ech! Why, what difference would it make to you since you ask for a bullet through your brains yourself?''

Stavrogin smiled strangely.

"If you were not such a buffoon I might perhaps have said yes now. . . . If you had only a grain of sense . . .''

"I am a buffoon, but I don't want you, my better half, to be one! Do you understand me?''

Stavrogin did understand, though perhaps no one else did. Shatov, for instance, was astonished when Stavrogin told him that Pyotr Stepanovitch had enthusiasm.

"Go to the devil now, and to-morrow perhaps I may wring something out of myself. Come to-morrow.''

"Yes? Yes?''

"How can I tell! . . . Go to hell. Go to hell.'' And he walked out of the room.

"Perhaps, after all, it may be for the best,'' Pyotr Stepano-vitch muttered to himself as he hid the revolver.

III

He rushed off to overtake Lizaveta Nikolaevna. She had not got far away, only a few steps, from the house. She had been detained by Alexey Yegorytch, who was following a step behind her, in a tail-coat, and without a hat; his head was bowed respectfully. He was persistently entreating her to wait for a carriage; the old man was alarmed and almost in tears.

"Go along. Your master is asking for tea, and there's no one to give it to him,'' said Pyotr Stepanovitch, pushing him away. He took Liza's arm.

She did not pull her arm away, but she seemed hardly to know what she was doing; she was still dazed.

"To begin with, you are going the wrong way,'' babbled Pyotr Stepanovitch. "We ought to go this way, and not by the garden, and, secondly, walking is impossible in any case. It's over two miles, and you are not properly dressed. If you would wait a second, I came in a droshky; the horse is in the yard. I'll get it instantly, put you in, and get you home so that no one sees you.''

"How kind you are,'' said Liza graciously.

"Oh, not at all. Any humane man in my position would do the same. . . .''

174

Liza looked at him, and was surprised.

"Good heavens! Why, I thought it was that old man here still."

"Listen. I am awfully glad that you take it like this, because it's all such a frightfully stupid convention, and since it's come to that, hadn't I better tell the old man to get the carriage at once? It's only a matter of ten minutes and we'll turn back and wait in the porch, eh?"

"I want first . . . where are those murdered people?"

"Ah! What next? That was what I was afraid of. . . . No, we'd better leave those wretched creatures alone; it's no use your looking at them."

"I know where they are. I know that house."

"Well? What if you do know it? Come: it's raining, and there's a fog. (A nice job this sacred duty I've taken upon myself.) Listen, Lizaveta Nikolaevna; It's one of two alternatives. Either you come with me in the droshky—in that case wait here, and don't take another step, for if we go another twenty steps we must be seen by Mavriky Nikolaevitch."

"Mavriky Nikolaevitch! Where? Where?"

"Well, if you want to go with him, I'll take you a little farther, if you like, and show you where he sits, but I don't care to go up to him just now. No, thank you."

"He is waiting for me. Good God!" she suddenly stopped, and a flush of colour flooded her face.

"Oh! Come now. If he is an unconventional man! You know, Lizaveta Nikolaevna, it's none of my business. I am a complete outsider, and you know that yourself. But, still, I wish you well. . . . If your 'fairy boat' has failed you, if it has turned out to be nothing more than a rotten old hulk, only fit to be chopped up . . ."

"Ah! That's fine, that's lovely," cried Liza.

"Lovely, and yet your tears are falling. You must have spirit. You must be as good as a man in every way. In our age, when woman . . . Foo, hang it," Pyotr Stepanovitch was on the point of spitting. "And the chief point is that there is nothing to regret. It may all turn out for the best. Mavriky Nikolaevitch is a man. . . . In fact, he is a man of feeling though not talkative, but that's a good thing, too, as long as he has no conventional notions, of course. . . ."

"Lovely, lovely!" Liza laughed hysterically.

"Well, hang it all . . . Lizaveta Nikolaevna," said Pyotr Stepanovitch, suddenly piqued. "I am simply here on your account. . . . It's nothing to me. . . . I helped you yesterday, when you wanted it yourself. To-day . . . well, you can see Mavriky Nikolaevitch from here; there he's sitting; he doesn't see us. I say, Lizaveta Nikolaevna, have you ever read 'Polenka Saxe'?''

"What's that?''

"It's the name of a novel, 'Polenka Saxe'. I read it when I was a student. . . . In it a very wealthy official of some sort, Saxe, arrested his wife at a summer villa for infidelity. . . . But, hang it; it's no consequence! You'll see, Mavriky Nikolae-vitch will make you an offer before you get home. He doesn't see us yet.''

"Ach! Don't let him see us!'' Liza cried suddenly, like a man creature. "Come away, come away! To the woods, to the fields!''

And she ran back.

"Lizaveta Nikolaevna, this is such cowardice,'' cried Pyotr Stepanovitch, running after her. "And why don't you want him to see you? On the contrary, you must look him straight in the face, with pride. . . . If it's some feeling about *that* . . . some maidenly . . . that's such a prejudice, so out of date. . . . But where are you going? Where are you going? Ech! she is running! Better go back to Stavrogin's and take my droshky. . . . Where are you going? That's the way to the fields! There! She's fallen down! . . .''

He stopped. Liza was flying along like a bird, not conscious where she was going, and Pyotr Stepanovitch was already fifty paces behind her. She stumbled over a mound of earth and fell down. At the same moment there was the sound of a terrible shout from behind. It came from Mavriky Nikolaevitch, who had seen her flight and her fall, and was running to her across the field. In a flash Pyotr Stepanovitch had retired into Stavrogin's gateway to make haste and get into his droshky.

Mavriky Nikolaevitch was already standing in terrible alarm by Liza, who had risen to her feet; he was bending over her and holding her hands in both of his. All the incredible sur-roundings of this meeting overwhelmed him, and tears were rolling down his cheeks. He saw the woman for whom he had such reverent devotion running madly across the fields, at such an hour, in such weather, with nothing over her dress, the gay dress she wore the day before now crumpled and muddy from her fall. . . . He could not utter a word; he took off his great-

176

coat, and with trembling hands put it round her shoulders. Suddenly he uttered a cry, feeling that she had pressed her lips to his hand.

"Liza," he cried, "I am no good for anything, but don't drive me away from you!"

"Oh, no! Let us make haste away from here. Don't leave me!" and, seizing his hand, she drew him after her. "Mavriky Nikolaevitch," she suddenly dropped her voice timidly, "I kept a bold face there all the time, but now I am afraid of death. I shall die soon, very soon, but I am afraid, I am afraid to die . . ." she whispered, pressing his hand tightly.

"Oh, if there were someone," he looked round in despair. "Some passer-by! You will get your feet wet, you . . . will lose your reason!"

"It's all right; it's all right," she tried to reassure him. "That's right. I am not so frightened with you. Hold my hand, lead me. . . . Where are we going now? Home? No! I want first to see the people who have been murdered. His wife has been murdered, they say, and he says he killed her himself. But that's not true, is it? I want to see for myself those three who've been killed . . . on my account . . . it's because of them his love for me has grown cold since last night. . . . I shall see and find out everything. Make haste, make haste, I know the house . . . there's a fire there. . . . Mavriky Nikolaevitch, my dear one, don't forgive me in my shame! Why forgive me? Why are you crying? Give me a blow and kill me here in the field, like a dog!"

"No one is your judge now," Mavriky Nikolaevitch pronounced firmly. "God forgive you. I least of all can be your judge."

But it would be strange to describe their conversation. And meanwhile they walked hand in hand quickly, hurrying as though they were crazy. They were going straight towards the fire. Mavriky Nikolaevitch still had hopes of meeting a cart at least, but no one came that way. A mist of fine, drizzling rain enveloped the whole country, swallowing up every ray of light, every gleam of colour, and transforming everything into one smoky, leaden, indistinguishable mass. It had long been daylight, yet it seemed as though it were still night. And suddenly in this cold foggy mist there appeared coming towards them a strange and absurd figure. Picturing it now I think I should not have believed my eyes if I had been in Lizaveta Nikolaevna's place, yet she uttered a cry of joy and recognised the approaching figure at once. It was Stepan Trofimovitch. How he had gone off, how the insane, impracticable idea of his flight came to be carried out, of that later. I will only mention that he was in a fever that morning, yet even illness did not prevent his starting. He was walking resolutely on the damp ground. It was evident that he had planned the enterprise to the best of his ability, alone with his inexperience and lack of practical sense. He wore "travelling dress", that is, a greatcoat with a wide patent-leather belt, fastened with a buckle, and a pair of new high boots pulled over his trousers. Probably he had for some time past pictured a traveller as looking like this, and the belt and high boots with the shining tops like a hussar's, in which he could hardly walk, had been ready some time before. A broad-brimmed hat, a knitted scarf, twisted close round his neck, a stick in his right hand, and an exceedingly small but extremely tightly packed bag in his left, completed his get-up. He had, besides, in the same right hand, an open umbrella. These three objects—the umbrella, the stick, and the bag—had been very awkward to carry for the first mile, and had begun to be heavy by the second.

"Can it really be you?" cried Liza, looking at him with distressed wonder, after her first rush of instinctive gladness.

"*Lise*," cried Stepan Trofimovitch, rushing to her almost in delirium too. "*Chère, chère*. . . . Can you be out, too . . . in such a fog? You see the glow of fire. *Vous êtes malheureuse, n'est-ce pas?* I see, I see. Don't tell me, but don't question me either. *Nous sommes tous malheureux, mais il faut les pardonner tous. Pardonnons, Lise,* and let us be free for ever. To be quit of the world and be completely free. *Il faut pardonner, pardonner, et pardonner!*"

"But why are you kneeling down?"

"Because, taking leave of the world, I want to take leave of all my past in your person!" He wept and raised both her hands to his tear-stained eyes. "I kneel to all that was beautiful in my life. I kiss and give thanks! Now I've torn myself in half; left behind a mad visionary who dreamed of soaring to the sky. *Vingt-deux ans,* here. A shattered, frozen old man. A tutor *chez ce marchand, s'il existe pourtant ce marchand.* . . . But how drenched you are, *Lise!*" he cried, jumping on to his feet, feeling that his knees too were soaked by the wet earth. "And how is it possible . . . you are in such a dress . . . and on foot, and in these fields? . . . You are crying! *Vous êtes malheureuse.* Bah, I did hear something. . . . But

178

where have you come from now?'' He asked hurried questions with an uneasy air, looking in extreme bewilderment at Mavriky Nikolaevitch. *"Mais savez-vous l'heure qu'il est?"*

"Stepan Trofimovitch, have you heard anything about the people who've been murdered? . . . Is it true? Is it true?''

"These people! I saw the glow of their work all night. They were bound to end in this. . . .'' His eyes flashed again. "I am fleeing away from madness, from a delirious dream. I am fleeing away to seek for Russia. *Existe-t-elle, la Russie? Bah! C'est vous, cher capitaine!* I've never doubted that I should meet you somewhere on some high adventure. . . . But take my umbrella, and—why must you be on foot? For God's sake, do at least take my umbrella, for I shall hire a carriage somewhere in any case. I am on foot because Stasie (I mean, Nastasya) would have shouted for the benefit of the whole street if she'd found out I was going away. So I slipped away as far as possible incognito. I don't know; in the 'Voice' they write of there being brigands everywhere, but I thought surely I shouldn't meet a brigand the moment I came out on the road. *Chère Lise,* I thought you said something of some-one's being murdered. Oh, *mon Dieu!* You are ill!''

"Come along, come along!'' cried Liza, almost in hysterics, drawing Mavriky Nikolaevitch after her again. "Wait a minute, Stepan Trofimovitch!'' she came back suddenly to him. "Stay, poor darling, let me sign you with the cross. Perhaps it would be better to put you under control, but I'd rather make the sign of the cross over you. You, too, pray for 'poor' Liza—just a little, don't bother too much about it. Mavriky Nikolae-vitch, give that baby back his umbrella. You must give it him. That's right. . . . Come, let us go, let us go!''

They reached the fatal house at the very moment when the huge crowd, which had gathered round it, had already heard a good deal of Stavrogin, and of how much it was to his interest to murder his wife. Yet, I repeat, the immense majority went on listening without moving or uttering a word. The only people who were excited were bawling drunkards and excitable in-dividuals of the same sort as the gesticulating cabinet-maker. Everyone knew the latter as a man really of mild disposition, but he was liable on occasion to get excited and to fly off at a tangent if anything struck him in a certain way. I did not see Liza and Mavriky Nikolaevitch arrive. Petrified with amaze-ment, I first noticed Liza some distance away in the crowd, and I did not at once catch sight of Mavriky Nikolaevitch. I fancy

179

there was a moment when he fell two or three steps behind her or was pressed back by the crush. Liza, forcing her way through the crowd, seeing and noticing nothing round her, like one in a delirium, like a patient escaped from a hospital, attracted attention only too quickly, of course. There arose a hubbub of loud talking and at last sudden shouts. Someone bawled out: "It's Stavrogin's woman!" And on the other side: "It's not enough to murder them, she wants to look at them!" All at once I saw an arm raised above her head from behind and suddenly brought down upon it. Liza fell to the ground. We heard a fearful scream from Mavriky Nikolaevitch as he dashed to her assistance and struck with all his strength the man who stood between him and Liza. But at that instant the same cabinet-maker seized him with both arms from behind. For some minutes nothing could be distinguished in the scrimmage that followed. I believe Liza got up, but was knocked down by another blow. Suddenly the crowd parted and a small space was left empty round Liza's prostrate figure, and Mavriky Nikolaevitch, frantic with grief and covered with blood, was standing over her, screaming, weeping, and wringing his hands. I don't remember exactly what followed after; I only remember that they began to carry Liza away. I ran after her. She was still alive and perhaps still conscious. The cabinet-maker and three other men in the crowd were seized. These three still deny having taken any part in the dastardly deed, stubbornly maintaining that they have been arrested by mistake. Perhaps it's the truth. Though the evidence against the cabinet-maker is clear, he is so irrational that he is still unable to explain what happened coherently. I too, as a spectator, though at some distance, had to give evidence at the inquest. I declared that it had all happened entirely accidentally through the action of men perhaps moved by ill-feeling, yet scarcely conscious of what they were doing—drunk and irresponsible. I am of that opinion to this day.

CHAPTER IV

THE LAST RESOLUTION

I

THAT morning many people saw Pyotr Stepanovitch. All who saw him remembered that he was in a particularly excitable state. At two o'clock he went to see Gaganov, who had arrived from the country only the day before, and whose house was full of visitors hotly discussing the events of the previous day. Pyotr Stepanovitch talked more than anyone and made them listen to him. He was always considered among us as a "chatterbox of a student with a screw loose", but now he talked of Yulia Mihailovna, and in the general excitement the theme was an enthralling one. As one who had recently been her intimate and confidential friend, he disclosed many new and unexpected details concerning her; incidentally (and of course unguardedly) he repeated some of her own remarks about persons known to all in the town, and thereby piqued their vanity. He dropped it all in a vague and rambling way, like a man free from guile driven by his sense of honour to the painful necessity of clearing up a perfect mountain of misunderstandings, and so simple-hearted that he hardly knew where to begin and where to leave off. He let slip in a rather unguarded way, too, that Yulia Mihailovna knew the whole secret of Stavrogin and that she had been at the bottom of the whole intrigue. She had taken him in too, for he, Pyotr Stepanovitch, had also been in love with this unhappy Liza, yet he had been so hoodwinked that he had *almost* taken her to Stavrogin himself in the carriage. "Yes, yes, it's all very well for you to laugh, gentlemen, but if only I'd known, if I'd known how it would end!" he concluded. To various excited inquiries about Stavrogin he bluntly replied that in his opinion the catastrophe to the Lebyadkins was a pure coincidence, and that it was all Lebyadkin's own fault for displaying his money. He explained this particularly well. One of his listeners observed that it was no good his "pretending"; that he had eaten and drunk and almost slept at Yulia Mihailovna's, yet now he was the first to blacken her character, and that this was by no means such a fine thing to do as he supposed. But Pyotr Stepanovitch immediately defended himself.

"I ate and drank there not because I had no money, and it's not my fault that I was invited there. Allow me to judge for myself how far I need to be grateful for that."

The general impression was in his favour. "He may be rather absurd, and of course he is a nonsensical fellow, yet still he is not responsible for Yulia Mihailovna's foolishness. On the contrary, it appears that he tried to stop her."

About two o'clock the news suddenly came that Stavrogin, about whom there was so much talk, had suddenly left for Petersburg by the midday train. This interested people immensely; many of them frowned. Pyotr Stepanovitch was so much struck that I was told he turned quite pale and cried out strangely: "Why, how could they have let him go?" He hurried away from Gaganov's forthwith, yet he was seen in two or three other houses.

Towards dusk he succeeded in getting in to see Yulia Mihailovna, though he had the greatest pains to do so, as she had absolutely refused to see him. I heard of this from the lady herself only three weeks afterwards, just before her departure for Petersburg. She gave me no details, but observed with a shudder that "he had on that occasion astounded her beyond all belief". I imagine that all he did was to terrify her by threatening to charge her with being an accomplice if she "said anything". The necessity for this intimidation arose from his plans at the moment, of which she, of course, knew nothing; and only later, five days afterwards, she guessed why he had been so doubtful of her reticence and so afraid of a new outburst of indignation on her part.

Between seven and eight o'clock, when it was dark, all the five members of the quintet met together at Ensign Erkel's lodgings in a little crooked house at the end of the town. The meeting had been fixed by Pyotr Stepanovitch himself, but he was unpardonably late, and the members waited over an hour for him. This Ensign Erkel was that young officer who had sat the whole evening at Virginsky's with a pencil in his hand and a note-book before him. He had not long been in the town; he lodged alone with two old women, sisters, in a secluded by-street and was shortly to leave the town; a meeting at his house was less likely to attract notice than anywhere. This strange boy was distinguished by extreme taciturnity: he was capable of sitting for a dozen evenings in succession in noisy company, with the most extraordinary conversation going on around him, without uttering a word, though he listened with extreme attention, watching the speakers with his childlike eyes. His face was very pretty and even had a certain look of cleverness. He did not belong to the quintet; it was supposed that he had some special job of a purely practical character. It is known now that he had nothing of the sort and probably did not understand his position himself. It was simply that he was filled with hero-worship for Pyotr Stepanovitch, whom he had only lately met. If he had met a monster of iniquity who had incited him to found a band of brigands on the pretext of some romantic and socialistic object, and as a test had bidden him rob and murder the first peasant he met, he would certainly have obeyed and done it. He had an invalid mother to whom he sent half of his scanty pay—and how she must have kissed that poor flaxen head, how she must have trembled and prayed over it! I go into these details about him because I feel very sorry for him.

"Our fellows" were excited. The events of the previous night had made a great impression on them, and I fancy they were in a panic. The simple disorderliness in which they had so zealously and systematically taken part had ended in a way they had not expected. The fire in the night, the murder of the Lebyadkins, the savage brutality of the crowd with Liza, had been a series of surprises which they had not anticipated in their programme. They hotly accused the hand that had guided them of despotism and duplicity. In fact, while they were waiting for Pyotr Stepanovitch they worked each other up to such a point that they resolved again to ask him for a definite explanation, and if he evaded again, as he had done before, to dissolve the quintet and to found instead a new secret society "for the propaganda of ideas" and on their own initiative on the basis of democracy and equality. Liputin, Shigalov, and the authority on the peasantry supported this plan; Lyamshin said nothing, though he looked approving. Virginsky hesitated and wanted to hear Pyotr Stepanovitch first. It was decided to hear Pyotr Stepanovitch, but still he did not come; such casualness added fuel to the flames. Erkel was absolutely silent and did nothing but order the tea, which he brought from the landladies in glasses on a tray, not bringing in the samovar nor allowing the servant to enter.

Pyotr Stepanovitch did not turn up till half-past eight. With rapid steps he went up to the circular table before the sofa round which the company were seated; he kept his cap in his hand and refused tea. He looked angry, severe and supercilious. He must have observed at once from their faces that they were "mutinous".

"Before I open my mouth, you've got something hidden; out with it."

Liputin began "in the name of all", and declared in a voice quivering with resentment "that if things were going on like that they might as well blow their brains out". Oh, they were not at all afraid to blow their brains out, they were quite ready to, in fact, but only to serve the common cause (a general movement of approbation). So he must be more open with them, so that they might always know beforehand, "or else what would things be coming to?" (Again a stir and some guttural sounds.) To behave like this was humiliating and dangerous. "We don't say so because we are afraid, but if one acts and the rest are only pawns, then one would blunder and all would be lost." (Exclamations. "Yes, yes." General approval.)

"Damn it all, what do you want?"

"What connection is there between the common cause and the petty intrigues of Mr. Stavrogin?" cried Liputin, boiling over. "Suppose he is in some mysterious relation to the centre, if that legendary centre really exists at all, it's no concern of ours. And meantime a murder has been committed, the police have been roused; if they follow the thread they may find what it starts from."

"If Stavrogin and you are caught, we shall be caught too," added the authority on the peasantry.

"And to no good purpose for the common cause," Virginsky concluded despondently.

"What nonsense! The murder is a chance crime; it was committed by Fedka for the sake of robbery."

"H'm! Strange coincidence, though," said Liputin, wriggling.

"And if you will have it, it's all through you."

"Through us?"

"In the first place, you, Liputin, had a share in the intrigue yourself; and the second chief point is, you were ordered to get Lebyadkin away and given money to do it; and what did you do? If you'd got him away nothing would have happened."

"But wasn't it you yourself who suggested the idea that it would be a good thing to set him on to read his verses?"

"An idea is not a command. The command was to get him away."

184

"Command! Rather a queer word. . . . On the contrary, your orders were to delay sending him off."

"You made a mistake and showed your foolishness and self-will. The murder was the work of Fedka, and he carried it out alone for the sake of robbery. You heard the gossip and believed it. You were scared. Stavrogin is not such a fool, and the proof of that is he left the town at twelve o'clock after an interview with the vice-governor; if there were anything in it they would not let him go to Petersburg in broad daylight."

"But we are not making out that Mr. Stavrogin committed the murder himself," Liputin rejoined spitefully and unceremoniously. "He may have known nothing about it, like me; and you know very well that I know nothing about it, though I am mixed up in it like mutton in a hash."

"Whom are you accusing?" said Pyotr Stepanovitch, looking at him darkly.

"Those whose interest it is to burn down towns."

"You make matters worse by wriggling out of it. However, won't you read this and pass it to the others, simply as a fact of interest?"

He pulled out of his pocket Lebyadkin's anonymous letter to Lembke and handed it to Liputin. The latter read it, was evidently surprised, and passed it thoughtfully to his neighbour; the letter quickly went the round.

"Is that really Lebyadkin's handwriting?" observed Shigalov.

"It is," answered Liputin and Tolkatchenko (the authority on the peasantry).

"I simply brought it as a fact of interest and because I knew you were so sentimental over Lebyadkin," repeated Pyotr Stepanovitch, taking the letter back. "So it turns out, gentlemen, that a stray Fedka relieves us quite by chance of a dangerous man. That's what chance does sometimes! It's instructive, isn't it?"

The members exchanged rapid glances.

"And now, gentlemen, it's my turn to ask questions," said Pyotr Stepanovitch, assuming an air of dignity. "Let me know what business you had to set fire to the town without permission."

"What's this! We, we set fire to the town? That is laying the blame on others!" they exclaimed.

"I quite understand that you carried the game too far," Pyotr Stepanovitch persisted stubbornly, "but it's not a matter of petty scandals with Yulia Mihailovna. I've brought you here, gentlemen, to explain to you the greatness of the danger you have so stupidly incurred, which is a menace to much beside yourselves."

"Excuse me, we, on the contrary, were intending just now to point out to you the greatness of the despotism and unfairness you have shown in taking such a serious and also strange step without consulting the members," Virginsky, who had been hitherto silent, protested, almost with indignation.

"And so you deny it? But I maintain that you set fire to the town, you and none but you. Gentlemen, don't tell lies; I have good evidence. By your rashness you exposed the common cause to danger. You are only one knot in an endless network of knots—and your duty is blind obedience to the centre. Yet three men of you incited the Shpigulin men to set fire to the town without the least instruction to do so, and the fire has taken place."

"What three? What three of us?"

"The day before yesterday, at three o'clock in the night, you, Tolkatchenko, were inciting Fomka Zavyalov at the 'Forget-me-not'. "

"Upon my word!" cried the latter, jumping up, "I scarcely said a word to him, and what I did say was without intention, simply because he had been flogged that morning. And I dropped it at once; I saw he was too drunk. If you had not referred to it I should not have thought of it again. A word could not set the place on fire."

"You are like a man who should be surprised that a tiny spark could blow a whole powder magazine into the air."

"I spoke in a whisper in his ear, in a corner; how could you have heard of it?"

Tolkatchenko reflected suddenly.

"I was sitting there under the table. Don't disturb yourselves, gentlemen; I know every step you take. You smile sarcastically, Mr. Liputin? But I know, for instance, that you pinched your wife black and blue at midnight, three days ago, in your bedroom as you were going to bed."

Liputin's mouth fell open and he turned pale. "It was afterwards found out that he knew of this exploit of Liputin's from Agafya, Liputin's servant, whom he had paid from the beginning to spy on him; this only came out later.)

"May I state a fact?" said Shigalov, getting up.

"State it."

Shigalov sat down and pulled himself together.

"So far as I understand—and it's impossible not to understand it—you yourself at first and a second time later, drew with great eloquence, but too theoretically, a picture of Russia covered with an endless network of knots. Each of these centres of activity, proselytising and ramifying endlessly, aims by systematic denunciation to injure the prestige of local authority, to reduce the villages to confusion, to spread cynicism and scandals, together with complete disbelief in everything and an eagerness for something better, and finally, by means of fires, as a pre-eminently national method, to reduce the country at a given moment, if need be, to desperation. Are those your words which I tried to remember accurately? Is that the programme you gave us as the authorised representative of the central committee, which is to this day utterly unknown to us and almost like a myth?"

"It's correct, only you are very tedious."

"Everyone has a right to express himself in his own way. Giving us to understand that the separate knots of the general network already covering Russia number by now several hundred, and propounding the theory that if everyone does his work successfully, all Russia at a given moment, at a signal . . ."

"Ah, damn it all, I have enough to do without you!" cried Pyotr Stepanovitch, twisting in his chair.

"Very well, I'll cut it short and I'll end simply by asking if we've seen the disorderly scenes, we've seen the discontent of the people, we've seen and taken part in the downfall of local administration, and finally, we've seen with our own eyes the town on fire? What do you find amiss? Isn't that your programme? What can you blame us for?"

"Acting on your own initiative!" Pyotr Stepanovitch cried furiously. "While I am here you ought not to have dared to act without my permission. Enough. We are on the eve of betrayal, and perhaps to-morrow or to-night you'll be seized. So there. I have authentic information."

At this all were agape with astonishment.

"You will be arrested not only as the instigators of the fire but as a quintet. The traitor knows the whole secret of the network. So you see what a mess you've made of it!"

"Stavrogin, no doubt," cried Liputin.

"What . . . why Stavrogin?" Pyotr Stepanovitch seemed suddenly taken aback. "Hang it all," he cried, pulling himself together at once, "it's Shatov! I believe you all know now that Shatov in his time was one of the society. I must tell you that, watching him through persons he does not suspect, I found out to my amazement that he knows all about the organisation of the network and . . . everything, in fact. To save himself from being charged with having formerly belonged, he will give information against all. He has been hesitating up till now and I have spared him. Your fire has decided him: he is shaken and will hesitate no longer. To-morrow we shall be arrested as incendiaries and political offenders."

"Is it true? How does Shatov know?"

The excitement was indescribable.

"It's all perfectly true. I have no right to reveal the source from which I learnt it or how I discovered it, but I tell you what I can do for you meanwhile: through one person I can act on Shatov so that without his suspecting it he will put off giving information, but not more than for twenty-four hours."

All were silent.

"We really must send him to the devil!" Tolkatchenko was the first to exclaim.

"It ought to have been done long ago," Lyamshin put in malignantly, striking the table with his fist.

"'But how is it to be done?" muttered Liputin.

Pyotr Stepanovitch at once took up the question and unfolded his plan. The plan was the following day at nightfall to draw Shatov away to a secluded spot to hand over the secret printing press which had been in his keeping and was buried there, and there "to settle things". He went into various essential details which we will omit here, and explained minutely Shatov's present ambiguous attitude to the central society, of which the reader knows already.

"That's all very well," Liputin observed irresolutely, "but since it will be another adventure . . . of the same sort . . . it will make too great a sensation."

"No doubt," assented Pyotr Stepanovitch, "but I've provided against that. We have the means of averting suspicion completely."

And with the same minuteness he told them about Kirillov, of his intention to shoot himself, and of his promise to wait for a signal from them and to leave a letter behind him taking on himself anything they dictated to him (all of which the reader knows already).

"His determination to take his own life—a philosophic, or as I should call it, insane decision—has become known *there*," Pyotr Stepanovitch went on to explain. "*There* not a thread,

188

not a grain of dust is overlooked; everything is turned to the service of the cause. Foreseeing how useful it might be and satisfying themselves that his intention was quite serious, they had offered him the means to come to Russia (he was set for some reason on dying in Russia), gave him a commission which he promised to carry out (and he had done so), and had, moreover, bound him by a promise, as you already know, to commit suicide only when he was told to. He promised everything. You must note that he belongs to the organisation on a particular footing and is anxious to be of service; more than that I can't tell you. To-morrow, *after Shatov's affair*, I'll dictate a note to him saying that he is responsible for his death. That will seem very plausible: they were friends and travelled together to America, there they quarrelled; and it will all be explained in the letter . . . and . . . and perhaps, if it seems feasible, we might dictate something more to Kirillov—something about the manifestos, for instance, and even perhaps about the fire. But I'll think about that. You needn't worry yourselves, he has no prejudices; he'll sign anything.''

There were expressions of doubt. It sounded a fantastic story. But they had all heard more or less about Kirillov; Liputin more than all.

"He may change his mind and not want to," said Shigalov; "he is a madman anyway, so he is not much to build upon."

"Don't be uneasy, gentlemen, he will want to," Pyotr Stepanovitch snapped out. "I am obliged by our agreement to give him warning the day before, so it must be to-day. I invite Liputin to go with me at once to see him and make certain, and he will tell you, gentlemen, when he comes back—to-day if need be—whether what I say is true. However," he broke off suddenly with intense exasperation, as though he suddenly felt he was doing people like them too much honour by wasting time in persuading them, "however, do as you please. If you don't decide to do it, the union is broken up—but solely through your insubordination and treachery. In that case we are all independent from this moment. But under those circumstances, besides the unpleasantness of Shatov's betrayal and its consequences, you will have brought upon yourselves another little unpleasantness of which you were definitely warned when the union was formed. As far as I am concerned, I am not much afraid of you, gentlemen. . . . Don't imagine that I am so involved with you. . . . But that's no matter."

"Yes, we decide to do it," Liputin pronounced.

189

"There's no other way out of it," muttered Tolkatchenko, "and if only Liputin confirms about Kirillov, then . . ."

"I am against it; with all my soul and strength I protest against such a murderous decision," said Virginsky, standing up.

"But?" asked Pyotr Stepanovitch. . . ."

"*But* what?"

"You said *but* . . . and I am waiting."

"I don't think I did say *but* . . . I only meant to say that if you decide to do it, then . . ."

"Then?"

Virginsky did not answer.

"I think that one is at liberty to neglect danger to one's own life," said Erkel, suddenly opening his mouth, "but if it may injure the cause, then I consider one ought not to dare to neglect danger to one's life. . . ."

He broke off in confusion, blushing. Absorbed as they all were in their own ideas, they all looked at him in amazement— it was such a surprise that he too could speak.

"I am for the cause," Virginsky pronounced suddenly.

Everyone got up. It was decided to communicate once more and make final arrangements at midday on the morrow, though without meeting. The place where the printing press was hidden was announced and each was assigned his part and his duty. Liputin and Pyotr Stepanovitch promptly set off together to Kirillov.

II

All our fellows believed that Shatov was going to betray them; but they also believed that Pyotr Stepanovitch was playing with them like pawns. And yet they knew, too, that in any case they would all meet on the spot next day and that Shatov's fate was sealed. They suddenly felt like flies caught in a web by a huge spider; they were furious, but they were trembling with terror.

Pyotr Stepanovitch, of course, had treated them badly; it might all have gone off far more harmoniously and *easily* if he had taken the trouble to embellish the facts ever so little. Instead of putting the facts in a decorous light, as an exploit worthy of ancient Rome or something of the sort, he simply appealed to their animal fears and laid stress on the danger to their own skins, which was simply insulting; of course there was a struggle for existence in everything and there was no other principle in nature, they all knew that, but still . . .

But Pyotr Stepanovitch had no time to trot out the Romans; he was completely thrown out of his reckoning. Stavrogin's flight had astounded and crushed him. It was a lie when he said that Stavrogin had seen the vice-governor; what worried Pyotr Stepanovitch was that Stavrogin had gone off without seeing anyone, even his mother—and it was certainly strange that he had been allowed to leave without hindrance. (The authorities were called to account for it afterwards.) Pyotr Stepanovitch had been making inquiries all day, but so far had found out nothing, and he had never been so upset. And how could he, how could he give up Stavrogin all at once like this! That was why he could not be very tender with the quintet. Besides, they tied his hands: he had already decided to gallop after Stavrogin at once; and meanwhile he was detained by Shatov; he had to cement the quintet together once for all, in case of emergency. "Pity to waste them, they might be of use." That, I imagine, was his way of reasoning.

As for Shatov, Pyotr Stepanovitch was firmly convinced that he would betray them. All that he had told the others about it was a lie: he had never seen the document nor heard of it, but he thought it as certain as that twice two makes four. It seemed to him that what had happened—the death of Liza, the death of Marya Timofyevna—would be too much for Shatov, and that he would make up his mind at once. Who knows? perhaps he had grounds for supposing it. It is known, too, that he hated Shatov personally; there had at some time been a quarrel between them, and Pyotr Stepanovitch never forgave an offence. I am convinced, indeed, that this was his leading motive.

We have narrow brick pavements in our town, and in some streets only raised wooden planks instead of a pavement. Pyotr Stepanovitch walked in the middle of the pavement, taking up the whole of it, utterly regardless of Liputin, who had no room to walk beside him and so had to hurry a step behind or run in the muddy road if he wanted to speak to him. Pyotr Stepanovitch suddenly remembered how he had lately splashed through the mud to keep pace with Stavrogin, who had walked, as he was doing now, taking up the whole pavement. He recalled the whole scene, and rage choked him.

But Liputin, too, was choking with resentment. Pyotr Stepanovitch might treat the others as he liked, but him! Why, he *knew* more than all the rest, was in closer touch with the work and taking more intimate part in it than anyone, and hitherto his services had been continual, though indirect. Oh, he knew that even now Pyotr Stepanovitch might ruin him *if it came to the worst*. But he had long hated Pyotr Stepanovitch, and not because he was a danger but because of his overbearing manner. Now, when he had to make up his mind to such a deed, he raged inwardly more than all the rest put together. Alas! he knew that next day "like a slave" he would be the first on the spot and would bring the others, and if he could somehow have murdered Pyotr Stepanovitch before the morrow, without ruining himself, of course, he would certainly have murdered him.

Absorbed in his sensations, he trudged dejectedly after his tormentor, who seemed to have forgotten his existence, though he gave him a rude and careless shove with his elbow now and then. Suddenly Pyotr Stepanovitch halted in one of the principal thoroughfares and went into a restaurant.

"What are you doing?" cried Liputin, boiling over. "This is a restaurant."

"I want a beefsteak."

"Upon my word! It is always full of people."

"What if it is?"

"But . . . we shall be late. It's ten o'clock already."

"You can't be too late to go there."

"But I shall be late! They are expecting me back."

"Well, let them; but it would be stupid of you to go to them. With all your bobbery I've had no dinner. And the later you go to Kirillov's the more sure you are to find him."

Pyotr Stepanovitch went to a room apart. Liputin sat in an easy chair on one side, angry and resentful, and watched him eating. Half an hour and more passed. Pyotr Stepanovitch did not hurry himself; he ate with relish, rang the bell, asked for a different kind of mustard, then for beer, without saying a word to Liputin. He was pondering deeply. He was capable of doing two things at once—eating with relish and pondering deeply. Liputin loathed him so intensely at last that he could not tear himself away. It was like a nervous obsession. He counted every morsel of beefsteak that Pyotr Stepanovitch put into his mouth; he loathed him for the way he opened it, for the way he chewed, for the way he smacked his lips over the fat morsels, he loathed the steak itself. At last things began to swim before his eyes; he began to feel slightly giddy; he felt hot and cold run down his spine by turns.

"You are doing nothing; read that," said Pyotr Stepanovitch suddenly, throwing him a sheet of paper. Liputin went nearer to the candle. The paper was closely covered with bad handwriting, with corrections in every line. By the time he had mastered it Pyotr Stepanovitch had paid his bill and was ready to go. When they were on the pavement Liputin handed him back the paper.

"Keep it; I'll tell you afterwards. . . . What do you say to it, though?"

Liputin shuddered all over.

"In my opinion . . . such a manifesto . . . is nothing but a ridiculous absurdity."

His anger broke out; he felt as though he were being caught up and carried along.

"If we decide to distribute such manifestos," he said, quivering all over, "we'll make ourselves contemptible by our stupidity and incompetence."

"H'm! I think differently," said Pyotr Stepanovitch, walking on resolutely.

"So do I; surely it isn't your work?"

"That's not your business."

"I think too that doggerel, 'A Noble Personality', is the most utter trash possible, and it couldn't have been written by Herzen."

"You are talking nonsense; it's a good poem."

"I am surprised, too, for instance," said Liputin, still dashing along with desperate leaps, "that it is suggested that we should act so as to bring everything to the ground. It's natural in Europe to wish to destroy everything because there's a proletariat there, but we are only amateurs here and in my opinion are only showing off."

"I thought you were a Fourierist."

"Fourier says something quite different, quite different."

"I know it's nonsense."

"No, Fourier isn't nonsense. . . . Excuse me, I can't believe that there will be a rising in May."

Liputin positively unbuttoned his coat, he was so hot.

"Well, that's enough; but now, that I mayn't forget it," said Pyotr Stepanovitch, passing with extraordinary coolness to another subject, "you will have to print this manifesto with your own hands. We're going to dig up Shatov's printing press, and you will take it to-morrow. As quickly as possible you must print as many copies as you can, and then distribute them all the winter. The means will be provided. You must do as many copies as possible, for you'll be asked for them from other places."

"No, excuse me; I can't undertake such a . . . I decline."

"You'll take it all the same. I am acting on the instructions of the central committee, and you are bound to obey."

"And I consider that our centres abroad have forgotten what Russia is like and have lost all touch, and that's why they talk such nonsense. . . . I even think that instead of many hundreds of quintets in Russia, we are the only one that exists, and there is no network at all," Liputin gasped finally.

"The more contemptible of you, then, to run after the cause without believing in it . . . and you are running after me now like a mean little cur."

"No, I'm not. We have a full right to break off and found a new society."

"Fool!" Pyotr Stepanovitch boomed at him threateningly all of a sudden, with flashing eyes.

They stood facing one another for some time. Pyotr Stepanovitch turned and pursued his way confidently.

The idea flashed through Liputin's mind: "Turn and go back; if I don't turn now I shall never go back." He pondered this for ten steps, but at the eleventh a new and desperate idea flashed into his mind: he did not turn and did not go back.

They were approaching Filipov's house, but before reaching it they turned down a side street, or, to be more accurate, an inconspicuous path under a fence, so that for some time they had to walk along a steep slope above a ditch where they could not keep their footing without holding the fence. At a dark corner in the slanting fence Pyotr Stepanovitch took out a plank, leaving a gap, through which he promptly scrambled. Liputin was surprised, but he crawled through after him; then they replaced the plank after them. This was the secret way by which Fedka used to visit Kirillov.

"Shatov mustn't know that we are here," Pyotr Stepanovitch whispered sternly to Liputin.

III

Kirillov was sitting on his leather sofa drinking tea, as he always was at that hour. He did not get up to meet them, but gave a sort of start and looked at the new-comers anxiously.

"You are not mistaken," said Pyotr Stepanovitch, "it's just that I've come about."

"To-day?"

"No, no, to-morrow . . . about this time." And he hurriedly sat down at the table, watching Kirillov's agitation with some uneasiness. But the latter had already regained his composure and looked as usual.

"These people still refuse to believe in you. You are not vexed at my bringing Liputin?"

"To-day I am not vexed; to-morrow I want to be alone."

"But not before I come, and therefore in my presence."

"I should prefer not in your presence."

"You remember you promised to write and to sign all I dictated."

"I don't care. And now will you be here long?"

"I have to see one man and to remain half an hour, so whatever you say I shall stay that half-hour."

Kirillov did not speak. Liputin meanwhile sat down on one side under the portrait of the bishop. That last desperate idea gained more and more possession of him. Kirillov scarcely noticed him. Liputin had heard of Kirillov's theory before and always laughed at him; but now he was silent and looked gloomily round him.

"I've no objection to some tea," said Pyotr Stepanovitch, moving up. "I've just had some steak and was reckoning on getting tea with you."

"Drink it. You can have some if you like."

"You used to offer it to me," observed Pyotr Stepanovitch sourly.

"That's no matter. Let Liputin have some too."

"No, I . . . can't."

"Don't want to or can't?" said Pyotr Stepanovitch, turning quickly to him.

"I am not going to here," Liputin said expressively.

Pyotr Stepanovitch frowned.

"There's a flavour of mysticism about that; goodness knows what to make of you people!"

No one answered; there was a full minute of silence.

"But I know one thing," he added abruptly, "that no superstition will prevent any one of us doing his duty."

"Has Stavrogin gone?" asked Kirillov.

"Yes."

"He's done well."

Pyotr Stepanovitch's eyes gleamed but he restrained himself.

"I don't care what you think as long as everyone keeps his word."

"I'll keep my word."

"I always knew that you would do your duty like an independent and progressive man."

"You are an absurd fellow."

"That may be; I am very glad to amuse you. I am always glad if I can give people pleasure."

"You are very anxious I should shoot myself and are afraid I might suddenly not?"

"Well, you see, it was your own doing—connecting your plan with our work. Reckoning on your plan we have already done something, so that you couldn't refuse now because you've let us in for it."

"You've no claim at all."

"I understand, I understand; you are perfectly free, and we don't come in so long as your free intention is carried out."

"And am I to take on myself all the nasty things you've done?"

"Listen, Kirillov, are you afraid? If you want to cry off, say so at once."

"I am not afraid."

"I ask because you are making so many inquiries."

"Are you going soon?"

"Asking questions again?"

Kirillov scanned him contemptuously.

"You see," Pyotr Stepanovitch went on, getting angrier and angrier, and unable to take the right tone, "you want me to go away, to be alone, to concentrate yourself, but all that's a bad sign for you—for you above all. You want to think a great deal. To my mind you'd better not think. And really you make me uneasy."

"There's only one thing I hate, that at such a moment I should have a reptile like you beside me."

"Oh, that doesn't matter. I'll go away at the time and stand on the steps if you like. If you are so concerned about trifles when it comes to dying, then . . . it's all a very bad sign. I'll go out on to the steps and you can imagine I know nothing about it, and that I am a man infinitely below you."

"No, not infinitely; you've got abilities, but there's a lot you don't understand because you are a low man."

"Delighted, delighted. I told you already I am delighted to provide entertainment . . . at such a moment."

"You don't understand anything."

"That is, I . . . well, I listen with respect, anyway."

"You can do nothing; even now you can't hide your petty spite, though it's not to your interest to show it. You'll make me cross, and then I may want another six months."

Pyotr Stepanovitch looked at his watch.

"I never understood your theory, but I know you didn't invent it for our sakes, so I suppose you would carry it out apart from us. And I know too that you haven't mastered the idea but the idea has mastered you, so you won't put it off."

"What? The idea has mastered me?"

"Yes."

"And not I mastered the idea? That's good. You have a little sense. Only you tease me and I am proud."

"That's a good thing, that's a good thing. Just what you need, to be proud."

"Enough. You've drunk your tea; go away."

"Damn it all, I suppose I must"—Pyotr Stepanovitch got up—"though it's early. Listen, Kirillov. Shall I find that man —you know whom I mean—at Myasnitchiha's? Or has she too been lying?"

"You won't find him, because he is here and not there."

"Here! Damn it all, where?"

"Sitting in the kitchen, eating and drinking."

"How dared he?" cried Pyotr Stepanovitch, flushing angrily. "It was his duty to wait . . . what nonsense! He has no passport, no money!"

"I don't know. He came to say good-bye; he is dressed and ready. He is going away and won't come back. He says you are a scoundrel and he doesn't want to wait for your money."

"Ha ha! He is afraid that I'll . . . But even now I can . . . if . . . Where is he, in the kitchen?"

Kirillov opened a side door into a tiny dark room; from this room three steps led straight to the part of the kitchen where the cook's bed was usually put, behind the partition. Here, in the corner under the ikons, Fedka was sitting now, at a bare deal table. Before him stood a pint bottle, a plate of bread, and some cold beef and potatoes on an earthenware dish. He was eating in a leisurely way and was already half drunk, but he was wearing his sheepskin coat and was evidently ready for a journey. A samovar was boiling the other side of the screen, but it was

197

THE POSSESSED

not for Fedka, who had every night for a week or more zealously blown it up and got it ready for "Alexey Nilitch, for he's such a habit of drinking tea at nights". I am strongly disposed to believe that, as Kirillov had not a cook, he had cooked the beef and potatoes that morning with his own hands for Fedka.

"What notion is this?" cried Pyotr Stepanovitch, whisking into the room. "Why didn't you wait where you were ordered?"

And swinging his fist, he brought it down heavily on the table. Fedka assumed an air of dignity.

"You wait a bit, Pyotr Stepanovitch, you wait a bit," he began, with a swaggering emphasis on each word, "it's your first duty to understand here that you are on a polite visit to Mr. Kirillov, Alexey Nilitch, whose boots you might clean any day, because beside you he is a man of culture and you are only—foo!"

And he made a jaunty show of spitting to one side. Haughtiness and determination were evident in his manner, and a certain very threatening assumption of argumentative calm that suggested an outburst to follow. But Pyotr Stepanovitch had no time to realise the danger, and it did not fit in with preconceived ideas. The incidents and disasters of the day had quite turned his head. Liputin, at the top of the three steps, stared inquisitively down from the little dark room.

"Do you or don't you want a trustworthy passport and good money to go where you've been told? Yes or no?"

"D'you see, Pyotr Stepanovitch, you've been deceiving me from the first, and so you've been a regular scoundrel to me. For all the world like a filthy human louse—that's how I look on you. You've promised me a lot of money for shedding innocent blood and swore it was for Mr. Stavrogin, though it turns out to be nothing but your want of breeding. I didn't get a farthing out of it, let alone fifteen hundred, and Mr. Stavrogin hit you in the face, which has come to our ears. Now you are threatening me again and promising me money—what for, you don't say. And I shouldn't wonder if you are sending me to Petersburg to plot some revenge in your spite against Mr. Stavrogin, Nikolay Vsyevolodovitch, reckoning on my simplicity. And that proves you are the chief murderer. And do you know what you deserve for the very fact that in the depravity of your heart you've given up believing in God Himself, the true Creator? You are no better than an idolater and are on a level with the Tatar and the Mordva. Alexey Nilitch, who is a philosopher, has expounded the true God, the Creator, many a time to you, as well as the creation of the world and the fate that's to come and the transformation of every sort of creature and every sort of beast out of the Apocalypse, but you've persisted like a senseless idol in your deafness and your dumbness and have brought Ensign Erkel to the same, like the veriest evil seducer and so-called atheist. . . ."

"Ah, you drunken dog! He strips the ikons of their setting and then preaches about God!"

"D'you see, Pyotr Stepanovitch, I tell you truly that I have stripped the ikons, but I only took out the pearls; and how do you know? Perhaps my own tear was transformed into a pearl in the furnace of the Most High to make up for my sufferings, seeing I am just that very orphan, having no daily refuge. Do you know from the books that once, in ancient times, a merchant with just such tearful sighs and prayers stole a pearl from the halo of the Mother of God, and afterwards, in the face of all the people, laid the whole price of it at her feet, and the Holy Mother sheltered him with her mantle before all the people, so that it was a miracle, and the command was given through the authorities to write it all down word for word in the Imperial books. And you let a mouse in, so you insulted the very throne of God. And if you were not my natural master, whom I dandled in my arms when I was a stripling, I would have done for you now, without budging from this place!"

Pyotr Stepanovitch flew into a violent rage.

"Tell me, have you seen Stavrogin to-day?"

"Don't you dare to question me. Mr. Stavrogin is fairly amazed at you, and he had no share in it even in wish, let alone instructions or giving money. You've presumed with me."

"You'll get the money and you'll get another two thousand in Petersburg, when you get there, in a lump sum, and you'll get more."

"You are lying, my fine gentleman, and it makes me laugh to see how easily you are taken in. Mr. Stavrogin stands at the top of the ladder above you, and you yelp at him from below like a silly puppy dog, while he thinks it would be doing you an honour to spit at you."

"But do you know," cried Pyotr Stepanovitch in a rage, "that I won't let you stir a step from here, you scoundrel, and I'll hand you straight over to the police."

Fedka leapt on to his feet and his eyes gleamed with fury. Pyotr Stepanovitch pulled out his revolver. Then followed a rapid and revolting scene: before Pyotr Stepanovitch could take aim, Fedka swung round and in a flash struck him on the cheek with all his might. Then there was the thud of a second blow, a third, then a fourth, all on the cheek. Pyotr Stepanovitch was dazed; with his eyes starting out of his head, he muttered something, and suddenly crashed full length to the ground.

"There you are; take him," shouted Fedka with a triumphant swagger; he instantly took up his cap, his bag from under the bench, and was gone. Pyotr Stepanovitch lay gasping and unconscious. Liputin even imagined that he had been murdered. Kirillov ran headlong into the kitchen.

"Water!" he cried, and ladling some water in an iron dipper from a bucket, he poured it over the injured man's head. Pyotr Stepanovitch stirred, raised his head, sat up, and looked blankly about him.

"Well, how are you?" asked Kirillov. Pyotr Stepanovitch looked at him intently, still not recognising him; but seeing Liputin peeping in from the kitchen, he smiled his hateful smile and suddenly got up, picking up his revolver from the floor.

"If you take it into your head to run away to-morrow like that scoundrel Stavrogin," he cried, pouncing furiously on Kirillov, pale, stammering, and hardly able to articulate his words, "I'll hang you . . . like a fly . . . or crush you . . . if it's at the other end of the world . . . do you understand?"

And he held the revolver straight at Kirillov's head; but almost at the same minute, coming completely to himself, he drew back his hand, thrust the revolver into his pocket, and without saying another word ran out of the house. Liputin followed him. They clambered through the same gap and again walked along the slope holding to the fence. Pyotr Stepanovitch strode rapidly down the street so that Liputin could scarcely keep up with him. At the first crossing he suddenly stopped.

"Well?" He turned to Liputin with a challenge.

Liputin remembered the revolver and was still trembling all over after the scene he had witnessed; but the answer seemed to come of itself irresistibly from his tongue:

"I think . . . I think that . . ."

"Did you see what Fedka was drinking in the kitchen?"

"What he was drinking? He was drinking vodka."

"Well then, let me tell you it's the last time in his life he will drink vodka. I recommend you to remember that and reflect on it. And now go to hell; you are not wanted till to-morrow. But mind now, don't be a fool!''

Liputin rushed home full speed.

IV

He had long had a passport in readiness made out in a false name. It seems a wild idea that this prudent little man, the petty despot of his family, who was, above all things, a sharp man of business and a capitalist, and who was an official too (though he was a Fourierist), should long before have conceived the fantastic project of procuring this passport in case of emergency, that he might escape abroad by means of it *if* . . . he did admit the possibility of this *if*, though no doubt he was never able himself to formulate what this *if* might mean.

But now it suddenly formulated itself, and in a most unexpected way. That desperate idea with which he had gone to Kirillov's after that ''fool'' he had heard from Pyotr Stepanovitch on the pavement, had been to abandon everything at dawn next day and to emigrate abroad. If anyone doubts that such fantastic incidents occur in everyday Russian life, even now, let him look into the biographies of all the Russian exiles abroad. Not one of them escaped with more wisdom or real justification. It has always been the unrestrained domination of phantoms and nothing more.

Running home, he began by locking himself in, getting out his travelling-bag, and feverishly beginning to pack. His chief anxiety was the question of money, and how much he could rescue from the impending ruin—and by what means. He thought of it as ''rescuing'', for it seemed to him that he could not linger an hour, and that by daylight he must be on the high road. He did not know where to take the train either; he vaguely determined to take it at the second or third big station from the town, and to make his way there on foot, if necessary. In that way, instinctively and mechanically he busied himself in his packing with a perfect whirl of ideas in his head—and suddenly stopped short, gave it all up, and with a deep groan stretched himself on the sofa.

He felt clearly, and suddenly realised that he might escape, but that he was by now utterly incapable of deciding whether he ought to make off *before* or *after* Shatov's death; that he was simply a lifeless body, a crude inert mass; that he was being moved by an awful outside power; and that, though he had a passport to go abroad, that though he could run away from Shatov (otherwise what need was there of such haste?), yet he would run away, not from Shatov, not before his murder, but *after* it, and that that was determined, signed, and sealed.

In insufferable distress, trembling every instant and wondering at himself, alternately groaning aloud and numb with terror, he managed to exist till eleven o'clock next morning locked in and lying on the sofa; then came the shock he was awaiting, and it at once determined him. When he unlocked his door and went out to his household at eleven o'clock they told him that the runaway convict and brigand, Fedka, who was a terror to everyone, who had pillaged churches and only lately been guilty of murder and arson, who was being pursued and could not be captured by our police, had been found at daybreak murdered, five miles from the town, at a turning off the high road, and that the whole town was talking of it already. He rushed headlong out of the house at once to find out further details, and learned, to begin with, that Fedka, who had been found with his skull broken, had apparently been robbed and, secondly, that the police already had strong suspicion and even good grounds for believing that the murderer was one of the Shpigulin men called Fomka, the very one who had been his accomplice in murdering the Lebyadkins and setting fire to their house, and that there had been a quarrel between them on the road about a large sum of money stolen from Lebyadkin, which Fedka was supposed to have hidden. Liputin ran to Pyotr Stepanovitch's lodgings and succeeded in learning at the back door, on the sly, that though Pyotr Stepanovitch had not returned home till about one o'clock at night, he had slept there quietly all night till eight o'clock next morning. Of course, there could be no doubt that there was nothing extraordinary about Fedka's death, and that such careers usually have such an ending; but the coincidence of the fatal words that "it was the last time Fedka would drink vodka", with the prompt fulfilment of the prediction, was so remarkable that Liputin no longer hesitated. The shock had been given; it was as though a stone had fallen upon him and crushed him for ever. Returning home, he thrust his travelling-bag under the bed without a word, and in the evening at the hour fixed he was the first to appear at the appointed spot to meet Shatov, though it's true he still had his passport in his pocket.

CHAPTER V

A WANDERER

I

THE catastrophe with Liza and the death of Marya Timofyevna made an overwhelming impression on Shatov. I
have already mentioned that that morning I met him in passing; he seemed to me not himself. He told me among other
things that on the evening before at nine o'clock (that is, three
hours before the fire had broken out) he had been at Marya
Timofyevna's. He went in the morning to look at the corpses,
but as far as I know gave no evidence of any sort that morning.
Meanwhile, towards the end of the day there was a perfect
tempest in his soul, and . . . I think I can say with certainty
that there was a moment at dusk when he wanted to get up, go
out and tell everything. What that *everything* was, no one but
he could say. Of course he would have achieved nothing, and
would have simply betrayed himself. He had no proofs whatever with which to convict the perpetrators of the crime, and,
indeed, he had nothing but vague conjectures to go upon,
though to him they amounted to complete certainty. But he
was ready to ruin himself if he could only "crush the
scoundrels"—his own words. Pyotr Stepanovitch had guessed
fairly correctly at this impulse in him, and he knew himself that
he was risking a great deal in putting off the execution of his
new awful project till next day. On his side there was, as usual,
great self-confidence and contempt for all these "wretched
creatures" and for Shatov in particular. He had for years
despised Shatov for his "whining idiocy", as he had expressed
it in former days abroad, and he was absolutely confident that
he could deal with such a guileless creature, that is, keep an eye
on him all that day, and put a check on him at the first sign of
danger. Yet what saved "the scoundrels" for a short time was
something quite unexpected which they had not foreseen. . . .

Towards eight o'clock in the evening (at the very time when
the quintet was meeting at Erkel's, and waiting in indignation
and excitement for Pyotr Stepanovitch) Shatov was lying in
the dark on his bed with a headache and a slight chill; he was
tortured by uncertainty, he was angry, he kept making up his
mind, and could not make it up finally, and felt, with a curse,
that it would all lead to nothing. Gradually he sank into a brief

doze and had something like a nightmare. He dreamt that he was lying on his bed, tied up with cords and unable to stir, and meantime he heard a terrible banging that echoed all over the house, a banging on the fence, at the gate, at his door, in Kirillov's lodge, so that the whole house was shaking, and a far-away familiar voice that wrung his heart was calling to him piteously. He suddenly woke and sat up in bed. To his surprise the banging at the gate went on, though not nearly so violently as it had seemed in his dream. The knocks were repeated and persistent, and the strange voice "that wrung his heart" could still be heard below at the gate, though not piteously but angrily and impatiently, alternating with another voice, more restrained and ordinary. He jumped up, opened the casement pane and put his head out.

"Who's there?" he called, literally numb with terror.

"If you are Shatov," the answer came harshly and resolutely from below, "be so good as to tell me straight out and honestly whether you agree to let me in or not?"

It was true: he recognised the voice!

"Marie! . . . Is it you?"

"Yes, yes, Marya Shatov, and I assure you I can't keep the driver a minute longer."

"This minute . . . I'll get a candle," Shatov cried faintly. Then he rushed to look for the matches. The matches, as always happens at such moments, could not be found. He dropped the candlestick and the candle on the floor and as soon as he heard the impatient voice from below again, he abandoned the search and dashed down the steep stairs to open the gate.

"Be so good as to hold the bag while I settle with this blockhead," was how Madame Marya Shatov greeted him below, and she thrust into his hands a rather light cheap canvas handbag studded with brass nails, of Dresden manufacture. She attacked the driver with exasperation.

"Allow me to tell you, you are asking too much. If you've been driving me for an extra hour through these filthy streets, that's your fault, because it seems you didn't know where to find this stupid street and imbecile house. Take your thirty kopecks and make up your mind that you'll get nothing more."

"Ech, lady, you told me yourself Voznesensky Street and this is Bogoyavlensky; Voznesensky is ever so far away. You've simply put the horse into a steam."

"Voznesensky, Bogoyavlensky—you ought to know all those stupid names better than I do, as you are an inhabitant; besides,

you are unfair, I told you first of all Filipov's house and you
declared you knew it. In any case you can have me up
to-morrow in the local court, but now I beg you to let me
alone."

"Here, here's another five kopecks." With eager haste
Shatov pulled a five-kopeck piece out of his pocket and gave
it to the driver.

"Do me a favour, I beg you, don't dare to do that!" Madame
Shatov flared up, but the driver drove off and Shatov, taking
her hand, drew her through the gate.

"Make haste, Marie, make haste . . . that's no matter,
and . . . you are wet through. Take care, we go up here—
how sorry I am there's no light—the stairs are steep, hold tight,
hold tight! Well, this is my room. Excuse my having no
light. . . . One minute!"

He picked up the candlestick but it was a long time before
the matches were found. Madame Shatov stood waiting in the
middle of the room, silent and motionless.

"Thank God, here they are at last!" he cried joyfully, lighting up the room. Marya Shatov took a cursory survey of his
abode.

"They told me you lived in a poor way, but I didn't expect
it to be as bad as this," she pronounced with an air of disgust,
and she moved towards the bed.

"Oh, I am tired!" She sat down on the hard bed, with an
exhausted air. "Please put down the bag and sit down on the
chair yourself. Just as you like though; you are in the way
standing there. I have come to you for a time, till I can get
work, because I know nothing of this place and I have no
money. But if I shall be in your way I beg you again, be so
good as to tell me so at once, as you are bound to do if you
are an honest man. I could sell something to-morrow and pay
for a room at an hotel, but you must take me to the hotel yourself. . . . Oh, but I am tired!"

Shatov was all of a tremor.

"You mustn't, Marie, you mustn't go to an hotel! An hotel!
What for? What for?"

He clasped his hands imploringly. . . .

"Well, if I can get on without the hotel . . . I must, anyway, explain the position. Remember, Shatov, that we lived
in Geneva as man and wife for a fortnight and a few days;
it's three years since we parted, without any particular quarrel
though. But don't imagine that I've come back to renew any

205

of the foolishness of the past. I've come back to look for work, and that I've come straight to this town is just because it's all the same to me. I've not come to say I am sorry for anything; please don't imagine anything so stupid as that.''

"Oh, Marie! This is unnecessary, quite unnecessary," Shatov muttered vaguely.

"If so, if you are so far developed as to be able to understand that, I may allow myself to add, that if I've come straight to you now and am in your lodging, it's partly because I always thought you were far from being a scoundrel and were perhaps much better than other . . . blackguards!''

Her eyes flashed. She must have had to bear a great deal at the hands of some "blackguards".

"And please believe me, I wasn't laughing at you just now when I told you you were good. I spoke plainly, without fine phrases and I can't endure them. But that's all nonsense. I always hoped you would have sense enough not to pester me. . . . Enough, I am tired.''

And she bent on him a long, harassed and weary gaze. Shatov stood facing her at the other end of the room, which was five paces away, and listened to her timidly with a look of new life and unwonted radiance on his face. This strong, rugged man, all bristles on the surface, was suddenly all softness and shining gladness. There was a thrill of extraordinary and unexpected feeling in his soul. Three years of separation, three years of the broken marriage had effaced nothing from his heart. And perhaps every day during those three years he had dreamed of her, of that beloved being who had once said to him: "I love you." Knowing Shatov I can say with certainty that he could never have allowed himself even to dream that a woman might say to him: "I love you." He was savagely modest and chaste, he looked on himself as a perfect monster, detested his own face as well as his character, compared himself to some freak only fit to be exhibited at fairs. Consequently he valued honesty above everything and was fanatically devoted to his convictions; he was gloomy, proud, easily moved to wrath, and sparing of words. But here was the one being who had loved him for a fortnight (that he had never doubted, never!), a being he had always considered immeasurably above him in spite of his perfectly sober understanding of her errors; a being to whom he could forgive everything, *everything* (of that there could be no question; indeed it was quite the other way, his idea was that he was entirely to blame); this woman,

THE POSSESSED

this Marya Shatov, was in his house, in his presence again . . .
it was almost inconceivable! He was so overcome, there was so
much that was terrible and at the same time so much happiness
in this event that he could not, perhaps would not—perhaps was
afraid to—realise the position. It was a dream. But when she
looked at him with that harassed gaze he suddenly understood
that this woman he loved so dearly was suffering, perhaps had
been wronged. His heart went cold. He looked at her features
with anguish: the first bloom of youth had long faded from this
exhausted face. It's true that she was still good-looking—in
his eyes a beauty, as she had always been. In reality she was a
woman of twenty-five, rather strongly built, above the medium
height (taller than Shatov), with abundant dark brown hair, a
pale oval face, and large dark eyes now glittering with feverish
brilliance. But the light-hearted, naïve and good-natured energy
he had known so well in the past was replaced now by a sullen
irritability and disillusionment, a sort of cynicism which was not
yet habitual to her herself, and which weighed upon her. But
the chief thing was that she was ill, that he could see clearly. In
spite of the awe in which he stood of her he suddenly went up to
her and took her by both hands.

"Marie . . . you know . . . you are very tired, perhaps,
for God's sake, don't be angry. . . . If you'd consent to have
some tea, for instance, eh? Tea picks one up so, doesn't it? If
you'd consent!"

"Why talk about consenting? Of course I consent, what a
baby you are still. Get me some if you can. How cramped you
are here. How cold it is!"

"Oh, I'll get some logs for the fire directly, some logs . . .
I've got logs." Shatov was all astir. "Logs . . . that is . . .
but I'll get tea directly," he waved his hand as though with
desperate determination and snatched up his cap.

"Where are you going? So you've no tea in the house?"

"There shall be, there shall be, there shall be, there shall be
everything directly. . . . I . . ." he took his revolver from the
shelf, "I'll sell this revolver directly . . . or pawn it. . . ."

"What foolishness and what a time that will take! Take my
money if you've nothing, there's eighty kopecks here, I think;
that's all I have. This is like a madhouse."

"I don't want your money, I don't want it, I'll be
here directly, in one instant. I can manage without the
revolver. . . ."

And he rushed straight to Kirillov's. This was probably two

207

hours before the visit of Pyotr Stepanovitch and Liputin to Kirillov. Though Shatov and Kirillov lived in the same yard they hardly ever saw each other, and when they met they did not nod or speak; they had been too long "lying side by side" in America. . . .

"Kirillov, you always have tea; have you got tea and a samovar?"

Kirillov, who was walking up and down the room, as he was in the habit of doing all night, stopped and looked intently at his hurried visitor, though without much surprise.

"I've got tea and sugar and a samovar. But there's no need of the samovar, the tea is hot. Sit down and simply drink it."

"Kirillov, we lay side by side in America. . . . My wife has come to me . . . I . . . give me the tea. . . . I shall want the samovar."

"If your wife is here you want the samovar. But take it later. I've two. And now take the teapot from the table. It's hot, boiling hot. Take everything, take the sugar, all of it. Bread . . . there's plenty of bread; all of it. There's some veal. I've a rouble."

"Give it me, friend, I'll pay it back to-morrow! Ach, Kirillov!"

"Is it the same wife who was in Switzerland? That's a good thing. And your running in like this, that's a good thing too."

"Kirillov!" cried Shatov, taking the teapot under his arm and carrying the bread and sugar in both hands. "Kirillov, if . . . if you could get rid of your dreadful fancies and give up your atheistic ravings . . . oh, what a man you'd be, Kirillov!"

"One can see you love your wife after Switzerland. It's a good thing you do—after Switzerland. When you want tea, come again. You can come all night, I don't sleep at all. There'll be a samovar. Take the rouble, here it is. Go to your wife, I'll stay here and think about you and your wife."

Marya Shatov was unmistakably pleased at her husband's haste and fell upon the tea almost greedily, but there was no need to run for the samovar; she drank only half a cup and swallowed a tiny piece of bread. The veal she refused with disgust and irritation.

"You are ill, Marie, all this is a sign of illness," Shatov remarked timidly as he waited upon her.

"Of course I'm ill, please sit down. Where did you get the tea if you haven't any?"

208

THE POSSESSED

Shatov told her about Kirillov briefly. She had heard something of him.

"I know he is mad; say no more, please; there are plenty of fools. So you've been in America? I heard, you wrote."

"Yes, I . . . I wrote to you in Paris."

"Enough, please talk of something else. Are you a Slavophil in your convictions?"

"I . . . I am not exactly. . . . Since I cannot be a Russian, I became a Slavophil." He smiled a wry smile with the effort of one who feels he has made a strained and inappropriate jest.

"Why, aren't you a Russian?"

"No, I'm not."

"Well, that's all foolishness. Do sit down, I entreat you. Why are you all over the place? Do you think I am light-headed? Perhaps I shall be. You say there are only you two in the house."

"Yes. . . . Downstairs . . ."

"And both such clever people. What is there downstairs? You said downstairs?"

"No, nothing."

"Why nothing? I want to know."

"I only meant to say that now we are only two in the yard, but that the Lebyadkins used to live downstairs. . . ."

"That woman who was murdered last night?" she started suddenly. "I heard of it. I heard of it as soon as I arrived. There was a fire here, wasn't there?"

"Yes, Marie, yes, and perhaps I am doing a scoundrelly thing this moment in forgiving the scoundrels. . . ." He stood up suddenly and paced about the room, raising his arms as though in a frenzy.

But Marie had not quite understood him. She heard his answers inattentively; she asked questions but did not listen.

"Fine things are being done among you! Oh, how contemptible it all is! What scoundrels men all are! But do sit down, I beg you, oh, how you exasperate me!" and she let her head sink on the pillow, exhausted.

"Marie, I won't. . . . Perhaps you'll lie down, Marie?"

She made no answer and closed her eyes helplessly. Her pale face looked death-like. She fell asleep almost instantly. Shatov looked round, snuffed the candle, looked uneasily at her face once more, pressed his hands tight in front of him and walked on tiptoe out of the room into the passage. At the top of the stairs he stood in the corner with his face to the wall and re-

209

mained so for ten minutes without sound or movement. He would have stood there longer, but he suddenly caught the sound of soft cautious steps below. Someone was coming up the stairs. Shatov remembered he had forgotten to fasten the gate.

"Who's there?" he asked in a whisper. The unknown visitor went on slowly mounting the stairs without answering. When he reached the top he stood still; it was impossible to see his face in the dark; suddenly Shatov heard the cautious question:

"Ivan Shatov?"

Shatov said who he was, but at once held out his hand to check his advance. The latter took his hand, and Shatov shuddered as though he had touched some terrible reptile.

"Stand here," he whispered quickly. "Don't go in, I can't receive you just now. My wife has come back. I'll fetch the candle."

When he returned with the candle he found a young officer standing there; he did not know his name, but he had seen him before.

"Erkel," said the lad, introducing himself. "You've seen me at Virginsky's."

"I remember; you sat writing. Listen," said Shatov in sudden excitement, going up to him frantically, but still talking in a whisper. "You gave me a sign just now when you took my hand. But you know I can treat all these signals with contempt! I don't acknowledge them. . . . I don't want them. . . . I can throw you downstairs this minute, do you know that?"

"No, I know nothing about that and I don't know what you are in such a rage about," the visitor answered without malice and almost ingenuously. "I have only to give you a message, and that's what I've come for, being particularly anxious not to lose time. You have a printing press which does not belong to you, and of which you are bound to give an account, as you know yourself. I have received instructions to request you to give it up to-morrow at seven o'clock in the evening to Liputin. I have been instructed to tell you also that nothing more will be asked of you."

"Nothing?"

"Absolutely nothing. Your request is granted, and you are struck off our list. I was instructed to tell you that positively."

"Who instructed you to tell me?"

"Those who told me the sign."

"Have you come from abroad?"

"I . . . I think that's no matter to you."

"Oh, hang it! Why didn't you come before if you were told to?"

"I followed certain instructions and was not alone."

"I understand, I understand that you were not alone. Eh . . . hang it! But why didn't Liputin come himself?"

"So I shall come for you to-morrow at exactly six o'clock in the evening, and we'll go there on foot. There will be no one there but us three."

"Will Verhovensky be there?"

"No, he won't. Verhovensky is leaving the town at eleven o'clock to-morrow morning."

"Just what I thought!" Shatov whispered furiously, and he struck his fist on his hip. "He's run off, the sneak!"

He sank into agitated reflection. Erkel looked intently at him and waited in silence.

"But how will you take it? You can't simply pick it up in your hands and carry it."

"There will be no need to. You'll simply point out the place and we'll just make sure that it really is buried there. We only know whereabouts the place is, we don't know the place itself. And have you pointed the place out to anyone else yet?"

Shatov looked at him.

"You, you, a chit of a boy like you, a silly boy like you, you too have been caught in that net like a sheep? Yes, that's just the young blood they want! Well, go along. E-ech! that scoundrel's taken you all in and run away."

Erkel looked at him serenely and calmly, but did not seem to understand.

"Verhovensky, Verhovensky has run away!" Shatov growled fiercely.

"But he is still here, he is not gone away. He is not going till to-morrow," Erkel observed softly and persuasively. "I particularly begged him to be present as a witness; my instructions all referred to him (he explained frankly like a young and inexperienced boy). But I regret to say he did not agree on the ground of his departure, and he really is in a hurry."

Shatov glanced compassionately at the simple youth again, but suddenly gave a gesture of despair as though he thought "they are not worth pitying".

"All right, I'll come," he cut him short. "And now get away, be off."

"So I'll come for you at six o'clock punctually." Erkel made a courteous bow and walked deliberately downstairs.

"Little fool!" Shatov could not help shouting after him from the top.

"What is it?" responded the lad from the bottom.

"Nothing, you can go."

"I thought you said something."

II

Erkel was a "little fool" who was only lacking in the higher form of reason, the ruling power of the intellect; but of the lesser, the subordinate reasoning faculties, he had plenty—even to the point of cunning. Fanatically, childishly devoted to "the cause" or rather in reality to Pyotr Verhovensky, he acted on the instructions given to him when at the meeting of the quintet they had agreed and had distributed the various duties for the next day. When Pyotr Stepanovitch gave him the job of messenger, he succeeded in talking to him aside for ten minutes.

A craving for active service was characteristic of this shallow, unreflecting nature, which was for ever yearning to follow the lead of another man's will, of course for the good of "the common" or "the great" cause. Not that that made any difference, for little fanatics like Erkel can never imagine serving a cause except by identifying it with the person who, to their minds, is the expression of it. The sensitive, affectionate and kind-hearted Erkel was perhaps the most callous of Shatov's would-be murderers, and, though he had no personal spite against him, he would have been present at his murder without the quiver of an eyelid. He had been instructed, for instance, to have a good look at Shatov's surroundings while carrying out his commission, and when Shatov, receiving him at the top of the stairs, blurted out to him, probably unaware in the heat of the moment, that his wife had come back to him—Erkel had the instinctive cunning to avoid displaying the slightest curiosity, though the idea flashed through his mind that the fact of his wife's return was of great importance for the success of their undertaking.

And so it was in reality; it was only that fact that saved the "scoundrels" from Shatov's carrying out his intention, and at the same time helped them "to get rid of him". To begin with, it agitated Shatov, threw him out of his regular routine, and deprived him of his usual clear-sightedness and caution. Any

THE POSSESSED

idea of his own danger would be the last thing to enter his head at this moment when he was absorbed with such different considerations. On the contrary, he eagerly believed that Pyotr Verhovensky was running away the next day: it fell in exactly with his suspicions! Returning to the room he sat down again in a corner, leaned his elbows on his knees and hid his face in his hands. Bitter thoughts tormented him. . . .

Then he would raise his head again and go on tiptoe to look at her. "Good God! she will be in a fever by to-morrow morning; perhaps it's begun already! She must have caught cold. She is not accustomed to this awful climate, and then a third-class carriage, the storm, the rain, and she has such a thin little pelisse, no wrap at all. . . . And to leave her like this, to abandon her in her helplessness! Her bag, too, her bag—what a tiny, light thing, all crumpled up, scarcely weighs ten pounds! Poor thing, how worn out she is, how much she's been through! She is proud, that's why she won't complain. But she is irritable, very irritable. It's illness; an angel will grow irritable in illness. What a dry forehead, it must be hot—how dark she is under her eyes, and . . . and yet how beautiful the oval of her face is and her rich hair, how . . ."

And he made haste to turn away his eyes, to walk away as though he were frightened at the very idea of seeing in her anything but an unhappy, exhausted fellow-creature who needed help—"how could he think of hopes, oh, how mean, how base is man!" And he would go back to his corner, sit down, hide his face in his hands and again sink into dreams and reminiscences . . . and again he was haunted by hopes.

"Oh, I am tired, I am tired," he remembered her exclamations, her weak broken voice. "Good God! Abandon her now, and she has only eighty kopecks; she held out her purse, a tiny old thing! She's come to look for a job. What does she know about jobs? What do they know about Russia? Why, they are like naughty children, they've nothing but their own fancies made up by themselves, and she is angry, poor thing, that Russia is not like their foreign dreams! The luckless, innocent creatures! . . . It's really cold here, though."

He remembered that she had complained, that he had promised to heat the stove. "There are logs here, I can fetch them if only I don't wake her. But I can do it without waking her. But what shall I do about the veal? When she gets up perhaps she will be hungry. . . . Well, that will do later: Kirillov doesn't go to bed all night. What could I cover her with,

213

she is sleeping so soundly, but she must be cold, ah, she must be cold!'' And once more he went to look at her; her dress had worked up a little and her right leg was half uncovered to the knee. He suddenly turned away almost in dismay, took off his warm overcoat, and, remaining in his wretched old jacket, covered it up, trying not to look at it.

A great deal of time was spent in lighting the fire, stepping about on tiptoe, looking at the sleeping woman, dreaming in the corner, then looking at her again. Two or three hours had passed. During that time Verhovensky and Liputin had been at Kirillov's. At last he, too, began to doze in the corner. He heard her groan; she waked up and called him; he jumped up like a criminal.

"Marie, I was dropping asleep. . . Ah, what a wretch I am, Marie!''

She sat up, looking about her with wonder, seeming not to recognise where she was, and suddenly leapt up in indignation and anger.

"I've taken your bed, I fell asleep so tired I didn't know what I was doing; how dared you not wake me? How could you dare imagine I meant to be a burden to you?''

"How could I wake you, Marie?''

"You could, you ought to have! You've no other bed here, and I've taken yours. You had no business to put me into a false position. Or do you suppose that I've come to take advantage of your charity? Kindly get into your bed at once and I'll lie down in the corner on some chairs.''

"Marie, there aren't chairs enough, and there's nothing to put on them.''

"Then simply on the floor. Or you'll have to lie on the floor yourself. I want to lie on the floor at once, at once!''

She stood up, tried to take a step, but suddenly a violent spasm of pain deprived her of all power and all determination, and with a loud groan she fell back on the bed. Shatov ran up, but Marie, hiding her face on the pillow, seized his hand and gripped and squeezed it with all her might. This lasted a minute.

"Marie darling, there's a Doctor Frenzel living here, a friend of mine. . . . I could run for him.''

"Nonsense!''

"What do you mean by nonsense? Tell me, Marie, what is it hurting you? For we might try fomentations . . . on the stomach, for instance. . . . I can do that without a doctor. . . . Or else mustard poultices.''

"What's this?" she asked strangely, raising her head and looking at him in dismay.

"What's what, Marie?" said Shatov, not understanding. "What are you asking about? Good heavens! I am quite bewildered, excuse my not understanding."

"Ach, let me alone; it's not your business to understand. And it would be too absurd . . ." she said with a bitter smile. "Talk to me about something. Walk about the room and talk. Don't stand over me and don't look at me, I particularly ask you that for the five-hundredth time?"

Shatov began walking up and down the room, looking at the floor, and doing his utmost not to glance at her.

"There's—don't be angry, Marie, I entreat you—there's some veal here, and there's tea not far off. . . . You had so little before."

She made an angry gesture of disgust. Shatov bit his tongue in despair.

"Listen, I intend to open a bookbinding business here, on rational co-operative principles. Since you live here what do you think of it, would it be successful?"

"Ech, Marie, people don't read books here, and there are none here at all. And are they likely to begin binding them?"

"Who are they?"

"The local readers and inhabitants generally, Marie."

"Well, then, speak more clearly. *They* indeed, and one doesn't know who they are. You don't know grammar!"

"It's in the spirit of the language," Shatov muttered.

"Oh, get along with your spirit, you bore me. Why shouldn't the local inhabitant or reader have his books bound?"

"Because reading books and having them bound are two different stages of development, and there's a vast gulf between them. To begin with, a man gradually gets used to reading, in the course of ages of course, but takes no care of his books and throws them about, not thinking them worth attention. But binding implies respect for books, and implies that not only he has grown fond of reading, but that he looks upon it as something of value. That period has not been reached anywhere in Russia yet. In Europe books have been bound for a long while."

"Though that's pedantic, anyway, it's not stupid, and reminds me of the time three years ago; you used to be rather clever sometimes three years ago."

She said this as disdainfully as her other capricious remarks.

215

"Marie, Marie," said Shatov, turning to her, much moved, "oh, Marie! If you only knew how much has happened in those three years! I heard afterwards that you despised me for changing my convictions. But what are the men I've broken with? The enemies of all true life, out-of-date Liberals who are afraid of their own independence, the flunkeys of thought, the enemies of individuality and freedom, the decrepit advocates of deadness and rottenness! All they have to offer is senility, a glorious mediocrity of the most bourgeois kind, contemptible shallowness, a jealous equality, equality without individual dignity, equality as it's understood by flunkeys or by the French in '93. And the worst of it is there are swarms of scoundrels among them, swarms of scoundrels!"

"Yes, there are a lot of scoundrels," she brought out abruptly with painful effort. She lay stretched out, motionless, as though afraid to move with her head thrown back on the pillow, rather on one side, staring at the ceiling with exhausted but glowing eyes. Her face was pale, her lips were dry and hot.

"You recognise it, Marie, you recognise it," cried Shatov. She tried to shake her head, and suddenly the same spasm came over her again. Again she hid her face in the pillow, and again for a full minute she squeezed Shatov's hand till it hurt. He had run up, beside himself with alarm.

"Marie, Marie! But it may be very serious, Marie!"

"Be quiet . . . I won't have it, I won't have it," she screamed almost furiously, turning her face upwards again. "Don't dare to look at me with sympathy! Walk about the room, say something, talk. . . ."

Shatov began muttering something again, like one distraught.

"What do you do here?" she asked, interrupting him with contemptuous impatience.

"I work in a merchant's office. I could get a fair amount of money even here if I cared to, Marie."

"So much the better for you. . . ."

"Oh, don't suppose I meant anything, Marie. I said it without thinking."

"And what do you do besides? What are you preaching? You can't exist without preaching, that's your character!"

"I am preaching God, Marie."

"In whom you don't believe yourself. I never could see the idea of that."

"Let's leave that, Marie; we'll talk of that later."

"What sort of person was this Marya Timofyevna here?"

216

"We'll talk of that later too, Marie."

"Don't dare to say such things to me! Is it true that her death may have been caused by . . . the wickedness . . . of these people?"

"Not a doubt of it," growled Shatov.

Marie suddenly raised her head and cried out painfully:

"Don't dare speak of that to me again, don't dare to, never, never!"

And she fell back in bed again, overcome by the same convulsive agony; it was the third time, but this time her groans were louder; in fact, she screamed.

"Oh, you insufferable man! Oh, you unbearable man," she cried, tossing about recklessly, and pushing away Shatov as he bent over her.

"Marie, I'll do anything you like. . . . I'll walk about and talk. . . ."

"'Surely you must see that it has begun!"

"What's begun, Marie?"

"How can I tell? Do I know anything about it? . . . I curse myself! Oh, curse it all from the beginning!"

"Marie, if you'd tell me what's beginning . . . or else I . . . if you don't, what am I to make of it?"

"You are a useless, theoretical babbler. Oh, curse everything on earth!"

"Marie, Marie!" He seriously thought that she was beginning to go mad.

"Surely you must see that I am in the agonies of childbirth," she said, sitting up and gazing at him with a terrible, hysterical vindictiveness that distorted her whole face. "I curse him before he is born, this child!"

"Marie," cried Shatov, realising at last what it meant. "Marie . . . but why didn't you tell me before?" He pulled himself together at once and seized his cap with an air of vigorous determination.

"How could I tell when I came in here? Should I have come to you if I'd known? I was told it would be another ten days! Where are you going? . . . Where are you going? You mustn't dare!"

"To fetch a midwife! I'll sell the revolver. We must get money before anything else now."

"Don't dare to do anything, don't dare to fetch a midwife! Bring a peasant woman, any old woman, I've eighty kopecks in my purse. . . . Peasant women have babies without midwives.

217

. . . And if I die, so much the better. . . ."

"You shall have a midwife and an old woman too. But how am I to leave you alone, Marie!"

But reflecting that it was better to leave her alone now in spite of her desperate state than to leave her without help later, he paid no attention to her groans, nor her angry exclamations, but rushed downstairs, hurrying all he could.

III

First of all he went to Kirillov. It was by now about one o'clock in the night. Kirillov was standing in the middle of the room.

"Kirillov, my wife is in childbirth."

"How do you mean?"

"Childbirth, bearing a child!"

"You . . . are not mistaken?"

"Oh, no, no, she is in agonies! I want a woman, any old woman, I must have one at once. . . Can you get one now? You used to have a lot of old women. . . ."

"Very sorry that I am no good at childbearing," Kirillov answered thoughtfully; "that is, not at childbearing, but at doing anything for childbearing . . . or . . . no, I don't know how to say it."

"You mean you can't assist at a confinement yourself? But that's not what I've come for. An old woman, I want a woman, a nurse, a servant!"

"You shall have an old woman, but not directly, perhaps . . . If you like I'll come instead. . . ."

"Oh, impossible; I am running to Madame Virginsky, the midwife, now."

"A horrid woman!"

"Oh, yes, Kirillov, yes, but she is the best of them all. Yes, it'll all be without reverence, without gladness, with contempt, with abuse, with blasphemy in the presence of so great a mystery, the coming of a new creature! Oh, she is cursing it already!"

"If you like I'll . . ."

"No, no, but while I'm running (oh, I'll make Madame Virginsky come), will you go to the foot of my staircase and quietly listen? But don't venture to go in, you'll frighten her; don't

go in on any account, you must only listen . . . in case anything dreadful happens. If anything very bad happens, then
run in."

"I understand. I've another rouble. Here it is. I meant to
have a fowl to-morrow, but now I don't want to, make haste,
run with all your might. There's a samovar all the night."

Kirillov knew nothing of the present design against Shatov,
nor had he had any idea in the past of the degree of danger that
threatened him. He only knew that Shatov had some old scores
with "those people", and although he was to some extent involved with them through instructions he had received from
abroad (not that these were of much consequence, however,
for he had never taken any direct share in anything), yet of late
he had given it all up, having left off doing anything especially
for the "cause", and devoted himself entirely to a life of contem-
plation. Although Pyotr Stepanovitch had at the meeting invited Liputin to go with him to Kirillov's to make sure that
the latter would take upon himself, at a given moment, the
responsibility for the "Shatov business", yet in his interview
with Kirillov he had said no word about Shatov nor alluded to
him in any way—probably considering it impolitic to do so,
and thinking that Kirillov could not be relied upon. He put off
speaking about it till next day, when it would be all over and
would therefore not matter to Kirillov; such at least was Pyotr
Stepanovitch's judgment of him. Liputin, too, was struck by
the fact that Shatov was not mentioned in spite of what Pyotr
Stepanovitch had promised, but he was too much agitated to
protest.

Shatov ran like a hurricane to Virginsky's house, cursing the
distance and feeling it endless.

He had to knock a long time at Virginsky's; everyone had
been asleep a long while. But Shatov did not scruple to bang
at the shutters with all his might. The dog chained up in the
yard dashed about barking furiously. The dogs caught it up
all along the street, and there was a regular babel of barking.

"Why are you knocking and what do you want?" Shatov
heard at the window at last Virginsky's gentle voice, betraying
none of the resentment appropriate to the "outrage". The
shutter was pushed back a little and the casement was opened.

"Who's there, what scoundrel is it?" shrilled a female voice
which betrayed all the resentment appropriate to the "outrage".
It was the old maid, Virginsky's relation.

"I am Shatov, my wife has come back to me and she is just confined. . . ."

"Well, let her be, get along."

"I've come for Arina Prohorovna; I won't go without Arina Prohorovna!"

"She can't attend to everyone. Practice at night is a special line. Take yourself off to Maksheyev's and don't dare to make that din," rattled the exasperated female voice. He could hear Virginsky checking her; but the old maid pushed him away and would not desist.

"I am not going away!" Shatov cried again.

"Wait a little, wait a little," Virginsky cried at last, over-powering the lady. "I beg you to wait five minutes, Shatov. I'll wake Arina Prohorovna. Please don't knock and don't shout. . . . Oh, how awful it all is!"

After five endless minutes, Arina Prohorovna made her appearance.

"Has your wife come?" Shatov heard her voice at the window and to his surprise it was not at all ill-tempered, only as usual peremptory, but Arina Prohorovna could not speak except in a peremptory tone.

"Yes, my wife, and she is in labour."

"Marya Ignatyevna?"

"Yes, Marya Ignatyevna. Of course it's Marya Ignatyevna."

A silence followed. Shatov waited. He heard a whispering in the house.

"Has she been here long?" Madame Virginsky asked again.

"She came this evening at eight o'clock. Please make haste."

Again he heard whispering, as though they were consulting.

"Listen, you are not making a mistake? Did she send you for me herself?"

"No, she didn't send for you, she wants a peasant woman, so as not to burden me with expense, but don't be afraid, I'll pay you."

"Very good, I'll come, whether you pay or not. I always thought highly of Marya Ignatyevna for the independence of her sentiments, though perhaps she won't remember me. Have you got the most necessary things?"

"I've nothing, but I'll get everything, everything."

"There is something generous even in these people," Shatov reflected, as he set off to Lyamshin's. "The convictions and the man are two very different things, very likely I've been very unfair to them! . . . We are all to blame, we are all to blame

. . . and if only all were convinced of it!"

He had not to knock long at Lyamshin's; the latter, to Shatov's surprise, opened his casement at once, jumping out of bed, barefoot and in his night clothes at the risk of catching cold; and he was hypochondriacal and always anxious about his health. But there was a special cause for such alertness and haste: Lyamshin had been in a tremor all the evening, and had not been able to sleep for excitement after the meeting of the quintet; he was haunted by the dread of uninvited and un-desired visitors. The news of Shatov's giving information tor-mented him more than anything. . . . And suddenly there was this terrible loud knocking at the window as though to justify his fears.

He was so frightened at seeing Shatov that he at once slammed the casement and jumped back into bed. Shatov began furi-ously knocking and shouting.

"How dare you knock like that in the middle of the night?" shouted Lyamshin, in a threatening voice, though he was numb with fear, when at least two minutes later he ventured to open the casement again, and was at last convinced that Shatov had come alone.

"Here's your revolver for you; take it back, give me fifteen roubles."

"What's the matter, are you drunk? This is outrageous, I shall simply catch cold. Wait a minute, I'll just throw my rug over me."

"Give me fifteen roubles at once. If you don't give it me, I'll knock and shout till daybreak; I'll break your window-frame."

"And I'll shout police and you'll be taken to the lock-up."

"And am I dumb? Can't I shout 'police' too? Which of us has most reason to be afraid of the police, you or I?"

"And you can hold such contemptible opinions! I know what you are hinting at. . . . Stop, stop, for God's sake don't go on knocking! Upon my word, who has money at night? What do you want money for, unless you are drunk?"

"My wife has come back. I've taken ten roubles off the price, I haven't fired it once; take the revolver, take it this minute!"

Lyamshin mechanically put his hand out of the casement and took the revolver; he waited a little, and suddenly thrusting his head out of the casement, and with a shiver running down his spine, faltered as though he were beside himself.

"You are lying, your wife hasn't come back to you. . . . It's . . . it's simply that you want to run away."

"You are a fool. Where should I run to? It's for your Pyotr Verhovensky to run away, not for me. I've just been to the midwife, Madame Virginsky, and she consented at once to come to me. You can ask them. My wife is in agony; I need the money; give it me!"

A swarm of ideas flared up in Lyamshin's crafty mind like a shower of fireworks. It all suddenly took a different colour, though still panic prevented him from reflecting.

"But how . . . you are not living with your wife?"

"I'll break your skull for questions like that."

"Oh, dear, I understand, forgive me, I was struck all of a heap. . . But I understand, I understand . . . is Arina Prohorovna really coming? You said just now that she had gone? You know, that's not true. You see, you see, you see what lies you tell at every step."

"By now, she must be with my wife . . . don't keep me . . . it's not my fault you are a fool."

"That's a lie, I am not a fool. Excuse me, I really can't . . ."

And utterly distraught he began shutting the casement again for the third time, but Shatov gave such a yell that he put his head out again.

"But this is simply an unprovoked assault! What do you want of me, what is it, what is it, formulate it? And think, only think, it's the middle of the night!"

"I want fifteen roubles, you sheep's-head!"

"But perhaps I don't care to take back the revolver. You have no right to force me. You bought the thing and the matter is settled, and you've no right. . . . I can't give you a sum like that in the night, anyhow. Where am I to get a sum like that?"

"You always have money. I've taken ten roubles off the price, but everyone knows you are a skinflint."

"Come the day after to-morrow, do you hear, the day after to-morrow at twelve o'clock, and I'll give you the whole of it, that will do, won't it?"

Shatov knocked furiously at the window-frame for the third time.

"Give me ten roubles, and to-morrow early the other five."

"No, the day after to-morrow the other five, to-morrow I swear I shan't have it. You'd better not come, you'd better not come."

"Give me ten, you scoundrel!"

"Why are you so abusive? Wait a minute, I must light a candle; you've broken the window. . . . Nobody swears like that at night. Here you are!" He held a note to him out of the window.

Shatov seized it—it was a note for five roubles.

"On my honour I can't do more, if you were to murder me, I couldn't; the day after to-morrow I can give you it all, but now I can do nothing."

"I am not going away!" roared Shatov.

"Very well, take it, here's some more, see, here's some more, and I won't give more. You can shout at the top of your voice, but I won't give more, I won't, whatever happens, I won't, I won't."

He was in a perfect frenzy, desperate and perspiring. The two notes he had just given him were each for a rouble. Shatov had seven roubles altogether now.

"Well, damn you, then, I'll come to-morrow. I'll thrash you, Lyamshin, if you don't give me the other eight."

"You won't find me at home, you fool!" Lyamshin reflected quickly.

"'Stay, stay!" he shouted frantically after Shatov, who was already running off. "Stay, come back. Tell me, please, is it true what you said that your wife has come back?"

"Fool!" cried Shatov, with a gesture of disgust, and ran home as hard as he could.

IV

I may mention that Arina Prohorovna knew nothing of the resolutions that had been taken at the meeting the day before. On returning home overwhelmed and exhausted, Virginsky had not ventured to tell her of the decision that had been taken, yet he could not refrain from telling her half—that is, all that Verhovensky had told them of the certainty of Shatov's intention to betray them; but he added at the same time that he did not quite believe it. Arina Prohorovna was terribly alarmed. This was why she decided at once to go when Shatov came to fetch her, though she was tired out, as she had been hard at work at a confinement all the night before. She had always been convinced that "a wretched creature like Shatov was capable of any political baseness", but the arrival of Marya Ignatyevna put things in a different light. Shatov's alarm, the despairing tone of his entreaties, the way he begged for help, clearly showed a complete change of feeling in the traitor: a man who was ready to betray himself merely for the sake of ruining others would, she thought, have had a different air and tone. In short, Arina Prohorovna resolved to look into the matter for herself, with her own eyes. Virginsky was very glad of her decision, he felt as though a hundredweight had been lifted off him! He even began to feel hopeful: Shatov's appearance seemed to him utterly incompatible with Verhovensky's supposition.

Shatov was not mistaken: on getting home he found Arina Prohorovna already with Marie. She had just arrived, had contemptuously dismissed Kirillov, whom she found hanging about the foot of the stairs, had hastily introduced herself to Marie, who had not recognised her as her former acquaintance, found her in "a very bad way", that is ill-tempered, irritable and in "a state of cowardly despair", and within five minutes had completely silenced all her protests.

"Why do you keep on that you don't want an expensive midwife?" she was saying at the moment when Shatov came in. "That's perfect nonsense, it's a false idea arising from the abnormality of your condition. In the hands of some ordinary old woman, some peasant midwife, you'd have fifty chances of going wrong and then you'd have more bother and expense than with a regular midwife. How do you know I am an expensive midwife? You can pay afterwards; I won't charge you much and I answer for my success; you won't die in my hands, I've seen worse cases than yours. And I can send the baby to a foundling asylum to-morrow, if you like, and then to be brought up in the country, and that's all it will mean. And meantime you'll grow strong again, take up some rational work, and in a very short time you'll repay Shatov for sheltering you and for the expense, which will not be so great."

"It's not that . . . I've no right to be a burden. . . ."

"Rational feelings and worthy of a citizen, but you can take my word for it, Shatov will spend scarcely anything, if he is willing to become ever so little a man of sound ideas instead of the fantastic person he is. He has only not to do anything stupid, not to raise an alarm, not to run about the town with his tongue out. If we don't restrain him he will be knocking up all the doctors of the town before the morning; he waked all the dogs in my street. There's no need of doctors, I've said already. I'll answer for everything. You can hire an old woman if you like to wait on you, that won't cost much. Though he too can do something besides the silly things he's been doing. He's got hands and feet, he can run to the chemist's without offending your feelings by being too benevolent. As though it were a case of benevolence! Hasn't he brought you into this position? Didn't he make you break with the family in which you were a governess, with the egoistic object of marrying you? We heard of it, you know . . . though he did run for me like one possessed and yell so all the street could hear. I won't force myself upon anyone and have come only for your sake, on the principle that all of us are bound to hold together! And I told him so before I left the house. If you think I am in the way, good-bye, I only hope you won't have trouble which might so easily be averted."

And she positively got up from the chair. Marie was so helpless, in such pain, and—the truth must be confessed—so frightened of what was before her that she dared not let her go. But this woman was suddenly hateful to her, what she said was not what she wanted, there was something quite different in Marie's soul. Yet the prediction that she might possibly die in the hands of an inexperienced peasant woman overcame her aversion. But she made up for it by being more exacting and more ruthless than ever with Shatov. She ended by forbidding him not only to look at her, but even to stand facing her. Her pains became more violent. Her curses, her abuse became more and more frantic.

"Ech, we'll send him away," Arina Prohorovna rapped out. "I don't know what he looks like, he is simply frightening you; he is as white as a corpse! What is it to you, tell me please, you absurd fellow? What a farce!"

Shatov made no reply, he made up his mind to say nothing.

"I've seen many a foolish father, half crazy in such cases. But they, at any rate . . ."

"Be quiet or leave me to die! Don't say another word! I won't have it, I won't have it!" screamed Marie.

"It's impossible not to say another word, if you are not out of your mind, as I think you are in your condition. We must talk of what we want, anyway: tell me, have you anything ready? You answer, Shatov, she is incapable."

"Tell me what's needed?"

"That means you've nothing ready." She reckoned up all that was quite necessary, and one must do her the justice to say she only asked for what was absolutely indispensable, the barest necessaries. Some things Shatov had. Marie took her key and held it out to him, for him to look in her bag. As his hands shook he was longer than he should have been opening the unfamiliar lock. Marie flew into a rage, but when Arina Prohorovna rushed up to take the key from him, she would not allow her on any account to look into her bag and with peevish cries and tears insisted that no one should open the bag but Shatov.

Some things he had to fetch from Kirillov's. No sooner had Shatov turned to go for them than she began frantically calling him back and was only quieted when Shatov had rushed impetuously back from the stairs, and explained that he would only be gone a minute to fetch something indispensable and would be back at once.

"Well, my lady, it's hard to please you," laughed Arina Prohorovna, "one minute he must stand with his face to the wall and not dare to look at you, and the next he mustn't be gone for a minute, or you begin crying. He may begin to imagine something. Come, come, don't be silly, don't blubber, I was laughing, you know."

"He won't dare to imagine anything."

"Tut, tut, tut, if he didn't love you like a sheep he wouldn't run about the streets with his tongue out and wouldn't have roused all the dogs in the town. He broke my window-frame."

V

He found Kirillov still pacing up and down his room so preoccupied that he had forgotten the arrival of Shatov's wife, and heard what he said without understanding him.

"Oh, yes!" he recollected suddenly, as though tearing himself with an effort and only for an instant from some absorbing idea, "yes . . an old woman. . . . A wife or an old woman? Stay a minute: a wife and an old woman, is that it? I remember. I've been, the old woman will come, only not just now. Take the pillow. Is there anything else? Yes. . . . Stay, do you have moments of the eternal harmony, Shatov?"

"You know, Kirillov, you mustn't go on staying up every night."

Kirillov came out of his reverie and, strange to say, spoke far more coherently than he usually did; it was clear that he had formulated it long ago and perhaps written it down.

"There are seconds—they come five or six at a time—when you suddenly feel the presence of the eternal harmony perfectly attained. It's something not earthly—I don't mean in the sense that it's heavenly—but in that sense that man cannot endure it in his earthly aspect. He must be physically changed or die. This feeling is clear and unmistakable; it's as though you apprehend all nature and suddenly say: 'Yes, that's right.' God, when He created the world, said at the end of each day of creation: 'Yes, it's right, it's good.' It . . . it's not being deeply moved, but simply joy. You don't forgive anything because there is no more need of forgiveness. It's not that you love—oh, there's something in it higher than love—what's most awful is that it's terribly clear and such joy. If it lasted more than five seconds, the soul could not endure it and must perish. In those five seconds I live through a lifetime, and I'd give my whole life for them, because they are worth it. To endure ten seconds one must be physically changed. I think man ought to give up having children—what's the use of children, what's the use of evolution when the goal has been attained? In the gospel it is written that there will be no child-bearing in the resurrection, but that men will be like the angels of the Lord. That's a hint. Is your wife bearing a child?"

"Kirillov, does this often happen?"

"Once in three days, or once a week."

"Don't you have fits, perhaps?"

"No."

"Well, you will. Be careful, Kirillov. I've heard that's just how fits begin. An epileptic described exactly that sensation before a fit, word for word as you've done. He mentioned five seconds, too, and said that more could not be endured. Remember Mahomet's pitcher from which no drop of water was spilt while he circled Paradise on his horse. That was a case of five seconds too; that's too much like your eternal harmony, and Mahomet was an epileptic. Be careful, Kirillov, it's epilepsy!"

"It won't have time," Kirillov smiled gently.

VI

The night was passing. Shatov was sent hither and thither, abused, called back. Marie was reduced to the most abject terror for life. She screamed that she wanted to live, that "she must, she must", and was afraid to die. "I don't want to, I don't want to!" she repeated. If Arina Prohorovna had not been there, things would have gone very badly. By degrees she gained complete control of the patient—who began to obey every word, every order from her like a child. Arina Prohorovna ruled by sternness not by kindness, but she was first-rate at her work. It began to get light . . . Arina Prohorovna suddenly imagined that Shatov had just run out on to the stairs to say his prayers and began laughing. Marie laughed too, spitefully, malignantly, as though such laughter relieved her. At last they drove Shatov away altogether. A damp, cold morning dawned. He pressed his face to the wall in the corner just as he had done the evening before when Erkel came. He was trembling like a leaf, afraid to think, but his mind caught at every thought as it does in dreams. He was continually being carried away by day-dreams, which snapped off short like a rotten thread. From the room came no longer groans but awful animal cries, unendurable, incredible. He tried to stop up his ears, but could not, and he fell on his knees, repeating unconsciously: "Marie, Marie!" Then suddenly he heard a cry, a new cry, which made Shatov start and jump up from his knees, the cry of a baby, a weak discordant cry. He crossed himself and rushed into the room. Arina Prohorovna held in her hands a little red wrinkled creature, screaming, and moving its little arms and legs, fearfully helpless, and looking as though it could be blown away by a puff of wind, but screaming and seeming to assert its full right to live. Marie was lying as though insensible, but a minute later she opened her eyes, and bent a strange, strange look on Shatov: it was something quite new, that look. What it meant exactly he was not able to understand yet, but he had never known such a look on her face before.

"Is it a boy? Is it a boy?" she asked Arina Prohorovna in an exhausted voice.

"It is a boy," the latter shouted in reply, as she bound up the child.

When she had bound him up and was about to lay him across the bed between the two pillows, she gave him to Shatov for a minute to hold. Marie signed to him on the sly as though afraid of Arina Prohorovna. He understood at once and brought the baby to show her.

"How . . . pretty he is," she whispered weakly with a smile.

"Foo, what does he look like?" Arina Prohorovna laughed

gaily in triumph, glancing at Shatov's face. "What a funny face!"

"You may be merry, Arina Prohorovna. . . . It's a great joy," Shatov faltered with an expression of idiotic bliss, radiant at the phrase Marie had uttered about the child.

"Where does the great joy come in?" said Arina Prohorovna good-humouredly, bustling about, clearing up, and working like a convict.

"The mysterious coming of a new creature, a great and inexplicable mystery; and what a pity it is, Arina Prohorovna, that you don't understand it."

Shatov spoke in an incoherent, stupefied and ecstatic way. Something seemed to be tottering in his head and welling up from his soul apart from his own will.

"There were two and now there's a third human being, a new spirit, finished and complete, unlike the handiwork of man; a new thought and a new love . . . it's positively frightening. . . . And there's nothing grander in the world."

"Ech, what nonsense he talks! It's simply a further development of the organism, and there's nothing else in it, no mystery," said Arina Prohorovna with genuine and good-humoured laughter. "If you talk like that, every fly is a mystery. But I tell you what: superfluous people ought not to be born. We must first remould everything so that they won't be superfluous and then bring them into the world. As it is, we shall have to take him to the Foundling the day after to-morrow. . . . Though that's as it should be."

"I will never let him go to the Foundling," Shatov pronounced resolutely, staring at the floor.

"You adopt him as your son?"

"He is my son."

"Of course he is a Shatov, legally he is a Shatov, and there's no need for you to pose as a humanitarian. Men can't get on without fine words. There, there, it's all right, but look here, my friends," she added, having finished clearing up at last, "it's time for me to go. I'll come again this morning, and again in the evening, if necessary, but now, since everything has gone off so well, I must run off to my other patients, they've been expecting me long ago. I believe you got an old woman somewhere, Shatov; an old woman is all very well, but don't you, her tender husband, desert her; sit beside her, you may be of use; Marya Ignatyevna won't drive you away, I fancy. . . . There, there, I was only laughing."

229

At the gate, to which Shatov accompanied her, she added to him alone:

"You've given me something to laugh at for the rest of my life; I shan't charge you anything; I shall laugh at you in my sleep! I have never seen anything funnier than you last night."

She went off very well satisfied. Shatov's appearance and conversation made it clear as daylight that this man "was going in for being a father and a ninny". She ran home on purpose to tell Virginsky about it, though it was shorter and more direct to go to another patient.

"Marie, she told you not to go to sleep for a little time, though, I see, it's very hard for you," Shatov began timidly. "I'll sit here by the window and take care of you, shall I?"

And he sat down by the window behind the sofa so that she could not see him. But before a minute had passed she called him and fretfully asked him to arrange her pillow. He began arranging it. She looked angrily at the wall.

"That's not right, that's not right. . . . What hands!"

Shatov did it again.

"Stoop down to me," she said wildly, trying hard not to look at him.

He started but stooped down.

"More . . . not so . . . nearer," and suddenly her left arm was impulsively thrown round his neck and he felt her warm moist kiss on his forehead.

"Marie!"

Her lips were quivering, she was struggling with herself, but suddenly she raised herself and said with flashing eyes:

"Nikolay Stavrogin is a scoundrel!" And she fell back helplessly with her face in the pillow, sobbing hysterically, and tightly squeezing Shatov's hand in hers.

From that moment she would not let him leave her; she insisted on his sitting by her pillow. She could not talk much, but she kept gazing at him and smiling blissfully. She seemed suddenly to have become a silly girl. Everything seemed transformed. Shatov cried like a boy, then talked of God knows what, wildly, crazily, with inspiration, kissed her hands; she listened entranced, perhaps not understanding him, but caressingly ruffling his hair with her weak hand, smoothing it and admiring it. He talked about Kirillov, of how they would now begin "a new life" for good, of the existence of God, of the goodness of all men. . . . She took out the child again to gaze at it rapturously.

"Marie," he cried, as he held the child in his arms, "all the old madness, shame, and deadness is over, isn't it? Let us work hard and begin a new life, the three of us, yes, yes! . . . Oh, by the way, what shall we call him, Marie?"

"What shall we called him?" she repeated with surprise, and there was a sudden look of terrible grief in her face.

She clasped her hands, looked reproachfully at Shatov and hid her face in the pillow.

"Marie, what is it?" he cried with painful alarm.

"How could you, how could you . . Oh, you ungrateful man!"

"Marie, forgive me, Marie . . . I only asked you what his name should be. I don't know. . . ."

"Ivan, Ivan." She raised her flushed and tear-stained face. "How could you suppose we should call him by another *horrible* name?"

"Marie, calm yourself; oh, what a nervous state you are in!"

"That's rude again, putting it down to my nerves. I bet that if I'd said his name was to be that other . . . horrible name, you'd have agreed at once and not have noticed it even! Oh, men, the mean ungrateful creatures, they are all alike!"

A minute later, of course, they were reconciled. Shatov persuaded her to have a nap. She fell asleep but still kept his hand in hers; she waked up frequently, looked at him, as though afraid he would go away, and dropped asleep again.

Kirillov sent an old woman "to congratulate them" as well as some hot tea, some freshly-cooked cutlets, and some broth and white bread for Marya Ignatyevna. The patient sipped the broth greedily, the old woman undid the baby's wrappings and swaddled it afresh, Marie made Shatov have a cutlet too.

Time was passing. Shatov, exhausted, fell asleep himself in his chair, with his head on Marie's pillow. So they were found by Arina Prohorovna, who kept her word. She waked them up gaily, asked Marie some necessary questions, examined the baby, and again forbade Shatov to leave her. Then, jesting at the "happy couple", with a shade of contempt and superciliousness she went away as well satisfied as before.

It was quite dark when Shatov waked up. He made haste to light the candle and ran for the old woman; but he had hardly begun to go down the stairs when he was struck by the sound of the soft, deliberate steps of someone coming up towards him. Erkel came in.

"Don't come in," whispered Shatov, and impulsively seizing

231

him by the hand he drew him back towards the gate. "Wait here, I'll come directly, I'd completely forgotten you, completely! Oh, how you brought it back!"

He was in such haste that he did not even run into Kirillov's, but only called the old woman. Marie was in despair and indignation that "he could dream of leaving her alone".

"But," he cried ecstatically, "this is the very last step! And then for a new life and we'll never, never think of the old horrors again!"

He somehow appeased her and promised to be back at nine o'clock; he kissed her warmly, kissed the baby and ran down quickly to Erkel.

They set off together to Stavrogin's park at Skvoreshniki, where, in a secluded place at the very edge of the park where it adjoined the pine-wood, he had, eighteen months before, buried the printing press which had been entrusted to him. It was a wild and deserted place, quite hidden and at some distance from the Stavrogins' house. It was two or perhaps three miles from Filipov's house.

"Are we going to walk all the way? I'll take a cab."

"I particularly beg you not to," replied Erkel. "They insisted on that. A cabman would be a witness."

"Well . . . bother! I don't care, only to make an end of it."

They walked very fast.

"Erkel, you little boy," cried Shatov, "have you ever been happy?"

"You seem to be very happy just now," observed Erkel with curiosity.

CHAPTER VI

A BUSY NIGHT

I

DURING that day Virginsky had spent two hours in running round to see the members of the quintet and to inform them that Shatov would certainly not give information, because his wife had come back and given birth to a child, and no one "who knew anything of human nature" could suppose that Shatov could be a danger at this moment. But to his discomfiture he found none of them at home except Erkel and Lyam-

shin. Erkel listened in silence, looking candidly into his eyes,
and in answer to the direct question "Would he go at six o'clock
or not?" he replied with the brightest of smiles that "of course
he would go".

Lyamshin was in bed, seriously ill, as it seemed, with his head
covered with a quilt. He was alarmed at Virginsky's coming
in, and as soon as the latter began speaking he waved him off
from under the bedclothes, entreating him to let him alone. He
listened to all he said about Shatov, however, and seemed for
some reason extremely struck by the news that Virginsky had
found no one at home. It seemed that Lyamshin knew already
(through Liputin) of Fedka's death, and hurriedly and incoherently told Virginsky about it, at which the latter seemed
struck in his turn. To Virginsky's direct question: "Should
they go or not?" he began suddenly waving his hands again,
entreating him to let him alone, and saying that it was not his
business, and that he knew nothing about it.

Virginsky returned home dejectedly and greatly alarmed. It
weighed upon him that he had to hide it from his family; he
was accustomed to tell his wife everything; and if his feverish
brain had not hatched a new idea at that moment, a new plan
of conciliation for further action, he might have taken to his
bed like Lyamshin. But this new idea sustained him; what's
more, he began impatiently awaiting the hour fixed, and set
off for the appointed spot earlier than was necessary.

It was a very gloomy place at the end of the huge park.
I went there afterwards on purpose to look at it. How sinister
it must have looked on that chill autumn evening! It was at
the edge of an old wood belonging to the Crown. Huge ancient
pines stood out as vague sombre blurs in the darkness. It was
so dark that they could hardly see each other two paces off, but
Pyotr Stepanovitch, Liputin, and afterwards Erkel, brought
lanterns with them. At some unrecorded date in the past a rather
absurd-looking grotto had for some reason been built here of
rough unhewn stones. The table and benches in the grotto had
long ago decayed and fallen. Two hundred paces to the right
was the bank of the third pond of the park. These three ponds
stretched one after another for a mile from the house to the
very end of the park. One could scarcely imagine that any
noise, a scream, or even a shot, could reach the inhabitants of
the Stavrogins' deserted house. Nikolay Vsyevolodovitch's
departure the previous day and Alexey Yegorytch's absence left
only five or six people in the house, all more or less invalided,

so to speak. In any case it might be assumed with perfect confidence that if cries or shouts for help were heard by any of the inhabitants of the isolated house they would only have excited terror; no one would have moved from his warm stove or snug shelf to give assistance.

By twenty past six almost all of them except Erkel, who had been told off to fetch Shatov, had turned up at the trysting-place. This time Pyotr Stepanovitch was not late; he came with Tolkatchenko. Tolkatchenko looked frowning and anxious; all his assumed determination and insolent bravado had vanished. He scarcely left Pyotr Stepanovitch's side, and seemed to have become all at once immensely devoted to him. He was continually thrusting himself forward to whisper fussily to him, but the latter scarcely answered him, or muttered something irritably to get rid of him.

Shigalov and Virginsky had arrived rather before Pyotr Stepanovitch, and as soon as he came they drew a little apart in profound and obviously intentional silence. Pyotr Stepanovitch raised his lantern and examined them with unceremonious and insulting minuteness. "They mean to speak," flashed through his mind.

"Isn't Lyamshin here?" he asked Virginsky. "Who said he was ill?"

"I am here," responded Lyamshin, suddenly coming from behind a tree. He was in a warm greatcoat and thickly muffled in a rug, so that it was difficult to make out his face even with a lantern.

"So Liputin is the only one not here?"

Liputin too came out of the grotto without speaking. Pyotr Stepanovitch raised the lantern again.

"Why were you hiding in there? Why didn't you come out?"

"I imagine we still keep the right of freedom . . . of our actions," Liputin muttered, though probably he hardly knew what he wanted to express.

"Gentlemen," said Pyotr Stepanovitch, raising his voice for the first time above a whisper, which produced an effect, "I think you fully understand that it's useless to go over things again. Everything was said and fully thrashed out yesterday, openly and directly. But perhaps—as I see from your faces— someone wants to make some statement; in that case I beg you to make haste. Damn it all! there's not much time, and Erkel may bring him in a minute. . . ."

"He is sure to bring him," Tolkatchenko put in for some reason.

"If I am not mistaken, the printing press will be handed over, to begin with?" inquired Liputin, though again he seemed hardly to understand why he asked the question.

"Of course. Why should we lose it?" said Pyotr Stepanovitch, lifting the lantern to his face. "But, you see, we all agreed yesterday that it was not really necessary to take it. He need only show you the exact spot where it's buried; we can dig it up afterwards for ourselves. I know that it's somewhere ten paces from a corner of this grotto. But, damn it all! how could you have forgotten, Liputin? It was agreed that you should meet him alone and that we should come out afterwards. . . . It's strange that you should ask—or didn't you mean what you said?"

Liputin kept gloomily silent. All were silent. The wind shook the tops of the pine-trees.

"I trust, however, gentlemen, that every one will do his duty," Pyotr Stepanovitch rapped out impatiently.

"I know that Shatov's wife has come back and has given birth to a child," Virginsky said suddenly, excited and gesticulating and scarcely able to speak distinctly. "Knowing what human nature is, we can be sure that now he won't give information . . . because he is happy. . . So I went to everyone this morning and found no one at home, so perhaps now nothing need be done. . . ."

He stopped short with a catch in his breath.

"If you suddenly became happy, Mr. Virginsky," said Pyotr Stepanovitch, stepping up to him, "would you abandon—not giving information; there's no question of that—but any perilous public action which you had planned before you were happy and which you regarded as a duty and obligation in spite of the risk and loss of happiness?"

"No, I wouldn't abandon it! I wouldn't on any account!" said Virginsky with absurd warmth, twitching all over.

"You would rather be unhappy again than be a scoundrel?"

"Yes, yes. . . . Quite the contrary. . . . I'd rather be a complete scoundrel . . . that is not . . . not a scoundrel at all, but on the contrary completely unhappy rather than a scoundrel."

"Well, then, let me tell you that Shatov looks on this betrayal as a public duty. It's his most cherished conviction, and the proof of it is that he runs some risk himself; though, of course,

235

they will pardon him a great deal for giving information. A man like that will never give up the idea. No sort of happiness would overcome him. In another day he'll go back on it, reproach himself, and will go straight to the police. What's more, I don't see any happiness in the fact that his wife has come back after three years' absence to bear him a child of Stavrogin's.''

"But no one has seen Shatov's letter," Shigalov brought out all at once, emphatically.

"I've seen it," cried Pyotr Stepanovitch. "It exists, and all this is awfully stupid, gentlemen."

"And I protest . . ." Virginsky cried, boiling over suddenly. "I protest with all my might. . . . I want . . . this is what I want. I suggest that when he arrives we all come out and question him; if it's true, we induce him to repent of it; and if he gives you his word of honour, let him go. In any case we must have a trial; it must be done after trial. We mustn't lie in wait for him and then fall upon him."

"Risk the cause on his word of honour—that's the acme of stupidity! Damnation, how stupid it all is now, gentlemen! And a pretty part you are choosing to play at the moment of danger!"

"I protest, I protest!" Virginsky persisted.

"Don't bawl, anyway; we shan't hear the signal. Shatov, gentlemen. . . . (Damnation, how stupid this is now!) I've told you already that Shatov is a Slavophil, that is, one of the stupidest set of people. . . . But, damn it all, never mind, that's no matter! You put me out! . . . Shatov is an embittered man, gentlemen, and since he has belonged to the party, anyway, whether he wanted to or no, I had hoped till the last minute that he might have been of service to the cause and might have been made use of as an embittered man. I spared him and was keeping him in reserve, in spite of most exact instructions. . . . I've spared him a hundred times more than he deserved! But he's ended by betraying us. . . . But, hang it all, I don't care! You'd better try running away now, any of you! No one of you has the right to give up the job! You can kiss him if you like, but you haven't the right to stake the cause on his word of honour! That's acting like swine and spies in government pay!"

"Who's a spy in government pay here?" Liputin filtered out.

"You, perhaps. You'd better hold your tongue, Liputin; you talk for the sake of talking, as you always do. All men are spies, gentlemen, who funk their duty at the moment of danger.

There will always be some fools who'll run in a panic at the last moment and cry out: 'Aie, forgive me, and I'll give them all away!' But let me tell you, gentlemen, no betrayal would win you a pardon now. Even if your sentence were mitigated it would mean Siberia; and, what's more, there's no escaping the weapons of the other side—and their weapons are sharper than the government's."

Pyotr Stepanovitch was furious and said more than he meant to. With a resolute air Shigalov took three steps towards him.

"Since yesterday evening I've thought over the question," he began, speaking with his usual pedantry and assurance. (I believe that if the earth had given way under his feet he would not have raised his voice nor have varied one tone in his methodical exposition.) "Thinking the matter over, I've come to the conclusion that the projected murder is not merely a waste of precious time which might be employed in a more suitable and befitting manner, but presents, moreover, that deplorable deviation from the normal method which has always been most prejudicial to the cause and has delayed its triumph for scores of years, under the guidance of shallow thinkers and pre-eminently of men of political instead of purely socialistic leanings. I have come here solely to protest against the projected enterprise, for the general edification, intending then to withdraw at the actual moment, which you, for some reason I don't understand, speak of as a moment of danger to us. I am going—not from fear of that danger nor from a sentimental feeling for Shatov, whom I have no inclination to kiss, but solely because all this business from beginning to end is in direct contradiction to my programme. As for my betraying you and my being in the pay of the government, you can set your mind completely at rest. I shall not betray you."

He turned and walked away.

"Damn it all, he'll meet them and warn Shatov!" cried Pyotr Stepanovitch, pulling his revolver. They heard the click of the trigger.

"You may be confident," said Shigalov, turning once more, "that if I meet Shatov on the way I may bow to him, but I shall not warn him."

"But do you know, you may have to pay for this, Mr. Fourier?"

"I beg you to observe that I am not Fourier. If you mix me up with that mawkish theoretical twaddler, you simply prove that you know nothing of my manuscript, though it has been in

237

your hands. As for your vengeance, let me tell you that it's a mistake to cock your pistol: that's absolutely against your interests at the present moment. But if you threaten to shoot me to-morrow, or the day after, you'll gain nothing by it but unnecessary trouble. You may kill me, but sooner or later you'll come to my system all the same. Good-bye."

At that instant a whistle was heard in the park, two hundred paces away from the direction of the pond. Liputin at once answered, whistling also as had been agreed the evening before. (As he had lost several teeth and distrusted his own powers, he had this morning bought for a farthing in the market a child's clay whistle for the purpose.) Erkel had warned Shatov on the way that they would whistle as a signal, so that the latter felt no uneasiness.

"Don't be uneasy, I'll avoid them and they won't notice me at all," Shigalov declared in an impressive whisper; and thereupon deliberately and without haste he walked home through the dark park.

Everything, to the smallest detail of this terrible affair, is now fully known. To begin with, Liputin met Erkel and Shatov at the entrance to the grotto. Shatov did not bow or offer him his hand, but at once pronounced hurriedly in a loud voice:

"Well, where have you put the spade, and haven't you another lantern? You needn't be afraid, there's absolutely no one here, and they wouldn't hear at Skvoreshniki now if we fired a cannon here. This is the place, here this very spot."

And he stamped with his foot ten paces from the end of the grotto towards the wood. At that moment Tolkatchenko rushed out from behind a tree and sprang at him from behind, while Erkel seized him by the elbows. Liputin attacked him from the front. The three of them at once knocked him down and pinned him to the ground. At this point Pyotr Stepanovitch darted up with his revolver. It is said that Shatov had time to turn his head and was able to see and recognise him. Three lanterns lighted up the scene. Shatov suddenly uttered a short and desperate scream. But they did not let him go on screaming. Pyotr Stepanovitch firmly and accurately put his revolver to Shatov's forehead, pressed it to it, and pulled the trigger. The shot seems not to have been loud; nothing was heard at Skvoreshniki, anyway. Shigalov, who was scarcely three paces away, of course heard it—he heard the shout and the shot, but, as he testified afterwards, he did not turn nor even stop. Death was almost instantaneous. Pyotr Stepanovitch was the only

238

one who preserved all his faculties, but I don't think he was quite cool. Squatting on his heels, he searched the murdered man's pockets hastily, though with steady hand. No money was found (his purse had been left under Marya Ignatyevna's pillow). Two or three scraps of paper of no importance were found: a note from his office, the title of some book, and an old bill from a restaurant abroad which had been preserved, goodness knows why, for two years in his pocket. Pyotr Stepanovitch transferred these scraps of paper to his own pocket, and suddenly noticing that they had all gathered round, were gazing at the corpse and doing nothing, he began rudely and angrily abusing them and urging them on. Tolkatchenko and Erkel recovered themselves, and running to the grotto brought instantly from it two stones which they had got ready there that morning. These stones, which weighed about twenty pounds each, were securely tied with cord. As they intended to throw the body in the nearest of the three ponds, they proceeded to tie the stones to the head and feet respectively. Pyotr Stepanovitch fastened the stones while Tolkatchenko and Erkel only held and passed them. Erkel was foremost, and while Pyotr Stepanovitch, grumbling and swearing, tied the dead man's feet together with the cord and fastened the stone to them—a rather lengthy operation—Tolkatchenko stood holding the other stone at arm's-length, his whole person bending forward, as it were, deferentially, to be in readiness to hand it without delay. It never once occurred to him to lay his burden on the ground in the interval. When at last both stones were tied on and Pyotr Stepanovitch got up from the ground to scrutinise the faces of his companions, something strange happened, utterly unexpected and surprising to almost everyone.

As I have said already, all except perhaps Tolkatchenko and Erkel were standing still doing nothing. Though Virginsky had rushed up to Shatov with the others he had not seized him nor helped to hold him. Lyamshin had joined the group after the shot had been fired. Afterwards, while Pyotr Stepanovitch was busy with the corpse—for perhaps ten minutes—none of them seemed to have been fully conscious. They grouped themselves around and seemed to have felt amazement rather than anxiety or alarm. Liputin stood foremost, close to the corpse. Virginsky stood behind him, peeping over his shoulder with a peculiar, as it were unconcerned, curiosity; he even stood on tiptoe to get a better view. Lyamshin hid behind Virginsky. He took an apprehensive peep from time to time and slipped behind him again at once. When the stones had been tied on and Pyotr Stepanovitch had risen to his feet, Virginsky began faintly shuddering all over, clasped his hands, and cried out bitterly at the top of his voice:

"It's not the right thing, it's not, it's not at all!" He would perhaps have added something more to his belated exclamation, but Lyamshin did not let him finish: he suddenly seized him from behind and squeezed him with all his might, uttering an unnatural shriek. There are moments of violent emotion, of terror, for instance, when a man will cry out in a voice not his own, unlike anything one could have anticipated from him, and this has sometimes a very terrible effect. Lyamshin gave vent to a scream more animal than human. Squeezing Virginsky from behind more and more tightly and convulsively, he went on shrieking without a pause, his mouth wide open and his eyes starting out of his head, keeping up a continual patter with his feet, as though he were beating a drum. Virginsky was so scared that he too screamed out like a madman, and with a ferocity, a vindictiveness that one could never have expected of Virginsky. He tried to pull himself away from Lyamshin, scratching and punching him as far as he could with his arms behind him. Erkel at last helped to pull Lyamshin away. But when, in his terror, Virginsky had skipped ten paces away from him, Lyamshin, catching sight of Pyotr Stepanovitch, began yelling again and flew at him. Stumbling over the corpse he fell upon Pyotr Stepanovitch, pressing his head to the latter's chest and gripping him so tightly in his arms that Pyotr Stepanovitch, Tolkatchenko, and Liputin could all of them do nothing at the first moment. Pyotr Stepanovitch shouted, swore, beat him on the head with his fists. At last, wrenching himself away, he drew his revolver and put it in the open mouth of Lyamshin, who was still yelling and was by now tightly held by Tolkatchenko, Erkel, and Liputin. But Lyamshin went on shrieking in spite of the revolver. At last Erkel, crushing his silk handkerchief into a ball, deftly thrust it into his mouth and the shriek ceased. Meantime Tolkatchenko tied his hands with what was left of the rope.

"It's very strange," said Pyotr Stepanovitch, scrutinising the madman with uneasy wonder. He was evidently struck. "I expected something very different from him," he added thoughtfully.

They left Erkel in charge of him for a time. They had to make haste to get rid of the corpse: there had been so much noise that someone might have heard. Tolkatchenko and Pyotr Stepanovitch took up the lanterns and lifted the corpse by the head, while Liputin and Virginsky took the feet, and so they carried it away. With the two stones it was a heavy burden, and the distance was more than two hundred paces. Tolkatchenko was the strongest of them. He advised them to keep in step, but no one answered him and they all walked anyhow. Pyotr Stepanovitch walked on the right and, bending forward, carried the dead man's head on his shoulder, while with the left hand he supported the stone. As Tolkatchenko walked more than half the way without thinking of helping him with the stone, Pyotr Stepanovitch at last shouted at him with an oath. It was a single, sudden shout. They all went on carrying the body in silence, and it was only when they reached the pond that Virginsky, stooping under his burden and seeming to be exhausted by the weight of it, cried out again in the same loud and wailing voice:

"It's not the right thing, no, no, it's not the right thing!"

The place to which they carried the dead man at the extreme end of the rather large pond, which was the farthest of the three from the house, was one of the most solitary and unfrequented spots in the park, especially at this late season of the year. At that end the pond was overgrown with weeds by the banks. They put down the lantern, swung the corpse and threw it into the pond. They heard a muffled and prolonged splash. Pyotr Stepanovitch raised the lantern and everyone followed his example, peering curiously to see the body sink, but nothing could be seen: weighted with the two stones, the body sank at once. The big ripples spread over the surface of the water and quickly passed away. It was over.

"Now we can separate, gentlemen," said Pyotr Stepanovitch, addressing them. "You must certainly be feeling that pride of a free spirit which is inseparable from the fulfilment of a duty freely undertaken. If you are unhappily at this moment too much agitated for such feelings, you will certainly feel them to-morrow, when, in fact, it would be shameful not to feel them. As for Lyamshin's too disgraceful over-excitement, I am willing to put it down to delirium, especially as they say he has been really ill all day. And one instant of free reflection will convince you, Virginsky, that in the interests of the cause we could not have trusted to any word of honour, but had to act as we did. Subsequent events will convince you that he was a traitor. I am ready to overlook your exclamations. As for danger, there is

THE POSSESSED

no reason to anticipate it. It would occur to no one to suspect any of us if you'll behave sensibly; so that it really depends on yourselves and on the conviction in which I hope you will be fully confirmed to-morrow. One of the reasons why you have banded yourselves together into a separate branch of a free organisation representing certain views was to support each other in the cause by your energy at any crisis and if need be to watch over one another. The highest responsibility is laid upon each of you. You are called upon to bring new life into the party, which has grown decrepit and stinking with stagnation. Keep that always before your eyes to give you strength. All that you have to do meanwhile is to bring about the downfall of everything—both the government and its moral standards. None will be left but us, who have prepared ourselves beforehand to take over the government. The intelligent we shall bring over to our side, and as for the fools, we shall mount upon their shoulders. You must not be shy of that. We've got to re-educate a generation to make them worthy of freedom. We shall have many thousands of Shatovs to contend with. We shall organise to control public opinion; it's shameful not to snatch at anything that lies idle and gaping at us. I'm going at once to Kirillov, and by the morning a document will be in existence in which he will as he dies take it all on himself by way of an explanation to the police. Nothing can be more probable than such a solution. To begin with, he was on bad terms with Shatov; they had lived together in America, so they've had time to quarrel. It was well known that Shatov had changed his convictions, so there was hostility between them on that ground and fear of treachery—that is, the most relentless hostility. All that will be stated in writing. Finally, it will be mentioned that Fedka had been lodging with him at Filipov's, so all this will completely avert all suspicion from you, because it will throw all those sheep's-heads off the scent. We shall not meet to-morrow, gentlemen; I am going into the country for a very short time, but the day after you will hear from me. I should advise you to spend to-morrow at home. Now we will separate, going back by twos by different paths. You, Tolkatchenko, I'll ask to look after Lyamshin and take him home. You may have some influence over him; and above all make him understand what harm he is doing himself by his cowardice. Your kinsman Shigalov, Virginsky, I am as unwilling to distrust as I am you; he will not betray us. I can only regret his action. He has not, however, announced that he will leave the society, so it would be premature to bury him. Well, make haste, gentlemen. Though they are sheep's-heads, there's no harm in prudence. . . ."

Virginsky went off with Erkel, who before giving up Lyamshin to Tolkatchenko brought him to Pyotr Stepanovitch, reporting to the latter that Lyamshin had come to his senses, was penitent and begged forgiveness, and indeed had no recollection of what had happened to him. Pyotr Stepanovitch walked off alone, going round by the farther side of the pond, skirting the park. This was the longest way. To his surprise Liputin overtook him before he got half-way home.

"Pyotr Stepanovitch! Pyotr Stepanovitch! Lyamshin will give information!"

"No, he will come to his senses and realise that he will be the first to go to Siberia if he did. No one will betray us now. Even you won't."

"What about you?"

"No fear! I'll get you all out of the way the minute you attempt to turn traitors, and you know that. But you won't turn traitors. Have you run a mile and a half to tell me that?"

"Pyotr Stepanovitch, Pyotr Stepanovitch, perhaps we shall never meet again!"

"What's put that into your head?"

"Only tell me one thing."

"Well, what? Though I want you to take yourself off."

"One question, but answer it truly: are we the only quintet in the world, or is it true that there are hundreds of others? It's a question of the utmost importance to me, Pyotr Stepanovitch."

"I see that from the frantic state you are in. But do you know, Liputin, you are more dangerous than Lyamshin?"

"I know, I know; but the answer, your answer!"

"You are a stupid fellow! I should have thought it could make no difference to you now whether it's the only quintet or one of a thousand."

"That means it's the only one! I was sure of it . . ." cried Liputin. "I always knew it was the only one, I knew it all along." And without waiting for any reply he turned and quickly vanished into the darkness.

Pyotr Stepanovitch pondered a little.

"No, no one will turn traitor," he concluded with decision, "but the group must remain a group and obey, or I'll . . . What a wretched set they are though!"

He first went home, and carefully, without haste, packed his
trunk. At six o'clock in the morning there was a special train
from the town. This early morning express only ran once a
week, and was only a recent experiment. Though Pyotr
Stepanovitch had told the members of the quintet that he was
only going to be away for a short time in the neighbourhood, his
intentions, as appeared later, were in reality very different.
Having finished packing, he settled accounts with his landlady,
to whom he had previously given notice of his departure, and
drove in a cab to Erkel's lodgings, near the station. And then
just upon one o'clock at night he walked to Kirillov's, approaching as before by Fedka's secret way.

Pyotr Stepanovitch was in a painful state of mind. Apart
from other extremely grave reasons for dissatisfaction (he was
still unable to learn anything of Stavrogin), he had, it seems—
for I cannot assert it for a fact—received in the course of that
day, probably from Petersburg, secret information of a danger
awaiting him in the immediate future. There are, of course,
many legends in the town relating to this period; but if any facts
were known, it was only to those immediately concerned. I can
only surmise as my own conjecture that Pyotr Stepanovitch
may well have had affairs going on in other neighbourhoods as
well as in our town, so that he really may have received such a
warning. I am convinced, indeed, in spite of Liputin's cynical
and despairing doubts, that he really had two or three other
quintets; for instance, in Petersburg and Moscow, and if not
quintets at least colleagues and correspondents, and possibly was
in very curious relations with them. Not more than three days
after his departure an order for his immediate arrest arrived
from Petersburg—whether in connection with what had happened among us, or elsewhere, I don't know. This order only
served to increase the overwhelming, almost panic terror which
suddenly came upon our local authorities and the society of the
town, till then so persistently frivolous in its attitude, on the discovery of the mysterious and portentous murder of the student
Shatov—the climax of the long series of senseless actions in our
midst—as well as the extremely mysterious circumstances that
accompanied that murder. But the order came too late: Pyotr
Stepanovitch was already in Petersburg, living under another
name, and, learning what was going on, he made haste to make

his escape abroad. . . . But I am anticipating in a shocking way.

He went in to Kirillov, looking ill-humoured and quarrelsome. Apart from the real task before him, he felt, as it were, tempted to satisfy some personal grudge, to avenge himself on Kirillov for something. Kirillov seemed pleased to see him; he had evidently been expecting him a long time with painful impatience. His face was paler than usual; there was a fixed and heavy look in his black eyes.

"I thought you weren't coming," he brought out drearily from his corner of the sofa, from which he had not, however, moved to greet him.

Pyotr Stepanovitch stood before him and, before uttering a word, looked intently at his face.

"Everything is in order, then, and we are not drawing back from our resolution. Bravo!" He smiled an offensively patronising smile. "But, after all," he added with unpleasant jocosity, "if I am behind my time, it's not for you to complain: I made you a present of three hours."

"I don't want extra hours as a present from you, and you can't make me a present . . . you fool!"

"What?" Pyotr Stepanovitch was startled, but instantly controlled himself. "What huffiness! So we are in a savage temper?" he rapped out, still with the same offensive superciliousness. "At such a moment composure is what you need. The best thing you can do is to consider yourself a Columbus and me a mouse, and not to take offence at anything I say. I gave you that advice yesterday."

"I don't want to look upon you as a mouse."

"What's that, a compliment? But the tea is cold—and that shows that everything is topsy-turvy. Bah! But I see something in the window, on a plate." He went to the window. "Oh oh, boiled chicken and rice! . . . But why haven't you begun upon it yet? So we are in such a state of mind that even chicken . . ."

"I've dined, and it's not your business. Hold your tongue!"

"Oh, of course; besides, it's no consequence—though for me at the moment it is of consequence. Only fancy, I scarcely had any dinner, and so if, as I suppose, that chicken is not wanted now . . . eh?"

"Eat it if you can."

"Thank you, and then I'll have tea."

He instantly settled himself at the other end of the sofa and fell upon the chicken with extraordinary greediness; at the same time he kept a constant watch on his victim. Kirillov looked at him fixedly with angry aversion, as though unable to tear himself away.

"I say, though," Pyotr Stepanovitch fired off suddenly, while he still went on eating, "what about our business? We are not crying off, are we? How about that document?"

"I've decided in the night that it's nothing to me. I'll write it. About the manifestos?"

"Yes, about the manifestos too. But I'll dictate it. Of course, that's nothing to you. Can you possibly mind what's in the letter at such a moment?"

"That's not your business."

"It's not mine, of course. It need only be a few lines, though: that you and Shatov distributed the manifestos and with the help of Fedka, who hid in your lodgings. This last point about Fedka and your lodgings is very important—the most important of all, indeed. You see, I am talking to you quite openly."

"Shatov? Why Shatov? I won't mention Shatov for anything."

"What next! What is it to you? You can't hurt him now."

"His wife has come back to him. She has waked up and has sent to ask me where he is."

"She has sent to ask you where he is? H'm . . . that's unfortunate. She may send again; no one ought to know I am here."

Pyotr Stepanovitch was uneasy.

"She won't know, she's gone to sleep again. There's a mid-wife with her, Arina Virginsky."

"So that's how it was. . . . She won't overhear, I suppose? I say, you'd better shut the front door."

"She won't overhear anything. And if Shatov comes I'll hide you in another room."

"Shatov won't come; and you must write that you quarrelled with him because he turned traitor and informed the police . . . this evening . . . and caused his death."

"He is dead!" cried Kirillov, jumping up from the sofa.

"He died at seven o'clock this evening, or rather, at seven o'clock yesterday evening, and now it's one o'clock."

"You have killed him! . . . And I foresaw it yesterday!"

"No doubt you did! With this revolver here." (He drew out his revolver as though to show it, but did not put it back again and still held it in his right hand as though in readiness.)

246

THE POSSESSED

"You are a strange man, though, Kirillov; you knew yourself that the stupid fellow was bound to end like this. What was there to foresee in that? I made that as plain as possible over and over again. Shatov was meaning to betray us; I was watching him, and it could not be left like that. And you too had instructions to watch him; you told me so yourself three weeks ago. . . ."

"Hold your tongue! You've done this because he spat in your face in Geneva!"

"For that and for other things too—for many other things; not from spite, however. Why do you jump up? Why look like that? Oh oh, so that's it, is it?"

He jumped up and held out his revolver before him. Kirillov had suddenly snatched up from the window his revolver, which had been loaded and put ready since the morning. Pyotr Stepanovitch took up his position and aimed his weapon at Kirillov. The latter laughed angrily.

"Confess, you scoundrel, that you brought your revolver because I might shoot you. . . . But I shan't shoot you . . . though . . . though . . ."

And again he turned his revolver upon Pyotr Stepanovitch, as it were rehearsing, as though unable to deny himself the pleasure of imagining how he would shoot him. Pyotr Stepanovitch, holding his ground, waited for him, waited for him till the last minute without pulling the trigger, at the risk of being the first to get a bullet in his head: it might well be expected of "the maniac". But at last "the maniac" dropped his hand, gasping and trembling and unable to speak.

"You've played your little game and that's enough." Pyotr Stepanovitch, too, dropped his weapon. "I knew it was only a game; only you ran a risk, let me tell you: I might have fired."

And he sat down on the sofa with a fair show of composure and poured himself out some tea, though his hand trembled a little. Kirillov laid his revolver on the table and began walking up and down.

"I won't write that I killed Shatov . . . and I won't write anything now. You won't have a document!"

"I shan't?"

"No, you won't."

"What meanness and what stupidity!" Pyotr Stepanovitch turned green with resentment. "I foresaw it, though. You've not taken me by surprise, let me tell you. As you please, however. If I could make you do it by force, I would. You are a scoundrel, though." Pyotr Stepanovitch was more and more carried away and unable to restrain himself. "You asked us for money out there and promised us no end of things. . . . I won't go away with nothing, however: I'll see you put the bullet through your brains first, anyway."

"I want you to go away at once." Kirillov stood firmly before him.

"No, that's impossible." Pyotr Stepanovitch took up his revolver again. "Now in your spite and cowardice you may think fit to put it off and to turn traitor to-morrow, so as to get money again; they'll pay you for that, of course. Damn it all, fellows like you are capable of anything! Only don't trouble yourself; I've provided for all contingencies: I am not going till I've dashed your brains out with this revolver, as I did to that scoundrel Shatov, if you are afraid to do it yourself and put off your intention, damn you!"

"You are set on seeing my blood, too?"

"I am not acting from spite; let me tell you, it's nothing to me. I am doing it to be at ease about the cause. One can't rely on men; you see that for yourself. I don't understand what fancy possesses you to put yourself to death. It wasn't my idea; you thought of it yourself before I appeared, and talked of your intention to the committee abroad before you said anything to me. And you know, no one has forced it out of you; no one of them knew you, but you came to confide in them yourself, from sentimentalism. And what's to be done if a plan of action here, which can't be altered now, was founded upon that with your consent and upon your suggestion? . . . your suggestion, mind that! You have put yourself in a position in which you know too much. If you are an ass and go off to-morrow to inform the police, that would be rather a disadvantage to us; what do you think about it? Yes, you've bound yourself; you've given your word, you've taken money. That you can't deny. . . ."

Pyotr Stepanovitch was much excited, but for some time past Kirillov had not been listening. He paced up and down the room, lost in thought again.

"I am sorry for Shatov," he said, stopping before Pyotr Stepanovitch again.

"Why so? I am sorry, if that's all, and do you suppose . . ."

"Hold your tongue, you scoundrel," roared Kirillov, making an alarming and unmistakable movement; "I'll kill you."

248

THE POSSESSED

"There, there, there! I told a lie, I admit it; I am not sorry at all. Come, that's enough, that's enough." Pyotr Stepanovitch started up apprehensively, putting out his hand.

Kirillov subsided and began walking up and down again. "I won't put it off; I want to kill myself now: all are scoundrels."

"Well, that's an idea; of course all are scoundrels; and since life is a beastly thing for a decent man . . ."

"Fool, I am just such a scoundrel as you, as all, not a decent man. There's never been a decent man anywhere."

"He's guessed the truth at last! Can you, Kirillov, with your sense, have failed to see till now that all men are alike, that there are none better or worse, only some are stupider than others, and that if all are scoundrels (which is nonsense, though) there oughtn't to be any people that are not?"

"Ah! Why, you are really in earnest?" Kirillov looked at him with some wonder. "You speak with heat and simply. . . . Can it be that even fellows like you have convictions?"

"Kirillov, I've never been able to understand why you mean to kill yourself. I only know it's from conviction . . . strong conviction. But if you feel a yearning to express yourself, so to say, I am at your service. . . . Only you must think of the time."

"What time is it?"

"Oh oh, just two." Pyotr Stepanovitch looked at his watch and lighted a cigarette.

"It seems we can come to terms after all," he reflected.

"I've nothing to say to you," muttered Kirillov.

"I remember that something about God comes into it . . . you explained it to me once—twice, in fact. If you shoot yourself, you become God; that's it, isn't it?"

"Yes, I become God."

Pyotr Stepanovitch did not even smile; he waited. Kirillov looked at him subtly.

"You are a political impostor and intriguer. You want to lead me on into philosophy and enthusiasm and to bring about a reconciliation so as to disperse my anger, and then, when I am reconciled with you, beg from me a note to say I killed Shatov."

Pyotr Stepanovitch answered with almost natural frankness.

"Well, supposing I am such a scoundrel. But at the last moments does that matter to you, Kirillov? What are we quarrelling about? Tell me, please. You are one sort of man

249

and I am another—what of it? And what's more, we are both of us . . ."

"Scoundrels."

"Yes, scoundrels if you like. But you know that that's only words."

"All my life I wanted it not to be only words. I lived because I did not want it to be. Even now every day I want it to be not words."

"Well, everyone seeks to be where he is best off. The fish . . . that is, everyone seeks his own comfort, that's all. That's been a commonplace for ages and ages."

"Comfort, do you say?"

"Oh, it's not worth while quarrelling over words."

"No, you were right in what you said; let it be comfort. God is necessary and so must exist."

"Well, that's all right, then."

"But I know He doesn't and can't."

"That's more likely."

"Surely you must understand that a man with two such ideas can't go on living?"

"Must shoot himself, you mean?"

"Surely you must understand that one might shoot oneself for that alone? You don't understand that there may be a man, one man out of your thousands of millions, one man who won't bear it and does not want to."

"All I understand is that you seem to be hesitating. . . . That's very bad."

"Stavrogin, too, is consumed by an idea," Kirillov said gloomily, pacing up and down the room. He had not noticed the previous remark.

"What?" Pyotr Stepanovitch pricked up his ears. "What idea? Did he tell you something himself?"

"No, I guessed it myself: if Stavrogin has faith, he does not believe that he has faith. If he hasn't faith, he does not believe that he hasn't."

"Well, Stavrogin has got something else wiser than that in his head," Pyotr Stepanovitch muttered peevishly, uneasily watching the turn the conversation had taken and the pallor of Kirillov.

"Damn it all, he won't shoot himself!" he was thinking. "I always suspected it; it's a maggot in the brain and nothing more; what a rotten lot of people!"

"You are the last to be with me; I shouldn't like to part on

250

bad terms with you," Kirillov vouchsafed suddenly.

Pyotr Stepanovitch did not answer at once. "Damn it all, what is it now?" he thought again.

"I assure you, Kirillov, I have nothing against you personally as a man, and always . . ."

"You are a scoundrel and a false intellect. But I am just the same as you are, and I will shoot myself while you will remain living."

"You mean to say, I am so abject that I want to go on living."

He could not make up his mind whether it was judicious to keep up such a conversation at such a moment or not, and resolved "to be guided by circumstances". But the tone of superiority and of contempt for him, which Kirillov had never disguised, had always irritated him, and now for some reason it irritated him more than ever—possibly because Kirillov, who was to die within an hour or so (Pyotr Stepanovitch still reckoned upon this), seemed to him, as it were, already only half a man, some creature whom he could not allow to be haughty.

"You seem to be boasting to me of your shooting yourself."

"I've always been surprised at everyone's going on living," said Kirillov, not hearing his remark.

"H'm! Admitting that's an idea, but . . ."

"You ape, you assent to get the better of me. Hold your tongue; you won't understand anything. If there is no God, then I am God."

"There, I could never understand that point of yours: why are you God?"

"If God exists, all is His will and from His will I cannot escape. If not, it's all my will and I am bound to show self-will."

"Self-will? But why are you bound?"

"Because all will has become mine. Can it be that no one in the whole planet, after making an end of God and believing in his own will, will dare to express his self-will on the most vital point? It's like a beggar inheriting a fortune and being afraid of it and not daring to approach the bag of gold, thinking himself too weak to own it. I want to manifest my self-will. I may be the only one, but I'll do it."

"Do it by all means."

"I am bound to shoot myself because the highest point of my self-will is to kill myself with my own hands."

251

"But you won't be the only one to kill yourself; there are lots of suicides."

"With good cause. But to do it without any cause at all, simply for self-will, I am the only one."

"He won't shoot himself," flashed across Pyotr Stepano-vitch's mind again.

"Do you know," he observed irritably, "if I were in your place I should kill someone else to show my self-will, not myself. You might be of use. I'll tell you whom, if you are not afraid. Then you needn't shoot yourself to-day, perhaps. We may come to terms."

"To kill someone would be the lowest point of self-will, and you show your whole soul in that. I am not you: I want the highest point and I'll kill myself."

"He's come to it of himself," Pyotr Stepanovitch muttered malignantly.

"I am bound to show my unbelief," said Kirillov, walking about the room. "I have no higher idea than disbelief in God. I have all the history of mankind on my side. Man has done nothing but invent God so as to go on living, and not kill himself; that's the whole of universal history up till now. I am the first one in the whole history of mankind who would not invent God. Let them know it once for all."

"He won't shoot himself," Pyotr Stepanovitch thought anxiously.

"Let whom know it?" he said, egging him on. "It's only you and me here: you mean Liputin?"

"Let everyone know; all will know. There is nothing secret that will not be made known. *He* said so."

And he pointed with feverish enthusiasm to the image of the Saviour, before which a lamp was burning. Pyotr Stepanovitch lost his temper completely.

"So you still believe in Him, and you've lighted the lamp; 'to be on the safe side', I suppose?"

The other did not speak.

"Do you know, to my thinking, you believe perhaps more thoroughly than any priest."

"Believe in whom? In *Him?* Listen." Kirillov stood still, gazing before him with fixed and ecstatic look. "Listen to a great idea: there was a day on earth, and in the midst of the earth there stood three crosses. One on the Cross had such faith that he said to another: 'To-day thou shalt be with me in Paradise.' The day ended; both died and passed away and found neither Paradise nor resurrection. His words did not come true. Listen: that Man was the loftiest of all on earth, He was that which gave meaning to life. The whole planet, with everything on it, is mere madness without that Man. There has never been any like Him before or since, never, up to a miracle. For that is the miracle, that there never was or never will be another like Him. And if that is so, if the laws of nature did not spare even Him, have not spared even their miracle and made even Him live in a lie and die for a lie, then all the planet is a lie and rests on a lie and on mockery. So then, the very laws of the planet are a lie and the vaudeville of devils. What is there to live for? Answer, if you are a man."

"That's a different matter. It seems to me you've mixed up two different causes, and that's a very unsafe thing to do. But excuse me, if you are God? If the lie were ended and if you realised that all the falsity comes from the belief in that former God?"

"So at last you understand!" cried Kirillov rapturously. "So it can be understood if even a fellow like you understands. Do you understand now that the salvation for all consists in proving this idea to everyone? Who will prove it? I! I can't understand how an atheist could know that there is no God and not kill himself on the spot. To recognise that there is no God and not to recognise at the same instant that one is God oneself is an absurdity, else one would certainly kill oneself. If you recognise it you are sovereign, and then you won't kill yourself but will live in the greatest glory. But one, the first, must kill himself, for else who will begin and prove it? So I must certainly kill myself, to begin and prove it. Now I am only a god against my will and I am unhappy, because I am *bound* to assert my will. All are unhappy because all are afraid to express their will. Man has hitherto been so unhappy and so poor because he has been afraid to assert his will in the highest point and has shown his self-will only in little things, like a schoolboy. I am awfully unhappy, for I'm awfully afraid. Terror is the curse of man. . . . But I will assert my will, I am bound to believe that I don't believe. I will begin and will make an end of it and open the door, and will save. That's the only thing that will save mankind and will re-create the next generation physically; for with his present physical nature man can't get on without his former God, I believe. For three years I've been seeking for the attribute of my godhead and I've found it; the attribute of my godhead is self-will! That's all

253

I can do to prove in the highest point my independence and my new terrible freedom. For it is very terrible. I am killing myself to prove my independence and my new terrible freedom."

His face was unnaturally pale, and there was a terribly heavy look in his eyes. He was like a man in delirium. Pyotr Stepanovitch thought he would drop on to the floor.

"Give me the pen!" Kirillov cried suddenly, quite unexpectedly, in a positive frenzy. "Dictate; I'll sign anything. I'll sign that I killed Shatov even. Dictate while it amuses me. I am not afraid of what the haughty slaves will think! You will see for yourself that all that is secret shall be made manifest! And you will be crushed. . . . I believe, I believe!"

Pyotr Stepanovitch jumped up from his seat and instantly handed him an inkstand and paper, and began dictating, seizing the moment, quivering with anxiety.

"I, Alexey Kirillov, declare . . ."

"Stay; I won't! To whom am I declaring it?"

Kirillov was shaking as though he were in a fever. This declaration and the sudden strange idea of it seemed to absorb him entirely, as though it were a means of escape by which his tortured spirit strove for a moment's relief.

"To whom am I declaring it? I want to know to whom?"

"To no one, everyone, the first person who reads it. Why define it? The whole world!"

"The whole world! Bravo! And I won't have any repentance. I don't want penitence and I don't want it for the police!"

"No, of course, there's no need of it, damn the police! Write, if you are in earnest!" Pyotr Stepanovitch cried hysterically.

"Stay! I want to put at the top a face with the tongue out."

"Ech, what nonsense," cried Pyotr Stepanovitch crossly, "you can express all that without the drawing, by—the tone."

"By the tone? That's true. Yes, by the tone, by the tone of it. Dictate, the tone."

"I, Alexey Kirillov," Pyotr Stepanovitch dictated firmly and peremptorily, bending over Kirillov's shoulder and following every letter which the latter formed with a hand trembling with excitement, "I, Kirillov, declare that to-day, the —th October, at about eight o'clock in the evening, I killed the student Shatov in the park for turning traitor and giving information of the manifestos and of Fedka, who has been lodging with us for ten days in Filipov's house. I am shooting myself to-day with my revolver, not because I repent and am afraid of you, but because when I was abroad I made up my mind to put an end to my life.''

"Is that all?" cried Kirillov with surprise and indignation.

"Not another word," cried Pyotr Stepanovitch, waving his hand, attempting to snatch the document from him.

"Stay." Kirillov put his hand firmly on the paper. "Stay it's nonsense! I want to say with whom I killed him. Wh' Fedka? And what about the fire? I want it all and I want to be abusive in tone, too, in tone!"

"Enough, Kirillov, I assure you it's enough," cried Py)tr Stepanovitch almost imploringly, trembling lest he should tear up the paper; "that they may believe you, you must say it as obscurely as possible, just like that, simply in hints. You must only give them a peep of the truth, just enough to tantalise them. They'll tell a story better than ours, and of course they'll believe themselves more than they would us; and, you know, it's better than anything—better than anything! Let me have it, it's splendid as it is; give it to me, give it to me!"

And he kept trying to snatch the paper. Kirillov listened open-eyed and appeared to be trying to reflect, but he seemed beyond understanding now.

"Damn it all," Pyotr Stepanovitch cried all at once, ill-humouredly, "he hasn't signed it! Why are you staring like that? Sign!"

"I want to abuse them," muttered Kirillov. He took the pen, however, and signed. "I want to abuse them."

"Write *'Vive la république'*, and that will be enough."

"Bravo!" Kirillov almost bellowed with delight. *'Vive la république démocratique sociale et universelle ou la mort!'* No, no, that's not it. *'Liberté, égalité, fraternité ou la mort.'* There, that's better, that's better." He wrote it gleefully under his signature.

"Enough, enough," repeated Pyotr Stepanovitch.

"Stay, a little more. I'll sign it again in French, you know. *'De Kirilloff, gentilhomme russe et citoyen du monde.'* Ha ha!" He went off in a peal of laughter. "No, no, no; stay. I've found something better than all. Eureka! *'Gentilhomme, séminariste russe et citoyen du monde civilisé!'* That's better than any. . . ." He jumped up from the sofa and suddenly, with a rapid gesture, snatched up the revolver from the window,

255

ran with it into the next room, and closed the door behind him. Pyotr Stepanovitch stood for a moment, pondering and gazing at the door.

"If he does it at once, perhaps he'll do it, but if he begins thinking, nothing will come of it."

Meanwhile he took up the paper, sat down. and looked at it again. The wording of the document pleased him again.

"What's needed for the moment? What's wanted is to throw them all off the scent and keep them busy for a time. The park? There's no park in the town and they'll guess it's Skvoreshniki of themselves. But while they are arriving at that, time will be passing; then the search will take time too; then when they find the body it will prove that the story is true, and it will follow that it's all true, that it's true about Fedka too. And Fedka explains the fire, the Lebyadkins; so that it was all being hatched here, at Filipov's, while they overlooked it and saw nothing—that will quite turn their heads! They will never think of the quintet; Shatov and Kirillov and Fedka and Lebyadkin, and why they killed each other—that will be another question for them. Oh, damn it all, I don't hear the shot!"

Though he had been reading and admiring the wording of it, he had been listening anxiously all the time, and he suddenly flew into a rage. He looked anxiously at his watch; it was getting late and it was fully ten minutes since Kirillov had gone out. . . . Snatching up the candle, he went to the door of the room where Kirillov had shut himself up. He was just at the door when the thought struck him that the candle had burnt out, that it would not last another twenty minutes, and that there was no other in the room. He took hold of the handle and listened warily; he did not hear the slightest sound. He suddenly opened the door and lifted up the candle: something uttered a roar and rushed at him. He slammed the door with all his might and pressed his weight against it; but all sounds died away and again there was deathlike stillness.

He stood for a long while irresolute, with the candle in his hand. He had been able to see very little in the second he held the door open, but he had caught a glimpse of the face of Kirillov standing at the other end of the room by the window, and the savage fury with which the latter had rushed upon him. Pyotr Stepanovitch started, rapidly set the candle on the table, made ready his revolver, and retreated on tiptoe to the farthest corner of the room, so that if Kirillov opened the door and

256

rushed up to the table with the revolver he would still have time to be the first to aim and fire.

Pyotr Stepanovitch had by now lost all faith in the suicide. "He was standing in the middle of the room, thinking," flashed like a whirlwind through Pyotr Stepanovitch's mind, "and the room was dark and horrible too. . . . He roared and rushed at me. There are two possibilities: either I interrupted him at the very second when he was pulling the trigger or . . . or he was standing planning how to kill me. Yes, that's it, he was planning it. . . . He knows I won't go away without killing him if he funks it himself—so that he would have to kill me first to prevent my killing him. . . . And again, again there is silence. I am really frightened: he may open the door all of a sudden. . . . The nuisance of it is that he believes in God like any priest. . . . He won't shoot himself for anything! There are lots of these people nowadays 'who've come to it of themselves'. A rotten lot! Oh, damn it, the candle, the candle! It'll go out within a quarter of an hour for certain. . . . I must put a stop to it; come what may, I must put a stop to it. . . . Now I can kill him. . . . With that document here no one would think of my killing him. I can put him in such an attitude on the floor with an unloaded revolver in his hand that they'd be certain he'd done it himself. . . . Ach, damn it! how is one to kill him? If I open the door he'll rush out again and shoot me first. Damn it all, he'll be sure to miss!"

He was in agonies, trembling at the necessity of action and his own indecision. At last he took up the candle and again approached the door with the revolver held up in readiness; he put his left hand, in which he held the candle, on the door-handle. But he managed awkwardly: the handle clanked, there was a rattle and a creak. "He will fire straightway," flashed through Pyotr Stepanovitch's mind. With his foot he flung the door open violently, raised the candle, and held out the re-volver; but no shot nor cry came from within. . . . There was no one in the room.

He started. The room led nowhere. There was no exit, no means of escape from it. He lifted the candle higher and looked about him more attentively: there was certainly no one. He called Kirillov's name in a low voice, then again louder; no one answered.

"Can he have got out by the window?" The casement in one window was, in fact, open. "Absurd! He couldn't have got away through the casement." Pyotr Stepanovitch crossed the room and went up to the window. "He couldn't possibly." All at once he turned round quickly and was aghast at something extraordinary.

Against the wall facing the windows on the right of the door stood a cupboard. On the right side of this cupboard, in the corner formed by the cupboard and the wall, stood Kirillov, and he was standing in a very strange way; motionless, perfectly erect, with his arms held stiffly at his sides, his head raised and pressed tightly back against the wall in the very corner, he seemed to be trying to conceal and efface himself. Everything seemed to show that he was hiding, yet somehow it was not easy to believe it. Pyotr Stepanovitch was standing a little sideways to the corner, and could only see the projecting parts of the figure. He could not bring himself to move to the left to get a full view of Kirillov and solve the mystery. His heart began beating violently, and he felt a sudden rush of blind fury: he started from where he stood, and, shouting and stamping with his feet, he rushed to the horrible place.

But when he reached Kirillov he stopped short again, still more overcome, horror-stricken. What struck him most was that, in spite of his shout and his furious rush, the figure did not stir, did not move in a single limb—as though it were of stone or of wax. The pallor of the face was unnatural, the black eyes were quite unmoving and were staring away at a point in the distance. Pyotr Stepanovitch lowered the candle and raised it again, lighting up the figure from all points of view and scrutinising it. He suddenly noticed that, although Kirillov was looking straight before him, he could see him and was perhaps watching him out of the corner of his eye. Then the idea occurred to him to hold the candle right up to the wretch's face, to scorch him and see what he would do. He suddenly fancied that Kirillov's chin twitched and that something like a mocking smile passed over his lips—as though he had guessed Pyotr Stepanovitch's thought. He shuddered and, beside himself, clutched violently at Kirillov's shoulder.

Then something happened so hideous and so soon over that Pyotr Stepanovitch could never afterwards recover a coherent impression of it. He had hardly touched Kirillov when the latter bent down quickly and with his head knocked the candle out of Pyotr Stepanovitch's hand; the candlestick fell with a clang on the ground and the candle went out. At the same moment he was conscious of a fearful pain in the little finger of his left hand. He cried out, and all that he could remember was that,

beside himself, he hit out with all his might and struck three blows with the revolver on the head of Kirillov, who had bent down to him and had bitten his finger. At last he tore away his finger and rushed headlong to get out of the house, feeling his way in the dark. He was pursued by terrible shouts from the room.

"Directly, directly, directly, directly." Ten times. But he still ran on, and was running into the porch when he suddenly heard a loud shot. Then he stopped short in the dark porch and stood deliberating for five minutes; at last he made his way back into the house. But he had to get the candle. He had only to feel on the floor on the right of the cupboard for the candlestick; but how was he to light the candle? There suddenly came into his mind a vague recollection: he recalled that when he had run into the kitchen the day before to attack Fedka he had noticed in passing a large red box of matches in a corner on a shelf. Feeling with his hands, he made his way to the door on the left leading to the kitchen, found it, crossed the passage, and went down the steps. On the shelf, on the very spot where he had just recalled seeing it, he felt in the dark a full unopened box of matches. He hurriedly went up the steps again without striking a light, and it was only when he was near the cupboard, at the spot where he had struck Kirillov with the revolver and been bitten by him, that he remembered his bitten finger, and at the same instant was conscious that it was unbearably painful. Clenching his teeth, he managed somehow to light the candle end, set it in the candlestick again, and looked about him: near the open casement, with his feet towards the right-hand corner, lay the dead body of Kirillov. The shot had been fired at the right temple and the bullet had come out at the top on the left, shattering the skull. There were splashes of blood and brains. The revolver was still in the suicide's hand on the floor. Death must have been instantaneous. After a careful look round, Pyotr Stepanovitch got up and went out on tiptoe, closed the door, left the candle on the table in the outer room, thought a moment, and resolved not to put it out, reflecting that it could not possibly set fire to anything. Looking once more at the document left on the table, he smiled mechanically and then went out of the house, still for some reason walking on tiptoe. He crept through Fedka's hole again and carefully replaced the posts after him.

Precisely at ten minutes to six Pyotr Stepanovitch and Erkel were walking up and down the platform at the railway station beside a rather long train. Pyotr Stepanovitch was setting off and Erkel was saying good-bye to him. The luggage was in, and his bag was in the seat he had taken in a second-class carriage. The first bell had rung already; they were waiting for the second. Pyotr Stepanovitch looked about him, openly watching the passengers as they got into the train. But he did not meet anyone he knew well; only twice he nodded to acquaintances—a merchant whom he knew slightly, and then a young village priest who was going to his parish two stations away. Erkel evidently wanted to speak of something of importance in the last moments, though possibly he did not himself know exactly of what, but he could not bring himself to begin! He kept fancying that Pyotr Stepanovitch seemed anxious to get rid of him and was impatient for the last bell.

"You look at everyone so openly," he observed with some timidity, as though he would have warned him.

"Why not? It would not do for me to conceal myself at present. It's too soon. Don't be uneasy. All I am afraid of is that the devil might send Liputin this way; he might scent me out and race off here."

"Pyotr Stepanovitch, they are not to be trusted," Erkel brought out resolutely.

"Liputin?"

"None of them, Pyotr Stepanovitch."

"Nonsense! they are all bound by what happened yesterday. There isn't one who would turn traitor. People won't go to certain destruction unless they've lost their reason."

"Pyotr Stepanovitch, but they will lose their reason."

Evidently that idea had already occurred to Pyotr Stepanovitch too, and so Erkel's observation irritated him the more.

"You are not in a funk too, are you, Erkel? I rely on you more than on any of them. I've seen now what each of them is worth. Tell them to-day all I've told you. I leave them in your charge. Go round to each of them this morning. Read them my written instructions to-morrow, or the day after, when you are all together and they are capable of listening again . . . and believe me, they will be by to-morrow, for they'll be in an awful funk, and that will make them as soft as wax. . . . The great thing is that you shouldn't be downhearted."

"Ach, Pyotr Stepanovitch, it would be better if you weren't going away."

"But I am only going for a few days; I shall be back in no time."

"Pyotr Stepanovitch," Erkel brought out warily but resolutely, "what if you were going to Petersburg? Of course, I understand that you are only doing what's necessary for the cause."

"I expected as much from you, Erkel. If you have guessed that I am going to Petersburg you can realise that I couldn't tell them yesterday, at that moment, that I was going so far for fear of frightening them. You saw for yourself what a state they were in. But you understand that I am going for the cause, for work of the first importance, for the common cause, and not to save my skin, as Liputin imagines."

"Pyotr Stepanovitch, what if you were going abroad? I should understand . . . I should understand that you must be careful of yourself because you are everything and we are nothing. I shall understand, Pyotr Stepanovitch."

The poor boy's voice actually quivered.

"Thank you, Erkel. . . . Aie, you've touched my bad finger." (Erkel had pressed his hand awkwardly; the bad finger was discreetly bound up in black silk.) "But I tell you positively again that I am going to Petersburg only to sniff round, and perhaps shall only be there for twenty-four hours and then back here again at once. When I come back I shall stay at Gaganov's country place for the sake of appearances. If there is any notion of danger, I should be the first to take the lead and share it. If I stay longer in Petersburg I'll let you know at once . . . in the way we've arranged, and you'll tell them."

The second bell rang.

"Ah, then there's only five minutes before the train starts. I don't want the group here to break up, you know. I am not afraid; don't be anxious about me. I have plenty of such centres, and it's not much consequence; but there's no harm in having as many centres as possible. But I am quite at ease about you, though I am leaving you almost alone with those idiots. Don't be uneasy; they won't turn traitor, they won't have the pluck. . . . Ha ha, you going to-day too?" he cried suddenly in a quite different, cheerful voice to a very young man, who came up gaily to greet him. "I didn't know you were going by the express too. Where are you off to . . . to your mother's?"

261

The mother of the young man was a very wealthy landowner in a neighbouring province, and the young man was a distant relation of Yulia Mihailovna's and had been staying about a fortnight in our town.

"No, I am going farther, to R——. I've eight hours to live through in the train. Off to Petersburg?" laughed the young man.

"What makes you suppose I must be going to Petersburg?" said Pyotr Stepanovitch, laughing even more openly.

The young man shook his gloved finger at him.

"Well, you're guessed right," Pyotr Stepanovitch whispered to him mysteriously. "I am going with letters from Yulia Mihailovna and have to call on three or four personages, as you can imagine—bother them all, to speak candidly. It's a beastly job!"

"But why is she in such a panic? Tell me," the young man whispered too. "She wouldn't see even me yesterday. I don't think she has anything to fear for her husband, quite the contrary; he fell down so creditably at the fire—ready to sacrifice his life, so to speak."

"Well, there it is," laughed Pyotr Stepanovitch. "You see, she is afraid that people may have written from here already . . . that is, some gentlemen. . . . The fact is, Stavrogin is at the bottom of it, or rather Prince K. . . . Ech, it's a long story; I'll tell you something about it on the journey if you like—as far as my chivalrous feelings will allow me, at least. . . . This is my relation, Lieutenant Erkel, who lives down here."

The young man, who had been stealthily glancing at Erkel, touched his hat; Erkel made a bow.

"But I say, Verhovensky, eight hours in the train is an awful ordeal. Berestov, the colonel, an awfully funny fellow, is travelling with me in the first class. He is a neighbour of ours in the country, and his wife is a Garin (*née* de Garine), and you know he is a very decent fellow. He's got ideas too. He's only been here a couple of days. He's passionately fond of whist; couldn't we get up a game, eh? I've already fixed on a fourth—Pripuhlov, our merchant from T——with a beard, a millionaire—I mean it, a real millionaire; you can take my word for it. . . . I'll introduce you; he is a very interesting money-bag. We shall have a laugh."

"I shall be delighted, and I am awfully fond of cards in the train, but I am going second class."

"Nonsense, that's no matter. Get in with us. I'll tell them

directly to move you to the first class. The chief guard would do anything I tell him. What have you got? . . . a bag? a rug?"

"First-rate. Come along!"

Pyotr Stepanovitch took his bag, his rug, and his book, and at once and with alacrity transferred himself to the first class. Erkel helped him. The third bell rang.

"Well, Erkel." Hurriedly, and with a preoccupied air, Pyotr Stepanovitch held out his hand from the window for the last time. "You see, I am sitting down to cards with them."

"Why explain, Pyotr Stepanovitch? I understand, I understand it all!"

"Well, au revoir," Pyotr Stepanovitch turned away suddenly on his name being called by the young man, who wanted to introduce him to his partners. And Erkel saw nothing more of Pyotr Stepanovitch.

He returned home very sad. Not that he was alarmed at Pyotr Stepanovitch's leaving them so suddenly, but . . . he had turned away from him so quickly when that young swell had called to him and . . . he might have said something different to him, not "Au revoir", or . . . or at least have pressed his hand more warmly. That last was bitterest of all. Something else was beginning to gnaw in his poor little heart, something which he could not understand himself yet, something connected with the evening before.

CHAPTER VII

STEPAN TROFIMOVITCH'S LAST WANDERING

I

I AM persuaded that Stepan Trofimovitch was terribly frightened as he felt the time fixed for his insane enterprise drawing near. I am convinced that he suffered dreadfully from terror, especially on the night before he started—that awful night. Nastasya mentioned afterwards that he had gone to bed late and fallen asleep. But that proves nothing; men sentenced to death sleep very soundly, they say, even the night before their execution. Though he set off by daylight, when a nervous man is always a little more confident (and the major, Virginsky's relative, used to give up believing in God every morning when the night was over), yet I am convinced he could never, without horror, have imagined himself alone on the high road in such a position. No doubt a certain desperation in his feelings softened at first the terrible sensation of sudden solitude in which he at once found himself as soon as he had left Nastasya, and the corner in which he had been warm and snug for twenty years. But it made no difference; even with the clearest recognition of all the horrors awaiting him he would have gone out to the high road and walked along it! There was something proud in the undertaking which allured him in spite of everything. Oh, he might have accepted Varvara Petrovna's luxurious provision and have remained living on her charity, *"comme un humble dependant"*. But he had not accepted her charity and was not remaining! And here he was leaving her of himself, and holding aloft the "standard of a great idea, and going to die for it on the open road". That is how he must have been feeling; that's how his action must have appeared to him.

Another question presented itself to me more than once. Why did he run away, that is, literally run away on foot, rather than simply drive away? I put it down at first to the impracticability of fifty years and the fantastic bent of his mind under the influence of strong emotion. I imagined that the thought of posting tickets and horses (even if they had bells) would have seemed too simple and prosaic to him; a pilgrimage, on the other hand, even under an umbrella, was ever so much more picturesque and in character with love and resentment. But now that everything is over, I am inclined to think that it all came about in a much simpler way. To begin with, he was afraid to hire horses because Varvara Petrovna might have heard of it and prevented him from going by force; which she certainly would have done, and he certainly would have given in, and then farewell to the great idea for ever. Besides, to take tickets for anywhere he must have known at least where he was going. But to think about that was the greatest agony to him at that moment; he was utterly unable to fix upon a place. For if he had to fix on any particular town his enterprise would at once have seemed in his own eyes absurd and impossible; he felt that very strongly. What should he do in that particular town rather than in any other? Look out for *ce marchand?* But what *marchand?* At that point his second and most terrible question cropped up. In reality there was nothing he dreaded more than *ce marchand*, whom he had rushed off to seek so recklessly, though, of course, he was terribly afraid of finding him. No, better simply the high road, better simply to set off for it, and walk along it and to think of nothing so long as he could put off thinking. The high road is something very, very long, of which one cannot see the end—like human life, like human dreams. There is an idea in the open road, but what sort of idea is there in travelling with posting tickets? Posting tickets mean an end to ideas. *Vive la grande route* and then as God wills.

After the sudden and unexpected interview with Liza which I have described, he rushed on, more lost in forgetfulness than ever. The high road passed half a mile from Skvoreshniki and, strange to say, he was not at first aware that he was on it. Logical reasoning or even distinct consciousness was unbearable to him at this moment. A fine rain kept drizzling, ceasing, and drizzling again; but he did not even notice the rain. He did not even notice either how he threw his bag over his shoulder, nor how much more comfortably he walked with it so. He must have walked like that for nearly a mile or so when he suddenly stood still and looked round. The old road, black, marked with wheel-ruts and planted with willows on each side, ran before him like an endless thread; on the right hand were bare plains from which the harvest had long ago been carried; on the left there were bushes and in the distance beyond them a copse. And far, far away a scarcely perceptible line of the railway, running aslant, and on it the smoke of a train, but no sound was heard. Stepan Trofimovitch felt a little timid, but only for a moment. He heaved a vague sigh, put down his bag beside a willow, and sat down to rest. As he moved to sit down he was conscious of being chilly and wrapped himself in his rug; noticing at the same time that it was raining, he put up his umbrella. He sat like that for some time, moving his lips from time to time and firmly grasping the umbrella handle. Images of all sorts passed in feverish procession before him, rapidly succeeding one another in his mind.

"Lise, Lise," he thought, "and with her *ce Maurice*. . . . Strange people. . . . But what was the strange fire, and what were they talking about, and who were murdered? I fancy Nastasya has not found out yet and is still waiting for me with my coffee . . . cards? Did I really lose men at cards? H'm! Among us in Russia in the times of serfdom, so called. . . . My God, yes—Fedka!"

He started all over with terror and looked about him. "What

if that Fedka is in hiding somewhere behind the bushes? They say he has a regular band of robbers here on the high road. Oh, mercy, I . . . I'll tell him the whole truth then, that I was to blame . . . and that I've been miserable about him *for ten years*. More miserable than he was as a soldier, and . . . I'll give him my purse. H'm! *J'ai en tout quarante roubles; il prendra les roubles et il me tuera tout de même."*

In his panic he for some reason shut up the umbrella and laid it down beside him. A cart came into sight on the high road in the distance coming from the town.

"Grâce à Dieu, that's a cart and it's coming at a walking pace; that can't be dangerous. The wretched little horses here . . . I always said that breed . . . It was Pyotr Ilyitch though, he talked at the club about horse-breeding and I trumped him, *et puis* . . . but what's that behind? . . . I believe there's a woman in the cart. A peasant and a woman, *cela commence à être rassurant.* The woman behind and the man in front—*c'est très rassurant.* There's a cow behind the cart tied by the horns, *c'est rassurant au plus haut degré."*

The cart reached him; it was a fairly solid peasant cart. The woman was sitting on a tightly stuffed sack and the man on the front of the cart with his legs hanging over towards Stepan Trofimovitch. A red cow was, in fact, shambling behind, tied by the horns to the cart. The man and the woman gazed open-eyed at Stepan Trofimovitch, and Stepan Trofimovitch gazed back at them with equal wonder, but after he had let them pass twenty paces, he got up hurriedly all of a sudden and walked after them. In the proximity of the cart it was natural that he should feel safer, but when he had overtaken it he became oblivious of everything again and sank back into his disconnected thoughts and fancies. He stepped along with no suspicion, of course, that for the two peasants he was at that instant the most mysterious and interesting object that one could meet on the high road.

"What sort may you be, pray, if it's not uncivil to ask?" the woman could not resist asking at last when Stepan Trofimovitch glanced absent-mindedly at her. She was a woman of about seven-and-twenty, sturdily built, with black eyebrows, rosy cheeks, and a friendly smile on her red lips, between which gleamed white even teeth.

"You . . . you are addressing me?" muttered Stepan Trofimovitch with mournful wonder.

"A merchant, for sure," the peasant observed confidently.

266

He was a well-grown man of forty with a broad and intelligent face, framed in a reddish beard.

"No, I am not exactly a merchant, I . . . I . . . *moi, c'est autre chose.*" Stepan Trofimovitch parried the question some-how, and to be on the safe side he dropped back a little from the cart, so that he was walking on a level with the cow.

"Must be a gentleman," the man decided, hearing words not Russian, and he gave a tug at the horse.

"That's what set us wondering. You are out for a walk seem-ingly?" the woman asked inquisitively again.

"You . . . you ask me?"

"Foreigners come from other parts sometimes by the train; your boots don't seem to be from hereabouts. . . ."

"They are army boots," the man put in complacently and significantly.

"No, I am not precisely in the army, I . . ."

"What an inquisitive woman!" Stepan Trofimovitch mused with vexation. "And how they stare at me . . . *mais enfin.* In fact, it's strange that I feel, as it were, conscience-stricken before them, and yet I've done them no harm."

The woman was whispering to the man.

"If it's no offence, we'd give you a lift if so be it's agree-able."

Stepan Trofimovitch suddenly roused himself.

"Yes, yes, my friends, I accept it with pleasure, for I'm very tired; but how am I to get in?"

"How wonderful it is," he thought to himself, "that I've been walking so long beside that cow and it never entered my head to ask them for a lift. This 'real life' has something very original about it."

But the peasant had not, however, pulled up the horse.

"But where are you bound for?" he asked with some mis-trustfulness.

Stepan Trofimovitch did not understand him at once.

"To Hatovo, I suppose?"

"Hatov? No, not to Hatov's exactly? . . . And I don't know him though I've heard of him."

"The village of Hatovo, the village, seven miles from here."

"A village? *C'est charmant*, to be sure I've heard of it. . . ."

Stepan Trofimovitch was still walking, they had not yet taken him into the cart. A guess that was a stroke of genius flashed through his mind.

"You think perhaps that I am . . . I've got a passport and

THE POSSESSED

I am a professor, that is, if you like, a teacher . . . but a head teacher. I am a head teacher. *Oui c'est comme ça qu'on peut traduire.* I should be very glad of a lift and I'll buy you . . . I'll buy you a quart of vodka for it.''

"It'll be half a rouble, sir; it's a bad road.''

"Or it wouldn't be fair to ourselves,'' put in the woman.

"Half a rouble? Very good then, half a rouble. *C'est encore mieux; j'ai en tout quarante roubles mais . . .''*

The peasant stopped the horse and by their united efforts Stepan Trofimovitch was dragged into the cart, and seated on the sack by the woman. He was still pursued by the same whirl of ideas. Sometimes he was aware himself that he was terribly absent-minded, and that he was not thinking of what he ought to be thinking of and wondered at it. This consciousness of abnormal weakness of mind became at moments very painful and even humiliating to him.

"How . . . how is this you've got a cow behind?'' he suddenly asked the woman.

"What do you mean, sir, as though you'd never seen one,'' laughed the woman.

"We bought it in the town,'' the peasant put in. "Our cattle died last spring . . . the plague. All the beasts have died round us, all of them. There aren't half of them left, it's heart-breaking.''

And again he lashed the horse, which had got stuck in a rut.

"Yes, that does happen among you in Russia . . . in general we Russians . . . Well, yes, it happens,'' Stepan Trofimovitch broke off.

"If you are a teacher, what are you going to Hatovo for? Maybe you are going on farther.''

"I . . . I'm not going farther precisely. . . . *C'est-à-dire,* I'm going to a merchant's.''

"To Spasov, I suppose?''

"Yes, yes, to Spasov. But that's no matter.''

"If you are going to Spasov and on foot, it will take you a week in your boots,'' laughed the woman.

"I dare say, I dare say, no matter, *mes amis,* no matter.'' Stepan Trofimovitch cut her short impatiently.

"Awfully inquisitive people; but the woman speaks better than he does, and I notice that since February 19* their language has altered a little, and . . . and what business is it

* February 19, 1861, the day of the Emancipation of the Serfs, is meant.—Translator's note.

268

of mine whether I'm going to Spasov or not? Besides, I'll pay them, so why do they pester me?"

"If you are going to Spasov, you must take the steamer," the peasant persisted.

"That's true indeed," the woman put in with animation, "for if you drive along the bank it's twenty-five miles out of the way."

"Thirty-five."

"You'll just catch the steamer at Ustyevo at two o'clock tomorrow," the woman decided finally. But Stepan Trofimovitch was obstinately silent. His questioners, too, sank into silence. The peasant tugged at his horse at rare intervals; the peasant woman exchanged brief remarks with him. Stepan Trofimovitch fell into a doze. He was tremendously surprised when the woman, laughing, gave him a poke and he found himself in a rather large village at the door of a cottage with three wndows.

"You've had a nap, sir?"

"What is it? Where am I? Ah, yes! Well . . . never mind," sighed Stepan Trofimovitch, and he got out of the cart

He looked about him mournfully; the village scene seemed strange to him and somehow terribly remote.

"And the half-rouble, I was forgetting it!" he said to the peasant, turning to him with an excessively hurried gesture; he was evidently by now afraid to part from them.

"We'll settle indoors, walk in," the peasant invited him.

"It's comfortable inside," the woman said reassuringly.

Stepan Trofimovitch mounted the shaky steps. "How can it be?" he murmured in profound and apprehensive perplexity. He went into the cottage, however. *"Elle l'a voulu,"* he felt a stab at his heart and again he became oblivious of everything, even of the fact that he had gone into the cottage.

It was a light and fairly clean peasant's cottage, with three windows and two rooms; not exactly an inn, but a cottage at which people who knew the place were accustomed to stop on their way through the village. Stepan Trofimovitch, quite unembarrassed, went to the foremost corner; forgot to greet anyone, sat down and sank into thought. Meanwhile a sensation of warmth, extremely agreeable after three hours of travelling in the damp, was suddenly diffused throughout his person. Even the slight shivers that spasmodically ran down his spine—such as always occur in particularly nervous people when they are feverish and have suddenly come into a warm room from the cold—became all at once strangely agreeable. He raised his head and the delicious fragrance of the hot pancakes with which the woman of the house was busy at the stove tickled his nostrils. With a childlike smile he leaned towards the woman and suddenly said:

"What's that? Are they pancakes? *Mais . . . c'est charmant.*"

"Would you like some, sir?" the woman politely offered him at once.

"I should like some, I certainly should, and . . . may I ask you for some tea too?" said Stepan Trofimovitch, reviving.

"Get the samovar? With the greatest pleasure."

On a large plate with a big blue pattern on it were served the pancakes—regular peasant pancakes, thin, made half of wheat, covered with fresh hot butter, most delicious pancakes. Stepan Trofimovitch tasted them with relish.

"How rich they are and how good! And if one could only have *un doigt d'eau de vie.*"

"It's a drop of vodka you would like, sir, isn't it?"

"Just so, just so, a little, *un tout petit rien.*"

"Five farthings' worth, I suppose?"

"Five, yes, five, five, five, *un tout petit rien,*" Stepan Trofimovitch assented with a blissful smile.

Ask a peasant to do anything for you, and if he can, and will, he will serve you with care and friendliness; but ask him to fetch you vodka—and his habitual serenity and friendliness will pass at once into a sort of joyful haste and alacrity; he will be as keen in your interest as though you were one of his family. The peasant who fetches vodka—even though you are going to drink it and not he and he knows that beforehand—seems, as it were, to be enjoying part of your future gratification. Within three minutes (the tavern was only two paces away), a bottle and a large greenish wineglass were set on the table before Stepan Trofimovitch.

"Is that all for me?" He was extremely surprised. "I've always had vodka, but I never knew you could get so much for five farthings."

He filled the wineglass, got up and with a certain solemnity crossed the room to the other corner where his fellow-traveller, the black-browed peasant woman, who had shared the sack with him and bothered him with her questions, had ensconced herself. The woman was taken aback, and began to decline, but after having said all that was prescribed by politeness, she stood up and drank it decorously in three sips, as women do, and, with an expression of intense suffering on her face, gave back the wineglass and bowed to Stepan Trofimovitch. He returned the bow with dignity and returned to the table with an expression of positive pride on his countenance.

All this was done on the inspiration of the moment: a second before he had no idea that he would go and treat the peasant woman.

"I know how to get on with peasants to perfection, to perfection, and I've always told them so," he thought complacently, pouring out the rest of the vodka; though there was less than a glass left, it warmed and revived him, and even went a little to his head.

"*Je suis malade tout à fait, mais ce n'est pas trop mauvais d'être malade.*"

"Would you care to purchase?" a gentle feminine voice asked close by him.

He raised his eyes and to his surprise saw a lady—*une dame, et elle en avait l'air*, somewhat over thirty, very modest in appearance, dressed not like a peasant, in a dark gown with a grey shawl on her shoulders. There was something very kindly in her face which attracted Stepan Trofimovitch immediately. She had only just come back to the cottage, where her things had been left on a bench close by the place where Stepan Trofimovitch had seated himself. Among them was a portfolio, at which he remembered he had looked with curiosity on going in, and a pack, not very large, of American leather. From this pack she took out two nicely bound books with a cross engraved on the cover, and offered them to Stepan Trofimovitch.

"*Et . . . mais je crois que c'est l'Évangile* . . . with the greatest pleasure. . . . Ah, now I understand. . . . *Vous êtes ce qu'on appelle* a gospel-woman; I've read more than once. . . . Half a rouble?"

"Thirty-five kopecks," answered the gospel-woman.

"With the greatest pleasure. *Je n'ai rien contre l'Évangile,* and I've been wanting to re-read it for a long time. . . ."

The idea occurred to him at the moment that he had not read the gospel for thirty years at least, and at most had recalled some passages of it, seven years before, when reading Renan's "Vie de Jésus". As he had no small change he pulled out his four ten-rouble notes—all that he had. The woman of the house undertook to get change, and only then he noticed, looking round, that a good many people had come into the cottage, and that they had all been watching him for some time past, and seemed to be talking about him. They were talking too of the fire in the town, especially the owner of the cart who had only just returned from the town with the cow. They talked of arson, of the Shpigulin men.

"He said nothing to me about the fire when he brought me along, although he talked of everything," struck Stepan Trofimovitch for some reason.

"Master, Stepan Trofimovitch, sir, is it you I see? Well, I never should have thought it! . . . Don't you know me?" exclaimed a middle-aged man who looked like an old-fashioned house-serf, wearing no beard and dressed in an overcoat with a wide turn-down collar. Stepan Trofimovitch was alarmed at hearing his own name.

"Excuse me," he muttered, "I don't quite remember you."

"You don't remember me? I am Anisim, Anisim Ivanov. I used to be in the service of the late Mr. Gaganov, and many's the time I've seen you, sir, with Varvara Petrovna at the late Avdotya Sergyevna's. I used to go to you with books from her, and twice I brought you Petersburg sweets from her. . . ."

"Why, yes, I remember you, Anisim," said Stepan Trofimovitch, smiling. "Do you live here?"

"I live near Spasov, close to the V—— Monastery, in the service of Marfa Sergyevna, Avdotya Sergyevna's sister. Perhaps your honour remembers her; she broke her leg falling out of her carriage on her way to a ball. Now her honour lives near the monastery, and I am in her service. And now, as your honour sees, I am on my way to the town to see my kinsfolk."

"Quite so, quite so."

"I felt so pleased when I saw you, you used to be so kind to me," Anisim smiled delightedly. "But where are you travelling to, sir, all by yourself as it seems? . . . You've never been a journey alone, I fancy?"

Stepan Trofimovitch looked at him in alarm.

"You are going, maybe, to our parts, to Spasov?"

"Yes, I am going to Spasov. *Il me semble que tout le monde va à Spassof.*"

"You don't say it's to Fyodor Matveyevitch's? They will be pleased to see you. He had such a respect for you in old days; he often speaks of you now."

"Yes, yes, to Fyodor Matveyevitch's."

"To be sure, to be sure. The peasants here are wondering; they make out they met you, sir, walking on the high road. They are a foolish lot."

272

"I . . . I . . . Yes, you know, Anisim, I made a wager, you know, like an Englishman, that I would go on foot and I . . ."

The perspiration came out on his forehead

"To be sure, to be sure." Anisim listened with merciless curiosity. But Stepan Trofimovitch could bear it no longer. He was so disconcerted that he was on the point of getting up and going out of the cottage. But the samovar was brought in, and at the same moment the gospel-woman, who had been out of the room, returned. With the air of a man clutching at a straw he turned to her and offered her tea. Anisim submitted and walked away.

The peasants certainly had begun to feel perplexed: "What sort of person is he? He was found walking on the high road, he says he is a teacher, he is dressed like a foreigner, and has no more sense than a little child; he answers queerly, as though he had run away from someone, and he's got money!" An idea was beginning to gain ground that information must be given to the authorities, "especially as things weren't quite right in the town". But Anisim set all that right in a minute. Going into the passage he explained to everyone who cared to listen that Stepan Trofimovitch was not exactly a teacher but "a very learned man and busy with very learned studies, and was a landowner of the district himself, and had been living for twenty-two years with her excellency, the general's widow, the stout Madame Stavrogin, and was by way of being the most important person in her house, and was held in the greatest respect by everyone in the town. He used to lose by fifties and hundreds in an evening at the club of the nobility, and in rank he was a councillor, which was equal to a lieutenant-colonel in the army, which was next door to being a colonel. As for his having money, he had so much from the stout Madame Stavrogin that there was no reckoning it"—and so on and so on.

"*Mais c'est une dame et très comme il faut,*" thought Stepan Trofimovitch, as he recovered from Anisim's attack, gazing with agreeable curiosity at his neighbour, the gospel pedlar, who was, however, drinking the tea from a saucer and nibbling at a piece of sugar. "*Ce petit morceau de sucre, ce n'est rien. . . .* There is something noble and independent about her, and at the same time—gentle. *Le comme il faut tout pur,* but rather in a different style."

He soon learned from her that her name was Sofya Matveyevna Ulitin and she lived at K——, that she had a sister there, a widow; that she was a widow too, and that her husband, who was a sub-lieutenant risen from the ranks, had been killed at Sevastopol.

"But you are still so young, *vous n'avez pas trente ans.*"

"Thirty-four," said Sofya Matveyevna, smiling.

"What, you understand French?"

"A little. I lived for four years after that in a gentleman's family, and there I picked it up from the children."

She told him that being left a widow at eighteen she was for some time in Sevastopol as a nurse, and had afterwards lived in various places, and now she travelled about selling the gospel.

"*Mais, mon Dieu,* wasn't it you who had a strange adventure in our town, a very strange adventure?"

She flushed; it turned out that it had been she.

"*Ces vauriens, ces malheureux,*" he began in a voice quivering with indignation; miserable and hateful recollections stirred painfully in his heart. For a minute he seemed to sink into oblivion.

"Bah, but she's gone away again," he thought, with a start, noticing that she was not by his side. "She keeps going out and is busy about something; I notice that she seems upset too. . . . *Bah, je deviens égoïste!*"

He raised his eyes and saw Anisim again, but this time in the most menacing surroundings. The whole cottage was full of peasants, and it was evidently Anisim who had brought them all in. Among them were the master of the house, and the peasant with the cow, two other peasants (they turned out to be cab-drivers), another little man, half-drunk, dressed like a peasant but clean-shaven, who seemed like a townsman ruined by drink and talked more than any of them. And they were all discussing him, Stepan Trofimovitch. The peasant with the cow insisted on his point that to go round by the lake would be thirty-five miles out of the way, and that he certainly must go by steamer. The half-drunken man and the man of the house warmly retorted:

"Seeing that, though of course it will be nearer for his honour on the steamer over the lake; that's true enough, but maybe according to present arrangements the steamer doesn't go there, brother."

"It does go, it does, it will go for another week," cried Anisim, more excited than any of them.

"That's true enough, but it doesn't arrive punctually, seeing it's late in the season, and sometimes it'll stay three days together at Ustyevo."

"It'll be there to-morrow at two o'clock punctually. You'll be at Spasov punctually by the evening," cried Anisim, eager to do his best for Stepan Trofimovitch.

"*Mais qu'est-ce qu'il a, cet homme,*" thought Stepan Trofimovitch, trembling and waiting in terror for what was in store for him.

The cab-drivers, too, came forward and began bargaining with him; they asked three roubles to Ustyevo. The others shouted that that was not too much, that that was the fare, and that they had been driving from here to Ustyevo all the summer for that fare.

"But . . . it's nice here too. . . . And I don't want . . ." Stepan Trofimovitch mumbled in protest.

"Nice it is, sir, you are right there, it's wonderfully nice at Spasov now and Fyodor Matveyevitch will be so pleased to see you."

"*Mon Dieu, mes amis,* all this is such a surprise to me."

At last Sofya Matveyevna came back. But she sat down on the bench looking dejected and mournful.

"I can't get to Spasov!" she said to the woman of the cottage.

"Why, you are bound to Spasov, too, then?" cried Stepan Trofimovitch, starting.

It appeared that a lady had the day before told her to wait at Hatovo and had promised to take her to Spasov, and now this lady had not turned up after all.

"What am I to do now?" repeated Sofya Matveyevna.

"*Mais, ma chère et nouvelle amie,* I can take you just as well as the lady to that village, whatever it is, to which I've hired horses, and to-morrow—well, to-morrow, we'll go on together to Spasov."

"Why, are you going to Spasov too?"

"*Mais que faire, et je suis enchanté!* I shall take you with the greatest pleasure; you see they want to take me, I've engaged them already. Which of you did I engage?" Stepan Trofimovitch suddenly felt an intense desire to go to Spasov.

Within a quarter of an hour they were getting into a covered trap, he very lively and quite satisfied, she with her pack beside him, with a grateful smile on her face. Anisim helped them in.

"A good journey to you, sir," said he, bustling officiously round the trap, "it has been a treat to see you."

"Good-bye, good-bye, my friend, good-bye."

"You'll see Fyodor Matveyevitch, sir . . ."

"Yes, my friend, yes . . . Fyodor Petrovitch . . . only good-bye."

II

"You see, my friend . . . you'll allow me to call myself your friend, *n'est-ce pas?*" Stepan Trofimovitch began hurriedly as soon as the trap started. "You see I . . . *J'aime le peuple, c'est indispensable, mais il me semble que je ne l'avais jamais vu de près. Stasie . . . cela va sans dire qu'elle est aussi du peuple, mais le vrai peuple,* that is, the real ones, who are on the high road, it seems to me they care for nothing, but where exactly I am going . . . But let bygones be bygones. I fancy I am talking at random, but I believe it's from being flustered."

"You don't seem quite well." Sofya Matveyevna watched him keenly though respectfully.

"No, no, I must only wrap myself up, besides there's a fresh wind, very fresh in fact, but . . . let us forget that. That's not what I really meant to say. *Chère et incomparable amie,* I feel that I am almost happy, and it's your doing. Happiness is not good for me, for it makes me rush to forgive all my enemies at once. . . ."

"Why, that's a very good thing, sir."

"Not always, *chère innocente. L'Evangile . . . voyez-vous, désormais nous prêcherons ensemble* and I will gladly sell your beautiful little books. Yes, I feel that that perhaps is an idea, *quelque chose de très nouveau dans ce genre.* The peasants are religious, *c'est admis,* but they don't yet know the gospel. I will expound it to them. . . . By verbal explanation one might correct the mistakes in that remarkable book, which I am of course prepared to treat with the utmost respect. I will be of service even on the high road. I've always been of use, I always told *them* so *et à cette chère ingrate.* . . . Oh, we will forgive, we will forgive, first of all we will forgive all and always. . . . We will hope that we too shall be forgiven. Yes, for all, every one of us, have wronged one another, all are guilty!"

"That's a very good saying, I think, sir."

"Yes, yes. . . . I feel that I am speaking well. I shall speak to them very well, but what was the chief thing I meant to say?

276

I keep losing the thread and forgetting. . . . Will you allow me
to remain with you? I feel that the look in your eyes and . . .
I am surprised in fact at your manners. You are simple-
hearted, you call me 'sir', and turn your cup upside down on
your saucer . . . and that horrid lump of sugar; but there's
something charming about you, and I see from your
features . . . Oh, don't blush and don't be afraid of me as
a man. *Chère et incomparable, pour moi une femme c'est tout.*
I can't live without a woman, but only at her side, only at her
side. . . . I am awfully muddled, awfully. I can't remember
what I meant to say. Oh, blessed is he to whom God always
sends a woman and . . . and I fancy, indeed, that I am in
a sort of ecstasy. There's a lofty idea in the open road too!
That's what I meant to say, that's it—about the idea. Now
I've remembered it, but I kept losing it before. And why have
they taken us farther? It was nice there too, but here—*cela
devient trop froid. A propos, j'ai en tout quarante roubles et
voilà cet argent,* take it, take it, I can't take care of it, I shall
lose it or it will be taken away from me. . . . I seem to be
sleepy, I've a giddiness in my head. Yes, I am giddy, I am
giddy, I am giddy. Oh, how kind you are, what's that you are
wrapping me up in?"

"You are certainly in a regular fever and I've covered you
with my rug; only about the money, I'd rather . . ."

"Oh, for God's sake, *n'en parlons plus parce que cela me
fait mal.* Oh, how kind you are!"

He ceased speaking, and with strange suddenness dropped
into a feverish shivery sleep. The road by which they drove
the twelve miles was not a smooth one, and their carriage jolted
cruelly. Stepan Trofimovitch woke up frequently, quickly
raised his head from the little pillow which Sofya Matveyevna
had slipped under it, clutched her by the hand and asked
"Are you here?" as though he were afraid she had left him.
He told her, too, that he had dreamed of gaping jaws full of
teeth, and that he had very much disliked it. Sofya Matveyevna
was in great anxiety about him.

They were driven straight up to a large cottage with a
frontage of four windows and other rooms in the yard. Stepan
Trofimovitch waked up, hurriedly went in and walked straight
into the second room, which was the largest and best in the
house. An expression of fussiness came into his sleepy face.
He spoke at once to the landlady, a tall, thick-set woman of
forty with very dark hair and a slight moustache, and explained

that he required the whole room for himself, and that the door was to be shut and no one else was to be admitted, *"parce que nous avons à parler. Oui, j'ai beaucoup à vous dire, chère amie.* I'll pay you, I'll pay you,'' he said with a wave of dismissal to the landlady.

Though he was in a hurry, he seemed to articulate with difficulty. The landlady listened grimly, and was silent in token of consent, but there was a feeling of something menacing about her silence. He did not notice this, and hurriedly (he was in a terrible hurry) insisted on her going away and bringing them their dinner as quickly as possible, without a moment's delay.

At that point the moustached woman could contain herself no longer.

"This is not an inn, sir; we don't provide dinners for travellers. We can boil you some crayfish or set the samovar, but we've nothing more. There won't be fresh fish till to-morrow.''

But Stepan Trofimovitch waved his hands, repeating with wrathful impatience: "I'll pay, only make haste, make haste.'' They settled on fish, soup, and roast fowl; the landlady declared that fowl was not to be procured in the whole village; she agreed, however, to go in search of one, but with the air of doing him an immense favour.

As soon as she had gone Stepan Trofimovitch instantly sat down on the sofa and made Sofya Matveyevna sit down beside him. There were several arm-chairs as well as a sofa in the room, but they were of a most uninviting appearance. The room was rather a large one, with a corner, in which there was a bed, partitioned off. It was covered with old and tattered yellow paper, and had horrible lithographs of mythological subjects on the walls; in the corner facing the door there was a long row of painted ikons and several sets of brass ones. The whole room with its strangely ill-assorted furniture was an unattractive mixture of the town element and of peasant traditions. But he did not even glance at it all, nor look out of the window at the vast lake, the edge of which was only seventy feet from the cottage.

"At last we are by ourselves and we will admit no one! I want to tell you everything, everything from the very beginning.''

Sofya Matveyevna checked him with great uneasiness.

"Are you aware, Stepan Trofimovitch? . . .''

"Comment, vous savez déjà mon nom?'' He smiled with delight.

"I heard it this morning from Anisim Ivanovitch when

278

you were talking to him. But I venture to tell you for my part . . ."

And she whispered hurriedly to him, looking nervously at the closed door for fear anyone should overhear—that here in this village, it was dreadful. That though all the peasants were fishermen, they made their living chiefly by charging travellers every summer whatever they thought fit. The village was not on the high road but an out-of-the-way one, and people only called there because the steamers stopped there, and that when the steamer did not call—and if the weather was in the least unfavourable, it would not—then numbers of travellers would be waiting there for several days, and all the cottages in the village would be occupied, and that was just the villagers' opportunity, for they charged three times its value for everything; and their landlord here was proud and stuck up because he was, for these parts, very rich; he had a net which had cost a thousand roubles.

Stepan Trofimovitch looked almost reproachfully at Sofya Matveyevna's extremely excited face, and several times he made a motion to stop her. But she persisted and said all she had to say: she said she had been there before already in the summer "with a very genteel lady from the town", and stayed there too for two whole days till the steamer came, and what they had to put up with did not bear thinking of. "Here, Stepan Trofimovitch, you've been pleased to ask for this room for yourself alone. . . . I only speak to warn you. . . . In the other room there are travellers already. An elderly man and a young man and a lady with children, and by to-morrow before two o'clock the whole house will be filled up, for since the steamer hasn't been here for two days it will be sure to come to-morrow. So for a room apart and for ordering dinner, and for putting out the other travellers, they'll charge you a price unheard of even in the capital. . . ."

But he was in distress, in real distress. *"Assez, mon enfant,* I beseech you, *nous avons notre argent—et après, le bon Dieu.* And I am surprised that, with the loftiness of your ideas, you . . . *Assez, assez, vous me tourmentez,"* he articulated hysterically, "we have all our future before us, and you . . . you fill me with alarm for the future."

He proceeded at once to unfold his whole story with such haste that at first it was difficult to understand him. It went on for a long time. The soup was served, the fowl was brought in, followed at last by the samovar, and still he talked on. He

279

told it somewhat strangely and hysterically, and indeed he was ill. It was a sudden, extreme effort of his intellectual faculties, which was bound in his overstrained condition, of course—Sofya Matveyevna foresaw it with distress all the time he was talking—to result immediately afterwards in extreme exhaustion. He began his story almost with his childhood, when, "with fresh heart, he ran about the meadows; it was an hour before he reached his two marriages and his life in Berlin. I dare not laugh, however. It really was for him a matter of the utmost importance, and to adopt the modern jargon, almost a question of struggling for existence". He saw before him the woman whom he had already elected to share his new life, and was in haste to consecrate her, so to speak. His genius must not be hidden from her. . . . Perhaps he had formed a very exaggerated estimate of Sofya Matveyevna, but he had already chosen her. He could not exist without a woman. He saw clearly from her face that she hardly understood him, and could not grasp even the most essential part. *"Ce n'est rien, nous attendrons,"* and meanwhile she can feel it intuitively. . . . My friend, I need nothing but your heart!" he exclaimed, interrupting his narrative, "and that sweet enchanting look with which you are gazing at me now. Oh, don't blush! I've told you already . . ."

The poor woman who had fallen into his hands found much that was obscure, especially when his autobiography almost passed into a complete dissertation on the fact that no one had been ever able to understand Stepan Trofimovitch, and that "men of genius are wasted in Russia". It was all "so very intellectual", she reported afterwards dejectedly. She listened in evident misery, rather round-eyed. When Stepan Trofimovitch fell into a humorous vein and threw off witty sarcasms at the expense of our advanced and governing classes, she twice made grievous efforts to laugh in response to his laughter, but the result was worse than tears, so that Stepan Trofimovitch was at last embarrassed by it himself and attacked "the nihilists and modern people" with all the greater wrath and zest. At this point he simply alarmed her, and it was not until he began upon the romance of his life that she felt some slight relief, though that too was deceptive. A woman is always a woman even if she is a nun. She smiled, shook her head and then blushed crimson and dropped her eyes, which roused Stepan Trofimovitch to absolute ecstasy and inspiration so much that he began fibbing freely. Varvara Petrovna appeared in his story as an enchanting brunette (who had been the rage

THE POSSESSED

of Petersburg and many European capitals) and her husband
"had been struck down on the field of Sevastopol" simply
because he had felt unworthy of her love, and had yielded her
to his rival, that is, Stepan Trofimovitch. . . . "Don't be
shocked, my gentle one, my Christian," he exclaimed to Sofya
Matveyevna, almost believing himself in all that he was telling,
"it was something so lofty, so subtle, that we never spoke of it
to one another all our lives." As the story went on, the cause
of this position of affairs appeared to be a blonde lady (if not
Darya Pavlovna I don't know of whom Stepan Trofimovitch
could have been thinking), this blonde owed everything to the
brunette, and had grown up in her house, being a distant relation. The brunette, observing at last the love of the blonde girl
to Stepan Trofimovitch, kept her feelings locked up in her
heart. The blonde girl, noticing on her part the love of the
brunette to Stepan Trofimovitch, also locked her feelings in her
own heart. And all three, pining with mutual magnanimity,
kept silent in this way for twenty years, locking their feelings
in their hearts. "Oh, what a passion that was, what a passion
that was!" he exclaimed with a stifled sob of genuine ecstasy.
"I saw the full blooming of her beauty" (of the brunette's,
that is), "I saw daily with an ache in my heart how she passed
by me as though ashamed she was so fair" (once he said
"ashamed she was so fat"). At last he had run away, casting off all this feverish dream of twenty years—*vingt ans*—and
now here he was on the high road. . . .

Then in a sort of delirium he began explaining to Sofya
Matveyevna the significance of their meeting that day, "so
chance an encounter and so fateful for all eternity". Sofya
Matveyevna got up from the sofa in terrible confusion at last.
He had positively made an attempt to drop on his knees before
her, which made her cry. It was beginning to get dark. They
had been for some hours shut up in the room. . . .

"No, you'd better let me go into the other room," she faltered,
"or else there's no knowing what people may think. . . "

She tore herself away at last; he let her go, promising her to
go to bed at once. As they parted he complained that he had a
bad headache. Sofya Matveyevna had on entering the cottage
left her bag and things in the first room, meaning to spend the
night with the people of the house; but she got no rest.

In the night Stepan Trofimovitch was attacked by the malady
with which I and all his friends were so familiar—the summer
cholera, which was always the outcome of any nervous strain or

moral shocк with him. Poor Sofya Matveyevna did not sleep all night. As in waiting on the invalid she was obliged pretty often to go in and out of the cottage through the landlady's room, the latter, as well as the travellers who were sleeping there, grumbled and even began swearing when towards morning she set about preparing the samovar. Stepan Trofimovitch was half unconscious all through the attack; at times he had a vision of the samovar being set, or someone giving him something to drink (raspberry tea), and putting something warm to his stomach and his chest. But he felt almost every instant that *she* was here, beside him; that it was she going out and coming in, lifting him off the bed and settling him in it again. Towards three o'clock in the morning he began to be easier; he sat up, put his legs out of bed and thinking of nothing he fell on the floor at her feet. This was a very different matter from the kneeling of the evening; he simply bowed down at her feet and kissed the hem of her dress.

"Don't, sir, I am not worth it," she faltered, trying to get him back on to the bed.

"My saviour," he cried, clasping his hands reverently before her. *"Vous êtes noble comme une marquise!* I—I am a wretch. Oh, I've been dishonest all my life. . . ."

"Calm yourself!" Sofya Matveyevna implored him.

"It was all lies that I told you this evening—to glorify myself, to make it splendid, from pure wantonness—all, all, every word, oh, I am a wretch, I am a wretch!"

The first attack was succeeded in this way by a second—an attack of hysterical remorse. I have mentioned these attacks already when I described his letters to Varvara Petrovna. He suddenly recalled Lise and their meeting the previous morning. "It was so awful, and there must have been some disaster and I didn't ask, didn't find out! I thought only of myself. Oh, what's the matter with her? Do you know what's the matter with her?" he besought Sofya Matveyevna.

Then he swore that "he would never change", that he would go back to her (that is, Varvara Petrovna). "We" (that is, he and Sofya Matveyevna) "will go to her steps every day when she is getting into her carriage for her morning drive, and we will watch her in secret. . . . Oh, I wish her to smite me on the other cheek; it's a joy to wish it! I shall turn her my other cheek *comme dans votre livre!* Only now for the first time I understand what is meant by . . . turning the other cheek. I never understood before!"

The two days that followed were among the most terrible in Sofya Matveyevna's life; she remembers them with a shudder to this day. Stepan Trofimovitch became so seriously ill that he could not go on board the steamer, which on this occasion arrived punctually at two o'clock in the afternoon. She could not bring herself to leave him alone, so she did not leave for Spasov either. From her account he was positively delighted at the steamer's going without him.

"Well, that's a good thing, that's capital!" he muttered in his bed. "I've been afraid all the time that we should go. Here it's so nice, better than anywhere. . . . You won't leave me? Oh, you have not left me!"

It was by no means so nice "here", however. He did not care to hear of her difficulties; his head was full of fancies and nothing else. He looked upon his illness as something transitory, a trifling ailment, and did not think about it at all; he thought of nothing but how they would go and sell "these books". He asked her to read him the gospel.

"I haven't read it for a long time . . . in the original. Someone may ask me about it and I shall make a mistake; I ought to prepare myself after all."

She sat down beside him and opened the book.

"You read beautifully," he interrupted her after the first line. "I see, I see I was not mistaken," he added obscurely but ecstatically. He was, in fact, in a continual state of enthusiasm. She read the Sermon on the Mount.

"*Assez, assez, mon enfant,* enough. . . . Don't you think that *that* is enough?"

And he closed his eyes helplessly. He was very weak, but had not yet lost consciousness. Sofya Matveyevna was getting up, thinking that he wanted to sleep. But he stopped her.

"My friend, I've been telling lies all my life. Even when I told the truth I never spoke for the sake of the truth, but always for my own sake. I knew it before, but I only see it now. . . . Oh, where are those friends whom I have insulted with my friendship all my life? And all, all! *Savez-vous* . . . perhaps I am telling lies now; no doubt I am telling lies now. The worst of it is that I believe myself when I am lying. The hardest thing in life is to live without telling lies . . . and without believing in one's lies. Yes, yes, that's just it. . . . But wait a bit, that can all come afterwards. . . . We'll be together, together," he added enthusiastically.

"Stepan Trofimovitch," Sofya Matveyevna asked timidly,

"hadn't I better send to the town for the doctor?"

He was tremendously taken aback.

"What for? *Est-ce que je suis si malade? Mais rien de sérieux*. What need have we of outsiders? They may find, besides—and what will happen then? No, no, no outsiders and we'll be together."

"Do you know," he said after a pause, "read me something more, just the first thing you come across."

Sofya Matveyevna opened the Testament and began reading.

"Wherever it opens, wherever it happens to open," he repeated.

" 'And unto the angel of the church of the Laodiceans . . .' "

"What's that? What is it? Where is that from?"

"It's from the Revelation."

"Oh, je m'en souviens, oui, l'Apocalypse. Lisez, lisez, I am trying our future fortunes by the book. I want to know what has turned up. Read on from there. . . ."

" 'And unto the angel of the church of the Laodiceans write: These things saith the Amen, the faithful and true witness, the beginning of the creation of God;

" 'I know thy works, that thou art neither cold nor hot; I would thou wert cold or hot.

" 'So then because thou art lukewarm, and neither cold nor hot, I will spue thee out of my mouth.

" 'Because thou sayest, I am rich and increased with goods, and have need of nothing: and thou knowest not that thou art wretched, and miserable, and poor, and blind, and naked.' "

"That too . . . and that's in your book too!" he exclaimed, with flashing eyes and raising his head from the pillow. "I never knew that grand passage! You hear, better be cold, better be cold than lukewarm, than *only* lukewarm. Oh, I'll prove it! Only don't leave me, don't leave me alone! We'll prove it, we'll prove it!"

"I won't leave you, Stepan Trofimovitch. I'll never leave you!" She took his hand, pressed it in both of hers, and laid it against her heart, looking at him with tears in her eyes. ("I felt very sorry for him at that moment," she said, describing it afterwards.)

His lips twitched convulsively.

"But, Stepan Trofimovitch, what are we to do though? Oughtn't we to let some of your friends know, or perhaps your relations?"

But at that he was so dismayed that she was very sorry that

she had spoken of it again. Trembling and shaking, he besought her to fetch no one, not to do anything. He kept insisting: "No one, no one! We'll be alone, by ourselves, alone, *nous partirons ensemble.*"

Another difficulty was that the people of the house too began to be uneasy; they grumbled, and kept pestering Sofya Matveyevna. She paid them and managed to let them see her money. This softened them for the time, but the man insisted on seeing Stepan Trofimovitch's "papers". The invalid pointed with a supercilious smile to his little bag. Sofya Matveyevna found in it the certificate of his having resigned his post at the university, or something of the kind, which had served him as a passport all his life. The man persisted, and said that "he must be taken somewhere, because their house wasn't a hospital, and if he were to die there might be a bother. We should have no end of trouble." Sofya Matveyevna tried to speak to him of the doctor, but it appeared that sending to the town would cost so much that she had to give up all idea of the doctor. She returned in distress to her invalid. Stepan Trofimovitch was getting weaker and weaker.

"Now read me another passage. . . . About the pigs," he said suddenly.

"What?" asked Sofya Matveyevna, very much alarmed.

"About the pigs . . . that's there too . . . *ces cochons.* I remember the devils entered into swine and they all were drowned. You must read me that; I'll tell you why afterwards. I want to remember it word for word. I want it word for word."

Sofya Matveyevna knew the gospel well and at once found the passage in St. Luke which I have chosen as the motto of my record. I quote it here again:

" 'And there was there one herd of many swine feeding on the mountain; and they besought him that he would suffer them to enter into them. And he suffered them.

" 'Then went the devils out of the man and entered into the swine; and the herd ran violently down a steep place into the lake, and were choked.

" 'When they that fed them saw what was done, they fled, and went and told it in the city and in the country.

" ' Then they went out to see what was done; and came to Jesus and found the man, out of whom the devils were departed, sitting at the feet of Jesus, clothed, and in his right mind; and they were afraid.' "

"My friend," said Stepan Trofimovitch in great excitement, *"savez-vous,* that wonderful and . . . extraordinary passage has been a stumbling-block to me all my life . . . *dans ce livre* . . . so much so that I remembered those verses from childhood. Now an idea has occurred to me; *une comparaison.* A great number of ideas keep coming into my mind now. You see, that's exactly like our Russia, those devils that come out of the sick man and enter into the swine. They are all the sores, all the foul contagions, all the impurities, all the devils great and small that have multiplied in that great invalid, our beloved Russia, in the course of ages and ages. *Oui, cette Russie que j'aimais toujours.* But a great idea and a great Will will encompass it from on high, as with that lunatic possessed of devils . . . and all those devils will come forth, all the impurity, all the rottenness that was putrefying on the surface . . . and they will beg of themselves to enter into swine; and indeed maybe they have entered into them already! They are we, we and those . . . and Petrusha and *les autres avec lui* . . . and I perhaps at the head of them, and we shall cast ourselves down, possessed and raving, from the rocks into the sea, and we shall all be drowned—and a good thing too, for that is all we are fit for. But the sick man will be healed and 'will sit at the feet of Jesus', and all will look upon him with astonishment. . . . My dear, *vous comprendrez après,* but now it excites me very much. . . . *Vous comprendrez après. Nous comprendrons ensemble."*

He sank into delirium and at last lost consciousness. So it went on all the following day. Sofya Matveyevna sat beside him, crying. She scarcely slept at all for three nights, and avoided seeing the people of the house, who were, she felt, beginning to take some steps. Deliverance only came on the third day. In the morning Stepan Trofimovitch returned to consciousness, recognised her, and held out his hand to her. She crossed herself hopefully. He wanted to look out of the window. *"Tiens, un lac!"* he said. "Good heavens, I had not seen it before! . . ." At that moment there was the rumble of a carriage at the cottage door and a great hubbub in the house followed.

III

It was Varvara Petrovna herself. She had arrived, with Darya Pavlovna, in a closed carriage drawn by four horses, with two footmen. The marvel had happened in the simplest way: Anisim, dying of curiosity, went to Varvara Petrovna's the day after he reached the town and gossiped to the servants, telling them he had met Stepan Trofimovitch alone in a village, that the latter had been seen by peasants walking by himself on the high road, and that he had set off for Spasov by way of Ustyevo accompanied by Sofya Matveyevna. As Varvara Petrovna was, for her part, in terrible anxiety and had done everything she could to find her fugitive friend, she was at once told about Anisim. When she had heard his story, especially the details of the departure for Ustyevo in a cart in the company of some Sofya Matveyevna, she instantly got ready and set off post-haste for Ustyevo herself.

Her stern and peremptory voice resounded through the cottage; even the landlord and his wife were intimidated. She had only stopped to question them and make inquiries, being persuaded that Stepan Trofimovitch must have reached Spasov long before. Learning that he was still here and ill, she entered the cottage in great agitation.

"Well, where is he? Ah, that's you!" she cried, seeing Sofya Matveyevna, who appeared at that very instant in the doorway of the next room. "I can guess from your shameless face that it's you. Go away, you vile hussy! Don't let me find a trace of her in the house! Turn her out, or else, my girl, I'll get you locked up for good. Keep her safe for a time in another house. She's been in prison once already in the town; she can go back there again. And you, my good man, don't dare to let anyone in while I am here, I beg of you. I am Madame Stavrogin, and I'll take the whole house. As for you, my dear, you'll have to give me a full account of it all."

The familiar sounds overwhelmed Stepan Trofimovitch. He began to tremble. But she had already stepped behind the screen. With flashing eyes she drew up a chair with her foot, and, sinking back in it, she shouted to Dasha:

"Go away for a time! Stay in the other room. Why are you so inquisitive? And shut the door properly after you."

For some time she gazed in silence with a sort of predatory look into his frightened face.

"Well, how are you getting on, Stepan Trofimovitch? So you've been enjoying yourself?" broke from her with ferocious irony.

"*Chère,*" Stepan Trofimovitch faltered, not knowing what he was saying, "I've learnt to know real life in Russia . . . *et je prêcherai l'Evangile.*"

"Oh, shameless, ungrateful man!" she wailed suddenly, clasping her hands. "As though you had not disgraced me enough, you've taken up with . . . oh, you shameless old reprobate!"

"*Chère* . . ."

His voice failed him and he could not articulate a syllable but simply gazed with eyes wide with horror.

"Who is *she?*"

"*C'est un ange; c'était plus qu'un ange pour moi.* She's been all night . . . Oh, don't shout, don't frighten her, *chère, chère* . . ."

With a loud noise, Varvara Petrovna pushed back her chair, uttering a loud cry of alarm.

"Water, water!"

Though he returned to consciousness, she was still shaking with terror, and, with pale cheeks, looked at his distorted face. It was only then, for the first time, that she guessed the seriousness of his illness.

"Darya," she whispered suddenly to Darya Pavlovna, "send at once for the doctor, for Salzfish; let Yegorytch go at once. Let him hire horses here and get another carriage from the town. He must be here by night."

Dasha flew to do her bidding. Stepan Trofimovitch still gazed at her with the same wide-open, frightened eyes; his blanched lips quivered.

"Wait a bit, Stepan Trofimovitch, wait a bit, my dear!" she said, coaxing him like a child. "There, there, wait a bit! Darya will come back and . . . My goodness, the landlady, the landlady, you come, anyway, my good woman!"

In her impatience she ran herself to the landlady.

"Fetch *that woman* back at once, this minute. Bring her back, bring her back!"

Fortunately Sofya Matveyevna had not yet had time to get away and was only just going out of the gate with her pack and her bag. She was brought back. She was so panic-stricken that she was trembling in every limb. Varvara Petrovna pounced on her like a hawk on a chicken, seized her by the hand and dragged her impulsively to Stepan Trofimovitch.

"Here, here she is, then. I've not eaten her. You thought I'd eaten her."

Stepan Trofimovitch clutched Varvara Petrovna's hand, raised it to his eyes, and burst into tears, sobbing violently and convulsively.

"There, calm yourself, there, there, my dear, there, poor dear man! Ach, mercy on us! Calm yourself, will you?" she shouted frantically. "Oh, you bane of my life!"

"My dear," Stepan Trofimovitch murmured at last, addressing Sofya Matveyevna, "stay out there, my dear, I want to say something here. . ."

Sofya Matveyevna hurried out at once.

"*Chérie . . . chérie . . .*" he gasped.

"Don't talk for a bit, Stepan Trofimovitch, wait a little till you've rested. Here's some water. Do wait, will you!"

She sat down on the chair again. Stepan Trofimovitch held her hand tight. For a long while she would not allow him to speak. He raised her hand to his lips and fell to kissing it. She set her teeth and looked away into the corner of the room.

"*Je vous aimais,*" broke from him at last. She had never heard such words from him, uttered in such a voice.

"H'm!" she growled in response.

"*Je vous aimais toute ma vie . . . vingt ans!*"

She remained silent for two or three minutes.

"And when you were getting yourself up for Dasha you sprinkled yourself with scent," she said suddenly, in a terrible whisper.

Stepan Trofimovitch was dumbfounded.

"You put on a new tie . . ."

Again silence for two minutes.

"Do you remember the cigar?"

"My friend," he faltered, overcome with horror.

"That cigar at the window in the evening . . . the moon was shining . . . after the arbour . . . at Skvoreshniki? Do you remember, do you remember?" She jumped up from her place, seized his pillow by the corners and shook it with his head on it. "Do you remember, you worthless, worthless, ignoble, cowardly, worthless man, always worthless?" she hissed in her furious whisper, restraining herself from speaking loudly. At last she left him and sank on the chair, covering her face with her hands. "Enough!" she snapped out, drawing herself up. "Twenty years have passed, there's no calling them back. I am a fool too."

"*Je vous aimais.*" He clasped his hands again.

"Why do you keep on with your *aimais* and *aimais?* Enough!" she cried, leaping up again. "And if you don't go to sleep at once I'll . . . You need rest; go to sleep, go to sleep at once, shut your eyes. Ach, mercy on us, perhaps he wants some lunch! What do you eat? What does he eat? Ach, mercy on us! Where is that woman? Where is she?'

There was a general bustle again. But Stepan Trofimovitch faltered in a weak voice that he really would like to go to sleep *une heure,* and then *un bouillon, un thé . . . enfin il est si heureux.* He lay back and really did seem to go to sleep (he probably pretended to). Varvara Petrovna waited a little, and stole out on tiptoe from behind the partition.

She settled herself in the landlady's room, turned out the landlady and her husband, and told Dasha to bring her *that woman.* There followed an examination in earnest.

"Tell me all about it, my good girl. Sit down beside me; that's right. Well?"

"I met Stepan Trofimovitch . . ."

"Stay, hold your tongue! I warn you that if you tell lies or conceal anything, I'll ferret it out. Well?"

"Stepan Trofimovitch and I . . . as soon as I came to Hatovo . . ." Sofya Matveyevna began almost breathlessly.

"Stay, hold your tongue, wait a bit! Why do you gabble like that? To begin with, what sort of creature are you?"

Sofya Matveyevna told her after a fashion, giving a very brief account of herself, however, beginning with Sevastopol. Varvara Petrovna listened in silence, sitting up erect in her chair, looking sternly straight into the speaker's eyes.

"Why are you so frightened? Why do you look at the ground? I like people who look me straight in the face and hold their own with me. Go on."

She told of their meeting, of her books, of how Stepan Trofimovitch had regaled the peasant woman with vodka . . .

"That's right, that's right, don't leave out the slightest detail," Varvara Petrovna encouraged her.

At last she described how they had set off, and how Stepan Trofimovitch had gone on talking, "really ill by that time", and here had given an account of his life from the very beginning, talking for some hours.

"Tell me about his life."

Sofya Matveyevna suddenly stopped and was completely nonplussed.

"I can't tell you anything about that, madam," she brought out, almost crying; "besides, I could hardly understand a word of it."

"Nonsense! You must have understood something."

"He told a long time about a distinguished lady with black

hair." Sofya Matveyevna flushed terribly though she noticed Varvara Petrovna's fair hair and her complete dissimilarity with the "brunette" of the story.

"Black-haired? What exactly? Come, speak!"

"How this grand lady was deeply in love with his honour all her life long and for twenty years. but never dared to speak, and was shamefaced before him because she was a very stout lady. . . ."

"The fool!" Varvara Petrovna rapped out thoughtfully but resolutely.

Sofya Matveyevna was in tears by now.

"I don't know how to tell any of it properly, madam, because I was in a great fright over his honour; and I couldn't understand, as he is such an intellectual gentleman."

"It's not for a goose like you to judge of his intellect. Did he offer you his hand?"

The speaker trembled.

"Did he fall in love with you? Speak! Did he offer you his hand?" Varvara Petrovna shouted peremptorily.

"That was pretty much how it was," she murmured tearfully. "But I took it all to mean nothing, because of his illness," she added firmly, raising her eyes.

"What is your name?"

"Sofya Matveyevna, madam."

"Well, then, let me tell you, Sofya Matveyevna, that he is a wretched and worthless little man. . . . Good Lord! Do you look upon me as a wicked woman?"

Sofya Matveyevna gazed open-eyed.

"A wicked woman, a tyrant? Who has ruined his life?"

"How can that be when you are crying yourself, madam?"

Varvara Petrovna actually had tears in her eyes.

"Well, sit down, sit down, don't be frightened. Look me straight in the face again. Why are you blushing? Dasha, come here. Look at her. What do you think of her? Her heart is pure. . . ."

And to the amazement and perhaps still greater alarm of Sofya Matveyevna, she suddenly patted her on the cheek.

"It's only a pity she is a fool. Too great a fool for her age. That's all right, my dear, I'll look after you. I see that it's all nonsense. Stay near here for the time. A room shall be taken for you and you shall have food and everything else from me . . . till I ask for you."

Sofya Matveyevna stammered in alarm that she must hurry on.

"You've no need to hurry. I'll buy all your books, and meantime you stay here. Hold your tongue; don't make excuses. If I hadn't come you would have stayed with him all the same, wouldn't you?"

"I wouldn't have left him on any account," Sofya Matveyevna brought out softly and firmly, wiping her tears.

It was late at night when Doctor Salzfish was brought. He was a very respectable old man and a practitioner of fairly wide experience who had recently lost his post in the service in consequence of some quarrel on a point of honour with his superiors. Varvara Petrovna instantly and actively took him under her protection. He examined the patient attentively, questioned him, and cautiously pronounced to Varvara Petrovna that "the sufferer's" condition was highly dubious in consequence of complications, and that they must be prepared "even for the worst". Varvara Petrovna, who had during twenty years got accustomed to expecting nothing serious or decisive to come from Stepan Trofimovitch, was deeply moved and even turned pale.

"Is there really no hope?"

"Can there ever be said to be absolutely no hope? But . . ."

She did not go to bed all night, and felt that the morning would never come. As soon as the patient opened his eyes and returned to consciousness (he was conscious all the time, however, though he was growing weaker every hour), she went up to him with a very resolute air.

"Stepan Trofimovitch, one must be prepared for anything. I've sent for a priest. You must do what is right. . . ."

Knowing his convictions, she was terribly afraid of his refusing. He looked at her with surprise.

"Nonsense, nonsense!" she vociferated, thinking he was already refusing. "This is no time for whims. You have played the fool enough."

"But . . . am I really so ill, then?"

He agreed thoughtfully. And indeed I was much surprised to learn from Varvara Petrovna afterwards that he showed no fear of death at all. Possibly it was that he simply did not believe it, and still looked upon his illness as a trifling one.

He confessed and took the sacrament very readily. Everyone, Sofya Matveyevna, and even the servants, came to congratulate him on taking the sacrament. They were all moved to

292

tears looking at his sunken and exhausted face and his blanched
and quivering lips.

"*Oui, mes amis,* and I only wonder that you . . . take so
much trouble. I shall most likely get up to-morrow, and we
will . . . set off. . . . *Toute cette cérémonie* . . . for which,
of course, I feel every proper respect . . . was . . ."

"I beg you, father, to remain with the invalid," said Varvara
Petrovna hurriedly, stopping the priest, who had already taken
off his vestments. "As soon as tea has been handed, I beg you
to begin to speak of religion, to support his faith"

The priest spoke; everyone was standing or sitting round the
sick-bed.

"In our sinful days," the priest began smoothly, with a cup
of tea in his hand, "faith in the Most High is the sole refuge of
the race of man in all the trials and tribulations of life, as well
as its hope for that eternal bliss promised to the righteous."

Stepan Trofimovitch seemed to revive, a subtle smile strayed
on his lips.

"*Mon père, je vous remercie et vous êtes bien bon, mais . . .*"

"No *mais* about it, no *mais* at all!" exclaimed Varvara
Petrovna, bounding up from her chair. "Father," she said,
addressing the priest, "he is a man who . . . he is a man
who . . . You will have to confess him again in another hour!
That's the sort of man he is."

Stepan Trofimovitch smiled faintly.

"My friends," he said, "God is necessary to me, if only
because He is the only being whom one can love eternally."

Whether he was really converted, or whether the stately
ceremony of the administration of the sacrament had impressed
him and stirred the artistic responsiveness of his temperament
or not, he firmly and, I am told, with great feeling uttered
some words which were in flat contradiction with many of his
former convictions.

"My immortality is necessary if only because God will not be
guilty of injustice and extinguish altogether the flame of love
for Him once kindled in my heart. And what is more precious
than love? Love is higher than existence, love is the crown of
existence; and how is it possible that existence should not be
under its dominance? If I have once loved Him and rejoiced
in my love, is it possible that He should extinguish me and my
joy and bring me to nothingness again? If there is a God, then
I am immortal. *Voilà ma profession de foi.*"

"There is a God, Stepan Trofimovitch, I assure you there

293

is," Varvara Petrovna implored him. "Give it up, drop all your foolishness for once in your life!" (I think she had not quite understood his *profession de foi*.)

"My friend," he said, growing more and more animated, though his voice broke frequently, "as soon as I understood . . . that turning of the cheek, I . . . understood something else as well. *J'ai menti toute ma vie,* all my life, all! I should like . . . but that will do to-morrow. . . . To-morrow we will all set out."

Varvara Petrovna burst into tears. He was looking about for someone.

"Here she is, she is here!" She seized Sofya Matveyevna by the hand and led her to him. He smiled tenderly.

"Oh, I should dearly like to live again!" he exclaimed with an extraordinary rush of energy. "Every minute, every instant of life ought to be a blessing to man . . . they ought to be, they certainly ought to be! It's the duty of man to make it so; that's the law of his nature, which always exists even if hidden. . . . Oh, I wish I could see Petrusha . . . and all of them . . . Shatov . . ."

I may remark that as yet no one had heard of Shatov's fate—not Varvara Petrovna nor Darya Pavlovna, nor even Salzfish, who was the last to come from the town.

Stepan Trofimovitch became more and more excited, feverishly so, beyond his strength.

"The mere fact of the ever-present idea that there exists something infinitely more just and more happy than I am fills me through and through with tender ecstasy—and glorifies me —oh, whoever I may be, whatever I have done! What is far more essential for man than personal happiness is to know and to believe at every instant that there is somewhere a perfect and serene happiness for all men and for everything. . . . The one essential condition of human existence is that man should always be able to bow down before something infinitely great. If men are deprived of the infinitely great they will not go on living and will die of despair. The Infinite and the Eternal are as essential for man as the little planet on which he dwells. My friends, all, all: hail to the Great Idea! The Eternal, Infinite Idea! It is essential to every man, whoever he may be, to bow down before what is the Great Idea. Even the stupidest man needs something great. Petrusha . . . oh, how I want to see them all again! They don't know, they don't know that that same Eternal, Grand Idea lies in them all!"

Doctor Salzfish was not present at the ceremony. Coming in suddenly, he was horrified, and cleared the room, insisting that the patient must not be excited.

Stepan Trofimovitch died three days later, but by that time he was completely unconscious. He quietly went out like a candle that is burnt down. After having the funeral service performed, Varvara Petrovna took the body of her poor friend to Skvoreshniki. His grave is in the precincts of the church and is already covered with a marble slab. The inspiration and the railing will be added in the spring.

Varvara Petrovna's absence from town had lasted eight days. Sofya Matveyevna arrived in the carriage with her and seems to have settled with her for good. I may mention that as soon as Stepan Trofimovitch lost consciousness (the morning that he received the sacrament) Varvara Petrovna promptly asked Sofya Matveyevna to leave the cottage again, and waited on the invalid herself unassisted to the end, but she sent for her at once when he had breathed his last. Sofya Matveyevna was terribly alarmed by Varvara Petrovna's proposition, or rather command, that she should settle for good at Skvoreshniki, but the latter refused to listen to her protests.

"That's all nonsense! I will go with you to sell the gospel. I have no one in the world now."

"You have a son, however," Salzfish observed.

"I have no son!" Varvara Petrovna snapped out—and it was like a prophecy.

CHAPTER VIII

CONCLUSION

ALL the crimes and villainies that had been perpetrated were discovered with extraordinary rapidity, much more quickly than Pyotr Stepanovitch had expected. To begin with, the luckless Marya Ignatyevna waked up before daybreak on the night of her husband's murder, missed him and flew into indescribable agitation, not seeing him beside her. The woman who had been hired by Arina Prohorovna, and was there for the night, could not succeed in calming her, and as soon as it was daylight ran to fetch Arina Prohorovna herself, assuring the invalid that the latter knew where her husband was, and when he would be back. Meantime Arina Prohorovna was in some anxiety too;

THE POSSESSED

she had already heard from her husband of the deed perpetrated that night at Skvoreshniki. He had returned home about eleven o'clock in a terrible state of mind and body; wringing his hands, he flung himself face downwards on his bed and shaking with convulsive sobs kept repeating: "It's not right, it's not right, it's not right at all!" He ended, of course, by confessing it all to Arina Prohorovna—but to no one else in the house. She left him on his bed, sternly impressing upon him that "if he must blubber he must do it in his pillow so as not to be overheard, and that he would be a fool if he showed any traces of it next day". She felt somewhat anxious, however, and began at once to clear things up in case of emergency: she succeeded in hiding or completely destroying all suspicious papers, books, manifestos perhaps. At the same time she reflected that she, her sister, her aunt, her sister-in-law the student, and perhaps even her long-eared brother had really nothing much to be afraid of. When the nurse ran to her in the morning she went without a second thought to Marya Ignatyevna's. She was desperately anxious, moreover, to find out whether what her husband had told her that night in a terrified and frantic whisper, that was almost like delirium, was true—that is, whether Pyotr Stepanovitch had been right in his reckoning that Kirillov would sacrifice himself for the general benefit.

But she arrived at Marya Ignatyevna's too late: when the latter had sent off the woman and was left alone, she was unable to bear the suspense; she got out of bed, and throwing round her the first garment she could find, something very light and unsuitable for the weather, I believe, she ran down to Kirillov's lodge herself, thinking that he perhaps would be better able than anyone to tell her something about her husband. The terrible effect on her of what she saw there may well be imagined. It is remarkable that she did not read Kirillov's last letter, which lay conspicuously on the table, overlooking it, of course, in her fright. She ran back to her room, snatched up her baby, and went with it out of the house into the street. It was a damp morning, there was a fog. She met no passers-by in such an out-of-the-way street. She ran on breathless through the wet, cold mud, and at last began knocking at the doors of the houses. In the first house no one came to the door, in the second they were so long in coming that she gave it up impatiently and began knocking at a third door. This was the house of a merchant called Titov. Here she wailed and kept declaring incoherently that her husband was mur-

296

dered, causing a great flutter in the house. Something was
known about Shatov and his story in the Titov household; they
were horror-stricken that she should be running about the
streets in such attire and in such cold with the baby scarcely
covered in her arms, when, according to her story, she had
only been confined the day before. They thought at first that
she was delirious, especially as they could not make out whether
it was Kirillov who was murdered or her husband. Seeing that
they did not believe her she would have run on farther, but
they kept her by force, and I am told she screamed and
struggled terribly. They went to Filipov's, and within two
hours Kirillov's suicide and the letter he had left were known
to the whole town. The police came to question Marya Ignatyevna, who was still conscious, and it appeared at once that
she had not read Kirillov's letter, and they could not find out
from her what had led her to conclude that her husband had
been murdered. She only screamed that if Kirillov was murdered, then her husband was murdered, they were together.
Towards midday she sank into a state of unconsciousness from
which she never recovered, and she died three days later. The
baby had caught cold and died before her.

Arina Prohorovna, not finding Marya Ignatyevna and the
baby, and guessing something was wrong, was about to run
home, but she checked herself at the gate and sent the nurse to
inquire of the gentleman at the lodge whether Marya Ignatyevna
was not there and whether he knew anything about her. The
woman came back screaming frantically. Persuading her not to
scream and not to tell anyone by the time-honoured argument
that "she would get into trouble", she stole out of the yard.

It goes without saying that she was questioned the same
morning as having acted as midwife to Marya Ignatyevna; but
they did not get much out of her. She gave a very cool and
sensible account of all she had herself heard and seen at
Shatov's, but as to what had happened she declared that she
knew nothing, and could not understand it.

It may well be imagined what an uproar there was in the
town. A new "sensation", another murder! But there was
another element in this case: it was clear that a secret society
of murderers, incendiaries, and revolutionists did exist, did
actually exist. Liza's terrible death, the murder of Stavrogin's
wife, Stavrogin himself, the fire, the ball for the benefit of
the governesses, the laxity of manners and morals in Yulia
Mihailovna's circle. . . . Even in the disappearance of Stepan

Trofimovitch people insisted on scenting a mystery. All sorts of things were whispered about Nikolay Vsyevolodovitch. By the end of the day people knew of Pyotr Stepanovitch's absence too, and, strange to say, less was said of him than of anyone. What was talked of most all that day was "the senator". There was a crowd almost all day at Filipov's house. The police certainly were led astray by Kirillov's letter. They believed that Kirillov had murdered Shatov and had himself committed suicide. Yet, though the authorities were thrown into perplexity, they were not altogether hoodwinked. The word "park", for instance, so vaguely inserted in Kirillov's letter, did not puzzle anyone as Pyotr Stepanovitch had expected it would. The police at once made a rush for Skvoreshniki, not simply because it was the only park in the neighbourhood, but also led thither by a sort of instinct because all the horrors of the last few days were connected directly or indirectly with Skvoreshniki. That at least is my theory. (I may remark that Varvara Petrovna had driven off early that morning in chase of Stepan Trofimovitch, and knew nothing of what had happened in the town.)

The body was found in the pond that evening. What led to the discovery of it was the finding of Shatov's cap at the scene of the murder, where it had been with extraordinary careless-ness overlooked by the murderers. The appearance of the body, the medical examination and certain deductions from it roused immediate suspicions that Kirillov must have had accomplices. It became evident that a secret society really did exist of which Shatov and Kirillov were members and which was connected with the manifestos. Who were these accomplices? No one even thought of any member of the quintet that day. It was ascertained that Kirillov had lived like a hermit, and in so com-plete a seclusion that it had been possible, as stated in the letter, for Fedka to lodge with him for so many days, even while an active search was being made for him. The chief thing that worried everyone was the impossibility of discovering a connect-ing-link in this chaos.

There is no saying what conclusions and what disconnected theories our panic-stricken townspeople would have reached if the whole mystery had not been suddenly solved next day, thanks to Lyamshin.

He broke down. He behaved as even Pyotr Stepanovitch had towards the end begun to fear he would. Left in charge of Tolkatchenko, and afterwards of Erkel, he spent all the following day lying in his bed with his face turned to the wall, apparently calm, not uttering a word, and scarcely answering when he was spoken to This is how it was that he heard nothing all day of what was happening in the town. But Tolkatchenko, who was very well informed about everything, took into his head by the evening to throw up the task of watching Lyamshin which Pyotr Stepanovitch had laid upon him, and left the town, that is, to put it plainly, made his escape; the fact is, they lost their heads as Erkel had predicted they would. I may mention, by the way, that Liputin had disappeared the same day before twelve o'clock. But things fell out so that his disappearance did not become known to the authorities till the evening of the following day, when the police went to question his family, who were panic-stricken at his absence but kept quiet from fear of consequences. But to return to Lyamshin: as soon as he was left alone (Erkel had gone home earlier, relying on Tolkatchenko) he ran out of his house, and, of course, very soon learned the position of affairs. Without even returning home he too tried to run away without knowing where he was going. But the night was so dark and to escape was so terrible and difficult, that after going through two or three streets, he returned home and locked himself up for the whole night. I believe that towards morning he attempted to commit suicide but did not succeed. He remained locked up till midday—and then suddenly he ran to the authorities. He is said to have crawled on his knees, to have sobbed and shrieked, to have kissed the floor crying out that he was not worthy to kiss the boots of the officials standing before him. They soothed him, were positively affable to him. His examination lasted, I am told, for three hours. He confessed everything, everything, told every detail, everything he knew, every point, anticipating their questions, hurried to make a clean breast of it all, volunteering unnecessary information without being asked. It turned out that he knew enough, and presented things in a fairly true light: the tragedy of Shatov and Kirillov, the fire, the death of the Lebyadkins, and the rest of it were relegated to the background. Pyotr Stepanovitch, the secret society, the organisation, and the network were put in the first place. When asked what was the object of so many murders and scandals and dastardly outrages, he answered with feverish haste that "it was with the idea of systematically undermining the foundations, systematically destroying society and all principles; with the idea of nonplussing everyone and making hay of everything, and then, when society was tottering, sick and out of joint, cynical and sceptical though filled with an intense eagerness for self-preservation and for some guiding idea, suddenly to seize it in their hands, raising the standard of revolt and relying on a complete network of quintets, which were actively, meanwhile, gathering recruits and seeking out the weak spots which could be attacked". In conclusion, he said that here in our town Pyotr Stepanovitch had organised only the first experiment in such systematic disorder, so to speak as a programme for further activity, and for all the quintets—and that this was his own (Lyamshin's) idea, his own theory, "and that he hoped they would remember it and bear in mind how openly and properly he had given his information, and therefore might be of use hereafter". Being asked definitely how many quintets there were, he answered that there were immense numbers of them, that all Russia was overspread with a network, and although he brought forward no proofs, I believe his answer was perfectly sincere. He produced only the programme of the society, printed abroad, and the plan for developing a system of future activity roughly sketched in Pyotr Stepanovitch's own handwriting. It appeared that Lyamshin had quoted the phrase about "undermining the foundations", word for word from this document, not omitting a single stop or comma, though he had declared that it was all his own theory. Of Yulia Mihailovna he very funnily and quite without provocation volunteered the remark that "she was innocent and had been made a fool of". But, strange to say, he exonerated Nikolay Stavrogin from all share in the secret society, from any collaboration with Pyotr Stepanovitch. (Lyamshin had no conception of the secret and very absurd hopes that Pyotr Stepanovitch was resting on Stavrogin.) According to his story Nikolay Stavrogin had nothing whatever to do with the death of the Lebyadkins, which had been planned by Pyotr Stepanovitch alone and with the subtle aim of implicating the former in the crime, and therefore making him dependent on Pyotr Stepanovitch; but instead of the gratitude on which Pyotr Stepanovitch had reckoned with shallow confidence, he had roused nothing but indignation and even despair in "the generous heart of Nikolay Vsyevolodovitch". He wound up by a hint, evidently intentional, volunteered hastily, that Stavrogin was perhaps a very important personage, but that there was some secret about that, that he had been living among us, so to say, incognito, that he had some commission, and that very possibly he would come back

300

to us again from Petersburg. (Lyamshin was convinced that Stavrogin had gone to Petersburg), but in quite a different capacity and in different surroundings, in the suite of persons of whom perhaps we should soon hear, and that all this he had heard from Pyotr Stepanovitch, "Nikolay Vsyevolodovitch's secret enemy".

Here I will note that two months later, Lyamshin admitted that he had exonerated Stavrogin on purpose, hoping that he would protect him and would obtain for him a mitigation in the second degree of his sentence, and that he would provide him with money and letters of introduction in Siberia. From this confession it is evident that he had an extraordinarily exaggerated conception of Stavrogin's powers.

On the same day, of course, the police arrested Virginsky and in their zeal took his whole family too. (Arina Prohorovna, her sister, aunt, and even the girl student were released long ago; they say that Shigalov too will be set free very shortly because he cannot be classed with any of the other prisoners. But all that is so far only gossip.) Virginsky at once pleaded guilty. He was lying ill with fever when he was arrested. I am told that he seemed almost relieved; "it was a load off his heart", he is reported to have said. It is rumoured that he is giving his evidence without reservation, but with a certain dignity, and has not given up any of his "bright hopes", though at the same time he curses the political method (as opposed to the Socialist one), in which he had been unwittingly and heedlessly carried "by the vortex of combined circumstances". His conduct at the time of the murder has been put in a favourable light, and I imagine that he too may reckon on some mitigation of his sentence. That at least is what is asserted in the town.

But I doubt whether there is any hope for mercy in Erkel's case. Ever since his arrest he has been obstinately silent, or has misrepresented the facts as far as he could. Not one word of regret has been wrung from him so far. Yet even the sternest of the judges trying him has been moved to some compassion by his youth, by his helplessness, by the unmistakable evidence that he is nothing but a fanatical victim of a political impostor, and, most of all, by his conduct to his mother, to whom, as it appears, he used to send almost the half of his small salary. His mother is now in the town; she is a delicate and ailing woman, aged beyond her years; she weeps and positively grovels on the ground imploring mercy for her son. Whatever may happen, many among us feel sorry for Erkel.

Liputin was arrested in Petersburg, where he had been living for a fortnight. His conduct there sounds almost incredible and is difficult to explain. He is said to have had a passport in a forged name and quite a large sum of money upon him, and had every possibility of escaping abroad, yet instead of going he remained in Petersburg. He spent some time hunting for Stavrogin and Pyotr Stepanovitch. Suddenly he took to drinking and gave himself up to a debauchery that exceeded all bounds, like a man who had lost all reason and understanding of his position. He was arrested in Petersburg drunk in a brothel. There is a rumour that he has not by any means lost heart, that he tells lies in his evidence and is preparing for the approaching trial hopefully (?) and, as it were, triumphantly. He even intends to make a speech at the trial. Tolkatchenko, who was arrested in the neighbourhood ten days after his flight, behaves with incomparably more decorum; he does not shuffle or tell lies, he tells all he knows, does not justify himself, blames himself with all modesty, though he, too, has a weakness for rhetoric; he tells readily what he knows, and when knowledge of the peasantry and the revolutionary (?) elements among them is touched upon, he positively attitudinises and is eager to produce an effect. He, too, is meaning, I am told, to make a speech at the trial. Neither he nor Liputin seems very much afraid, curious as it seems.

I repeat that the case is not yet over. Now, three months afterwards, local society has had time to rest, has recovered, has got over it, has an opinion of its own, so much so that some people positively look upon Pyotr Stepanovitch as a genius or at least as possessed of "some characteristics of a genius". "Organisation!" they say at the club, holding up a finger. But all this is very innocent and there are not many people who talk like that. Others, on the other hand, do not deny his acuteness, but point out that he was utterly ignorant of real life, that he was terribly theoretical, grotesquely and stupidly one-sided, and consequently shallow in the extreme. As for his moral qualities all are agreed; about that there are no two opinions.

I do not know whom to mention next so as not to forget anyone. Mavriky Nikolaevitch has gone away for good, I don't know where. Old Madame Drozdov has sunk into dotage. . . . I have still one very gloomy story to tell, however. I will confine myself to the bare facts.

On her return from Ustyevo, Varvara Petrovna stayed at her

town house. All the accumulated news broke upon her at once
and gave her a terrible shock. She shut herself up alone. It
was evening; everyone was tired and went to bed early.

In the morning a maid with a mysterious air handed a note
to Darya Pavlovna. The note had, so she said, arrived the
evening before, but late, when all had gone to bed, so that she
had not ventured to wake her. It had not come by post, but
had been put in Alexey Yegorytch's hand in Skvoreshniki by
some unknown person. And Alexey Yegorytch had immediately set off and put it into her hands himself and had then
returned to Skvoreshniki.

For a long while Darya Pavlovna gazed at the letter with a
beating heart, and dared not open it. She knew from whom it
came: the writer was Nikolay Stavrogin. She read what was
written on the envelope: "To Alexey Yegorytch, to be given
secretly to Darya Pavlovna."

Here is the letter word for word, without the slightest correc-
tion of the defects in style of a Russian aristocrat who had
never mastered the Russian grammar in spite of his European
education.

"DEAR DARYA PAVLOVNA,—At one time you expressed a
wish to be my nurse and made me promise to send for you
when I wanted you. I am going away in two days and shall
not come back. Will you go with me?

"Last year, like Herzen, I was naturalised as a citizen of the
canton of Uri, and that nobody knows. There I've already
bought a little house. I've still twelve thousand roubles left;
we'll go and live there for ever. I don't want to go anywhere
else ever.

"It's a very dull place, a narrow valley, the mountains re-
strict both vision and thought. It's very gloomy. I chose the
place because there was a little house to be sold. If you don't
like it I'll sell it and buy another in some other place.

"I am not well, but I hope to get rid of hallucinations in that
air. It's physical, and as for the moral you know everything;
but do you know all?

"I've told you a great deal of my life, but not all. Even to
you! Not all. By the way, I repeat that in my conscience
I feel myself responsible for my wife's death. I haven't seen
you since then, that's why I repeat it. I feel guilty about Lizaveta Nikolaevna too; but you know about that; you foretold
almost all that.

"Better not come to me. My asking you to is a terrible mean-ness. And why should you bury your life with me? You are dear to me, and when I was miserable it was good to be beside you; only with you I could speak of myself aloud. But that proves nothing. You defined it yourself, 'a nurse'—it's your own expression; why sacrifice so much? Grasp this, too, that I have no pity for you since I ask you, and no respect for you since I reckon on you. And yet I ask you and I reckon on you. In any case I need your answer for I must set off very soon. In that case I shall go alone.

"I expect nothing of Uri; I am simply going. I have not chosen a gloomy place on purpose. I have no ties in Russia—everything is as alien to me there as everywhere. It's true that I dislike living there more than anywhere; but I can't hate any-thing even there!

"I've tried my strength everywhere. You advised me to do this 'that I might learn to know myself'. As long as I was experimenting for myself and for others it seemed infinite, as it has all my life. Before your eyes I endured a blow from your brother; I acknowledged my marriage in public. But to what to apply my strength, that is what I've never seen, and do not see now in spite of all your praises in Switzerland, which I believed in. I am still capable, as I always was, of desiring to do something good, and of feeling pleasure from it; at the same time I desire evil and feel pleasure from that too. But both feelings are always too petty, and are never very strong. My desires are too weak; they are not enough to guide me. On a log one may cross a river but not on a chip. I say this that you may not believe that I am going to Uri with hopes of any sort.

"As always I blame no one. I've tried the depths of de-bauchery and wasted my strength over it. But I don't like vice and I didn't want it. You have been watching me of late. Do you know that I looked upon our iconoclasts with spite, from envy of their hopes? But you had no need to be afraid. I could not have been one of them for I never shared anything with them. And to do it for fun, from spite I could not either, not because I was afraid of the ridiculous—I cannot be afraid of the ridiculous—but because I have, after all, the habits of a gentleman and it disgusted me. But if I had felt more spite and envy of them I might perhaps have joined them. You can judge how hard it has been for me, and how I've struggled from one thing to another.

304

"Dear friend! Great and tender heart which I divined! Perhaps you dream of giving me so much love and lavishing on me so much that is beautiful from your beautiful soul, that you hope to set up some aim for me at last by it? No, it's better for you to be more cautious, my love will be as petty as I am myself and you will be unhappy. Your brother told me that the man who loses connection with his country loses his gods, that is, all his aims. One may argue about everything endlessly, but from me nothing has come but negation, with no greatness of soul, no force. Even negation has not come from me. Everything has always been petty and spiritless. Kirillov, in the greatness of his soul, could not compromise with an idea, and shot himself; but I see, of course, that he was great-souled because he had lost his reason. I can never lose my reason, and I can never believe in an idea to such a degree as he did. I cannot even be interested in an idea to such a degree. I can never, never shoot myself.

"I know I ought to kill myself, to brush myself off the earth like a nasty insect; but I am afraid of suicide, for I am afraid of showing greatness of soul. I know that it will be another sham again—the last deception in an endless series of deceptions. What good is there in deceiving oneself? Simply to play at greatness of soul? Indignation and shame I can never feel, therefore not despair.

"Forgive me for writing so much. I wrote without noticing. A hundred pages would be too little and ten lines would be enough. Ten lines would be enough to ask you to be a nurse. Since I left Skvoreshniki I've been living at the sixth station on the line, at the stationmaster's. I got to know him in the time of debauchery five years ago in Petersburg. No one knows I am living there. Write to him. I enclose the address.

"NIKOLAY STAVROGIN."

Darya Pavlovna went at once and showed the letter to Varvara Petrovna. She read it and asked Dasha to go out of the room so that she might read it again alone; but she called her back very quickly.

"Are you going?" she asked almost timidly.

"I am going," answered Dasha.

"Get ready! We'll go together."

Dasha looked at her inquiringly.

"What is there left for me to do here? What difficulty will it make? I'll be naturalised in Uri, too, and live in the valley.

305

. . . Don't be uneasy, I won't be in the way."

They began packing quickly to be in time to catch the midday train. But in less than half an hour's time Alexey Yegorytch arrived from Skvoreshniki. He announced that Nikolay Vsyevolodovitch had suddenly arrived that morning by the early train, and was now at Skvoreshniki, but "in such a state that his honour did not answer any questions, walked through all the rooms and shut himself up in his own wing. . . ."

"Though I received no orders I thought it best to come and inform you," Alexey Yegorytch concluded with a very significant expression.

Varvara Petrovna looked at him searchingly and did not question him. The carriage was got ready instantly. Varvara Petrovna set off with Dasha. They say that she kept crossing herself on the journey.

In Nikolay Vsyevolodovitch's wing of the house all the doors were open and he was nowhere to be seen.

"Wouldn't he be upstairs?" Fomushka ventured.

It was remarkable that several servants followed Varvara Petrovna while the others all stood waiting in the drawing-room. They would never have dared to commit such a breach of etiquette before. Varvara Petrovna saw it and said nothing.

They went upstairs. There there were three rooms; but they found no one there.

"Wouldn't his honour have gone up there?" someone suggested, pointing to the door of the loft. And in fact, the door of the loft which was always closed had been opened and was standing ajar. The loft was right under the roof and was reached by a long, very steep and narrow wooden ladder. There was a sort of little room up there too.

"I am not going up there. Why should he go up there?" said Varvara Petrovna, turning terribly pale as she looked at the servants. They gazed back at her and said nothing. Dasha was trembling.

Varvara Petrovna rushed up the ladder; Dasha followed, but she had hardly entered the loft when she uttered a scream and fell senseless.

The citizen of the canton of Uri was hanging there behind the door. On the table lay a piece of paper with the words in pencil: "No one is to blame, I did it myself." Beside it on the table lay a hammer, a piece of soap, and a large nail—obviously an extra one in case of need. The strong silk cord upon which Nikolay Vsyevolodovitch had hanged himself had evidently been chosen and prepared beforehand and was thickly smeared with soap. Everything proved that there had been premeditation and consciousness up to the last moment.

At the inquest our doctors absolutely and emphatically rejected all idea of insanity.

This book, designed by
William B. Taylor,
is a production of
Edito-Service S.A., Geneva

Printed in Switzerland